The Doctor and Mr. Dylan

a novel by Rick Novak

PEGASUS BOOKS

Pegasus Books
3338 San Marino Ave
San Jose, CA 95127
www.pegasusbooks.net

First Edition: September 2014

Published in North America by Pegasus Books. For information, please contact Pegasus Books c/o Christopher Moebs, 3338 San Marino Ave, San Jose, CA 95127.

This book is a work of fiction. Any resemblance to actual persons, living or dead, events, or locales is entirely coincidental. Although the novel references the musician Bob Dylan and his music, the character in the novel is not to be confused with him.

Library of Congress Cataloguing-In-Publication Data
Rick Novak
The Doctor and Mr. Dylan/Rick Novak – 1st ed p. cm.
Library of Congress Control Number: 2014949756
ISBN – 978-1-941859-02-5

1. FICTION / Thrillers. 2. MEDICAL / Anesthesiology. 3. LAW / Criminal Law / General. 4. MUSIC / Genres & Styles / Rock / Folk & Traditional. 5. BIOGRAPHY & AUTOBIOGRAPHY / Composers & Musicians. 6. SPORTS & RECREATION / General.

10 9 8 7 6 5 4 3 2 1

Comments about The Doctor and Mr. Dylan and requests for additional copies, book club rates and author speaking appearances may be addressed to Rick Novak or Pegasus Books c/o Christopher Moebs, 3338 San Marino Ave, San Jose, CA, 95127, or you can send your comments and requests via e-mail to cmoebs@pegasusbooks.net.

Also available as an eBook from Internet retailers and from Pegasus Books

Printed in the United States of America

To my parents

Jennie and John Novak

WHO KILLED THE DOCTOR'S WIFE?

Stanford anesthesia professor Dr. Nico Antone believes his son's only chance to get accepted into a prestigious college is for Johnny to graduate at the top of the class in a small rural high school. The doctor leaves his wretched marriage in California to relocate to his boyhood hometown, Hibbing, Minnesota, also the boyhood home of rock legend Bob Dylan. His son becomes a small town academic star while Dr. Antone befriends Bobby Dylan, a nurse anesthetist renamed and reinvented as a younger version of the iconic singer. A love of Bob Dylan's music forms the basis for a tenuous friendship between the two men until Dr. Antone falls in love with Mr. Dylan's wife. When the doctor's estranged wife journeys from California to Minnesota and requires emergency surgery, Dr. Antone provides her anesthetic and she dies. Medical evidence points to a fatal drug administration and Antone is accused of first-degree murder.

The Doctor and Mr. Dylan examines the dark side of relationships between a doctor and his wife, a father and his son, and a man and his best friend. Set in a rural Northern Minnesota world reminiscent of the Coen brothers' *Fargo*, *The Doctor and Mr. Dylan* details scenes of family crises, operating room mishaps, and courtroom confrontation, and concludes in a final twist that will leave readers questioning what is of value in the world we live in.

The DOCTOR & Mr. DYLAN

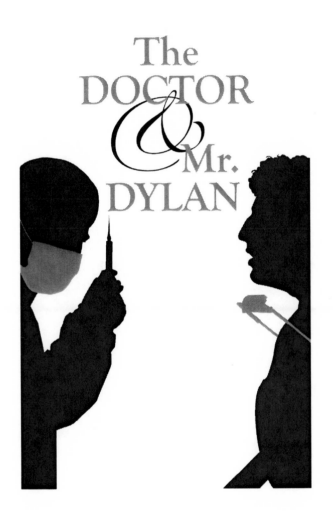

CHAPTER 1
GOING, GOING, GONE

first-degree murder n. an unlawful killing which is deliberate and premeditated (planned, after lying in wait, by poison or as part of a scheme)

My name is Dr. Nico Antone. I'm an anesthesiologist, and my job is to keep people alive. Nothing could inspire me to harm a patient. Alexandra Antone was my wife. Alexandra and I hadn't lived together for nearly a year. I dreaded every encounter with the woman. I wished she would board a boat, sail off into the sunset, and never return. She needed an urgent appendectomy on a snowy winter morning in a small Minnesota town. Anesthetist options were limited.

Life is a series of choices. I chose to be my wife's doctor. It was an opportunity to silence her, and I took it.

Before her surgery, Alexandra reclined awake on the operating room table. Her eyes were closed, and she was unaware I'd entered the room. She was dressed in a faded paisley surgical gown, and she looked like a spook—her hair flying out from a bouffant cap, her eye makeup smeared, and the creases on her forehead looking deeper than I'd ever seen them. I stood above her and felt an absurd distance from the whole situation.

Alexandra opened her eyes and moaned, "Oh, God. Can you people just get this surgery over with? I feel like crap. When is Nico going to get here?"

"I'm three feet away from you," I said.

Alexandra's face lit up at the sound of my voice. She craned her neck to look at me and said, "You're here. For a change I'm glad to see you."

I ground my teeth. My wife's condescending tone never ceased to irritate me. I turned away from her and said, "Give me a few minutes to review your medical records." She'd arrived at the Emergency Room with abdominal pain at 1 a.m., and an ultrasound confirmed that her appendix was inflamed. Other than an elevated white blood cell count, all her laboratory results were normal. She already had an intravenous line in place, and she'd received a dose of morphine in the Emergency Room.

"Are you in pain?" I said.

Her eyes were dull, narcotized—pinpoint pupils under drooping lids. "I like the morphine," she said. "Give me more."

Another command. For two decades she'd worked hard to control every aspect of my life. I ignored her request and said, "I need to go over a few things with you first. In a few minutes, I'll give you the anesthetic through your IV. You won't have any pain or awareness, and I'll be here with you the whole time you're asleep."

"Perfect," she oozed.

"When you wake up afterward, you'll feel drowsy and reasonably comfortable. As the general anesthetic fades and you awaken more, you may feel pain at the surgical site. You can request more morphine, and the nurse in the recovery room will give it to you."

"Yes. More morphine would be nice."

"During the surgery you'll have a breathing tube in your throat. I'll take it out before you wake up, and you'll likely have a sore throat after the surgery. About one patient out of ten is nauseated after anesthesia. These are the common risks. The chance of anything more serious going wrong with your heart, lungs or brain isn't zero, but it's very, very close to zero. Do you have any questions?"

"No," she sighed. "I'm sure you are very good at doing this. You've always been good at making me fall asleep."

I rolled my eyes at her feeble joke. I stood at the anesthesia workstation and reviewed my checklist. The anesthesia machine, monitors, airway equipment, and necessary drugs were set up and ready to go. I filled a 20 cc syringe with the sedative propofol and a second syringe with 40 mg of the paralyzing drug rocuronium.

"I'm going to let you breathe some oxygen now," I said as I lowered the anesthesia mask over Alexandra's face.

She said, "Remember, no matter how much you might hate me, Nico, I'm still the mother of your child."

Enough talk. I wanted her gone. I took a deep breath, exhaled slowly, and injected the anesthetic into her intravenous line. The milky whiteness of the propofol disappeared into the vein of her arm, and Alexandra Antone went to sleep for the last time.

CHAPTER 2
A PHARMACIST'S SON IN SOUTH DAKOTA

Eight months earlier

My cell phone pinged with a text message from my son Johnny. The text read:

911 call me

I was administering an anesthetic to a 41-year-old woman in an operating room at Stanford University, while a neurosurgeon worked to remove a meningioma tumor from her brain. I stood near my patient's feet in an anesthesia cockpit surrounded by two ventilator hoses, three intravenous lines, and four computer monitor screens. Ten syringes loaded with ten different drugs lay on the table before me. My job was to control my patient's breathing, blood pressure, and level of unconsciousness, but at that moment I could only stare at my cell phone as my heart rate climbed.

911 call me

911? My son was in trouble, and I was stuck in surgery, unable to leave. I wanted to contact Johnny as soon as possible, but my patient was asleep, paralyzed, and helpless. Her life was my responsibility. I scanned the operating room monitors and confirmed that her vital signs were perfect. I had to make a decision: should I call him now, or attend to my anesthetic and call after the surgery was over? My patient was stable, and my son was in danger. I pulled out my cell phone and dialed his number. He picked up after the first ring. "What is it, son?" I said.

"I'm screwed," Johnny wailed. "I just got my report card for the first semester and my grades totally suck. Mom is mega-pissed. She's going ballistic, and I'm screwed."

My shoulders slumped. This was 911 for a 17-year-old? "How bad were the grades?"

"I got six B's. I didn't get one A. I just met with my counselor and he says I'm ranked #101 in my high school class. I'm so doomed. Mom is so pissed. She called me a lazy shit."

I resisted my initial urge to scream at Johnny for scaring the hell out of me. The kid had no insight into what I did minute-to-minute in the hospital. Did he think his report card trumped my medical practice? Did he really think his report card full of B's was an emergency?

"I'm not sure what's worse, the grades or Mom's screaming about the grades," he said.

I imagined my wife having a temper tantrum about Johnny falling short of her straight-A's standard of excellence, and I knew the answer to that question. My wife could be a total bitch. "I'm sorry Mom got mad, Johnny, but..."

"No buts, Dad. You know Mom's idea of success is Ivy League or bust, and I'm a bust."

"Son, four of your six classes are Advanced Placement classes, and those grades aren't that bad."

"Dad, almost everyone in the school takes four AP classes. Every one of my friends got better grades than me. Ray, Brent, Robby, Olivia, Jessica, Sammy, and Adrian all got straight A's. Devon, Jackson, Pete, and Rod had all A's and one B. Even Diego had only two B's."

"But you..."

Johnny cut me off. "There's no 'buts,' Dad. I'm ranked in the middle of the pack in my class. I'm cooked. I'm ordinary. Forget Harvard and Princeton. I'm going to San Jose State."

My stomach dropped. Johnny was halfway through his junior year at Palo Alto Hills High School. The competition for elite college acceptance was on my son's mind every day, and on his mom's mind every minute. Johnny was a bright kid, but the school stood across the street from Stanford University and was packed wall-to-wall with the sons and daughters of Stanford MBAs, PhDs, lawyers, and doctors. Johnny's situation wasn't uncommon. You could be a pretty smart kid and still land somewhere in the middle of the class at P.A. Hills High.

"Everything will work out," I said. "There are plenty of great colleges. You'll see."

"Lame, Dad. Don't talk down to me. You stand there with your doctor job at Stanford and tell me that I'll be all right. I'll be the checkout guy at Safeway when you buy your groceries. That's where I'm heading."

Catastrophic thinking. Johnny Antone was holding a piece of paper in his hand—a piece of paper with some letters typed after his name—and he was translating it into an abject life of being average.

"Johnny, I can't talk about this any more right now. My patient ..."

"Whatever," Johnny answered.

I heard a click as he hung up. I hated it when he did that. In the operating room I had authority, and respect was a given. With my family, I was a punching bag for of all sorts of verbal blows from both my kid and my wife.

I reached down and turned off my cell phone. For now, the haven of the operating room would insulate me against assaults from the outside world.

Judith Chang was the neurosurgeon that day. Dr. Chang was the finest brain surgeon in the western United States, and was arguably the most outstanding female brain surgeon on the planet. She peered into a binocular microscope hour after hour, teasing the remnants of the tumor away from the patient's left frontal lobe. Dr. Chang always operated in silence, and her fingers moved in precise, calculated maneuvers. A 50-inch flat screen monitor on the wall of the operating room broadcast the image she saw from inside her microscope.

I paid little attention to the surgical images, which to me revealed nothing but incomprehensible blends of pink tissues.

My full attention was focused on my own 42-inch monitor screen which depicted the patient's electrocardiogram, blood pressure, and oxygen saturation, as well as the concentration of all gases moving in and out of her lungs. Everything was stable, and I was pleased.

It had been five hours since the initial skin incision. Dr. Chang pushed the microscope away and said, "We're done. The tumor's out."

"A cure?" I said.

"There was no invasion of the tumor into brain tissue or bone. She's cured." Dr. Chang had removed a 5 X 10-centimeter piece of the patient's skull to access the brain, and began the process of fitting the piece back into the defect in the skull—the placement not unlike finishing the last piece in a jigsaw puzzle. As Dr. Chang wired the bony plate into place, she said, "How's your family, Nico?"

She hadn't said a word to me in five hours, but once she was finished with the critical parts of surgery, Judith Chang had a reputation as a world-class chatterer. Some surgeons liked to listen to loud rock n' roll "closing music" as they sewed up a patient. Some surgeons preferred to tell raunchy jokes. Judith Chang enjoyed the sound of her own voice. We hadn't worked together for months, so we had a lot to catch up on.

"They're good," I said. "Johnny's in 11th grade. He's going to concerts, playing video games with friends, and sleeping until noon on weekends. Alexandra is working a lot, as usual. She just sold a house on your street."

"I heard about that property," Judith said. "You're a lucky guy. That house sold for close to $5 million. Her commission is more than some doctors earn in a year. In my next lifetime I'll be a big-time realtor like Alexandra. Does she give you half her income to spend?"

"In theory half that money is mine, but she invests the dough as soon as it hits her checking account."

"Smart. Is Johnny looking at colleges yet?"

Her question had eerie relevance, because I'd been ruminating over Johnny's phone call all morning. "That's a sensitive point. Johnny just got his mid-year report card, and he's freaking out."

"How bad was it?"

"Six B's. No A's. He's ranked #101 in a class of 480 students." I spilled out the whole story while Dr. Chang twisted the wires together to affix the bony plate into the patient's skull. I left out the "lazy shit" label from Johnny's mom.

Dr. Chang had no immediate answer, and I interpreted her silence as tacit damning of Johnny's fate. She opened her mouth and a flood of words began pouring out. "You know my twin daughters Meredith and Melody, who are sophomores at Stanford? They worked their butts off in high school. They were both straight-A students. Meredith captained the varsity water polo team, played saxophone in the jazz band, and started a non-profit charity foundation for an orphanage in Costa Rica. Melody was on the debate team and the varsity tennis team, and for three years she worked with Alzheimer patients at a nursing home in Palo Alto. Meredith and Melody were sweating bullets waiting to hear if Stanford would accept them, even though they were both legacies since I went to undergrad and med school here.

"The college admission game is a bitch, Nico. It's not like when we were kids. It's almost impossible to get into a great school without some kind of massive gimmick. It's a fact that Harvard rejects 75% of the high school valedictorians that apply. Can you believe that?"

I could believe it. And I didn't really care, since my only kid was at this moment freaking out because his grades qualified him for San Jose State, not the Ivy League. I didn't care to hear any more about the Chang daughters right now, either. To listen to Judith Chang, her daughters were the second and third coming of Judith Chang, destined for world domination. I was envious of the Chang sisters' academic successes—what parent wouldn't be? But I didn't want to compare them to my own son.

"What are Johnny's test scores like?" Dr. Chang said.

Ah, a bright spot, I thought. "He's always excelled at taking standardized tests. His SAT reading, math, and writing scores are all at the 98th percentile or better. His grade point average and class rank don't match his test scores."

"Does he have many extracurricular activities?"

"Johnny's extracurricular activities consist mostly of watching TV and playing games on his laptop. At the same time," I said, as if the combination of the two pastimes signaled a superior intellect.

Dr. Chang grew quiet again. More silent condemnation of my son's prospects. "Listen to me," she said. "My brother is a pharmacist in Sioux Falls, South Dakota. His son got accepted to Princeton, and let me tell you, my nephew isn't that bright. His test scores aren't anywhere near as high as Johnny's. But he just happens to live in South Dakota. He just happens to be a straight-A student in a rural state. He just happens to be one of the best students in South Dakota."

"How much do you think that matters?"

"It matters big time. The top schools want geographic variety in their student body. Stanford wants diversity. The Ivy League wants diversity. Princeton can find fifty kids from Palo Alto who meet their admission requirements. They want kids from all walks of life. They want … the son of a pharmacist from Podunk, South Dakota. If Johnny lived in South Dakota, with those test scores he'd be a shoo-in with the Ivy League admissions committees."

Judith Chang turned her back on the operating room table, and peeled off her surgical gloves. The bony plate was back in place, and her patient's skull was intact again. The surgical resident would conclude the task of sewing the skin closed. Dr. Chang paused for a moment, turned her palms upward, and said, "Just move to the Dakotas, Nico."

I stroked my chin. She made it sound so easy.

CHAPTER 3
QUEEN ALEXANDRA APPROXIMATELY

I drove my black BMW M6 convertible up the semicircular driveway to our Palo Alto home after work, and parked behind my wife's silver Aston Martin One-77. Together, the value of the two cars approximated the gross national products of some third world nations. Our home was a 7,000-square-foot Tuscan villa built on a hilltop west of the Stanford University campus. The Antone estate encompassed three acres of tranquility, and towered above an urban area of seven million Californians, most of whom were mired in less-than-tranquil rush hour traffic at that very moment.

Our living room featured thirty-foot-high ceiling-to-floor windows overlooking San Francisco Bay. The décor included opulent white Baker couches no one ever sat on and a Steinway grand piano no one ever played. I sped through the formal room at flank speed. I couldn't remember ever spending more than five minutes hanging out in this museum piece of showroom design.

I carried a large bag of Chinese take-out food from Chef Chu's, and set it down on the stainless steel countertop of our spotless, never-used kitchen. I made a beeline for the refrigerator, popped the top off a Corona and chugged half the bottle, still vibrating from my day in the operating room. I looked out the French doors toward the back patio.

Alexandra was lying on a lounge chair and sipping a tall drink through a straw. A broad-brimmed Panama hat graced her swirling mane of black hair. She wore a white one-piece swimming suit. It was an unseasonably warm day for January, and my wife never missed an opportunity to bronze her lanky limbs.

I walked up behind Alexandra, wrapped my arms around her neck, and kissed her left cheek. She held a cell phone against her right ear, and pushed me away while she continued her conversation. I frowned and said nothing. Was it so hard for Alexandra to pretend she loved me? I sank into a second chaise lounge beside her, closed my eyes and listened.

"That property is overpriced at $6.5 million," she said. "I know we can get it for 6.2. Put in the bid tonight and tell the seller they need to decide by tomorrow morning or the deal's off. Got it? Call me back when they cave. Ciao."

Alexandra set her phone down and lit a Marlboro Light 100. She inhaled with a violent effort, exhaled the smoke through her nostrils, dragon-like, and turned toward me. She wore broad Ray-Ban sunglasses. I couldn't tell if she was looking at me or if she was looking out over San Francisco Bay, a vista Alexandra may well have considered far more interesting.

"How are you?" she said.

"I had a busy day. Today I was in the neuro room…"

Her phone rang again, and she waved me off while taking the call. My heart sank anew. She listened for an extended time and then said, "I'll be there at 5. No problem. Thanks." She hung up and thrust her fist into the air. "Got a whale on the line," she said. "There's a couple from Taiwan who want to see the Jorgensen house tonight. Their agent drove them by the property this morning. They are very, very interested, and very, very wealthy. It's an all-cash deal. A blank check." She took a second long drag on her cigarette, and leaned toward me. At this angle, I could see my own reflection dwarfed in the lenses of her sunglasses. "This is big, Nico."

"How much is the Jorgensen house listed for?"

"Just under 8 mill. That's a quarter of a million dollar commission for yours truly."

Her monomaniacal pursuit of money baffled me. Alexandra Regina Antone was one of America's top real estate agents. Because of her explosive earning power, we lived in one of the nation's most expensive residential neighborhoods, a zip code where Silicon Valley's multimillionaire CEOs and venture capitalists lorded in their castles. The residential properties Alexandra bought and sold for her clients were in the $3 million to $10 million range, and she earned a 3% commission on each sale. She sold one or two houses each month, and her income for the past year topped $9 million.

Alexandra's salary dwarfed mine. None of my medical peers lived in this kind of luxury. To Alexandra, another $240,000 commission was headline news. It wasn't about the cash—this was about the glory of Alexandra and her talent. It was about the Queen of Palo Alto rising higher and higher on the pedestal she'd erected for herself.

"So, you were telling me about your day," Alexandra said, as she stretched her arms toward the sky and stifled a yawn.

"I did a craniotomy with Judith Chang. One case. It took all day."

She took a final drag on her Marlboro, shivered in disgust, and said, "Judith Chang is such a stiff. Always bragging about her robotic daughters. I don't know how you can do that job, locked in a windowless room with her hour after hour." Alexandra had zero interest in listening to medical stories. She changed the topic at once. "Did you hear about Johnny's report card?"

"I did. He's pretty upset. Johnny wishes his grades were better. I wish his grades were better. He said you yelled at him."

"Johnny's a slacker. God knows I tried to light a fire under him years ago, but you taught him how to watch ESPN instead of pushing academics."

"He said you called him a lazy shit."

"I did. He is a lazy shit."

"He's your son, for God's sakes. Johnny loves you and looks up to you. How do you think he feels when his mother says that?"

"I don't give a fuck how he feels. Johnny needs to hear it, and he needs to change. Clue in! You don't seem to get it, either. You think he's fine just the way he is. Well he isn't, Nico. Johnny's a spoiled brat, living in luxury on top of this hill. He has no incentive to work hard. He thinks he can live off my money forever."

Alexandra was dogmatic about the pathway to success. She was an unabashed academic snob—a graduate of Dartmouth College and Harvard Business School—and she'd have tattooed her Ivy League diplomas across her cleavage if she hadn't been too vain to disfigure her silicone orbs. I wasn't going to fight with her—I never won.

I shifted gears. "Dr. Chang had an interesting take on Johnny's grades. She said Johnny could get into any college he wanted to if we lived in South Dakota." I explained how Dr. Chang's nephew from Sioux Falls was accepted to Princeton.

Alexandra removed her hat, shook out her hair, and took off her sunglasses to reveal flashing brown eyes. "For a change, Judith Chang is right. Johnny's chances for success are slim on his current path. He has no chance at the Ivy League coming out of Palo Alto with his B average." She chewed on the earpiece of her Ray-Bans as she contemplated. "Why don't we send him to Minnesota to live with Dominic?"

"You're kidding," I said. My Uncle Dominic had a home near the Canadian border, in Hibbing, Minnesota, where I graduated from high school. Hibbing was a great place if you wanted to hunt partridge or ice fish for walleye pike, but the tiny village was a subarctic outpost light-years removed from the opulence Johnny grew up with in California.

"I'm not kidding. Johnny needs a gimmick for college admissions, and he has none. Hibbing could be his ticket."

"He can't just move up there with Dominic. Johnny's 17 years old. And Dominic moved to Arizona. His house is empty."

"Then take a year off. Go up there with him. Get your ass out of that windowless tomb of an operating room and take your son back to your childhood home."

I frowned. "What about you?"

"Are you kidding? I'm not going anywhere. My friends are here, my job is here. But you go right ahead, Nico."

Now it was my turn to stare off at the blue expanse of San Francisco Bay. Move back to the Iron Range of Northern Minnesota, to the land of rusted-out Fords and beer-swilling Vikings fans? What had my marriage come to? Before Johnny was born, Alexandra and I used to sit in these same chairs and drink margaritas together. Naked dips in this same pool led to nights of laughter and hot sex. Our current sex life had declined to hall sex, when I murmured "fuck you" under my breath after Alexandra walked past me in the hallway on her way to the second bedroom where she slept alone.

Alexandra was unrelenting. "Don't give Johnny an option. Tell him you're taking him to Minnesota to turn his life around, get some A's, and graduate number one in his class from Hibbing High School. Call Dominic tonight and make the arrangements. It'll be the best decision you've ever made. Trust me."

Trust me. Alexandra could sell bikinis to Eskimos. "You're OK with your husband and son moving 2,000 miles away?" I said.

She wrapped her arms around herself in an absurd parody of self-love and said, "Of course I'll miss you." Then she laid back onto the chaise lounge, the top third of her breasts busting out of her swimsuit top. She knit her hands behind her head, pushed her cleavage out into the January sunshine, and grinned in silence.

I watched the spectacle of her arching self-absorption and winced. Move 2,000 miles away? I was 2,000 miles away from this woman already.

"Hey guys," came a voice from behind us. Johnny was home from school. He walked onto the patio and stood between us. My mood improved at once. Our son was tall and muscular with perfect skin, dark wavy hair, and striking blue eyes. He wore his usual uniform of gym shorts and an oversized T-shirt. My love for Johnny was unlike any emotion I'd ever felt. Romantic love for a woman was a wonderful abyss—the subject matter of a million songs, books, movies, and television shows. I'd watched romantic love drift off into the ozone as years passed, but with my son I was in love forever. If Alexandra and I ever divorced, I'd carry on. If my son ever shut me out, I'd need electroshock therapy.

Johnny wasn't smiling. His shoulders drooped, his chin scraped his chest, and his gaze was locked onto the slate tiles under his well-worn Nike athletic shoes.

"How's the Boy with the B's doing?" Alexandra said.

Johnny regarded her through hooded eyes—James Dean with a cause. His upper lip curled skyward in a look of contempt. He was already smoldering from a bad day, and she was throwing kerosene on his fire.

She forged on, hawking optimism now. "Dad and I have a great plan for you that should make your report card problem of no consequence."

"Great plan?" Contempt turned to suspicion.

"Johnny, are you happy that your grades rank you in the middle of the pack at your school?" she said.

"You know I'm not," he sneered. I didn't have a 42-inch monitor displaying Johnny's vital signs, but I knew my son's blood pressure was escalating.

"Would you like to be accepted into a top college?"

"Duh. Of course, Mom."

"What if we told you there was a way for you to graduate at the top of your class and go on to one of America's best colleges?"

"I'd say you were smoking too much weed."

"No weed."

"How am I going to jump to the head of my class at Palo Alto Hills High?"

"Not Palo Alto Hills High School, Johnny. Hibbing High School."

Johnny looked from me to his mother and back again. "You two are messed up. Hibbing? Where the hell is that?"

"Hibbing is in Northern Minnesota. It's where your dad grew up. It could be worse. We're not sending you off to some military school in the badlands of Utah where you don't know anyone. Your dad will move to Minnesota with you."

"That's ridiculous... Dad?" he said, panic in his voice.

I opened my mouth, but Alexandra didn't give me a chance to weigh in. "There are consequences for your lack of effort in school, Johnny," she said. "We want you to get out of Palo Alto and compete for grades with the sons and daughters of some iron ore miners. Right, Nico?" She turned to me for affirmation.

Johnny's jaw sagged. "Dad?" he said again.

"I'm overdue for my sabbatical at the University," I said. "My Uncle Dominic has a house in Hibbing. With your brains, your test scores, and a lot of hard work, you could be a top student up there. Instead of being a middle-of-the-pack Palo Alto student, you could be...." At this point I decided to gamble and appeal to my son's ego and vanity, "You could be the valedictorian."

"Can the best students from a school like that get into a top college?"

"They can. When I was a senior at Hibbing High, two kids were accepted to Harvard. It's got to be the best high school in the northern half of Minnesota."

"Whoa. Harvard?"

"Yes, Harvard."

Johnny looked over at his mother. She smirked, as if she'd single-handedly masterminded a strategic maneuver worthy of Machiavelli.

"I'll have to think about this," Johnny said.

"I've got to shower and get ready for my meeting," Alexandra said. "Nico, you guys are on your own for dinner. Johnny, I'm sure you'll love Minnesota." She rolled off her lounge chair as Johnny covered his eyes and pressed his thumbs into his temples.

She walked away, and I admired the swagger of her slender hips and the bounce of her long tresses. I never got tired of looking at Alexandra, but it wasn't much fun living with a woman whose best friend was her mirror.

I turned to Johnny. "Want some Chinese food?" I said.

"I'll eat it in my room, Dad. I have a ton of homework. I'm really pissed off about everything and I don't want to talk anymore. First I get the crappy report card, and now you guys want to ship me off to the Yukon. All you guys care about is grades. You don't give two shits about whether I'm happy or not."

"That's not true."

"It is true. Just leave me alone. I'm going to my room. This B-student has a date with Hamlet." Johnny walked away, and I let him go. My B-student son needed more dates with the Danish prince.

I dished out a plate of Szechwan prawns and General Tso's chicken, and popped the top off a second Corona. The Golden State Warriors were playing the Miami Heat at 6 p.m. A second Corona, some Schezwan prawns, and the basketball game sounded like a decent evening.

After halftime, Johnny came shuffling down the hallway. He stretched out on the couch opposite me and opened his laptop. He was humming to himself, and his fingers were flying.

I was happy to see he'd cheered up. "Feeling better?" I said.

"Yep. The Chinese food hit the spot."

I waited for more conversation, but none was forthcoming. The Warriors connected on an alley-oop and an outrageous dunk. Johnny didn't look up.

"How's Amanda?" I said, trying to stoke up a dialogue. Amanda Feld was Johnny's girlfriend, a petite cross-country runner who gazed at Johnny like he was a Greek god. She hadn't been over for a couple of weeks, and Johnny hadn't brought up her name for longer than that.

"Amanda's history," Johnny said.

"History?"

"I broke up with her a month ago, Dad."

"What happened?"

"Nothing happened. It didn't work out."

"She was cute."

"Yep."

I waited for more of an explanation, but none came. Amanda's fate paralleled all the other breakups of the past year, when Johnny ended relationships with Samantha the cheerleader, Emily the debate star, and Jenna the girl across the street. Johnny seemed to attract girls by repelling them. The less interest he showed, the more the women orbited him. I was envious.

Johnny said, "The report card and class rank bullshit really wore me down today. Why should my whole future revolve around some alphabet letters on a page?"

"It doesn't. Your life is much more than your grades."

"Yeah, like what?"

I pointed my two forefingers at my son just like I had a thousand times in his life, and said, "You're a great kid. Don't ever forget it."

"Why do you always have to say that to me, Dad?"

"Because it's true. I want you to imprint it in your brain and never doubt it."

"Even if I can't get an A in one class?"

"Even if you can't get one A."

"I want to get A's. All A's. But transferring to Minnesota?" Johnny tapped the screen of his laptop and said, "I'm looking at the Weather Channel website. It's minus five degrees and snowing in Hibbing right now."

"Yep. That's why I left. In the winter the sun sets at 3:30 in the afternoon."

"That's insane."

"It ain't California."

He shook his head. "I'm going to sleep."

"Good night, son. I love you."

"Love you, too," Johnny said, and then he headed off toward his room.

I welcomed the tranquility from the two beers. My eyelids grew heavy, and I faded toward unconsciousness. My cell phone rang and woke me. I didn't recognize the number. I answered the call, and a male voice said, "Alexandra?"

"No, this is her husband's number. Who's calling?"

There was a click as the line went dead. The heaviness in my eyelids was gone. I found myself mistrusting my wife.

Again.

I woke in the middle of the night. I'd dozed off in my chair in front of the flickering television. A *Seinfeld* rerun was playing. I turned off the TV, tried my best to stay asleep, and stumbled down the hallway toward my bedroom. The door to Alexandra's bedroom was open, and her bed was untouched. I looked at my watch. It was 2:07 a.m.

A surge of annoyance ran through me. Where the devil was she at 2 o'clock in the morning on a Thursday night? My hopes for a quick return to slumber were dashed. I was full of adrenaline, and I wasn't going back to sleep anytime soon. I walked into her room and laid down on her bed. The familiar smell of her hair from the pillows jolted me. It had been a long time since we'd touched the same sheets together.

I heard a car door slam outside. A minute later, Alexandra stood in the bedroom doorway. She carried her high heel shoes in one hand and wore a black spaghetti strap cocktail dress. Those spectacular legs were glistening from mid-thigh on down.

She was startled to see me. "What are you doing in my room?" she said.

"Waiting up. Where were you?" My voice quivered with resentment.

"Oh, Jesus, Nico. I'm not a sixteen-year-old girl, and you're not my dad. I went out with the girls and had a couple of drinks and some laughs. It was fun. You should try it sometime."

"I don't believe you."

"Believe whatever you want. Can you get out of my room now so I can go to sleep?"

I turned on the overhead lights, and examined the illuminated spectacle of Alexandra Antone. Her arms were crossed, and she was smirking down at me. A streak of red lipstick stretched from her upper lip across her right cheek. Was she was playing kissy-face with the girls?

I lost it. "Are you playing me?" I said.

"What are you talking about?"

"Are you playing me for a fool? Who were you with?" She turned her back on me and walked into her closet. "You are such a buzzkill," she called out. "You always hate it when I have fun. I have a life. I'm sorry you're jealous."

I ran to her like a wild bull. I grabbed her by the arm and swung her around to face me. "Are you having an affair?" I screamed.

Dull eyes stared back at me. Alexandra blinked twice, shook her head in disgust, and said, "No, I'm not. And get your hands off of me, Nico. You're still the same small-town hick you've always been."

Her defiance infuriated me further. "I'm sick of you, and I'm sick of our bogus marriage."

She laughed at me and said, "You need to find somebody else. Someone who likes listening to your boring medical stories. Someone who wants to cook meat and potatoes for you. Someone who enjoys staying home and watching TV with you."

"I'm married to you. I'm not finding anybody else while I'm your husband."

"Are you my husband, Nico? Or my dependent?"

I saw flames. I picked up her six-foot-tall cast iron coat rack and rammed the shaft through the closet wall. The metal hung there, cleaving the room between us. "Are you crazy?" Her shriek was ear-splitting.

"At least I'm not a whore." With those words, I'd crossed the line. As of that moment, I knew I could no longer live with the woman. "If you want to stay out half the night like a tramp, don't bother to come home at all."

"I'm not going anywhere," she screeched. "You're the one who needs to move out. I paid for this damn house."

The hardwood floor creaked behind me, and a voice bellowed, "Shut the fuck up! Both of you!" It was Johnny, standing in the doorway in his undershorts. My world stopped. Alex and I stared at our son, and no words were offered.

Alexandra spoke at last. She said, "Whatever. Can you two get out of my bedroom now?"

Johnny shook his head and disappeared into the darkness of his own room. I was so embarrassed and furious I found it hard to breathe. The two most important relationships in my life were imploding before my eyes. I left Alexandra's room, and she shut her door behind me. I leaned against the closed door of Johnny's bedroom and said, "I'm sorry, son. I'm sorry you had to hear that."

"Then stop talking about it," he said. I waited there for five minutes. He made no further sound. I walked away, back to my isolation in the master bedroom.

I lay in the dark with a pillow over my eyes and replayed what had just gone down. My life was ridiculous. My separate-evening, separate-bedroom, give-your-husband-shit-whenever-possible marriage was ridiculous. How could Johnny have a healthy adolescence under these circumstances?

I had no answers. I was angry, depressed, and reeling. I reached into the drawer of my bedside table, pulled out my bottle of Ambien, popped two, and chased them with a swallow of water from last night's glass. I was an expert at anesthesia, even when I was the patient.

The next day I dragged myself through five routine surgeries although I was so angry it took all my will to concentrate on my craft. When I returned to my house that evening, Johnny was stretched out in my lounge chair. He was watching TV and typing into his laptop. He'd been asleep when I left for work that morning, so I hadn't seen him since the screaming session in the hallway. Alexandra was nowhere to be seen.

"Hey, Dad," Johnny said without looking up.

"Hello, son. Did you get some sleep after that whole episode last night?"

"I did. Mom gave me a ton of crap this morning for swearing at her and being disrespectful." His face soured. If there was more to say, he wasn't going there. He closed the laptop and said, "Other than that, it was a good day. I've been researching a lot of stuff about Hibbing on the Internet."

He had my attention.

"That was excellent Chinese food last night, wouldn't you agree?" he said.

"It was."

"It'll be our last decent Chinese food for awhile, Dad. I don't think there'll be any outstanding Chinese restaurants up there in Hibbing. I want to do it."

"Do it?"

"I want to get away from Palo Alto Hills High, away from Amanda Feld, and away from Mom. I want to go to Minnesota. Will you take me?" He held out his hand toward me. I stared at it and contemplated the implications of the gesture. Johnny was an impulsive kid, capable of making radical and irrational decisions in a heartbeat, but he'd never made a decision that impacted his life to this degree.

"You mean it?"

"I do. Can you walk away from your anesthesia job?"

"Well…" My thoughts were jumbled as I pondered the coin spinning through the air. Heads, I honored my love for my son and joined him in this adventure. Tails, I maintained my love for the warmth of California and my stable university job.

The tipping point was Alexandra. She was a toxic presence in my life. More than a marital separation, I needed an exorcism. It wasn't a question of love. I didn't even like her.

The coin landed on heads. I clasped Johnny's outstretched hand and said, "Let's do this, son. Let's move."

"Can't wait, Daddy-O," Johnny said.

"I'll call Uncle Dominic in the morning and set things up."

Johnny smiled and repeated again, "Can't wait."

CHAPTER 4
HIGHWAY 61 VISITED

I drove the black bullet of my BMW up Minnesota Highway 61, one hour north of Duluth and two hours short of the Canadian border. Johnny and I flew in from San Francisco to the Twin Cities that morning, and picked up the car from an interstate driving service in Minneapolis.

Our send-off in California was bitter. Alexandra dropped us off at the curb at San Francisco International Airport. She gave Johnny a big hug and said, "I love you, John-John. Call me every night."

"Love you too, Mom," he said. I watched their exchange with intrigue. Although he was eager to move thousands of miles away from her, Johnny still loved his mother. What can you say? She was the best mom he'd ever had.

As for me, I wasn't going to profess any love this morning. Alexandra faced me, her eyes vacant and cold. "Are you going to be OK without us?" I said.

"I'll be better than OK without you," she said, her voice dripping with its customary arrogance. "If I'm lucky, you'll never come back." She grabbed the door handle of her Aston Martin, jutted her chin toward the sky and said, "Go."

That's the way it ended. I watched her drive off, and I was jolted by an unexpected surge of glee. I felt an unfamiliar sense of freedom, like a captive hawk unhooded and released from its tether. I had no idea when I would see her again, and I wasn't in a hurry to find out.

Ten hours later, Johnny and I were driving north on a spectacular Minnesota winter day, with the blue expanse of Lake Superior sprawling ocean-like on our right and the setting sun disappearing behind the infinite expanse of pines on our left. I detoured up Highway 61 for the novelty of the famous road, so my son could witness the world's largest freshwater lake. The scenery was world class, but for me the highlight was spending time with Johnny uninterrupted by the distractions of a television, an Xbox, or cell phone calls. Exiled from California, Johnny had no friends except me, and I liked it that way.

He slumped in the passenger seat and stared out the side window. Despite the winter temperatures, he'd rolled down his window and the icy breeze from Highway 61 fluttered through his hair. I was in control of the music. For this occasion, it had to be Bob Dylan. I cued up *Highway 61 Revisited*, and blasted the title song though the speakers. I belted out the lyrics in a nasal twang: "Well Abe says, 'Where do you want this killin' done?' God says, 'Out on Highway 61.'" My "61" came out as a screeching "sexty-waawn," mimicking Dylan to the best of my ability.

"Bob Dylan wrote that song about this highway?" Johnny said.

"He did."

"It's a pretty creepy lyric. And you're screaming it out like it's an anthem. He's singing about killing a son?"

"It's from the Old Testament. God told Abraham to sacrifice his only son."

"So? Did he kill his son?"

"No. He was prepared to do it, to obey God, but at the last minute God sent an angel to stop him. Instead of killing his son, Abraham sacrificed a ram."

Johnny shook his head. "What kind of song is that? Sorry, Dad. I can't get into the Dylan thing. It's so hard to listen to the guy's voice. That screeching is pretty awful."

"Bob Dylan is one of the most imitated vocalists of the last hundred years. He gave every singer with a less-than-perfect voice a blueprint of how to sneer and twist off syllables."

"He's all mumbles to me."

"Try to get past the sound of his voice, and listen to the words. Dylan was the first songwriter to turn poetry into popular music."

"Who cares about poetry?"

"What is rap and hip-hop music but poetry? What do Jay Z or Kanye West do but chant some simple rhymes over a drum beat?"

Johnny looked unconvinced.

"Bob Dylan changed music forever. Before Dylan, the top singers were crooners like Frank Sinatra and Elvis Presley, guys with silky voices who performed songs written by unknown people. Then along came Dylan, coughing out "Blowin' in the Wind" with a voice like sandpaper on wood. He jammed his songs into your ears with that raspy nasal twang, and crossed you up with changes in inflection no one ever heard before."

"Why would anyone ever listen to that?"

"Great songs. 'The Times They Are A-Changin',' 'Mr. Tambourine Man,' 'Like a Rolling Stone.' Songs that influenced every writer that followed after him."

"It doesn't make sense to me. How can a guy who changed the world come out of all this?" Johnny said, waving his hands at the endless forests. "From up here in the sticks?"

"God only knows where genius is born, but education had something to do with it. Hibbing High School. The same classrooms and hallways you'll be in tomorrow."

I spun the steering wheel to the left as we departed Highway 61 and veered west toward the heart of the Superior National Forest. Lake County Highway 15 was a curving two-lane highway that slalomed over gentle hills and carved through wilderness untouched by 21st-Century development. It connected the two metropolises of Silver Bay and Hoyt Lakes, each with a population of about 2,000. The road was smooth and the setting was desolate. We hadn't seen another car in ten minutes. I compressed the accelerator pedal and watched the speedometer climb. "Hang on, son. We're going for triple digits."

When our speed hit 100 miles per hour, I looked over at Johnny. There was no trace of fear—he was loving it.

A sudden blaze of brown fur streaked across the road as the deer jumped out of the forest 100 yards in front of our car. "Shit!" I yelled, and stomped on the brakes so hard I thought my foot would break through the floorboard. Our car fishtailed counterclockwise. The rear wheels made a skid into the dirty snow on the side of the road, and our front fender slammed into the deer's flank. I heard the crunch of crumbling steel, and saw the deer's white tail slide up the windshield and over the top of the car. The airbags deployed, and twin balloons of white fabric blotted out the sun. The rear of the car wracked into something solid and stopped with a resounding thump.

I reached down and turned off the ignition. My hands were shaking. We'd hit the deer broadside at 100 mph. Highway 15 was now graced with one dead deer, one smashed-up BMW, and two happy-to-be-alive Antones. I took census of my four limbs and my vital functions. I didn't seem to be injured. I feared for Johnny. I elbowed my air bag aside, and looked over at the passenger seat. There was movement behind Johnny's air bag. I pushed the fabric aside, and saw my son crouched forward with his head between his knees.

"Are you all right?" I said.

Johnny was hyperventilating—a violent wind entered and exited his gaping mouth. Blood dripped from the right side of his chin. "Are you nuts, Dad?" he screamed. "You almost killed me. That was the scariest thing I've ever seen."

I was reeling. What kind of father was I? I'd almost offed us both. "I'm sorry," I said. "I didn't think…"

"You didn't think? Do you ever think? Oh, what the hell am I doing up here?" Johnny buried his face in his hands and wailed, "Everybody I know is in California. My mother is thousands of miles away. I'm up here in the woods with you, stuck in a ditch in outer Mongolia. We're going to freeze to death and die right here. I should never have left home."

I didn't know what to say. I started to reach out toward my son to comfort him, but Johnny grew more agitated, turned away, and wrestled with the airbag until he found the door latch. He pushed the door ajar, and burst out into the sub-freezing air outside.

I opened my own door and twisted my way out of the car. The right front quarter of the vehicle was buckled like an accordion. The deer lay mangled on the roadside at the rear of the car, its glassy eyes staring skyward into the void. Blood seeped from its ears, nose, and mouth. Its thorax was buckled, concave and deformed.

What a waste.

Behind me, Johnny said. "Dead deer. Totaled car. Stranded in the middle of nowhere. Great job, Dad."

"It all happened so fast…"

"No. You were driving like a maniac, and now we're stuck. We're so stuck. There's no people in these woods but lumberjacks. Lumberjacks who would be hunting this deer if you hadn't killed it." Johnny shook his head. He stuck out his jaw, square and resolute. "I'm done. I changed my mind. I want to go home."

I'd heard enough. "No. We're going to Hibbing," I barked. "It's what you and I decided to do. Together, that's what you and I decided."

"I'm un-deciding."

"It's too late for that. I'm pulling rank on you. We're in Minnesota, and we're staying in Minnesota." I walked back to the driver's door, unsheathed a small Swiss Army knife from my key chain, stabbed the point of the blade into the airbag, and slashed a 10-inch gouge in the material. I squeezed the remainder of the air out, compressed the bag into a dense lump the size of a basketball, and stuffed it back into its housing inside the steering wheel. I repeated the same treatment on the passenger airbag, and pushed the deflated fabric back into the dashboard.

"Get in," I commanded.

"You don't understand, Dad. What's the point of getting into this wreck of a car, marooned ass-end first in a snow bank?"

I ignored his sky-is-falling attitude, and pushed the ignition button. The engine sprang to life. I floored the accelerator pedal, and listened to the roar of the motor echo off the virgin pines around us.

"Get in," I repeated.

Johnny looked both ways on the deserted highway, and his shoulders slumped. He climbed into the passenger seat, with a look of hopeless resignation etched on his face. We were miles from the nearest town, and the deformed car was our only hope to limp out of the wilderness. I shifted the transmission into Drive and wondered if the right front tire would move within the mangled fender. With a lurch, the BMW rolled forward out of the snow bank. Lucky us. I whistled through my teeth and turned the automobile back onto Highway 15 for the last leg of our trip toward Hibbing.

I vowed that the next time I saw God, I'd run a little slower. Abraham sacrificed a ram instead of killing his son.

I settled for a deer.

CHAPTER 5
BOB DYLAN DRIVE

In Northern Minnesota, a "Ranger" is an inhabitant of the mining towns along the Mesabi, Vermillion, and Cuyuna Iron Ranges. Unlike a mountain range, a Minnesota iron range has no elevated topography, no grand vistas and no snow-capped peaks. An iron range is a geological phenomenon, named for the deposits of rich iron-laden minerals just beneath the earth's surface. Rangers take great pride in their iron mines. They'll tell you the American ships, tanks, and planes which won World Wars I and II were constructed from steel that originated in these Minnesota mines. No tunnels are required to mine Minnesota ore—a mere scraping of the top layer of trees and topsoil is all that's needed to expose the largest deposits of iron-containing rock in the United States.

Johnny and I passed the open pit of the Pillsbury Mine, five miles outside of Hibbing. Deep in the concavity of mines like this one, electric shovels the size of small office buildings excavated the iron-containing taconite rock, while the largest dump trucks on Earth carried 240-ton loads of rock to the mining factories on the edges of the pit.

Johnny pointed to a solitary billboard standing in the woods on the left side of the highway, and said, "Whoa, check that out." The billboard depicted a giant fetus in utero. The caption read, *Hello world. My heart was beating 18 days after conception.*

"Hmm. Disturbing," Johnny said. "What's the point of that?"

"Some folks up here don't believe in abortion. They believe life begins in the womb. I guess they pay for billboards to try to sway people to their way of thinking."

Two more curves up the road, the town of Hibbing spread out before us. A row of boxy stucco homes stood shoulder to shoulder, their canted roofs covered with fresh snow. A silver water tower bearing the stenciled name HIBBING crested a hilltop behind them. Our journey was at an end.

Bob Dylan once wrote, "*Hibbing's a good ol' town... I ran away from it when I was 10, 12, 13, 15, 15 ½, 17 an' 18. I been caught an' brought back all but once.*" I followed a similar path. I blew out of this town years ago, and clawed my way to a better life in California. I vowed never to return. That was before I had a son, a son who needed Hibbing.

I turned onto Howard Street, the main thoroughfare, and drove along the downtown strip of commercial buildings. Neon lights flashed the names of two banks, three restaurants, three taverns, and a liquor store. Six inches of new-fallen snow covered the surface of the two-laned street. Our tires made a scrunching sound as we drove. Mounds of ice and snow lined the perimeter of the road like levees isolating the street from the storefronts.

The vista was familiar, and it saddened me. Hibbing was unchanged from the Januarys of my youth. A woman dressed in a bulky goose-down parka crossed Howard Street in front of us, her scarf trailing in the wind behind her. I slowed to let her pass. She tested the snow-covered surface with exacting steps. Johnny followed the parka-clad woman's progress in wordless wonder.

I drove the 12-block length of Howard Street and made a left turn onto 1st Avenue, the second of Hibbing's two main business routes. Similar to Howard Street, 1st Avenue was home to three gas stations, four more bars, and two liquor stores.

"What do you think?" I said.

"There's not much here," Johnny said. "It looks like a ghost town. Black and white. Dark buildings and white snow. Lots of bars and liquor stores."

"Alcohol is a tonic against the tedium. It's a long winter up here."

"Iron miners drink a lot?"

"As long as there have been mining towns, there have been mining towns with taverns. But Hibbing is different. There are a lot of educated people here. Remember, this is the biggest urban area between Duluth and Winnipeg."

Johnny laughed. "That's not saying much, Daddy-O."

I turned off 1st Avenue and drove through six blocks of humble residential neighborhoods until I reached 7th Avenue, a narrow tunnel between rows of stark leafless trees. Stocky two-story homes lined up behind the trees like chess pieces behind pawns. Windows were miniscule. Walls were thick. The buildings were efficient barricades for holding in heat against brutal conditions. Hibbing houses weren't built for style; they were built to protect people from bitter cold.

After five or six blocks, the 7th Avenue street signs changed, and read Bob Dylan Drive. I parked the car when we reached the corner of 24th Street and Bob Dylan Drive. The corner house was a two-story grey cube lacking a single gable. Foot-long icicles hung from the roofline. No sign or placard designated the structure as a famous building.

"Why are we stopped here?" Johnny said.

"This was Bob Dylan's house."

"This was where he was born?"

"No. He was born in Duluth, 75 miles south of here. His parents moved to this house when Dylan was a boy. His real name was Robert Zimmerman, and this was his home back in 1959 when he graduated from Hibbing High School."

"So it's not a museum or anything." Johnny craned his neck to take in the particulars of the scene.

"No. It's someone's residence. I don't know who lives here now, but it's just a regular house."

As I spoke, a man came out of the front door. He tightened the hood of his parka against the wind and aimed a shovel at the snow on the walkway. After his second shovelful, he stopped and looked up at us in our bashed-in

BMW. A $120,000 German sports car with a smashed-in front end and California license plates couldn't be commonplace in Hibbing in January. On the other hand, I suspect an out-of-town vehicle perusing the old Zimmerman home was not unusual. Muslims made pilgrimages to Mecca. Dylan fans made pilgrimages to Hibbing.

The shoveler wore his hood pulled down over his eyebrows and a brown scarf wrapped snug over his mouth. Only his eyes were exposed to the frigid air. He continued to stare at Johnny and me.

Behind my windshield, I felt like a goldfish inside an aquarium. To ease the awkwardness of the moment, I waved at the man. The resident of 2425 Bob Dylan Drive only exhaled steam into the frigid Minnesota air. He did not wave back.

"Friendly guy," Johnny said.

"Cut him some slack. I'll bet every day some dude from New York, Pennsylvania, Illinois, England or Italy knocks on this guy's door and asks him if they can take a tour of the house. It must get old."

"Let's get out of here," Johnny said.

I put the car in gear and drove thirty seconds down the road to the intersection of Bob Dylan Drive and 21st Street. To our right, an imposing three-story red brick fortress sprawled over four square blocks. It was easily the largest building in town.

Johnny craned his neck up at the structure, and said, "What's this?"

"This is your new school."

"It looks like a castle. How can they have such a monster school in such a little town?"

"A hundred years ago the town of Hibbing was located two miles north of here. When the mining companies discovered the richest supply of iron ore in the United States in the soil below the existing town, they cut a deal. The mining companies agreed to move the entire village and build

Hibbing this wonderful high school in the new location as a reward for being relocated. C'mon, let's go take a look."

We walked up the front steps of the high school. At that moment, I was proud of my roots and proud of my alma mater. The front door was unlocked, and we stepped inside. I touched the brass railing with my bare hand, just like I had when I was 17 years old. The entryway was adorned with a tiled mosaic floor, a majestic marble staircase, and original oil paintings and murals on the walls depicting the history of the Iron Range.

"It looks like a museum," Johnny said.

"See that plaque? This building is on the National Register of Historic Places. Wait until you see the auditorium."

We walked to the end of the main hallway and passed through a set of double doors into the auditorium, an Art Deco wonder adorned by cut-glass chandeliers built in Czechoslovakia, and modeled after the ornate Capitol Theater in New York City. With a capacity of 1,800, the auditorium could seat every student in the school at once.

"This is where I received my high school diploma. And this is where Bob Dylan first performed and sang in public. They say he banged on the piano like a Little Richard clone."

Johnny said nothing. He was biting the nails of his right hand, and he looked nervous.

"You OK?" I said.

"I don't know. Now that I see this place, I'm getting worried. What if it doesn't work out for me here? I mean, wherever I go, I'm still Johnny Antone. What if I'm in the middle of the pack here, just like I was in Palo Alto? What if we moved here for nothing?"

"You've got what it takes, Johnny. You'll do great here. Let's go. I've got something else to show you." I led him out the front entrance of the school, and pointed across the street to a white colonial mansion on the corner of Bob Dylan Drive and 21st Street. It was twice the size of any house we'd seen in town. The front lawn was an expansive half-acre of drifted snow.

"That's Uncle Dom's house," I said.

"Nice."

"It's one of the most impressive homes in town. When I was a schoolboy, doctors were the wealthiest people, and Dr. Dominic Scipioni was the top surgeon in Hibbing."

We crossed the street together. Dom's front walk was covered by a foot of crusted snow, unbroken by a single footprint. Johnny tip-toed up the path, his Nike Air Jordans sinking in and filling with snow on every step. "Dom isn't doing a great job of keeping the snow off his walk," he said.

"He doesn't live here anymore, that's why we got the place. Dom has homes in Arizona and Montana. He keeps this family house for the nostalgia of the old homestead."

"What's the deal with this Uncle Dom, anyway?" Johnny said. "Is he your uncle, or is he my uncle?"

"He's nobody's uncle. Dom's not related to any of us, but he's always treated me like family. Dr. Dom was my role model and mentor ever since I was a teenager."

I bent over and peeled back the corner of the welcome mat. A shiny steel key lay underneath. "This is a sweet deal for us. We get one of the best houses in town, two blocks from the hospital and across the street from the high school, no questions asked. It'll be our Minnesota man-cave."

Johnny followed me into the house. The interior was meat-locker cold. We could see the water vapor of our breath. A lifelong ectomorph, I loathed hypothermia. I turned the thermostat up to 72 degrees and switched on the lights in the living room. "I recommend you proceed at once to the den in the basement. Dom has three big screen televisions, side by side by side. You can watch the NBA, the NHL, and the PGA Tour at the same time, by the mere effort of swiveling your neck a few degrees. And you want to know the best thing about Dom's house?"

"What's that?"

"There's no one here to yell at you."

"I'm with you there, Dad." Johnny descended the stairs into the basement.

I toured the living room. Dom's house lacked the towering ceilings of our glassed-in California home. The space felt claustrophobic with its tiny square windows, dark paneled walls, and smoke-stained brown-bricked fireplace. I knew every knot-hole in this room from my previous lifetime here, when Dom's family was my family. Once upon a time, this room represented the height of luxury to me.

I walked over to the framed black-and-white photograph I knew would be standing on the fireplace mantle. The photo portrayed a young man and a young woman dressed in formal attire. The dark-haired girl wore a square-necked white dress, and held a broad bouquet of flowers. Her lips were closed, and she had a solemn, far-away look in her eyes. The man wore a tuxedo and a goofy smile that was incongruous with the woman's apparent gloom.

A flood of grief overcame me. I'd traveled all day, and this picture was the tortured endpoint to my journey. It was Dom's house, and Dom could decorate the place as he pleased. Some people preferred to put their memories on their fireplace mantles. Some memories were better left hidden.

The boy in the picture was Nico Antone. And the girl? She was from another lifetime. I'd shoveled dirt over this unsmiling girl years ago. She was dead, and I needed her to stay dead.

CHAPTER 6
MR. DYLAN'S BLUES

Johnny and I ate breakfast together at 6:30 a.m. It was a complex meal—we split a six-pack of powdered sugar donuts from the Seven-Eleven and washed them down with two glasses of orange juice. The talc-like sugar dusted Johnny's upper lip and the collar of his San Francisco Giants T-shirt. The kitchen was quiet as a library. The only sounds were our glasses clacking against the tabletop. It was Johnny's first day of school and my first day to report to the local hospital. We were each journeying into the unknown, and the tension connected us.

I broke the silence. "Nervous?" I said.

"Nope."

I didn't believe it. Johnny's eyebrows cast dark shadows, shielding his sunken eyes in blackness. I waited a minute for a sequel to his monosyllabic teenage offering, but no conversation followed.

"Want me to walk over there with you?" I said. "Make sure the paperwork is all OK for your transfer?"

Johnny scoffed. "Are you kidding? I'm 17 years old, Dad, not 7. I'll figure it out." He pushed away from the table and left the kitchen. I watched him pace back and forth across the living room floor like a skydiver awaiting his turn to jump out of the plane. Then he grabbed the front door knob and said, "I hope this school doesn't suck, for both of our sakes." The door slammed shut, and I looked out the front window to see Johnny hopping through last night's frozen footprint holes in the snow. Steam rose from his wet hair. He wore a fleece turtleneck over a pair of cotton sweat pants, and no gloves, hat, or boots. I watched him bound two stairs at a time up the entryway of Hibbing High School.

I needed to be at Hibbing General Hospital before 7:30. I'd filled out all the necessary paperwork online. I'd already secured my medical staff privileges and my appointment to the anesthesia service. I wanted to arrive early to check out the facilities and meet the people I'd be working with in the coming months.

I dressed myself in a pair of Sorel boots, a North Face jacket, and one of Dom's Minnesota Vikings knit caps. A puff of wind from the north scorched my face as I headed out into the winter morning. The stark chill woke me up faster than two espressos. The hospital was a three-block hike from Dom's house, so it made sense to leave the battered BMW on the curb and walk to Hibbing General.

The hospital was an aging three-story building made of yellowed stone. The front doors were tall brown slabs flanked by two white Doric columns. I smiled at the polished surface of the brown wooden doors. I'd worked summers as a maintenance helper at the General during my college years. One day my foreman gave me a can of red paint and told me to paint these very doors. The next day the hospital administrator chewed our heads off for painting the hospital front doors the color of blood. He dispatched me to the front of the building with a paintbrush and a gallon of brown paint. The doors were still brown this very day.

I found the surgical locker room, a small space one-tenth the size of the men's locker room at Stanford. I selected a set of scrubs off the shelf and changed out of my street clothes. At Stanford the scrubs were bright royal blue. In Hibbing the scrubs were faded green and looked like they'd been in use since the day I was born in this very building.

I was edgy, even though I was overqualified to work at this little community hospital. At Stanford every nurse, doctor, and janitor knew my name. Here I'd have to earn the respect of dozens of people who'd never heard of me. Medical careers don't travel as well as business careers. A businessman in California could be promoted to a CEO job in Minneapolis, but doctors who moved from one state to another started at the bottom of the ladder, behind physicians who had reputations and referral patterns already established in the new community.

I entered the hallway of the operating room complex. Hibbing General had only six operating rooms, compared to the 40 rooms at Stanford. The schedule for the day was posted on a white board across from the central desk. My old med school classmate, Michael Perpich, the Chief of Staff at Hibbing General, was the surgeon working in operating room #1. Dr. Perpich was repairing an inguinal hernia on a 43-year-old man—a routine case. I could pop in and say hello without distracting Perp from his task.

I put on a surgical hat and mask and pushed open the door into O.R. #1. The operating room was small, a compact 30 feet by 30 feet. The linoleum floor showed brown stains from old iodine spills. The faded turquoise tile on the walls had witnessed thousands of hernia surgeries. Michael Perpich was bent over the patient's abdomen. He saw me walk through the door, and said, "Nico Antone. The Tone. Get your ass over here." A surgical mask covered his face, but I knew my friend was grinning.

"They said you needed some help to fix this hernia," I said.

"You're a God damned gas-passer. You couldn't fix this hernia if I held the book open for you."

"I'm here to see if your hands shake as much as they used to, Perp."

"I came here straight from the card room at the Corner Bar at dawn. Never felt better."

"You're so full of shit."

"Did you guys get situated over at Dom's?"

"We did. Johnny wasn't thrilled about waking up at 6 a.m., but he ran up the high school steps two at a time this morning."

"So he's a gunner. Just like his dad."

"I got by."

"You opened a textbook once a week in med school, and you still finished number one in our class. I can't believe you came back. When you left for California you said never wanted to see a snowflake again.'"

"Things change, Perp. My kid needs an upper-Midwest high school diploma."

"California kid comes to the wilderness to go to the head of the class, eh? I'll tell you one thing: the Hibbing teachers will shape him up. I had sergeants in the Army who were more mellow than the Hibbing faculty."

The scrub tech, a blonde woman wearing too many layers of blue eye shadow, said, "My son is a sophomore. He studies four hours every night."

"Nico, meet Heidi, my right-hand woman," Perpich said. "She's my assistant, my psychotherapist, and the encyclopedia of all gossip great and small in the village of Hibbing."

"Nice to meet you," I said.

"Heidi, this is Dr. Nicolai Antone, a welcome addition to the anesthesia staff. Dr. Antone and I went to med school together. He was an anesthesiologist in California, but now he's one of us, the slightly-better-than-average staff of Hibbing General. So you left Alexandra behind?"

"I did."

"Good move. Not much up here for princesses."

"You're married, Dr. Antone?" Heidi said.

"I am. My wife is back in California."

She fluttered mascara-laden eyelashes at me and said, "Welcome to Hibbing General. I look forward to working with you."

Perpich looked up toward the head of the operating room table and said, "Bobby, did he get his antibiotic?"

A wisp of a man—narrow and bony—stood at the head of the operating room table in the anesthesia cockpit of machines, monitors, intravenous drips, and drug cabinets. The man said, "She did. One gram of Kefzol at 7:45."

"Nico, I want you to meet Bobby Dylan, our Director of Nurse Anesthesia," Perpich said.

My head snapped back. I wondered if I trusted my ears. Bobby Dylan? The same name as the legendary musician? Here in Hibbing?

The nurse anesthetist ignored Perpich's cordial introduction and said nothing to me. I was miffed. Who did this guy think he was? He was only a nurse anesthetist. Why the ingratiating attitude toward me, a board-certified anesthesiologist physician?

It was a small hospital, and despite my negative first impression I felt compelled to meet my fellow anesthesia colleague. I walked around the operating room table and entered the anesthesia station. A blue paper hat and mask covered Dylan's face. His sole facial features were the recessed caves that housed his glossy fish eyes, and the speckled black and gray eyebrows that floated above them.

I extended my hand and said, "Greetings. I guess we'll be working together."

Dylan turned his back on me. The beep, beep, beep of the patient's pulse rate hung between us. He reached over and turned the knob on the anesthesia machine that titrated the oxygen flow. He coughed twice—loud, harsh, barking sounds, and said, "We opted out here, Mac."

"What?" I said. I wasn't sure what I had just heard.

"We opted out," Dylan repeated. He still wasn't looking at me. He picked up his clipboard and made some notations on the patient's chart with a pen.

I was getting more and more pissed off. My first impressions were confirmed. This guy was a dick. I didn't care if this was Dylan's anesthetic, his operating room, and his hospital. I was unaccustomed to this degree of condescension within two feet of an anesthesia machine. He turned up the intravenous propofol infusion and continued to ignore me, even though I was close enough to smell the staleness of his body odor.

I checked the settings on the anesthesia machine and monitors, looking for some sign that Dylan was as incompetent as an anesthetist as he was as a conversationalist.

He was using routine concentrations of standard anesthetic drugs. The ECG, blood pressure, and oxygen saturation numbers all showed normal values. Dylan wasn't a doctor, but at the moment he was delivering a routine anesthetic in a safe fashion.

I thought to myself, *Fuck you, you dirtball.* If this Bobby Dylan character wanted to be left alone, I was going to leave him alone. I said, "Hey Perp, I'll catch you when your case is done, OK?"

"Will do. I'll meet you in the lounge. Give me 30 minutes."

"See you there." My feathers were ruffled. It was great to see Michael Perpich again, but if my initial contact with this nurse anesthetist was any indication, my welcome in the Hibbing medical community was going to be as chilly as a January dawn. I made my way to the operating room lounge, a stark room with four walls of undecorated peach-colored wallboard. The sole furnishings were two long tables and a dozen chairs. All the chairs were empty. Sections of the *Duluth News Tribune* and the *Hibbing Daily Tribune* were strewn over the tabletops. The aroma of fresh brewed coffee filled the air. I poured myself a cup and selected a glazed doughnut from a platter.

I felt like a midcareer misfit, stuck in somebody else's workplace. I missed Stanford. On a professional level, this move to Minnesota looked to be a near-death experience for me.

Michael Perpich's clogs hammered the floor when he walked in. He pinched the back of my neck, snatched two doughnuts for himself, and plopped down in a chair across from me. "It's great to see you, Tone," he said. "I still can't believe it."

I hadn't sat eye to eye with Perp for years. With his surgical cloaking removed, he looked ten years older than me. The top of his head had more dandruff than hair, and the creases around his nose and mouth were deep and long. His smile was genuine, and I chose to disregard the ancient appearance of the only acquaintance I had within a thousand miles.

"Glad you're here," I said. "I'm counting on you to be my lifeline at this place." I waved my hand at the desolate room. "Does anybody else work here?"

"Of course. We have a full staff, like any other community hospital, but we're light on anesthesiologists. Your timing is perfect. Our last two anesthesiologists retired and moved to the Sun Belt in November. We have six nurse anesthetists, but for tough cases we need an M.D. anesthesiologist in town. Now we've got you."

"So the rest of the anesthesia staff is all nurses?"

"Yep. Six nurse anesthetists. They're a solid group. I haven't had too many problems with them."

I was unconvinced. Nurse anesthetists were registered nurses with a year or more of intensive care unit experience, followed by two or three years of training in a nurse anesthesia program. They learned how to anesthetize patients, but they weren't medical doctors. In some hospitals, anesthesiologists worked with nurse anesthetists in anesthesia care teams, a team model in which one M.D. anesthesiologist might supervise four nurse anesthetists working in four separate operating rooms. Because this hospital had no anesthesia doctors, the nurse anesthetists were working unsupervised.

"What's the deal with the Bobby Dylan guy?" I asked. "He stopped one step short of open hostility. Is he a prick, or what?"

"Sometimes he is."

"He didn't give me the time of day."

"It's a turf thing. This is his hospital. You're an outsider. The guy doesn't want you here."

"He's a nurse. How does he get off giving me a hard time?"

"Minnesota is an opt-out state, Nico. The Minnesota governor opted out of the requirement for a medical doctor to supervise nurse anesthetists. Bobby Dylan can give anesthesia here, just the same as you can, even though he's not a doctor."

We opted out here, Mac. The words Dylan had uttered to me. *Opted out.*

"So it's legal here for a nurse anesthetist to give an anesthetic without being supervised by a physician?"

"That's right."

"That's substandard care, if you ask me, and it still doesn't make this Bobby Dylan guy a doctor. If you had enough physician anesthesiologists in town, would you still let jokers like him give anesthetics alone, or would you replace him with a doctor?"

Perpich threw up his hands. "That's never going to happen, so who cares? Dylan has been here a long time. He hasn't had any deaths, he's kept his nose clean, and he's not going anywhere."

"Why is he named Bobby Dylan? That can't be for real."

Perpich shrugged again. "I don't know what his real name is, and I don't care. He showed up in Hibbing 8 or 10 years ago, and his license and paperwork all identified him as Bobby Dylan. I asked him if that was his real name or if he'd changed his name."

"And he said?"

"He said his name was Bobby Dylan. Period. He dodged any questions about his past. He was a nurse anesthetist in the Afghanistan War. He's got a wife and a daughter. He plays guitar and sings at a bar downtown. Plays all the original Dylan songs. People tell me he's pretty talented. Maybe he was a huge Bob Dylan fan and he just wanted to move to Dylan's hometown, take Dylan's name, and get a job here. If so, he's done all three."

I shook my head. "That's pretty weird stuff."

"It gets more weird. He bought the old Zimmerman house."

"You're kidding."

"Nope."

"He's a psycho," I said.

Perpich's eyes twinkled. "Up here, there are a lot of characters. Get used to it. He'll grow on you, once you accept the fact that he's your peer."

"My peer? I'll never accept that."

As if summoned by their conversation, Bobby Dylan came in through the doorway, poured himself a cup of coffee, and sat in the opposite corner of the room. He peeled off his surgical hat to reveal a fuzzball of curled black and gray hair. He took out a pen and started filling out a crossword puzzle from the morning paper. His mouth stretched into a long yawn. It was just another day for him. My presence was of no consequence.

"I'm going to make rounds on my patients upstairs on the surgical wards," Perpich said. "Will you be home tonight?"

"Where else would I be?"

"I'll drop by. I've got some housewarming presents for you."

"Can you bring us a digital video recorder? Dom doesn't have one."

"No DVR. Just make sure you're hungry."

"Sounds good. See you later."

Right after Perpich left, I heard a rumbling voice behind me say, "Doctor Antone?"

I turned. It was Mr. Dylan. His facial expression was a cross between a smirk and an all-knowing smile.

"Yes?" I said, puzzled at the encounter.

"I dissed you back there in the operating room. Sorry about that. I was concentrating on my patient, and no one told me you were coming to town. I expect this place is big enough for both of us. No hard feelings?"

I was suspicious. The curl of Dylan's upper lip seemed to say, *I don't like you one bit, but I'll pretend that I do just to fuck with you.* Before I could answer, he sat on the tabletop in front of me and asked, "Why does a California guy like you move to the Iron Range?"

"I grew up here. I missed the ice fishing and deer hunting."

"Bullshit."

"My son transferred into the 11th grade. We want him to graduate from Hibbing High."

"Let me guess. You think he'll be the smartest kid in town."

"I have no idea. We just got here."

Dylan twirled a wisp of his moustache between his fingers and thumb. "I'll bet $1000 you and your kid are gone by next January. This ain't no place for boys from Californeye-aye. No place at all."

"We'll adjust."

"You OK working here, where nurse anesthetists are your equals?"

I bit the inside of my cheek. "I'm not sure nurses and doctors are equal. I expect I'll get used to the fact that nurses can give their own anesthetics here."

"Of course you will. Just remember, you've got no power over me here. No power at all." Dylan winked and said, "Now, if you'll pardon me, I've got to go make me some money."

He walked away, and his words echoed in my ears: No power over me at all. My first impression was reconfirmed. This Bobby Dylan was trouble.

It was break time, and the lounge was filling up. An attractive woman sat down at the adjacent table. She had the palest of green eyes that precisely matched the color of her scrub shirt. She had flawless skin and adorable dimples, and the knack of smiling nonstop as she chatted.

I smiled to myself, and forgot about the onerous Mr. Dylan. The sight of a beautiful woman trumped all of life's ills. It really did.

CHAPTER 7
IN SOME FOOL'S HAND

The school bell rang at the end of the day, and I watched students stream down the front steps of Hibbing High. Johnny separated himself from the pack and ran across the street toward me. He hopped over the picket fence gate, skipped up the walkway of Dom's house, and burst through the front door. He was grinning like a lottery winner.

"How was your day?" I said.

"It was a life-changing experience."

"In what way?"

"In every way. The kids were friendly. The teachers were cool. I was afraid the teachers might be backward, like, maybe not even as smart as me. But they were sharp."

I was stunned. This was the same kid whose last words this morning were, "I hope this school doesn't suck, for both of our sakes."

"What were the classes like?"

"Calculus should be a breeze. They're doing stuff I already learned in Palo Alto. In English they're reading *King Lear.* They're in the middle of the play already, and I've got about 100 pages to catch up. In AP U.S History they're doing the Constitution, which I'm pretty comfortable with. In physics they're working on relativity. That was pretty hard to follow, but one of my classmates is going to help me figure it out."

"Great. So you made some new friends?"

"The kids were real chill. They couldn't believe I moved here from California. At lunch time they asked me a million questions. I was worried I'd be treated like an outsider, but instead I felt more like a celebrity."

Johnny's cell phone chirped. He pulled it out and his thumbs flew across the keyboard. His foot tapped the ground at a frantic pace.

"You sure look happy," I said. "Who are you texting?"

"Just someone. Hey, I've got a lot of homework to do, and I'd like to get started. One hundred pages of iambic pentameter, anybody?"

"I don't think so. I already finished 11th grade."

"You're my hero, Dad." As Johnny went inside I heard his cell phone chime again. I was thrilled. It was only the top of the first inning, but we seemed to be pitching a perfect game so far. Johnny was enthusiastic, studying without prompting, making friends, and not complaining about anything.

So far, so good.

A Ford Explorer pulled up to the curb, and Michael Perpich climbed out carrying a cardboard box and a six-pack of Pabst Blue Ribbon. He pushed past the front door, and the sixty-degree temperature gradient from outside to the interior of the house fogged his thick spectacles. He flipped the glasses up over his forehead and handed the box to me. "Welcome to the North Country," he said.

Something was alive and moving inside the box. I opened the lid and was greeted by the sight of a six crappies, a type of Minnesota game fish I hadn't seen since I was twelve years old. Their gills strained in agonal efforts to breathe air.

"These fish were swimming two hours ago," he said.

I pulled one of the crappies out of the box. It was greenish-brown, 10 inches long, with a broad tailfin and a white underbelly. "Who caught these?" I said.

"Not me. You saw how I spent my day. These are from my neighbor, an old guy who's a retired U.S. Steel welder. He goes fishing every day and hooks more than he can eat. He caught these this afternoon. We'll have to clean them ourselves. Remember how?"

"I haven't skinned a fish in twenty years, but I can do it. Do you think I forgot how to be a Ranger?"

"Let's see what you've got."

The box was lined with pages from the *Duluth News Tribune*. I spread the newspaper on the kitchen table, dumped the fish onto the paper, and pulled a 12-inch knife out of a kitchen drawer.

"For a change, a surgeon is going to watch an anesthesiologist cut," I said.

Perpich crossed his arms over his chest. He snickered and leaned back against the refrigerator to watch.

I laid the six fish in parallel on the tabletop. I turned the first crappie on its side, and brought the blade down hard to cut off its head. Ending its life didn't trouble me one bit. In my boyhood I'd killed hundreds of pike, ducks, and partridge, and even a deer or two. The act of beheading a living thing was barbaric, but this wasn't a loving creature, it was food. I tossed the fish head aside, gutted the body, and scaled the glistening skin. I grabbed a second crappie and repeated the process. In a flurry the paper was covered with five more fish heads, a mound of fish scales, and twelve fillets.

"For a gas passer, that was a nice job cutting," Perp said. "Let's fry these up. I need an egg, some flour and access to Dom's spice drawer. Your boy drink beer?"

"No. He's only 17."

"I know how old he is. I asked you if he drinks."

"He doesn't."

"I fry my fish in beer batter. Johnny can finish off the bottle if he wants. I recommend you teach him to drink. He's going to party up here with his friends. If he didn't drink in California, he's sure to find some keggers up here at somebody's lake cabin."

"He's a pretty straight kid."

"C'mon. He's in 11th grade. Look at you and Angel. You two were the straightest kids in the history of Hibbing, and look what trouble you got into."

"Who's Angel?" said a voice from the stairway. It was Johnny, peering down on us from on high, a quizzical look on his face.

Perp looked at Johnny, and glanced over at me. Perp raised his eyebrows as if to say, *He's your son. You answer.*

"Johnny, this is my friend from medical school, Dr. Michael Perpich. He's the Chief of Staff at the Hibbing hospital."

"Good to meet you, Dr. Perpich. So Dad got into trouble with somebody named Angel? Sounds like a good story. Who was Angel?"

I wanted to make this conversation go away as soon as possible. "Angel was Dom's daughter," I said in a flippant tone. *Next topic, please.*

"What kind of trouble did you get into with her?"

"I don't want to talk about it. She's dead now." I busied myself setting the table. *Next topic, please.*

"Jeez, I'm sorry," said Johnny. "What happened?"

"She died of cancer." *Next topic, please.*

There was only one family picture in the whole house. Johnny walked over to the fireplace and studied the solitary photo there. "Is this Angel?" he said.

"That's her," Perp said.

Johnny studied the photograph for more than a minute, but if he recognized the man in the picture, he didn't admit it. His cell phone chimed the arrival of yet another text message, and Johnny punched in a reply. The next topic had arrived, I thought with relief.

"Someone texting you from California?" I said.

"No. It's a friend I met at school today."

I waited for more information, but Johnny was distracted and quiet. His thumbs kept moving. I surmised that natural selection would favor future generations with pointed, pliant, and powerful thumbs. I was glad he lost interest in Angel, and made a mental note to remove the photo from the mantle and put it in a dark and dank drawer somewhere Johnny would never find it again.

Perp busied himself preparing beer batter and flipping the fish in a frying pan. A dollop of fish grease hit the left lens of Perp's eyeglasses, and he didn't bother to wipe it off. The smell of the sizzling beer batter filled my nostrils. I spread three dinner plates on the tiny pine table in the corner of the kitchen.

Perp set out three bottles of Pabst on the table. "Time to eat, boys," he said. He laid four crappie fillets on each plate.

Johnny eyed the fish with mistrust. "These were alive twenty minutes ago?" he said.

"It's your baptism into Up North culture," Perp said. He hoisted a beer bottle. "Let me offer a toast to Papa Antone and his son. May you love the North Country like I do."

We tapped bottles together, and I watched Johnny slug down a third of his Pabst Blue Ribbon without a grimace. *Where did he learn to do that?*

Johnny bit into his crappie and said, "Hey, I like it. It's not sushi, but if you wash it down with enough beer, it hits the spot."

"Enough beer? I didn't think you liked beer at all," I said.

"I had a beer or two at Amanda's house. You never offered me one at home before. Dr. Perpich, you're much more mellow than Dad."

"I am mellow."

"Dr. Perpich, can I ask you a question?" Johnny said.

"Sure."

"You helped Dad get his job at the hospital, right?"

"I did. He was an easy sell."

"Could you get me a job at the hospital? An orderly job, something like that?"

I almost fell over. My son, born into a world of entitlement, had never worked a day in his life. Nor had he ever expressed any interest in working.

Michael Perpich raised an eyebrow and looked at me. I nodded in affirmation.

"Why do you want a job at the hospital?" Perp said.

"A friend I met at school today works at the hospital on weekends. She said it was super interesting. I told her my dad was doctor who was going to be on staff there. She encouraged me to try to get a job at the hospital, too."

"What's your friend's name?"

"Echo."

"Echo?" I said.

"Yeah, Dad. Cool name, isn't it?"

It was a name seeped in Hibbing history. I'd read all of Bob Dylan's biographies, and tattooed his entire Hibbing back story on my brain. Echo was the name of Bob Zimmerman's girlfriend in high school. I'd never heard of another person named Echo, until now.

"Echo. Yeah, I know who she is," Perp said. "Good kid. Works hard. Tell you what, Johnny. I'll talk to the operating room management people first thing in the morning, and see if I can call in a favor for you."

"That would be great. Thanks."

Johnny finished his fish, drank half the beer, and departed for his bedroom either to read King Lear or to send another hundred text messages to Echo. I wouldn't bet which.

"I like your son," Perpich said. "I'm impressed that he wants to work at the hospital. Let me tell you, that Echo is a cute girl. If Johnny's hanging out with her already, he's a lucky kid. He doesn't have much trouble meeting girls, does he?"

"No. Johnny's always had a way with the ladies."

"Good for him," Perp said, setting his napkin down alongside his empty plate. "I need to get home. I want to see my kids before they go to bed."

"I don't expect you have a lot of free time with five kids. I don't know how you do it."

"Great wife, great life. You know how that goes. Sharon takes care of everything. My job is to bring home the money and teach the kids how to play hockey. That's about it."

"You're lucky. The only domestic work my wife ever did was hire the nannies."

"Your wife makes enough money to pay for an army of nannies, a cook, a housekeeper, ten gardeners and a pool boy. So it isn't all bad, right?"

"It isn't great. A lot of miserable wealthy couples would love to have the family life you have."

"The snow is always whiter on the other side of the fence, Tone. If those miserable wealthy couples want to wire any of their money to Michael Perpich, M.D., I'll be happy to take their troubles off their hands. I've got a ton of college tuition to pay for. You working tomorrow?"

"Yep. First case at 7:30."

"Excellent. I'll see you at the General."

One hour past dawn the next day, I was administering my first North Country anesthetic to a 50-year-old man undergoing a shoulder arthroscopy and rotator cuff repair. The surgeon, Dr. Luke Castro, had good hands and a professional demeanor. The surgery was going well, and the anesthetic was routine until I heard the screaming in the hallway outside.

The green-eyed nurse from the day before burst into my operating room and said, "Dr. Castro, we've got a major trauma up from the E.R. It was a car versus truck. The driver of the car is all busted up. They're wheeling him into room #4 now. We need a trauma surgeon stat."

Castro looked up from the surgery and said, "What are the injuries?"

"He has an open fracture to the femur and a possible tear of the femoral artery. There's also facial trauma."

"I'm in the middle of this case right now. Is Dr. Perpich around?"

"They're calling him, but he hasn't answered."

"Do you have an anesthetist to start the case?"

"Dylan is free. He's in room #4 already. We need a surgeon."

Castro said, "Damn it, Lena. Give me a minute to clean up the bleeding here, and I'll come over."

She left the room, and I had a bad feeling. Yes, they needed a surgeon as soon as possible, but before they could do any surgery there had to be a safe anesthetic. Anesthesia for elective, scheduled surgery is a controlled, predictable exercise. Elective surgery patients have appropriate preoperative assessment, including all necessary diagnostic and therapeutic measures, and their anesthesia can be initiated at a non-hectic pace.

Emergency surgery is another story. The patient often has acute illness and is decompensating in some way that pushes the surgical team to operate without delay. The patient might be bleeding to death, or their stomach might be full of pizza and beer, poised to be regurgitated into the lungs when the patient loses consciousness.

Emergency anesthesia separates experts from pretenders.

Bobby Dylan wasn't a doctor. He wasn't an anesthesiologist. How many emergency cases had this Dylan guy done? One hundred? Two hundred? How much could he handle?

My doubts were validated five minutes later. The green-eyed nurse stuck her head into the operating room again and said, "Bobby's lost the airway. He needs help. Can you come?"

I was in the middle of a stable anesthetic for shoulder surgery. If the patient was dying next door, the choice was a no-brainer. I had to leave. I told the nurse in my operating room to watch my patient's vital signs monitor, and I ran over to room #4. My heart was pounding. My routine morning had transformed into a battlefield drama.

Welcome to the world of North Country anesthesia.

Inside room #4, Bobby Dylan was hunched over a sphere of red hamburger meat that one hour before had been a man's head. The hamburger sphere was medium rare, covered in blood, and showed no signs of normal anatomy except for two brown eyes and a wide beak of a nose. Dylan was holding an oxygen mask over the meat. The vital signs monitor confirmed that the patient's oxygen saturation level was at a dangerous low level of 78%. Any number less than

90% meant the man's brain and heart were not receiving sufficient oxygen.

Dylan's eyes were wild and his hands weren't moving. He looked like a death row criminal stewing over his own mortality. His hands were dormant at a time when he needed to insert a breathing tube and save this man's life.

"Did you try to intubate him?" I said.

"I can't get his mouth open. There's something wrong with his jaw."

"Did you give him any drugs?"

"I put him asleep with a dose of propofol, but I can't ventilate him at all."

"Did you paralyze him?"

"No."

I put on a pair of gloves and tried to wrench the man's mouth open. Dylan was right. The jaw was anchored. The teeth were a pearly fence, barring entry. The patient's oxygen saturation dropped to 70%. At this rate, a cardiac arrest was imminent. "Get Castro in here," I said. "He needs to trach this guy." Brain cells died after mere minutes of oxygen deprivation. We needed an emergency airway tube. The man looked like he weighed 300 pounds, and he had a pendulous beard and a stubby neck. I couldn't feel his trachea below the chin. Cutting into his neck was going to be a serious challenge.

I struggled to fit an oxygen mask over the patient's face and tried to force oxygen through the mangled anatomy of what used to be a mouth. The patient was gasping for air. Bubbles of dark blood percolated from his nostrils like coffee grounds overrunning a pot.

Castro entered the room. "You need to trach this guy," I said.

He palpated the patient's neck and said, "I can't even feel the trachea under all this fat. This could be a flail. Someone retract his beard to the side. Give me a scalpel."

He made a slice across the man's throat. Blood pooled in the wound, and the assisting nurse sponged at the rising red tide. After a full minute, Castro was less than an inch deep into the pulp of the giant neck. The constant bleeding distorted and disguised all normal anatomy, and the windpipe was nowhere in sight.

Castro's efforts looked futile to me. "Do we have a fiberoptic laryngoscope?" I said.

"I'll go get it," a second nurse said.

We couldn't wait any longer. I selected a breathing tube from the anesthesia equipment cart and said, "Let me try something."

I inserted the tube into the patient's right nostril and advanced it through his nose. This maneuver wasn't without peril. If the man had fractured enough facial bones, the breathing tube could spear right through the nose and enter his brain. I rolled the dice—the threat of cardiac arrest was a powerful motivator.

I lowered my ear toward the man's face. The rasping sound of his labored breathing crowed through the lumen of the tube. The patient was sucking for his final breaths, like the fish in Dom's kitchen the night before. Every inhalation was an act of desperation.

At the moment when he sucked in his next breath, I pushed the tube hard into his nose. The patient inhaled the breathing tube into his windpipe, and a lungful of exhaled air shot out through the tube. I connected it to the oxygen circuit and began ventilating the man's lungs. His chest moved up and down, and the oxygen saturation climbed to 99% in the next minute.

A life saved.

My gamble had worked. It had been as much luck as skill. We'd come so close… too close…to the specter of brain death and cardiac arrest. The patient's oxygen level had been low for only a few minutes. This guy's brain would survive. I looked down at his right leg, and diagnosed the next crisis. The man's femur was deformed into an L-shape, snapped like a twig. Blood was drenching the bed sheets and dripping onto the floor tiles. His thigh was swollen to the size of a small beer keg.

I looked over at Mr. Dylan. His face was washed out and white. He avoided making eye contact with me, and said nothing. Dylan knew how close he'd come to disaster, and how inept he'd been during the crisis. He knew I'd saved his ass.

"You're going to need to get some blood into this guy fast," I said. "He'll bleed his entire blood volume into that thigh before you know it."

Dylan's blank, clueless look did not change.

"Do you have some blood coming? From the Blood Bank?"

Green Eyes said, "The E.R. typed and crossed him for four units of blood, but the blood isn't ready yet."

"O negative," I said. "Just get four units of O negative blood in here now. Pump it into this guy before he arrests, or you'll be doing CPR on an empty heart."

"Call the Blood Bank," Dylan blurted out. "Get me four units of O negative." The nurse anesthetist had snapped out of his stupor, and was showing signs of life and leadership at last.

"Do you guys have a Massive Transfusion Protocol?" I said.

"What's that?" Dylan said.

"It's standard stuff at a trauma center. An MTP pack contains four units each of O negative blood, fresh frozen plasma, and platelets. You transfuse the MTP pack in straight away if the patient has massive bleeding. It saves lives. Trauma patients can bleed to death in the first hour."

Dylan shook his head. "We don't have anything like that here."

"You need to have it. I'll work it out with the Blood Bank for the future. Right now, fire in four units of O negative blood and get the FFP and platelets up here as soon as you can."

"I will. Thanks," Dylan said.

"I've got a patient asleep across the hall," I said. "You going to be OK?"

"I'm good. Go." Dylan clamped five bony fingers across my shoulder and said, "Thanks, Doctor. I owe you."

"No problem." I went back to my own operating room. Nothing had changed. My patient was stable. I looked at my written record for the timing of my last documentation. I had been gone for ten minutes.

Ten minutes that felt like an hour.

Castro remained in O.R. #4 to sew the patient's neck back together after the failed tracheostomy attempt. I had no surgeon, and there was nothing for me to do but monitor my sleeping patient and wait. I sat down and took some deep breaths. I felt conflicting emotions of anxiety and pride. No one could bop in and out of a trauma scene like that without being changed by the adrenaline surge.

It was the sort of episode that defined a man's life—mine, Dylan's, and the patient's—while off the radar screen to the rest of the world. No one outside of the Hibbing General Hospital operating room suite had a clue about what we'd just lived through. The patient was oblivious, as were his relatives. Johnny, sitting in a classroom five blocks away, was oblivious. Alexandra, thousands of miles away, drinking her morning latte and puffing on a Marlboro Light, was just as oblivious. My disconnection from my small family never felt more profound. I was a skilled professional in the hospital, but outside these doors my mooring was tenuous.

The O.R. door opened. The green-eyed nurse entered the operating room and approached me. "That was pretty slick work in there, Doctor," she said. "I've never seen an intubation quite like that." Her masked face hovered so close I could count the turquoise flecks in her irises. I liked looking at her. She had young eyes, fascinating, intoxicating eyes.

"It was a long shot," I said. "I'm glad it worked."

"Where did you learn to do that?"

"I worked in a lot of intensive care units. The blind nasal technique works if a patient is awake and gasping for air. They inhale the tube down into their trachea."

She cocked her head, wondering that such a fairy tale could be true.

"How's the patient doing now?" I said.

"Bobby transfused the four units of O negative blood, just like you told him. Dr. Perpich just arrived. There weren't any pulses in the leg, so Dr. Perpich is doing an angiogram. It looks like he'll have to repair the femoral artery."

"What a mess. Why aren't you in there?"

"The dayshift nurses took over. I just got off night shift. It's time for me to go home."

She stood only inches away from me and made no move to leave. She leaned one elbow against my anesthesia machine, and let out a long sigh. The trauma patient episode had been stressful, and Green Eyes had suffered through it like I had. We had that crisis in common, this pixie of a woman and me. She was tiny, no more than five feet tall, with a thin and boyish figure. Her left hand was free of a ring.

I wanted to know her. I offered my hand and said, "I'm Nico Antone."

"My name is Lena Johnson." The clasp of her hand was warm, her skin soft. "I heard about you. They say you're from California."

"I am."

"If I had a job in California, I wouldn't leave it to come to Hibbing, Minnesota." She pronounced her home state Minnes-ooooh-tah, the word stretched out by an elongated O-sound. She stared back and waited for me to refute the obvious illogic of my translocation. The persistence of her stare made me uncomfortable. At last she asked, "Why did you move up here?"

"I grew up in Hibbing, and moved back so my son could graduate from high school here."

She lifted one eyebrow. "They don't have high schools in California?"

"It's a long story. My son and I decided it would be good for him to transfer to Hibbing High. It's a great school."

"I have a daughter in 11th grade."

"My son's in 11th grade. You and I can compare notes as the year goes on."

"Sounds good. Great work today, Dr. Antone. It's not every day you can save someone's life."

"Call me Nico."

"I'll call you Dr. Antone, Dr. Antone." She winked at me and walked away.

Our exchange was like electroshock therapy, bringing a wave of unexpected brightness into a tense morning. I couldn't remember Alexandra ever acknowledging that I'd saved anyone's life.

Dr. Castro reentered the room, and donned sterile gown and gloves again. "Everything OK next door?" I said.

"Yep. Perpich arrived. The femoral artery is torn. Once Perpich has repaired that, we'll deal with the broken leg and the facial trauma. You did a great job in there, Dr. Antone."

"Thanks."

Castro chuckled as he resumed the shoulder surgery. "Good God, that was like a fucking TV show episode. Dr. Nico Antone, M.D. In this episode, Dr. Fucking California saves the fucking day."

CHAPTER 8
HEAVEN'S DOOR

At ten o'clock that night, Johnny was quiet behind his bedroom door. I tapped on the frame and whispered his name. I eased the door open and saw Johnny sleeping on the bed, his right cheek plastered flat against the Second Act of *King Lear*. As timeless as Shakespeare's genius was, how many teenagers had he put to sleep? Perhaps someday the Bard would replace propofol as the anesthetic of choice for adolescents having surgery.

I turned off the light and made my way back to the living room. I wasn't tired, and at this hour there were no more sporting events on TV. I didn't feel like reading. I looked out the window at the pastoral winter setting. A full moon lit up the blanket of new snow that covered the yard, the driveway, and the top of my car. Nighttime seemed like day.

I wanted fresh air and some exercise. It was the perfect evening for both. I laced up my boots, put on my parka and gloves, and hit the street. I walked one block north to the storefront lights of Howard Street. The crunching of snow under my boots was an old sound from my youth. Every step sounded musical, the rhythmic backbeat to my North Country odyssey. I felt young, unfettered, and alive in Minnesota. There were no mirrors to fix me in time, and I felt like I was 18 years old again.

All commerce on Howard Street was shut down for the night, but the streetlights glowed amber, and I was drawn toward them. The Wells Fargo Bank sign sported the time and temperature—it was 10:12 p.m. and the temperature was a balmy 22 degrees Fahrenheit. A car or two passed by. I couldn't imagine where they were going. Who bothered to cruise the main street of the tiny village at this hour?

A green neon sign shined like a beacon atop a twenty-foot-tall pole one block in the distance. The sign read "Heaven's Door." The parking lot was full. I'd heard of the place. It was a casual restaurant and bar that specialized in hamburgers and pizza, beers and whiskey sours. As I grew nearer, I heard amplified guitar music and the sound of a man's baritone voice singing. A warm tingle glowed though me. The song was "Highway 61 Revisited," a memory from this week's journey north: "Well Abe says, 'Where do you want this killin' done?' God says, 'Out on Highway 61.'"

I looked in through the front window panels and saw a solo performer sitting on a stool. The man wore a black fedora, a black shirt, a matching vest, and a black string tie. He curled his lips against the microphone, and sneered the lyrics into the metal sphere while strumming an acoustic steel string guitar.

I was intrigued. Live music on a Tuesday night, three blocks from Dom's house? I walked in, peeled off my winter garb, and sat down on an empty stool near the door. The room was crowded with patrons bobbing their heads to the infectious beat of the music. The décor was best described as a Hard Rock Café motif featuring Bob Zimmerman and Bob Dylan memorabilia. The wall next to me was dense with museum items: A copy of Zimmerman's high school graduation picture with the caption "I want to be the next Little Richard," a faded article from The *Hibbing Daily Tribune* reporting a scathing review of Dylan's first album in 1961, a signed Fender guitar, and posters from Dylan concerts at Madison Square Garden and The Fillmore East.

The singer's voice was rich and resonant, and the words filled up the room like a warm fire. I'd heard the real Bob Dylan perform more than once, and had listened to Dylan's recordings thousands of times. The live voice I heard now was an uncanny mimicking of the youthful Bob Dylan's intonations, inflections, pronunciations, and phrasing, but compared to the original, this voice was... better. These vocals were reminiscent of Bob Dylan's crooning on "Lay,

Lady, Lay"—less nasal, with reduced gravel and more vibrato than most of Dylan's recordings. This singer had talent. I ordered a Bud Light on tap and settled back to be entertained.

The song ended, and the performer did something that Bob Dylan never did in concert—he talked to the audience. His voice was deep and fluid.

"Thank you," he said. "That's the only Biblical song I'll be singing tonight. I know you're all spiritually bankrupt this evening, and lustin' for some preachin', but I'm just here for one thing." A long pause. "I'm here to sing the religion of rock and roll. This here's a song I know you're all waiting for, so get on up off your chair and let's do some harmonizin'. I'm Bobby Dylan. Thanks for coming out tonight."

Bobby Dylan? I almost choked on my beer. I leaned forward to get a closer look at the singer. Beneath the shade of the fedora, the wisp of his beard and the broom of his bushy hair were unmistakable. It was him, the same nurse too inept to anesthetize the car crash victim in the operating room at Hibbing General this morning. The guy was not only a faux anesthesiologist, now he was a counterfeit Hibbing rock icon as well.

He strummed a familiar three-chord riff, then launched the Dylan masterpiece "Knockin' On Heaven's Door." His music worked magic on the room. As Bobby moved into the chorus, everyone in the tavern sang the title at the top of their lungs.

As agitated as I'd been when I learned the vocalist's identity, I found listening to a hundred inebriated voices shouting out the lyrics to the Dylan classic was a striking experience. "Knock, knock, knockin' on heaven's door." Goose bumps chased down my forearms, and I warmed to the energy around me. The sing-a-long linked the strangers into a congregation, and Bobby Dylan was their minister. On this wintry Tuesday night in this mining town on the edge of nowhere, they were alone no more.

I took another swig of my beer, felt the alcohol numb my brain, and tapped my fingers on the mug in time to the music. Mr. Dylan folded his body around his guitar, and closed his eyes as he led the patrons through the last lines of the chorus. When the final chord settled, he set down his instrument and said, "I'm gonna take a short break now. Don't go away."

He switched off the microphone and left the stage. Boisterous rounds of back-slapping and hand-shaking anointed him, as the crowd celebrated the performance of their Zimmerman clone.

Mr. Dylan exited the building through the front door, and perched himself on the brick ledge just outside my window. He lit up a cigarette and blew a trail of smoke into the dancing snowflakes descending on Howard Street. His face sported deep creases, with eyes that were slits against the nighttime breeze. I preferred listening to Mr. Dylan over looking at him, so I returned my attention back to the inside of the bar. The crowd was 80% men. Most of the women were wide-bodies—I didn't see any I'd care to chat up. The men weren't petite, either. The Mesabi Iron Range was home to real men—guys who drove trucks, repaired mining machinery, and were at ease with a shotgun.

Laughter filled the room. People were having a good time, and the booze was flowing. I wasn't accustomed to hanging around a bar by myself, but tonight it felt good. In one week I'd quit my job, traveled halfway across the country, and planted Johnny into my boyhood high school. For me, Heaven's Door was a reward and a celebration. I'd pulled off the Big Move with aplomb. "Great job, Nico," I said to myself, at once awash with pride.

I looked out the window as the snowfall thickened. Mr. Dylan took a deep drag off his smoke, flicked the butt onto the street, and reached into an inner coat pocket to fish out another. This second cigarette was different: thicker and home-rolled. He fired it up, drew in a deep inhale, and held his breath. I watched with fascination as Dylan exhaled twenty seconds later. He sucked in again, the joint glowing bright orange in the nighttime air as Mr. Dylan held a second lungful of smoke captive from the Minnesota night.

He blew out a thick cloud and started to giggle to himself. The giggle brought out a broad, shit-eating grin that morphed into a deep belly laugh. I chuckled to myself. What a piece of work this guy was. There was little doubt—Mr. Dylan was smoking marijuana right there on the main street of town, three blocks from the hospital where he knocked people unconscious every day. He held the joint cupped in his right hand, shielded from the world. Cars drove by, and individuals entered and left the club. No one looked twice, and no one seemed to care.

I had one more reason not to like the guy. On our first meeting, he was an arrogant prick. On our second meeting, Dylan was an underskilled health care provider. Now he'd revealed himself as a public pothead. Dylan swiveled his head and for the first time noticed I was watching him. His thick eyebrows descended into a dark V, and he locked eyes with me. He toked up with a mighty effort, rounded his eyes into a psycho-killer glare, and blew the smoke straight at the pane of glass that separated us. Then he leaned back and roared with laughter, impressed with the hilarity of the deed.

I could hear his guffawing through the glass. This wafer of a man emitted a laugh so coarse and guttural, so inconsistent with his reedy constitution, that it tickled neural pathways in my brain that had long been dormant. My reaction surprised me—I started laughing in concert with him. The scene was so absurd: a surrogate Dylan getting high on main street in a snowstorm in Hibbing, Minnesota. I hadn't laughed out loud for a long, long time.

Mr. Dylan extinguished the joint, and thirty seconds later materialized on the stool next to me. He still wore the same ludicrous smile, and I still found it infectious as hell.

"Good to see you at Heaven's Door, Doctor," he said.

"Good to be seen. Buy you a beer?"

"Don't drink."

I was surprised. "You stick to doobies, eh?"

"No doobies. Just roll-your-own tobackie."

"I doubt that." I hadn't stood outside with him, and I couldn't smell the smoke, but the combination of a musician smoking a hand-rolled joint and that same musician laughing with uproarious glee pointed to Mary Jane, not Marlboro. I pushed it a little further. "Aren't you a bit bold, smoking a joint right on Howard Street?"

The corners of Dylan's mouth curled up further. "It's not pot. Bobby D just likes to roll his own tobacco, that's all."

"And if I don't believe that?"

Dylan showed two rows of uneven teeth. "Then you are teeming with wisdom."

"You can call it wisdom. I'd call it an evolved skill at bullshit detection. How are you doing after that episode in the operating room today?"

"What episode?"

"The guy with the mashed up face. The guy from the car accident."

"Oh, him. He did fine." Dylan's face was proud, his chin held high.

"That could have ended bad."

"It would have worked out. I would've gotten a tube into him somehow."

I was aghast. The man had no insight into how close he'd come to an operating room death. "It looked to me like you had no clue what to do," I said, blunt as hell.

Dylan laughed and said, "You believe what you want to believe, Doctor. I've been in worse predicaments, and no one's died on me yet."

It was no use pushing the topic any further. The man had the humility of a peacock. I switched the conversation to music. "You play anything other than Dylan songs?"

"Bobby Dylan just plays Dylan. It can't be no other way." All the world was a stage, and this guy was staying in character. He wasn't going to be Joe Smith, Certified Nurse Anesthetist, or whatever his real name had been. He was determined to stay Bobby Dylan.

"Cynthia," Dylan called out toward the waitress, a plump blonde fifty-something who was collecting empty glasses from the next booth. "Bring my buddy here another beer."

"No. One's enough," I protested. "I've got to work early tomorrow."

"No earlier than I do. Loosen up, Doctor. You're on the Range now. Maybe you should come up on stage with me. Play tambourine or something."

"I play bass, when I'm not home reading anesthesia journals."

"I'm impressed you're not home reading one right now. There's hope for you yet." He reached over with the fingers of his right hand and pinched my cheek hard. "You're a funny guy, Doctor. What's a dude like you looking for, drinking by yourself in a saloon?"

"I'm not looking for anything."

"You a happy man, Doctor?"

"I suppose so. As happy as most people."

"What is happiness to you?"

I shrugged. "Family. Friends. A good job."

Dylan huffed. "Keep chasing that stuff, Doctor, and let me know if you ever get what you're looking for."

"What do you chase?"

"Me? Free will. To me, a man is a success if he gets up in the morning and goes to bed at night, and in between he does what he wants to do."

"I've heard that before. That's a Bob Dylan quote."

He looked at me as if I'd just claimed snow was black. "I know. I just said it."

"I mean, it's a quote from the real Bob Dylan. The rock singer."

"That's me. I'm here. Bobby Dylan."

It was no use. The man was out of touch with reality. Was he psychotic? The way he looked, acted, and talked reminded me of interactions I'd had with patients locked inside psychiatric wards. Patients who babbled about spiders from another planet or nocturnal visits from Jesus Christ.

Dylan stood up to return to the stage. "No one controls my ass, Doctor. That's the key to life. It's as simple as this." He raised his wrists and held them together, with his palms up and his left and right little fingers touching. Dylan bit his teeth into the imaginary handcuffs between the wrists, spit out the unseen shackle, and said "Poof," as his hands broke apart.

Dylan gave me a thumbs-up and left to weave his way through the tables back to the stage. He clipped a harmonica holder around his neck, strapped on the steel string, strummed a trio of chords and said, "This song goes out to that one special North Country woman who's always on my mind." He filled the air with his lush voice, and crooned the opening lines to Bob Dylan's "Girl From the North Country." "If you're traveling in the north country fair, Where the winds hit heavy on the borderline."

A second mug of Bud Light appeared on my table. I took a long drink and lost myself in the lyrics of a genius and the vocals of his talented namesake. It was late, it was wintry outside, and there were anesthetics to deliver in just eight hours, but I was drifting with the music and feeling better than I had in months.

The crowd waved their hands in time to the music. When chorus came around the second time, Mr. Dylan called out, "C'mon everyone," and the air was filled with the out-of-tune voices of happy Iron Rangers, singing an anthem to the girls they loved.

I didn't know a single person in this audience, but in my inebriated state, I found myself drawn into the fantasy that everyone in this room had a true love. Every man had his own Girl from the North Country, and every woman had her own Boy from the North Country. Their loves defined them, and their lives were special and worthwhile.

Bobby Dylan sang like a man in love, as he led the multitudes in this North Country anthem. The fervor in the congregation was infectious. I was glad to be there. I was glad to be alive.

I raised my glass in a salute to my colleague. Dylan wasn't much of an anesthetist, but he was one hell of a religious leader.

CHAPTER 9
I WOULD NOT FEEL SO ALL ALONE

Before sunrise Saturday morning, Johnny and I entered the Hibbing General Hospital locker room side by side. It was a notable event, the first time my son had ever accompanied me to a hospital. He wasn't there to observe my professional life, he was coming to work himself. In his former life in California, Johnny slept until noon every Saturday. The new Minnesota Johnny 2.0 pursued and welcomed this weekend orderly job. The work was unskilled labor at minimum wage, and it required both an alarm clock and a willingness to obey orders.

It was unclear to me why Johnny was interested at all.

Two minutes after we exited the locker room, the answer became all too apparent—a teenage Scandinavian Barbie Doll stepped out of the women's locker room. Her shoulder-length hair was tied back in a ponytail, and she walked with the jaunty step of a cheerleader. Her face lit up when she saw us. She grabbed Johnny's arm and said, "I'm so glad you're here. You're going to love this job. Is this your dad?"

I looked from the girl to Johnny, and waited for an introduction. Johnny blushed and said, "Yeah, this is my father. Echo, meet Dr. Antone. Dad, meet my friend Echo."

Echo fluttered long eyelashes at me and said, "Nice to meet you, Dr. Antone. Johnny told me all about you."

She clung to Johnny's arm, and after the initial pleasantries I became irrelevant. Echo was giggling and whispering into Johnny's ear. He was beaming like he'd just hit a walk-off home run in the bottom of the ninth inning.

"You'll see," she said to Johnny. "You'll be working around all these interesting surgeries, and you'll be making money at the same time. It's the most awesome job imaginable for a high school kid."

"I hope so," Johnny said, looking sheepish and nervous. "You know what you're doing here, but I'm a total rookie."

"I'll protect you," she said. "You'll do great."

I stood alongside them, but it wasn't a triangle. I was a spectator to a neighboring line segment. The two kids acted like they were best friends, even though Johnny and I had only been in town six days.

A scowling, hawk-faced nurse stepped up behind Echo and clapped her hands together with startling volume. "Good morning, everybody," she said. "This stranger must be Johnny Antone." She squared off against Johnny. "I'm Roberta Selvo, and I'm your boss. Welcome to the operating room suite." She turned to me and said, "Dr. Antone, I understand this is your son."

"He is indeed. Nepotism is alive and well in Hibbing."

A pained expression crossed her face. I wondered if she knew what nepotism meant. I tried a different approach. "Don't give him any preferential treatment. Make him do an honest day's work."

Roberta crossed her arms over her chest and said, "Your son will work like a man, or we'll send him down to slop plates in the hospital cafeteria. We've got sick patients here, and surgeons who like all the details perfect. Our operating room suite is no place for lazy teenagers."

Roberta Selvo was serious about her role. I liked that. There was nothing wrong with Johnny's first boss acting like a female version of General Patton. He shook his arm free from Echo's grasp and snapped his shoulders back. No lazy teenager he. My son molded himself into the image of a diligent, responsible employee.

"Come with me, you two," Roberta said. "They just finished an emergency Cesarean in O.R. #2, and the room needs to be turned over." She rotated her significant girth and headed for room #2. Echo followed her, and Johnny followed Echo. He offered no communication back toward me. The message was clear: *Let me go, Dad. I've got this covered.*

I checked out the operating room schedule for the morning. There was only one case scheduled today, a laparoscopic gall bladder resection, and I'd volunteered to do the anesthetic. If Johnny was going to be in the hospital, it made sense for me to be here, too.

I put on a scrub hat and mask, and entered room #3. I was pleased to see Lena was inside. She was preparing the video equipment for the surgery. As soon as I walked in she said, "Your son is a cutey. He's everything I heard he was."

"Thank you. Who did you hear that from?"

"From Echo, of course. She's my daughter."

Ah, small town life. It shouldn't have surprised me that the two best-looking females I'd seen in Hibbing were a mother and daughter combo. Peel off twenty years, and the mother was a copy of the daughter. I wondered what the real Lena looked like without the poufy hat, the surgical mask, and the baggy surgical scrubs.

"They send each other a thousand text messages a day," she said.

"They do?"

"They do. Echo talks about him all day long."

"What does she say?"

"She says he's funny, smart, and way more sophisticated than any of the other boys in town. Does Johnny talk about Echo?"

I pondered the miniseries of abbreviated conversations I'd had with Johnny since we'd hit the deer, and said, "My son puts his social life behind a brick wall, and I'm not invited over, through, or around that wall."

"That's too bad. I'll bet he talks to his mother."

"She's still in California."

"Close marriage, eh?"

I winced. "We have fewer battles living two time zones apart."

"Is that what it's all about? Avoiding battles?"

"Sometimes couples get along better when they see each other less."

"I get it. I'm a single parent myself. Is your wife going to move up here?"

"No, I don't think so." I was growing uncomfortable. It wasn't my style to share details of my marriage with people I didn't know well. I had no desire to play twenty questions with Lena right now. "I'd better set up my anesthesia equipment," I said, looking for a way out.

"Sure," she said. Lena turned her back on me and busied herself connecting the cables to the laparoscopy camera equipment and video screens. I opened the top drawer of my anesthesia cart and started drawing up medications for my anesthetic.

We were still alone in the room together, and the silence seemed awkward. Lena must have sensed this too, because she opened up again. "I have a question for you," she said. "The kids are studying together this weekend. You're new in town. Why don't you and Johnny come over to my house tomorrow night for dinner? It would be fun."

Fun? I imagined Echo and Johnny hanging all over each other, while Lena and I stood ten feet apart and tried to chat about the temperature outside.

She persisted. "I'm a good cook. You need to eat. We could have a glass of wine and a few laughs while Echo and Johnny do their calculus homework."

A glass of wine? I floundered a bit. I'd just told the woman I was married. I hadn't hit on her in any way, and yet she was pushing for an evening together. I opened my mouth to beg off, but before I could, Lena pulled down her mask to show me a thousand-candlewatt smile. "Relax, it's not a date," she said. "We'll just have some food and conversation."

What the hell? I had nothing else going on, and Johnny would be gonzo to hang out with his new girlfriend. Why shouldn't we spend an evening with these cute Minnesotans? "Sure," I said. "What time?"

"Seven o'clock? We live on 3rd Avenue. Johnny knows the place. He's been there already."

"Sounds good."

"It does sound good." She headed for the door. I watched her exit, each footstep landing with precision in front of the previous one. Her round bottom rocked with every stride. I grinned. My libido was tweaked in the middle of an operating room in this little town. I had to be honest with myself—Alexandra was a lost cause. Maybe someday Lena and I would be holding hands, and Echo and Johnny would be holding hands, and we'd all go on a double date to the movies together. The idea was so ridiculous that I threw back my head and laughed, my woes floating away like a helium balloon bound for the stratosphere.

At 7 p.m. that evening, I had my feet up and my fingers wrapped around a television remote control. Johnny breezed past, dressed in a winter coat and a ski hat. He hadn't shaved in two days, and he looked a year older than he had when we arrived in Hibbing.

"Where are you going?" I said.

"Out."

"Who are you doing out with?"

"Echo. I'll be back by eleven."

"You two are hitting it off, eh?"

"It's all good, Dad. Relax."

"It is all good. Have fun."

Johnny walked out with the swagger of a Hollywood movie star heading for the stage. He'd gone from spitting venom against an airbag to radiating confidence in less than a week. I had mixed emotions. With my son gone for the night, my absence of friends or family left me lonely and low. I'd lived this insipid reality back in California, with Johnny out on a date and Alexandra working in the evenings, but California was home. I had a routine there. I'd go to the gym, spring for a jog, write a paper, or watch a movie in my 7,000 square-foot mansion on the hill.

I didn't have an antidote for Minnesota loneliness.

I leaned on an old standby. Cable television was a godsend for bored and disconnected souls, no matter what state they lived in. I grabbed a beer out of the refrigerator and watched the puck drop on the Minnesota Wild vs. New York Rangers game. Beer and hockey seemed the best remedy available tonight.

My cell phone rang. The caller I.D. read *Hibbing General Hospital*. I sensed trouble. I wasn't on call, and no one at the hospital was supposed to be bothering me right now. The hospital operator was on the line. She said, "Dr. Antone, I have Bobby Dylan on the phone. He needs to talk to you."

"Put him through." I drained half the beer, and wondered what the hell Dylan's problem was. I wasn't in the mood for saving a nurse anesthetist with inadequate training from another medical calamity on my night off. I waited, skeptical about what I was about to be dragged into.

"Hello. This is Bobby Dylan," came the voice, cavernous and low. Two packs of Marlboro Lights so far today, I guessed. And maybe a joint or two.

"Nico Antone here. What's up?"

"I've got a Fender bass for you. 8 p.m. tonight. Heaven's Door. Be there."

Be there. A command, not an invitation.

"I'm not that good. You don't want me on stage."

"Three chords. That's all the songs will be tonight. Three chords. Can you sing?"

I laughed. "You don't want me to sing, either."

"Don't sing then. Just come play some backbeat and drain a few beers. Doctor, I'm going to show you how we have a good time on an Iron Range Saturday night. You got nothing better to do. See you at eight." He hung up.

The isolation of my Saturday night had been disrupted, challenged, and disrespected by a thirty-second phone call. My basement sanctuary of boob tube sports and Budweiser now seemed the domain of an isolated loser.

A commercial interrupted the hockey game. The ad showed an athletic young couple sailing a catamaran at a Club Med in Mexico. The girl was sun-bronzed and bursting out of a skimpy white bikini. The man had a knockout body to rival hers. I envied them both. They were actors. I supposed they lived somewhere in L.A. and didn't even know each other. Maybe they were sitting apart in two separate apartments at this moment, watching television just like I was.

Or maybe they were rollerblading along Venice Beach, flirting and laughing together just like in the commercial. My stomach tightened. The clock ticked off the wall above the couch. I felt a surge of profound sadness. The four walls offered no conversation.

I checked the time. It was ten minutes to seven. What was Alexandra doing on her Saturday night? With her work done for the week, she was no doubt indulging herself. I imagined Alexandra reclining in a chair and having her toenails done while she turned the pages of the latest Glamour magazine.

I hadn't talked to the woman since the airport in San Francisco. At the time I never wanted to see her again, but never was a fickle word. Now my thoughts tumbled like damp towels in a dryer. On an insane impulse, I dialed Alexandra's number.

She picked up on the fifth ring. "Hi, Nico," she said. "You guys OK?" She sounded bored. Preoccupied.

"We're fine. We had a good week. Did Johnny talk to you?"

"He did. He sounds quite happy. He said he met a nice girl." There was an awkward pause. I could hear her talking to someone in the background.

"Did I interrupt something?"

"I'm sitting at Claire's Salon. I'm getting my toenails done."

Bingo. My intuition was unfailing. There was another long pause. "Is Johnny with you right now?" she said. "He forgot to call me today."

She had nothing to say to me, so the requested substitution of Johnny for Nico was understandable. Alas, I had to disappoint her. "Johnny went out for the night."

"Good for him. What are you doing on your Saturday night in nowheresville?"

"I'm hanging out. Watching TV."

"No news there. Same old Nico. Watching TV while the rest of the world frolics."

Fuck you, I thought to myself. "Can you go two minutes without cutting me down?" I said.

"I'm not criticizing you. I'm just the play-by-play announcer, calling it like it is. Who can blame you for staying inside? What is it, fifty below zero up there when the sun goes down? I could never live there in a million years. It's unbelievable how different you and I are right now."

I crushed my empty beer can in my fist. She was a champion at poking me with a stick until I snarled. I had no desire to engage in negative dialogue, but she pushed on. "I've had a great week. I'm a complete person when you're not here, Nico. You and I are better off apart."

"Who is he?"

"There's no one person. I have a lot of friends who enjoy my company. We've had a dead marriage for a long time. I'm in the prime of my life. I need more from a man than I got from you. Stay where you are, Nico. We're both better off."

She was determined to make me eat shit and die, all before the toenail polish dried. I was getting more irate by the minute. I glared at what was now an irrelevant hockey game, and hated Alexandra more than ever. "I don't know what to say to you right now," I said. "I don't even know why I called you."

"I don't know why either. Tell Johnny I miss him. Have fun up there. Bye." The phone clicked off, and I stared at the television.

Have fun up there, indeed.

On the television, ten young men skated in circles. Thousands of adults screamed and cheered them on. *Who cares?* I thought. *Who the fuck cares?* I'd known for a long time that my marriage was a disaster, but now it was worse than ever. I wanted Alexandra to miss me after I left. Instead she'd inhaled toenail polish and concluded her husband should stay away forever.

I circled Dom's basement floor like a hungry tiger in a cage. I couldn't stay there alone for another minute. I switched off the television, threw on my polar weather gear, and headed to the street. A thousand stars jumped out of a jet-black sky. I picked up a chunk of frozen snow and hurled it at the stop sign on 21st Street. The chunk hit the O with a resounding clang. I was twelve years old again, throwing snowballs to my Minnesota Twins teammates, posing as the stop signs of Hibbing.

My boots traced a path toward the brighter lights of Howard Street. The parking lot outside Heaven's Door was jammed. I could hear the throb of live music from inside. The volume was louder tonight. Tuesday had been Bobby Dylan and an acoustic guitar. Tonight I heard electric guitars and a drummer. I took off my gloves, grabbed the doorknob, and entered another world.

The interior of Heaven's Door was a dank, sweltering cave. The room smelled of overripe armpits and spilled beer. The noise from the stage was deafening—amplified rock music filled my head. I covered my ears in protection. Rangers were elbow-to-elbow as they jumped to a Bo Diddly beat. Bobby Dylan stood center stage. He was hunched over a red Stratocaster, driving the music on with a look of manic intensity. He wore the same all-black shirt, hat, and necktie outfit he'd worn Tuesday night, but the contrast in the two performances was striking. Tuesday was an acoustic music sing-a-long. Tonight was a rock and roll rave.

Dylan's right arm swung in three wide arcs as he fired off a trio of windmill chords to finish off the song. The dance floor erupted in catcalls and clapping. A woman on my left rammed into me as she raised her arms over her head in a whooping celebration.

It had been an eternity since I'd had witnessed a scene like this. There wasn't a dance club with live music within ten miles of my house in Palo Alto, and I never ventured out to a San Francisco or San Jose nightclub. I angled my body through the crowd to get to the bar. I bought a beer, and the bartender handed me a 16-ounce plastic cup with suds dripping over the brim. The woman who'd bumped into me minutes earlier leaned her head against my shoulder and said, "Drink that fast, handsome, and let's do some dancing."

She was a chubby girl in her thirties. Beads of sweat dotted her upper lip. *What the heck*, I thought. "I'll take you up on that," I said, and tipped back my glass. With a skill unused since my college days, I chugged the entire beer in ten seconds, and placed the empty cup on the top of my head.

"That's talent, handsome." She grabbed the back of my head and pulled my face against hers. "I'm Ruthie," she said. "This your first time here?"

"Second," I said. I wiped her wetness off my forehead with the back of my hand. The odor of liquor on her breath overwhelmed me. At close range, the pores on her nose were so wide I could count them. She grappled onto my biceps like I was her lifeline. Ruthie was going to be hard to shake.

Liberty came in the person of Bobby Dylan, who pushed his way through the crowd toward us. I yelled out, "Can I make a request, sir? Can your band play the 'Beer Barrel Polka?' "

Dylan wrapped me in a bear hug, snaring Ruthie in the package. "I didn't think you'd make it, Doctor," he said.

"Best offer I had."

"You're gonna love it. Saturday night we rock. Your bass is right there." He pointed toward the stage, where a blue Fender four-string was propped on a stand next to the drum set.

"How will I know the songs?"

"We'll keep it simple for you. Everything we play will be in the key of G or B flat. You'll get it." He looked down at my companion and said, "You latched onto the good doctor tonight, eh Ruthie?"

"A doctor?" she said. "I was happy just looking at him. I didn't know he was a smart one, too."

Dylan peeled Ruthie's hands off me and said, "If you're lucky, the doctor will make a house call later on. Right now, he's with the band." His face blossomed into an evil grin. "Ready to hit it, Doc?"

"Let's do this." I followed him to the stage, and picked up the bass. I wrapped the strap around my neck, turned on the amplifier, and pounded out an 8-note riff from a time gone by. Ruthie moved to the front row and howled, "You go, Doctor!"

Dylan nodded in approval and said, "Is there anything you're not good at?"

Over a thumping run of bass notes, I said, "My wife says I suck at everything."

Dylan powered up his amp, hammered out a chain of power chords, and said, "Let her go, man. She's full of shit. I've known you one week, and I can see that you're a good guy."

Beyond the stage, people were fist-pumping to Dylan's chords. It was a vibrant young crowd tonight. Barrooms had changed. In my Minnesota youth, there were nine men to every one woman. Tonight Heaven's Door was teeming with women, and the ratio was closer to 1 to 1. The average age looked to be 25—Dylan and I were the two oldest men in the club. With the twin catalysts of alcohol and dim lighting we'd appear as young as the others.

The drummer and keyboard player joined us on stage. Dylan said, "Mikey and Luke, meet The Doctor. Boys, let's do a little rockin' blues. Woogie Boogie in B flat. Here we go. Hun, two, three, hah!"

The three men broke into an upbeat 12-bar blues, with the drummer driving the tempo fast and hard. After three measures, I learned the chord progression and joined in with the bass line. I reached over and turned up the volume knob on my amp to the max. The power of my notes shook the floorboards beneath me. Dylan looked over and winked in approval.

The dance floor became a mosh pit. At my feet, a muscular dude in a tattered Minnesota Twins T-shirt gyrated with a blonde in tight jeans and an even tighter red sweater. She melded her scarlet arms around his torso and dug her chin into his shoulder. The couple bounced and rebounded off every dancer within ten feet of them. At one point, the girl smiled up at me, rolled her tongue across her upper lip, and blew me a kiss.

I took my right hand off the bass strings and caught the kiss. I feigned a look of amazement toward her and angled my bass to the ceiling to validate my masculinity. It all felt wonderful. This big-fish-in-a-little-pond rock star gig was the best thing to happen to me in years. I was floating six inches off the stage. I looked over at Dylan. His head was bobbing to the beat, and his knees were going east and west at the same time.

"Go, Doctor, go," he shouted at me. My fingers flew over the strings to carve out a bass riff that blared through the refrigerator-sized speakers. I loved the power. From Elvis to Jagger to Maroon 5, this was what rock n' roll was all about. Forget the words. Give them a thundering beat, a dark room, and a chance to escape.

The primitive urges of the music stoked my disdain for my wife. Alexandra—strutting like a prostitute in her spaghetti-strapped cocktail dress down the hallway of our California home. Alexandra—beautiful and ornery. I hated her and I loved her. The wedding ring on my left hand was the tiniest handcuff in the world.

The hottie in the red sweater gyrated below, and the spectacle she presented motivated me to man up. I took my hands off the bass for five seconds, long enough to slip the wedding ring off my finger and drop it into the front pocket of my Levis. I jettisoned the shackle of my wedding band here in a town where I had a clean slate—a town where I sensed I could become someone special.

Like Johnny.

The band took a break after the set ended, and Dylan said, "Time to go outside, Doctor." We pushed through the back-slapping crowd, and I followed him onto the sidewalk facing Howard Street.

"Man, that was a rush," I said. "The applause, the attention, the music. I love it."

"Being on stage is a drug, Doctor. It's been my drug for years."

"You play here every week?"

"Yes, sir. I've been playing clubs and concerts all around the world since I left high school, but now I just play here. Twice a week. Acoustic set on Tuesdays, electric with the band on Saturdays. There's some nice tail here on Saturdays," he said, lighting a Marlboro. "Glad you came out tonight. You need it. Can't have you at home worshiping at the throne of the distant Mrs. Antone."

"No, sir."

"Tell her she needs to move up here or she's going to lose you. If she saw you on stage at Heaven's Door, her juices would be flowing. Bet on it."

I rolled my eyes. "She's too fucking good for this town. And she thinks she's too fucking good for me."

"Whoa. The doctor spews the F-bomb. Swearing like an iron miner."

"Only when I talk about my wife. I had a fight with her on the phone tonight. I've had it."

"Fighting with a wife is as predictable as the sunrise. She angry a lot?"

"Oh, yeah. Everything's always my fault."

Dylan chuckled, and took a big draw on his Marlboro. "No news there. Better to live on a corner of the roof than share a house with a quarrelsome wife.'"

"Where did you get that?"

"The Bible. Proverbs 21, verse 9. Thousands of years ago, Old Testament husbands had to deal with the same crap as we do. Those guys moved to the corner of the rooftop."

I laughed. "Now you're a Biblical scholar?"

"No scholar. Just a man who's been around the block a time or two."

"You married?"

"Separated."

"What happened?"

He shrugged. "I was happy with my marriage. Then my kid was born, and it was like the baby sucked my wife's brains out through her boobs. The woman was never the same after she got bit by the monster of motherhood."

"You getting divorced?"

"Who knows? It's been two years so far. We live in separate houses, but we still get together now and again. I still love her. I just can't live with the woman. She's crazy nuts sometimes." Dylan exhaled smoke straight up into the winter's sky, and looked forlorn. "When she was good, she was terrific. When she was bad, she was real bad. She seems calmer these days. They must have adjusted her medications." His eyes roamed the street, where a circle of young girls puffed on cigarettes and giggled. A tall brunette met his stare and waved at him. Dylan waved back.

"Some great tail here on Saturday nights," he repeated. "You could get fat just grazing on my leftovers, Doctor."

"I'm happy for you, but I'm not ready for that."

"You're ready. I saw your wedding ring go bye-bye tonight." He looked down his nose at my jewelry-free left hand. "I saw you checking out the local talent, and I don't blame you one bit. If you want me to introduce you to Peggy Stimac, just let me know."

"Who's Peggy Stimac?"

"The babe in the red sweater. Just left her old man last year. She likes to party. A handsome doctor from California..., she'd be happy to make your acquaintance."

"She's got a great body. She moves like an eel on the dance floor."

"Mmm mmm. She's the best this town has to offer. Your son wouldn't have to know, and no one else cares. A man's got needs, you know. A man's got needs." Dylan's eyes crinkled. Water droplets condensed on his moustache. I was intrigued by his mercurial nature: he was a Bible-quoting marital philosopher, a rollicking reefer-madman guitarist, a trembling nurse over his head in an emergency, and now an all-knowing rock n' roll pimp on a Saturday night.

Dylan stubbed out his cigarette butt against the brick wall and said, "I'm tired of watching all the women around this place hanging their heads in sorrow. Let's get back in there and let it loose." I followed him inside. He made a direct line to Peggy Stimac's table and said, "Peg, my buddy here wants to buy you a drink."

Peggy looked up, one eyebrow cocked, the corner of her mouth curious. "Who's your buddy?"

"Meet Nico Antone. Dr. Nico Antone. New in town. New in the band. Nico, meet Peggy."

The seat next to Peggy was open. I sat down to admire her from close range. She was ten years younger than Alexandra. Her rosy cheeks were baby doll smooth, and the pink pillows of her lips oozed toward me. Her long eyelashes dropped as she checked me out. After a quick up-down, her tongue flickered across her top lip again. She approved.

"I'll have a tequila if you're buying," Peggy said. I beckoned the waitress, who delivered two shots on a tray. Peggy wrapped an arm around my shoulder. She held a wedge of lime in front of my face and said, "Open your mouth, babe." She fit the lime between my teeth, sprinkled salt on the side of my neck, and lashed her raspy tongue across my skin to lick off the salt. She drained the tequila shot and fit her lips over the lime slice in my mouth. Darling Peggy sucked so hard I thought both the lime and my tongue would disappear down her throat.

"Nice," she said when she disengaged. "Now it's your turn, babe." She bit into a second wedge of lime, rubbed the salt across the top of her cleavage, and handed me the second glass of tequila. I knew the script. I sunk my face against her breasts to lick the salt, downed the tequila in one swallow, and sucked the lime juice from between her lips. While our lips met for this encore visit, I let my mouth linger and enjoyed the wetness.

The alcohol swept through my brain, and I felt wicked and omnipotent. Up on the stage, the keyboardist hit the opening chords to "Rainy Day Women #12 & 35." Bobby Dylan hollered into his microphone, "Let's go, Doctor. We need you up here."

"I have to play. Talk to you later," I told Peggy.

"I'll be here, Doctor," she said. She ran her finger over the rim of her glass, and traced the same finger across my lower lip. "I'll be here."

I rejoined the band, and Heaven's Door was rocking again. The crowd chanted the lyrics to Bob Dylan's classic along with us: "But I would not feel so all alone, Everybody must get stoned." It didn't get any better than this—leading a jam-packed barroom through the chorus to Dylan's anthem, in Dylan's hometown, on stage with my new friend, the Dylan impersonator extraordinaire. My California life seemed a faraway prison framed in palm trees and pain. Peggy Stimac smiled up at me, raised her empty glass in homage, and I sang only to her.

How did it feel? It felt terrific. Tonight, I did not feel so all alone.

CHAPTER 10
BLONDE AND BLONDE

I slept until noon the next day, a feat I hadn't accomplished for decades. My head was pounding from an evening of tequila shots washed down with Budweiser. My throat was Sahara dry from hours of screaming out lyrics to countless Dylan songs. Peggy Stimac came up on stage for the final encore, the taffy of her frame draped across my back, her perfumed hair tickling my nose.

She wanted me to take her home. I'd been too drunk to try. She was a dream girl, but at this point I was window shopping, not buying. If Peggy Stimac was to be my salvation, it would have to be another time, another place. This day was for sleep and for redemption. For the first time in years I hit the pillow without a thought about Alexandra Antone.

It felt great.

At the breakfast table, Johnny peered at me over a plate of steaming pancakes. He'd slept in ten minutes later than me. Breakfast was a word-free zone. I was nursing the worst hangover of my life, and Johnny was playing the part of a mute teenage boy after a late Sunday awakening. At last Johnny broke the silence. "Can I ask you a question, Dad?"

"Sure."

"People at the hospital were talking about a patient from a car crash who almost died in the operating room. I guess you put a breathing tube in through the guy's nose? Is it true that if you hadn't been there, the guy would have died? Did Echo's dad fuck up?"

"Echo's dad?" The sick feeling in the pit of my stomach doubled.

"Yeah, Echo's dad. Bobby Dylan, that nurse anesthetist."

"You're kidding. I met Echo's mom at the hospital. Her name isn't Dylan."

"Echo and her mom, their last name is Johnson. Echo said her dad changed his name from Johnson to Dylan. He started playing gigs two nights a week and telling everyone he was Bobby Dylan, the rock star, come back to Hibbing to play out his career. Then two years ago he moved out, left his wife, and bought the Zimmerman family home for more than it was worth."

"That's bizarre," I said. I rubbed my temples and tried to process what I'd just heard. There were a lot of overlapping relationships: Echo dating Johnny, Dylan and I in the band, Lena cooking for us tonight, Dylan and I and Lena all at the operating room together. Bobby Dylan's family and my family were intersecting.

"You didn't answer my question," Johnny said. "Would that patient have died?"

I rolled my lower lip inside out and chose my words with care. "It's possible," I said. "Probable even."

"Is he a hack? Dylan? I mean, he's not a doctor. He's a nurse doing a doctor's job, right?"

"I don't know if he's a hack. I can tell you he didn't have a clue how to handle that case. Dylan may not have any problems on the next thousand cases he does, but he didn't know what to do with that patient."

"Why is a nurse doing a doctor's job?"

"A state governor can opt out of the requirement for a physician to supervise anesthetic care in that state. The Minnesota governor opted out years ago."

"Why would he do that?"

"I presume it's because there aren't enough M.D. anesthesiologists to staff every little hospital in every tiny town in this state. I don't agree with the idea. Anesthesia is the practice of medicine, not a nursing pursuit. But according to the laws here, Mr. Dylan can give all the anesthesia care he wants."

"But you think he's incompetent."

"I don't know what I think. I'll need to make up my mind over the course of time."

"It bugs me," Johnny said, "because I really like Echo."

"What does that have to do with anything?"

"Our dads both give anesthesia, but you're a class act and her dad is a poser."

I decided not to fuel the comparison. Instead I bent the conversation in the direction I was most curious about. "How's Echo?"

"She's great. Nothing like the girls back home. She's so ... nice. She laughs at everything I say, and let's face it, Dad, she's beautiful."

Beautiful. I'd chosen a beautiful wife, and what good had it done me? I shuddered and said, "Don't lose your head over physical beauty, son."

"It's not just her looks, Dad. She's chill. We hung out together until eleven last night. Then after I got home, I called her and we talked on the phone until 3 o'clock this morning, Dad, she's great. Trust me."

Trust me. My 17-year-old son had it all figured out. My 17-year-old son understood women. Maybe I should take lessons from him.

"Her mom is chill, too," Johnny said. "She watched a movie with us last night. Lena says she's cooking a meal for all four of us tonight."

"Yep. Sounds like an excellent idea. No frozen pizza for the Antone men tonight."

"It'll be great, Dad."

Great. Hibbing High was great. Echo was great. Dinner would be great. I smiled. *Great.* An athlete's cliché gleaned from the hundreds of post-game interviews Johnny and I had watched together on ESPN. *Great.* A simple syllable, an overused syllable, but right now the word was spot on.

Our life was great.

Lena Johnson stirred spaghetti sauce with one hand and cradled a glass of Merlot in the other. She wore a lime green Patagonia fleece top with the collar zipped up to her chin. Her jeans were black Levis, one size too small, but I appreciated the fit. Johnny and Echo were in the next room watching television and laughing together, oblivious to the fact that their parents were in the same house.

"I heard you played in Bobby's band last night," Lena said.

"Word gets around fast."

"It's a small town. In a small town, people tend to keep score about what happens to their cast-off spouses."

"I didn't know he was your husband until this morning."

"He didn't tell you?"

"Nope. You didn't tell me at the hospital either."

She took a long pull on her wine. "I don't talk about him much. This town is too tiny for both of us."

"When are we eating, Mom?" Echo hollered from the next room.

"Five minutes," Lena answered. She refilled my glass, and picked a small piece of white lint from my shirt collar.

I watched her flick the lint into the garbage, and couldn't help but contrast her to Alexandra. My wife would never have wasted two seconds grooming me. Alexandra's time was spent cultivating the glory of Alexandra. My wife's body language oozed narcissism: *I'm special. I'm better than you.*

Lena's mannerisms oozed comfort. Her body language said, *Make yourself at ease. You're in a safe place.* It was foreign territory for me, and I liked it. She was a delight to look at, and Johnny was right—Lena Johnson was a delight to be around. She was charming and gracious. This was the same woman Bobby Dylan ran away from? This was the same woman he couldn't live with? Witnessing Lena's homemaking comforts made me certain, once again, that Bobby Dylan was bonkers. I couldn't imagine Lena Johnson driving her husband to live on the corner of a rooftop. If Dylan moved to the crest of some gable, it was because he had a few shingles loose.

"What do you think of Bobby?" she said.

"I didn't like him at first. He was pretty fun last night, though."

"That's Bobby. He's all about fun."

"What happened to you two?"

"He snapped. He was Bobby Johnson when I met him. I was in nursing school at the University of Minnesota, and he was doing his nurse anesthetist training there. We got married young. I wanted to have three or four kids and move to the suburbs. But right after Echo was born, Bobby enlisted in the Army reserves and got shipped off to Afghanistan as a nurse anesthetist. A suicide bomber blew up two of his best friends, and Bobby lost it. He came home in a straightjacket. He was hospitalized for a year in an inpatient mental hospital in South Carolina with Posttraumatic Stress Disorder. I moved back home to Hibbing. My mom helped me raise Echo, and I worked full time at the hospital here. When Bobby was discharged home, the doctors said the PTSD had resolved and he was OK to resume life in the real world. But he wasn't the same anymore. He'd changed his name to Bobby Dylan. Bobby Johnson was gone."

"How did he seem to you?"

"He was messed up. He convinced his doctors that he was sane, but I knew he wasn't."

"What do you mean?"

"The Bob Dylan thing is no ruse to him. He thinks he is the rock star, returned to his home town to retire as a part-time nurse and a part-time rock n' roll performer at Heaven's Door."

"You don't think it's an act?"

"No, sir. He's read every biography about Bob Dylan, and he's memorized every detail. He's convinced he's the real Dylan."

"He seems a little shaky in the operating room. Is he safe there?"

"I think he's safe. I mean, he hasn't killed anyone."

"He almost killed that car crash guy last week."

"You bailed him out, so we'll never know."

I nodded my head toward the other room, where Echo and Johnny were watching TV. "Is he a decent dad for Echo?"

"He manages. She lives at his house half the time. Bobby buys the groceries, makes the meals, and keeps the house clean. Echo loves him and accepts him for what he is. She never knew him in the Bobby Johnson days. She only knows her dad as Bobby Dylan. What can I do? My daughter needs a father, and he's the only one she's got. How's Bobby treating you?"

"He's treating me like a friend."

"Be careful. You're a threat to him. You have more medical training than Bobby does. He's got to feel inferior to you. The way you saved his patient's life? My God, it was your first week here, and you already showed him up."

"He's been humble and grateful since. It was nice of him to ask me to play in his band."

"Did Bobby get you laid last night?"

I cringed. "I'm married."

"That doesn't stop most people. Bobby slept around."

"I'm sorry to hear that."

"I never trusted the guy."

"I have a hard time picturing you two together," I said. "Bobby's rough around the edges, hair flying everywhere, gruff. You seem ... more sophisticated." I wanted to add "and a hell of a lot better looking than him," but I held back.

She sighed. "Bobby intrigued me. It was all about his rock n' roll. When I met him, he was singing in a Minneapolis club, and he was so sexy. His music made me fly. I loved him. I thought he was the one."

"And now? Is it hard to work at the same hospital as your ex-husband?"

She laughed. "He's not my ex-husband. We never divorced."

"Why not?"

"Bobby didn't want to sign the papers, and I didn't push it."

"You still love him?"

"Oh, God, no."

"Does he love you?"

"In his weird Bobby-like way, he does. He still sends me flowers on my birthday and on Valentine's Day. He still flirts with me."

I couldn't shake Bobby's version of his wife as a quarrelsome nag. I had to know Lena's version. "Did you two fight a lot?"

She nodded her head and said, "Did we ever. The crazy Dylan obsession was bad enough, but after I caught him in his third affair, I'd had enough. I threw his clothes in the snow bank and locked him out. Good riddance. Don't fuck with me."

Whoa. She is woman, hear her roar. The guise of the angelic nurse-mother was peeled back. I watched her face harden as she removed the cauldron of pasta from the stove and drained the noodles through a colander.

"Your turn," she said. "How did you meet your wife?"

"It was in San Francisco. I was out drinking with some friends at a place called the Balboa Café. Alexandra leaned over me at the bar and said, "Can a girl get a martini in this place without kissing someone's ass?" She was gorgeous. I bought her the martini, and I've been kissing her ass ever since. We got married a year later, and moved out of the city. I was a research fellow in the anesthesia department at Stanford, and Alexandra started a real estate company in downtown Palo Alto."

"Why did you two split up?"

"She's a workaholic who has no time for me. Alexandra makes a lot more money than I do, and she doesn't respect me at all. It's a dead marriage. It has been for a long time." I shrugged. "Shit happens."

Lena shrugged in return. "Shit does happen. Can you get the kids? It's time to eat."

I found Johnny and Echo sunken into the marshmallow cushions of a cream-colored couch. They were watching *The Simpsons* with their lanky limbs draped over each other and their fingers entwined. I envied everything I saw: their youthful beauty, their carefree laughter, and their obvious zeal for each other.

Lena's living room was one-tenth the size of my TV lounge in California. I stretched out my arms and almost touched the opposing walls. The most striking feature of the room was a lineup of three-foot-tall trophies covering a tabletop behind the couch. Each trophy featured a female figurine holding a broom in her outstretched arm.

"Who's the award-winner around here?" I said.

"Those are Echo's curling trophies," Johnny said. "Her team won the United States Junior Championship. Curling is this Canadian sport, kind of like shuffleboard on ice. I watched her team practice yesterday. She gets down in this yoga crouch and slides across the ice like a human arrow."

"I know all about curling," I said. "Curling is big up here. I'm impressed. We have a national champion in our midst."

Lena came up behind me and said, "Let's eat, guys." She touched my forearm, and her light caress made my skin tingle. It felt as if some angel had fluttered down and landed on the tiny hairs of my arm for a millisecond, and then flown away.

Echo and Lena led the way into the dining room. Johnny lingered behind and whispered into my ear, "This is so awesome, Dad. Everything. Coming to Minnesota was the best move we ever made."

"It is working out, isn't it?" I said. Life was changing, swirling like a Great Plains twister, dizzying me with newness. The two blonde Minnesota women awaited us at the dining table. I took my seat between them. Echo said, "I'll do grace." She held hands with Johnny and me. Lena did the same, and the four of us formed a circle of warmth around the steaming platter of pasta.

Echo prayed, "Dear Lord, thank you for this food, the roof over our heads, and my mother who takes wonderful care of me. Thank you for bringing Johnny and his dad into our lives. Help us to remember every day that all that is good comes from You. Amen."

"Amen," Lena said.

"Amen," Johnny and I mumbled in quiet unison. The Antone family had never bothered to sit down together for dinner, let alone close our eyes in prayer. We'd raised our son to know that God was out there somewhere, but the only true religion was the pursuit of material success. I could see from Johnny's face that he had no problem with Echo's spirituality. He would have chanted incantations to Satan if that pleased her.

We released each other's hands. Lena held onto mine a bit longer than she needed to. She picked up the platter of pasta and held it out toward Johnny. As she did, I took the opportunity to study Lena's profile—the swoop of blonde waves over her forehead, the tiny upturned nose, the pout of her ruby lower lip—and I could not look away. Our incomparable hostess had the face of a movie starlet.

"I've never been to California," Lena said. "But I feel like I have, since it seems every movie is filmed there."

I said, "It was the same for me when I grew up here. All the TV programs showed gorgeous people driving around California in red convertibles. Every New Year's Day the Rose Bowl game was on television. There was five feet of snow on the ground in Hibbing, but all the fans at the Rose Bowl were wearing T-shirts and shorts. I told myself, 'I'm going to move there,' and I did."

"The furthest west I've been is Fargo," Lena said. "I've never even seen an ocean."

"Echo and her mom could come out to Palo Alto with us this summer for a vacation," Johnny said.

"I'd like to go to Disneyland," Echo said.

"Disneyland is about 400 miles away from where we live," I said.

"We could take them on a drive down there. No problem," Johnny said. "Right, Dad?"

I tried to imagine all four of us driving down Interstate 5 toward L.A. Johnny, Echo, Lena, and me. And oh yeah, how about Alexandra, that woman who just happened to be living in my house back there in Palo Alto? That woman who just happened to be my wife?

I chose the high ground and said, "Right." The fraudulent tone of my voice said *great idea*, but the reality in my gut was *it's never gonna happen in a million years.*

Lena switched topics and said, "What's your favorite class at Hibbing High, Johnny?"

"Physics. It's tough, but Echo sits right behind me and whispers all the answers to me. She's the smartest kid in school. She really is."

Echo blushed. "Not since you moved to town."

Johnny countered, "I've never seen anyone study as hard as you. Tell my dad, Echo. Tell him your plan."

"I want to be a doctor some day," she said.

"Tremendous. Why did you decide on that?" I said.

"I've been diabetic since I was six years old, and I learned first-hand how important doctors are."

"You're all set for your medical school interviews," I said. "When the admissions officer asks, 'Why do you want to be a doctor?' you can say, 'I've had diabetes since I was six, and doctors saved my life. From that moment on, I've never wanted to be anything else.' The admissions officer will say to himself, 'We need more doctors like this young woman.'"

"That's funny," Echo said.

"Maybe you can convince Johnny to be a doc, too."

"Johnny can do anything he sets his mind to," she said. "He's a star."

Johnny blushed and feigned intent interest in his pasta.

"I want him to try curling," she said. "After dinner tonight, I'm taking him down to the curling club so he can give it a whirl."

"Watch out. She'll get you hooked," Lena said to Johnny.

"Maybe she will," Johnny said. "I hope she does."

Echo and Johnny were out the door five minutes after the dinner table was cleared, and I found myself alone with Lena. She refilled our wine glasses.

"Let's sit down and relax for a few minutes," she said. She walked into the living room, and sank into the white couch that Echo and Johnny had warmed up earlier. There were no other chairs in the room, so I sat beside her. Our arms were touching, and we molded into the cushions.

The room light was dim. Her hair floated inches from my face, and the scent of her, part vanilla, part animal, made my head swirl. How much wine had I drunk? Enough to eradicate most of my inhibitions. She cast me a brazen, inviting smile. She was a stranger, but at this point my world was adrift in strangers.

Lena kicked off her shoes, and ran the sole of her bare foot up the length of my calf. My heart thumped. She'd played the role of a homemaker all evening. Comfortable, hospitable, unthreatening. Now she bit into her lower lip, a hungry carnivore. We were alone, and it was now apparent Lena didn't intend to watch television. I was attracted to her—I longed to taste her lips, to touch her cheek. But just as I had with Peggy Stimac the night before, I felt an unseen barrier. I'd been attached to Alexandra for too long. I couldn't push things any further. I pogo-sticked to my feet and said, "What a fantastic evening. I'd better get going."

She looked puzzled and rejected. "You have to go?" Lena stood to face me, her face even with my chest. She craned her head up and looked at me, and the awkwardness of the moment paralyzed me. What was I doing? This wasn't a date. This wasn't the time for a good night kiss. What was it time for? Always the physician, always the professional, always the gentleman, I extended my right hand toward her and said, "Thanks so much."

"My pleasure, Dr. Antone."

"I told you to call me Nico."

"OK, from now on, you're Nico." She shook my hand, and instead of a handshake, she tickled the inside of my palm with the tips of her fingers. It was at once flirtatious and titillating. I giggled. She grew taller, onto her tiptoes. She reached up to caress my cheek with the lightest touch imaginable, and kissed me full on the mouth.

I made no move to break the embrace. She pressed her breasts against me. My intellect told me to run, but my emotions were in a jumble. I was a lonesome soul and I craved the connection.

Lena nibbled on my lower lip and whispered, "Do you like saunas, Nico?"

"I do."

"I have a sauna in the basement, and it's heated up and waiting. Come. Follow me." She took my hand and led me down a flight of stairs into a crude, unfinished basement. The only light was from a single bulb, swinging from the ceiling by its wire. She reached up, pulled a chain, and the light went off. The darkness was absolute. I heard the rustling of clothing. She grasped my hand again and guided it. Her nipple, firm and upturned, scraped against my palm. The warm peach of her breast, firm and foreign, filled my hand. Her breathing quickened in a crescendo that thrilled me, intoxicated me. In the blackness, the unseen unfolded like a dream sequence.

Lena's mouth covered mine, and her hands worked my belt buckle. My clothes hit the floor, and she pulled me through a doorway into a desert of infernal heat. The air was sordid, torched, difficult to inhale. My eyes stung with the temperature, but in the darkness they were useless anyway.

Lena's fingers dug into my back, and she wrapped her legs around me. Braided together, we settled downward onto the softness of a towel along a horizontal surface. I gasped in the oppressive heat. Lena Johnson was a fantasy, invisible to me and perfect. I gnawed the side of her neck like an animal. All patience descended into fury. She guided me into her—a violent, urgent, needy entry. I discarded years of frustration in mordant screams that shook the basement walls.

I'd been faithful to my wife our entire marriage, and I'd forgotten the feel, the scent, or the wetness of any woman before Alexandra. In the sightless abyss of this night, as blind as King Lear in the storm, I found Lena. I was overwhelmed and elated, touched by the wonder of physical love.

"Let's do this again sometime, Nico," she whispered into my ear.

"I'd love to," I said, and I meant it.

CHAPTER 11
A FRIEND OF MINE

The following morning I was back in the cockpit piloting a routine anesthetic. Michael Perpich was doing a partial colectomy on an 81-year-old man named Harlan Versich. Mr. Versich's bowel movements ceased seven days earlier, and he presented that morning with severe abdominal pain, distension, and vomiting. His intestinal obstruction could have been from a variety of diagnoses, but the unfortunate news for Mr. Versich was that the pathology was malignant—Perp found a large adenocarcinoma occluding the sigmoid colon.

The monitoring gauges on my anesthesia dashboard showed normal readings, and for the moment Mr. Versich was the most secure man in town—he had a board-certified anesthesiologist watching every heartbeat and every breath. I was in control of his physiology with my repertoire of inhaled gases and intravenous drugs, and I was focused on the challenge.

But I couldn't stop thinking about Lena Johnson.

The metronome beep, beep, beep of Harlan Versich's heart droned on, and I thought about Lena Johnson. The ventilator purred as it puffed eight breaths per minute into Mr. Versich's lungs, and I thought about Lena Johnson.

The phone on top of the anesthesia machine rang, and I answered it. I felt a pang of annoyance when I heard the voice—the caller was Bobby Dylan. My enchanted, obsessive loop of thoughts was centered on the allure of Lena's body, and I didn't want to interrupt them for a conversation with her estranged husband.

"Can you talk?" Dylan rasped.

"I guess so."

"I'm in room #4 right now. I'm doing a hip fracture on an 80-year-old, and she just tried to die on me. Her heart rate dropped and dropped until the monitor screen showed no EKG beats at all. Flat line."

"And?"

"It only lasted about 4 or 5 seconds. I shot in some atropine and her heartbeat came back up, but I have no idea what caused the whole episode. Should I call a cardiologist?"

"What are her vital signs now?"

"They're all normal."

"It might have only been a vasovagal episode, but you'd better have a cardiologist or internist follow her tonight to rule out a myocardial infarction. He'll put her in a monitored bed and draw some troponins."

"Will do. Thanks for the consult. You're a decisive guy. You must be from some hotsy-totsy hospital in California."

"I'll take that as a compliment."

"Hey, I got a phone call from your wife last night," Dylan said.

I almost fell off my chair. While I'd been with Lena, Mr. Dylan was talking to Alexandra? "What did she want?" I said.

"She's horny. She wants some action. And unless your dick is 2,000 miles long, I think the woman has a legitimate complaint."

"Alexandra never called you," I said, relieved by the hoax.

"No, not yet. But if she ever did call on Bobby Dylan, it would be the happiest day of her life."

"I hate my wife," I said.

"Of course you do. Heads it's love, tails it's hate."

"You'd hate her, too."

"I love all the ladies."

What would Dylan think if he knew about my sauna last night? It was an absurd question, and I knew the answer. Dylan would not appreciate me hooking up with Lena, his Girl from the North Country. I squirmed in my chair. I was uncomfortable with the duplicity of my friendship with Dylan and my intimacy with his wife. I didn't want to talk about women anymore right now.

"Heaven's Door tonight?" I asked, shifting the topic.

"Nope. Tonight I'm home watching the Minnesota-UMD hockey game. Why don't you come over? Have a couple of beers, watch the game, shoot the shit."

"I went to UMD. Big fan."

"I went to the University of Minnesota, and I'm an even bigger fan. Come and watch your alma mater get their asses kicked. Game starts at 7:30. I'm at 2425 7th Avenue, at the corner of 7th and 25th Street."

"I know the place. Bob Dylan's old house."

"Of course it is. I'm Bobby Dylan."

I rolled my eyes. *I'm Bobby Dylan*, indeed. Michael Perpich began stapling Harlan Versich's skin incision together. "Got to go," I told Dylan. "It's time to wake up this guy. See you tonight."

I finished three more anesthetics and left the operating room by 6 p.m. Back home I found Johnny frying hamburgers and heating up some frozen French fries. The house smelled like a diner, and my stomach rumbled in anticipation. I was blown away that Johnny was cooking at all. He never prepared meals in our Palo Alto kitchen. It was another good sign that small-town Minnesota values were rubbing off on the kid. I liked the change.

"Have a good day?" I said.

"Yep."

"What was the best thing that happened today?"

"Everything. Classes were good, lunchtime with friends was better."

"How's Echo?"

"Super."

I let "Super" hang in the air between us for a while. I could relate to my son's level of jubilance. The look on Johnny's face was telling. The kid was as infatuated with Echo as I was with her mom.

One week into our North Country adventure, Johnny had changed from a boy into a broad-shouldered, wide-eyed man, complete with a day's stubble on his chin and a cocksure look in his eyes. He removed the tray of fries out of the oven and spread them on two plates. He dropped a steaming hamburger patty between two pieces of bread, handed the plate to me and said, "It's feast time at the Antone Man Cave, Daddy-O."

The cuisine was primitive, but the effort and enthusiasm were laudable. "I'm impressed," I said, pouring a mound of ketchup onto my burger.

"Do you think we could host Echo and her mom here some night?" Johnny said.

"Sure. You could cook for them, return the favor. That was fun last night. I like them both."

"You should have come to the curling club with us last night."

The corners of my eyes crinkled into a reflective grin. I thought, *That's OK. I had a better time than that.* "What was it like?" I said.

"Echo's so good at the sport, she's a legend in this town. There are posters of her and her team all over the walls. Everyone at the club knows her. They treat her like a celebrity. She took me out on the ice and gave me an hour-long private lesson. She says I picked it up faster than anyone she's ever taught. I'm going to play in the Monday-Wednesday night league with some guys she introduced me to."

"I don't want this curling to get in the way of your schoolwork."

"It won't. School comes first. Tonight I finished all my homework before you got home. Echo is taking me to the curling club again tonight after dinner. It's fun."

I gave Johnny a thumbs-up and said, "Glad to hear it. You need a gimmick when it comes to getting into the top colleges. Curling could be a pretty good gimmick. There aren't a lot of curlers in the United States. You'll stand out in a crowd."

"Not everything is about college applications, Dad. I'm doing it because I like it."

"And you're doing it because of a certain blue-eyed Scandinavian gal."

"And that doesn't suck, Daddy-O. That doesn't suck."

I parked my car in the driveway of Mr. Dylan's house, and gaped at his garage door. The square wooden door was painted as a replica of Bob Dylan's classic *Blood on the Tracks* album cover, with the rock star's image in profile, hazy and cartoonish, and the singer's eyes hidden behind opaque sunglasses. The background color—a maroon hue of blood ancient and dried—was identical to the original album.

I'd walked or driven past this house a thousand times, but never been inside. Bob Zimmerman vacated his boyhood home decades before. What I was about to see lacked any history—it would be a nurse anesthetist's 21st-Century version of the Zimmerman home. I stood on the front walk and gazed north toward Hibbing High, two blocks in the distance. How many fathers had walked past this house, taken in the panorama of Hibbing High School in the distance, and wondered if their son or daughter could succeed like Bob Zimmerman had?

The front door opened, and Mr. Dylan stood on his stoop. He was dressed in bizarre attire—a faded, red-wine-colored University of Minnesota hockey jersey, oversized thermal snow pants, and a white CCM hockey helmet unstrapped at the neck. "Get in here, Doctor," he chided. "You already missed the first period."

"Nice outfit," I said.

"Damn right. I just took my Arctic Cat for a spin up to Carey Lake and back. The most fun a man can have with his clothes on."

The shining black and orange chassis of an Arctic Cat snowmobile stood parked next to the front door. In

California, men bought Harley Davidson motorcycles to prove their masculinity. In Minnesota, they bought Arctic Cats. "Looks like a powerful machine," I said.

"She goes ninety miles an hour if you crank her. One hundred and sixty horsepower. She's a rocket. Nothing wrong with having a rocket between your legs, right Doctor? C'mon, let's go in and watch the game."

I followed him inside the house, to a small square space dominated by a massive TV hanging on the only windowless wall. The room was lit like a Broadway stage, with a ceiling lamp, two standing lamps, and four lights on tables. I felt like putting on sunglasses. The décor was absurd, spartan, and all brown: brown chairs and sofa, brown wall-to-wall carpet, brown plaid curtains, and walls painted brown. The solitary accent piece was an oil painting of Echo on the wall adjacent to the front door. The image of her youthful face graced an inelegant room that was otherwise a man's space, a bachelor's space. A pair of brown Lazy Boy reclining chairs faced the television. Four remote controls sat on a small table along side it. Mission Control.

"The good guys are up 2-0 already," Dylan said. "Have a seat. Put your feet up." He handed me a bottle of Bud Light, and plopped down in the nearest reclining chair. A tug on the stick shift lever snapped the leg holder into the horizontal position. Dylan motioned me toward the second chair alongside him.

Four library books were stacked on the table between the two chairs. The books were fiction titles authored by well known popular scribes: James Patterson, David Baldacci, Dan Brown, and John Grisham. "While I'm home reading anesthesia journals, it looks like you're reading thrillers and mysteries," I said.

"I love a good yarn," Dylan said. "Nothing better than trying to get inside the author's head and figure out who did it."

"I haven't read a library book in twenty years."

"I read two or three a week. Can't afford to be buying a hundred and fifty books a year. I'm not a rich doctor like you, remember?"

I nestled down into my reclining chair. The vinyl squeaked as I pulled the stick shift to elevate my legs. It wasn't a classy piece of furniture, but I had to admit it was a superior way to relax. I liked the chair, liked the beer, and loved having someone to watch sports with again. Johnny Antone—super-student and Echo-addict—had no time to watch TV with me anymore. My time with Bobby was rain on the desert. Playing rock n' roll, talking about women, drinking, hanging out and watching hockey together—hanging out with Bobby felt like I was back in college with one of my mates again. I hadn't had a guy friend since my son was born.

I shielded my eyes from the blazing illumination in the room and said, "It's a little dark in here. Can you turn on a few more lights?"

"It's how I cope with winter," Dylan said. "In December, the sun sets at three in the afternoon, and it makes me crazy. The darkness makes me depressed. When I set the house blazing, it cheers me up."

"They call it SAD."

"Who calls it sad?"

"SAD stands for Seasonal Affective Disorder. It's a medical diagnosis for people who get depressed during the dark winter season. Doctors recommend treating SAD with light therapy, to trick the brain into forgetting it's winter."

"Hmm. I'm no doctor, but I sort of figured that out by myself. You docs come up with fancy names for things just to show off how you went to school for too many years, and how you memorized too many useless things."

"Who's the girl in the picture?" I said, tipping my beer bottle toward the painting of Echo. I feigned ignorance. Dylan didn't seem to know our kids were dating.

"That's my daughter, Echo. I'll bet you've seen her. She works part-time at the operating room. Best little girl in the world. Echo lives with me Wednesdays, Thursdays, and every other weekend. She's with her mother the other nights."

"I'd hate being away from Johnny half the nights."

"You get used to it. All those years I was on tour, I didn't see her for weeks at a time."

I raised an eyebrow. "On tour where?"

"All around the world. Concerts. Traveling."

"But you're a nurse."

"Now I'm a nurse, but I spent years touring and performing. I got burned out with the travel, so I came back here. But I still need to play. Heaven's Door is a kick—the adoration from the audience, the attention from the women. Ladies like me when I'm singing and playing my guitar. It's like the blazing lights in here." He waved his hands at the lamps. "The lights and the women, they keep me from getting down."

"Your wife wasn't enough?" If I'd had a woman as pretty as Lena, there was no way I'd have chased bimbo groupies.

He shook his head. "My wife was impossible, like a woman adrift in the middle of Lake Superior, so busy trying to keep her head above water that there was nothing left for me. Always struggling to get happy. I got sick of trying to keep her up."

I frowned. I had a difficult time picturing Lena as a drowning soul. It couldn't have been easy, living with this guy. I tried to imagine Lena rubbing her bare foot across Dylan's leg while the man lounged in full hockey regalia and bragged about the mirage of his rock star life. The image of Lena and Dylan together bugged me. Even though I'd only touched her once, I couldn't let go. I needed to know more. "What's your ex-wife up to now? It's a small town. You must know what she's doing."

He scoffed. "First off, she's not my ex-wife. She's my wife. She lives a mile away, in the house we used to share. Lena's a nurse. You must have seen her at the hospital. Best lookin' woman at the General. Her last name's Johnson."

"Oh, yes. I've met her. She's nice."

"Not always nice. The night she threw me out, she met me at the front door after a gig and bludgeoned me with a rolling pin." He peeled the hockey helmet off his forehead to reveal a well-healed longitudinal scar. "Twenty-five stitches in the General Emergency Room. When I came home afterwards, all my stuff was laying in a snow bank outside the front door. My guitars, my medical equipment, my clothes. Everything."

"Why did she do that?"

"She heard I was at the Holiday Inn with Carla Finn."

"Was she justified? Were you at the Holiday Inn with Carla Finn?"

Dylan took a puff on his cigarette and burped. "I don't even remember. I already told you, the ladies at the club like me. It's just sex. I love Lena, but she needed me on a short leash or else out in the snowbank. He bit at the imaginary shackles between his wrists again, and spit out the chain. "I prefer the snowbank."

I tried to process what I'd just heard. Dylan was a boorish, self-centered philanderer. Lena was as radiant as any light bulb in this room, upbeat, kind, and maternal. Hot as the sauna she'd stoked. If she had a temper, I admired her for throwing her unfaithful husband out.

"Does your wife have a boyfriend?" I said.

"Nah. Lena doesn't get out much. If she's dating someone, it's news to me. Another beer?"

"Sure." I followed him into the adjoining kitchen, a small room the size of my closet in California. The walls were white as a blizzard, and the sole furnishings were a dented metal folding table and two folding chairs. A Mr. Coffee percolator and two Minnesota Viking laminated placemats topped the table. I didn't see a dishwasher. A bottle of Ivory Liquid and a stained yellow sponge lay in the sink. It didn't look like Dylan entertained very often. He removed a second beer from the refrigerator, and handed it to me.

"Thanks," I said. "Is there a quiet room where I can call my patients for tomorrow?"

"Why do you want to do that?"

"I always call my patients the night before surgery. That way they know what to expect, and they can go to bed with some peace of mind."

"That's what you do?"

"Yes. You don't?"

"No way. I don't want to think about tomorrow until tomorrow. Matthew 6, verses 33-34. 'Therefore do not worry about tomorrow, for tomorrow will worry about itself. Each day has enough trouble of its own.' You can worry about Tuesday and Tuesday's surgeries. I'm still working on Monday." His voice dripped with contempt.

"Does it bother you that I'm a physician and you're not?"

"I can do anything you can," Dylan said. "You know it, and I know it too."

The answer was blunt, confrontational, and false. It rankled me. "How about the guy with the facial trauma? The guy you put to sleep but couldn't intubate?"

"I already thanked you for your help, Doctor. You got lucky with that nasal tube, and you know it. Next time, you'll be in a jam and I'll save your ass. Maybe in the operating room, maybe on Howard Street. Maybe you'd better go home and read some more anesthesia journals, so you can stay smarter than dumbass nurse anesthetists like me. You think it's a mistake, letting non-doctors practice medicine, don't you?"

"Yes, I do."

"Get over it. There aren't enough docs who want to work in a rusty-ass mining town like this. Patients either get me or they get nothing. Embrace it."

"Embrace this," I said with a grin, flipping Dylan my middle finger.

"Nice gratitude, Doctor. I give you two beers, I let you watch my Gophers rip your Bulldogs, and you do me wrong. I think I'd better get back to my easy chair and have a good cry."

"Where can I go to call my patients?"

"Be gone. Go to the other end of the house." He pointed through a doorway. I walked toward the rear of the house, and found the hallway walls covered with an array of framed photographs, each one canted at various non-horizontal angles. All the pictures were vintage shots from Bob Zimmerman's youth and the rock star Bob Dylan's concert career. They were aligned in chronologic order, starting with high school pics on the left. I recognized some of the photos from Dylan biographies I had read, but several of them were unique snapshots I'd never seen.

"Hey, Bobby, can you come down here?" I called out.

"What's up?" he said, leaning his head against the doorframe.

"I'm checking out these pictures. Where did you get this one?" I pointed to a photo of a youthful Bob Zimmerman sitting on a park bench with his arm around another kid. A golf bag leaned against the bench between them.

"That's a picture of my brother and me waiting to tee off at the Hibbing Municipal golf course when we were kids."

I did a double take. This was a picture of the real Bob Zimmerman. My nurse anesthetist friend didn't appreciate that he and the rock star were two different people.

I pointed out this fact to my new friend. "But it's not you. This is Bob Zimmerman as a boy."

"It's me." Dylan yawned, tired of this interrogation.

"And all these of these other pictures?" I asked, fearing I already knew the answer.

"They're different excerpts from my music career. I like this one of Neil Young and me backstage at The Last Waltz Concert. And I love this one of George Harrison and me at the Concert for Bangladesh. I miss George, God bless him."

The look on Dylan's face was serene and sympathetic. "This is my favorite in the whole collection," he said, pointing to the farthest picture on his end of the hallway. It was an 8 X 10 black and white photo of a younger nurse anesthetist Bobby Dylan, dressed in scrubs. He was beaming and sitting cheek-to-cheek next to a girlish and puffy Lena

Johnson. Lena was dressed in a hospital gown, and she cradled a tiny baby in her arms.

"That was the day my baby girl was born. Greatest day in my life." He nodded his head in confirmation, and repeated, "Greatest day in my life."

The entire collection of hallway photos left me perplexed and uneasy. The bona-fide picture of Bobby, Lena, and Echo hung alongside thirty pictures of the rock star Bob Dylan, and this nurse anesthetist could not distinguish himself from the rock star. My friend seemed to be out of touch with reality. He seemed delusional. It was possible the man was psychotic.

I spotted a copy of *No Direction Home*, a biography of Bob Dylan written by Robert Shelton, on the hallway bookshelf. I pulled the book out, and opened it. "The Bob Dylan in this book," I said. "What do you think of him?"

He glanced at the cover of the book, and shrugged his shoulders. "That's my biography, that's what I think. Some parts are accurate. Some are bullshit."

"You have the same name, but it's not really about you. Right?"

Dylan face crinkled into an eat-shit-and-die expression. "What are you driving at? You don't believe me?"

"I believe you're a nurse anesthetist in Hibbing. I don't believe you're the world famous rock star."

He threw back his head and laughed. "I'm the rock n' roll Bob Dylan. Hell, you've been on stage with me. Is it so hard to believe that I'd come back to roost in my old home town?"

I felt a chill go up my spine. He hadn't just adopted Bobby Dylan's name. He was living a fantasy that he occupied Bob Dylan's life. I'd heard enough. It was pointless arguing with him.

I looked at my watch, and said, "I should be heading home."

Dylan nodded in assent. "Game's over, anyway. Minnesota's ahead 7-2. Tough luck for your team. You working tomorrow?"

"Every day."

"Me, too. I'll see you in the O.R." He clapped his hand on my shoulder, and said, "And tomorrow night we'll be on stage."

"You said Tuesday was acoustic night. You sing by yourself on Tuesdays."

"I've got a stand-up acoustic bass just waiting to be plucked. Play with me. We'll light it up."

"I'm not sure."

"Nico, this town is 16,000 brave souls on the southern fringe of the polar ice cap, on the road to nowhere. There's nothing else for them or us to do on Tuesday nights. Turn off your TV, walk on over to Heaven's Door, and we'll make some music. On stage at eight o'clock. Deal?" Dylan grinned that twisted smile, and I was drawn in again. I couldn't say no. The man was crazy, but he had one endearing quality.

He thought Nico Antone was special.

CHAPTER 12
PEEKING THROUGH A KEYHOLE

My suitcase was packed and stowed in the back seat of the BMW. Johnny jumped into the passenger seat and said, "When are you coming back, Dad?"

"I'm returning on the 7 p.m. plane from Minneapolis tomorrow night."

"Business trip?"

"I have to meet with the dean of the medical school to talk about my job. I took a one-year leave of absence to come to Minnesota, and the dean needs a firm commitment for when I'm coming back. If I return within twelve months my job is secure, but to do that I'd have to leave you here to finish your senior year without me."

"Can you get an extension?"

"I don't know. That's why I'm going back to meet with him."

"If you have to move back to California, I could always live with Echo and her mom."

"That gets complicated. Echo lives with her dad half the time."

"I could stay with Lena full time, no problem. There's no way I'm staying with her dad. He's too creepy for me."

"Why don't we just wait and see what happens, Johnny. Tonight you'll be staying with Echo and her mom. Let's see how that goes." I rolled the BMW up to the front steps of the Hibbing Curling Club, and turned off the engine.

"I'll be fine while you're gone, Dad. Studying and curling, that's what I'll be doing."

"You enjoy curling?"

"I like it a lot, and I'm good at it. I'm almost the best guy on my team already. Echo's friends—the boy's team that won the State Championship last year—one of them tore his ACL skiing last week. They're looking for a replacement, and they're trying me out tonight."

"Join the defending Minnesota State Champions? You've only been playing for two months."

"I've been playing every day for two months. A team has four guys on it, and I'll be the front man for the other three champions. I'm an OK shooter, but the guys say they've never seen anyone sweep as hard as me, and they like that."

"A sweeping specialist?"

"No. Everyone on the team throws two rocks. My job is to make the first two shots, and then sweep the last six rocks. What time does your plane leave, Dad? Do you have time to come in and watch?"

"My plane leaves at 8."

"Come in then. I want you to see us play."

I followed Johnny inside the Hibbing Curling Club. The sign hanging over the entryway read: *Home of the 1976 World Champion Bruce Roberts Team.* I knew the Hibbing Club was a perennial contender for national titles. I'd forgotten club members had won a past world championship. Up North people were jazzed about curling, a winter recreation they could do after the sun went down and before the beer started flowing.

The interior of the Club resembled an inner city bowling alley. It smelled of stale tobacco smoke and spilled beer. Thirty or forty men were milling about, carrying brooms as they descended past glass doors leading to the curling sheets four steps below. There were seven curling lanes, or sheets, separated by pillars that held up the low-hanging ceiling. I sat down next to an old man in a fedora, and checked the clock. I had time to watch for fifteen minutes or so.

"Never saw you here before," the old man said to me.

"First time," I said. "I don't know that much about curling. I'm just here to watch my son. That's him with the wavy hair and the royal blue sweater."

"The game's like shuffleboard on ice," he said. "See the bulls-eye targets at both ends of the sheet of ice? Players try to slide granite stones as close as possible to the center of that bulls-eye. The two teams alternate shots, and try to knock out the other's stones. It's a simple game on the surface, but it's complicated as chess if you dig deeper."

"Did you play?"

"Sure, sure. I curled up until I was 85, and then I hung it up. Didn't want to slip on the ice and break a hip."

"My name's Nico Antone."

"Francis Baratto," he said, shaking my hand. "Your kid has a nice slide."

"Thanks." I turned my attention to observing the game. Many of the curlers were overweight men in baggy sweaters, but Johnny's teammates were three lean teenagers who looked like proper athletes. Johnny began the game by delivering the first stone. I leaned forward in my seat. Johnny appeared confident and laser focused on his target on the other end of the rink.

Francis continued educating me. "Your kid's got a Teflon slider on the sole of his left foot. Watch. He'll push off with his right foot, put all his weight on that Teflon on his left foot, and slide down the ice toward the target."

Below us, Johnny stood up for a small backswing, and then launched into a streamlined sliding position that was a cross between a yoga stretch and a praying mantis lurking for food. His left foot lay flat against the ice, his left knee was pressed to his chest, and his right leg stretched out behind him like a rudder at the aft of a ship. Johnny gripped the red handle of the rock in front of him and slid down the ice at a startling speed. After a 40-foot slide he released the stone, and it traveled the length of the sheet in a gentle left-to-right curl until it stopped on the front edge of the bulls-eye.

"Great shot, Tone," his teammates said in unison. Johnny raised one finger in acknowledgement. Like an emotionless assassin after a hit, he moved into position to await his next assignment. He didn't glance up to the viewing area. He seemed unconcerned with my approval.

Tone? My old college nickname, reborn in my son. Great shot, Tone. In less than two months, Johnny had grown into the local social network of this odd sport. Chalk another one up for Minnesota. My son had found his niche here.

"That's a perfect shot," Francis said. "See the way his shot curved to the right as it traveled down the ice? That's why they call the sport curling."

A second member of the red team delivered a shot. Johnny and a third teammate bent over the path of the stone and polished the ice with brooms that looked like oversized toothbrushes. Johnny leaned into his work and worked with the fury of a boxer pummeling an opponent on the ropes. The shot knocked two blue stones out of play. Johnny raised his broom high and called out, "Nice shot, Gary." His look was triumphant and serious.

"Your son's one hell of a sweeper," Francis said. "How many years has he curled?"

"Two months."

"Two months? Wow. He takes to this game. He really takes to it."

"Thanks." I was impressed, too. Johnny fit in. He was part of the scene, indistinguishable from Gary and the others. It was hard to believe this was the same kid that used to spend his winter evenings playing Call of Duty on the living room Xbox.

I'd seen enough. It was time to catch my plane. I knocked on the window that separated the viewing area from the arena ice, and gave Johnny a big thumbs up. He returned a hearty smile. I pointed to my watch and gestured toward the exit. He waved goodbye.

"Thanks for explaining things to me," I said to Francis. "I've got to leave for the airport."

"The airport? Where you flying to at this time of night?"

"To Minneapolis, and then from Minneapolis to San Francisco."

"San Francisco? What the hell you want to go there for?" Francis shook his head. He pulled a small glass jar out of his pocket, and unscrewed the lid. He hawked a big goober of chewing tobacco juice into the jar, and screwed the lid back on top of it. He shook his head again and said, "Nothing but kooks in San Francisco."

I couldn't see any point in arguing with him. His mind was pretty well made up. If Francis Barrato ever heard my story he'd no doubt realize I was one of those kooks. I bid him goodbye, and left for the parking lot.

As I drove toward the airport, my thoughts turned to the people I was leaving behind in Hibbing. The weather sucked—it was five degrees below zero. The wind was whipping snow across Highway 37 in my path. But in Johnny, Lena, and Dylan, I had three people I missed already.

I pulled into the driveway of my Palo Alto home at 1 a.m. Pacific Standard Time. I was surprised to see a silver Porsche 911 Carrera parked in front of our house. I didn't recognize the car. It wasn't new, so it couldn't be Alexandra's. The woman hadn't driven a used car in her life. I had a sickening feeling in my gut, and I ground my teeth hard. I should have pressed the accelerator down, driven to a nearby hotel, and confronted the unsavory circumstances after the sun came up.

But I didn't. Instead, I turned off the engine and sat alone in the moonlight. My heart was pounding, and there was no release for the adrenaline. I'd flown 1,600 miles to get to this point, and I was going to enter my home.

I unlocked the front door and turned on the entryway light. The furnishings were new. Three new long white couches formed an equilateral seating triangle in front of the fireplace. A six-foot-tall wooden sculpture of a leaping horse stood in front of the picture window that overlooked the Bay. The changes were absurd, and I loathed them. Alexandra knew how to sell houses. She had no idea how to decorate them.

I slipped off my dress shoes and tiptoed down the Oriental carpeting that lined the hallway toward the bedrooms. The door to Alexandra's room was open. The sound of heavy snoring—male snoring—resonated from inside. I balled my right fist and sucked in my breath. This was going to be ugly. This was my house. This was my wife. There would be consequences for the snorer, and for Alexandra.

I returned to the living room and picked up the fireplace poker, all the while fearing what I was capable of at a moment like this. I knew I should walk out the front door now, before I lost my temper, but my weeks in the North Country had affected me. I couldn't let this go. I was Odysseus returned from Troy. I seized the iron poker, strode into Alexandra's room, snapped the lights on, and screamed, "I'm home!"

The man woke up first. He shielded his eyes from the glare, and puffed up his naked chest like a rooster. The blackest of beards framed his gaping mouth. He roared, "What the hell?"

Alexandra rolled over him to face me, her face lined with creases from sleeping hard. She blinked herself into consciousness and drawled, "Jesus Christ, Nico, what are you doing here?"

"How about I'm here because it's my house? What are you doing, you piece of shit whore?"

"Hey man, stay cool," the bearded rooster said.

"Don't call me a whore, you limp-dicked weasel," Alexandra shrieked. She pulled the plug on a brass lamp from her bedside table and hurled it across the bedroom at me. Her ridiculous silicon breasts flapped in the breeze as she swung her arm. The false melons bounced across the rooster's shoulder.

The lamp smashed into a full-length mirror behind me. I raised the fireplace iron over the wreckage of the glass and the wreckage of my marriage. My eyes flickered back and forth between the rooster and the hen. My heart raced and sweat poured from under my arms. I drew back the poker like a baseball player stepping up to the plate. I'd hit home runs as a youth—my rejoicing teammates mobbing me at the dugout steps. If I reprised that baseball swing at my wife and her lover right here right now, I'd wind up alone and shackled in a jail cell—an image more awful than the naked duo before me.

I dropped the poker, and left the house.

My meeting with the dean of the medical school the next morning passed by in a fog. I remember little of the encounter except the dean's insensitive words. He folded his hands on his desk and said, "Dr. Antone, it's simple arithmetic. You have ten months to go. If you exceed your 12-month sabbatical, your faculty position here will be forfeited. You're welcome to reapply in the future if you choose to, but there are no guarantees as to the success of your application."

"I need to stay in Minnesota until one year from June."

"It's your life, and it's your career. Make your own decision. I can only tell you what the rules are. You'll need to return by next January to retain your job." He shook my hand and looked right through me. I was an insignificant speck in his universe.

Dejected, I left the medical school and drove to the Stanford Shopping Center, where I eradicated my negative energy and a significant amount of money doing something the old Nico Antone never wasted a minute on: I went shopping. I blitzed in and out of Neiman Marcus in thirty minutes. I carried a slim gift-wrapped box, and the bounce had returned to my step. It was a warm winter day under a flawless blue California sky.

I could not wait to return to the snows of Minnesota.

The temperature was sixty degrees colder when I walked up Lena's front steps that evening. I could see the flickering of her television screen through a gap in the front curtains. I peeked through the tiny window at the top of the front door. Lena was asleep, curled up under a blanket on her couch.

Last night, I'd awakened a woman in her house. Unlike last night, this woman wouldn't throw a lamp at me.

Why did Alexandra's infidelity bother me so much? I was no saint myself. I spent as much time in Lena's bed as I could, whenever Echo slept the night at her dad's house. I'd return home right after the lovemaking so Johnny wouldn't know what I was up to. Sometimes I slept until near dawn and snuck back into Dom's house before Johnny woke. I was like a schoolboy myself, stealing around in the middle of the night, hiding condoms in a shoebox in the trunk of my BMW.

Alexandra was a bad dream, a distant tormentor I couldn't shake from my memory. Had I expected that she would sit around night after night in that empty mansion, crying over my picture? Of course Alexandra was going to party when I moved away, but the grim reality of being a cuckold eviscerated me.

I needed to hold Lena again. I wanted to resume this new life that felt so natural.

I had a key to her house, and I let myself in. I tiptoed with stealth across the room and knelt at her side. She was breathing in quiet puffs. I touched her lips with a single finger, and Lena's eyes fluttered open. She smiled at me, kissed my finger and said, "Hi, handsome."

"I came here straight from the airport. I didn't want to wait until tomorrow to see you."

"Mmm. I'm glad you did."

"I brought you something." I handed Lena the package from Neiman Marcus. She opened the Hermes box and lifted out an Italian silk scarf, woven in interlocking paisley swirls of gold and green.

She ran the fabric across her face and said, "It's the most beautiful thing I've ever touched." She wrapped the scarf around her neck and pulled it into a loose knot above her breasts. "You could never find anything like this in Northern Minnesota. Never." She ran her fingers through my hair and said, "And there's nothing like you in Northern Minnesota, either. How was your trip?"

"My trip sucked. I had a rocky time with Alexandra, and the dean won't guarantee me my faculty job if I stay away for more than a year." Then I told her about the bedroom scene, my voice a dry croak as I relived the sordid details.

"That's an awful story. You could have gone O.J. on them."

"I'm too smart for that. It's over. That's the bottom line."

Her eyebrows rose a millimeter. She leaned into me and busied her fingers stroking the knot in her new scarf. "Everything happens for a reason. It's a good thing you found out about Alexandra." Lena rolled over on top of me and said, "Welcome home."

"It is home," I said, and I meant it.

CHAPTER 13
WATCHING THE RIVER FLOW

Rays of morning sun streaked through Lena's open bedroom window, across the billowing white duvet cover. My scrub clothes and her T-shirt and shorts lay in a lump next to the bed. Birds cheeped outside her window. It was summer in Minnesota, the days were long, and life was simple. I kissed the inside of Lena's forearm and watched her dimples rise into a smile. We lay skin to skin in the afterglow of sex, and my mind was at ease. It was an opportune moment for a man to express his love for a woman, but I held my tongue. I felt an intense attraction to Lena, unlike any love I'd ever felt for a woman, but I wanted nothing more from Lena than I had right now—a clandestine relationship, concealed from our children and her husband. Sex and companionship. It made sense to conceal the poker hand of my emotions. Silence kept the power in my court.

Lena chose to tamper with the moment. "I love you," she said.

I was trapped. What to say? "I'm so happy with you," I said.

"I just told you I loved you. Do you love me?"

I was on the spot. How could I not parrot those same words? I looked into the sea foam of her irises, and felt a fluttering in my chest, but not from love. It was uneasiness. Instead of speaking, I kissed her, and I reached between her legs for the wonder she never denied me.

But this time she did deny me. She tightened her thighs together and said, "Do you love me, Nico?"

I winced. "I have a hard time expressing my emotions. I'm crazy about you."

"I love you," she persisted.

My heart rate climbed. I sat up in bed and said nothing. Our morning had shifted from idyllic to awkward. Her face curled into a distasteful scowl. She pulled the sheets up to her chin. I wanted to crawl out the window.

"Does it bother you that I haven't divorced Bobby yet?" she said.

"No. I'm just happy that we're together."

"I'll break it off. For us."

"That's up to you. You and Bobby have had separate lives for what, two years now?"

"How about you and Alexandra?"

"What about her?"

"Are you waiting for her to file for divorce? Or will you?"

"Good God, I don't know." I rolled over in bed and turned my back to Lena. Just hearing Alexandra's name bouncing off these walls made me agitated. "I don't want to talk about her. I don't even want to think about her." The muscles in my jaw tightened.

"I'm afraid you'll go back to California in a year, and I'll never see you again."

"You'll always see me."

She spun me around with violent force, her face millimeters from mine. "I don't believe that. You'll go back to California. You're not going to stay up here forever."

"Don't worry about forever right now. I'm here. You're here. We're good."

"When Johnny and Echo leave for college, I want to move to California with you."

I sighed. "It may not be that simple. I have to move back this January. If I don't return to my faculty job when my 12 months are up, I lose my professorship, my seniority, my Stanford title. Everything."

"But you have lots of money."

"Alexandra has lots of money. I need my own job."

"What are you trying to say?"

"I'm going to move back before Johnny graduates. I'm hoping Johnny can stay here with you."

"We love Johnny. I'd be happy to have him. You can come visit every weekend."

"I'll do my best."

"Will you move back into your house in California?"

"No. I expect I'll get a smaller place on campus."

"So Alexandra stays in your mansion on the hill, and you're out? That's ridiculous. You're the doctor."

"She makes twenty times as much money as I do. She can afford the mansion. I don't care."

"You need to start caring. Take it from me. I've been living in 9 X 12-foot rooms all my life. Scraping ice off my windshield all my life. You don't get it, honey. Let me show you something." She rolled out of bed, left the room, and returned a minute later. She handed me a flat package, two feet long by three feet wide, wrapped in simple white tissue. I ripped off the paper to reveal an oil painting in an aged wooden frame. The painting depicted a blazing sunset over a turquoise ocean. The sun's golden light filtered through the branches of three tall palm trees on the shore.

"It's California as I picture it," Lena said. "Beautiful, serene, idyllic, warm. Every night I go to sleep imagining you and me under those palm trees."

I was stupefied. I held the framed picture at arm's length. No one had ever given me artwork before, let alone while I was lying naked in bed. "Where did you find this?"

"I painted it for you. I painted it for us."

The painting had an amateurish edge to it—no one would mistake it for a Van Gogh. It was art, but more so, it was an invitation. *Take care of me.* I felt a churning in my gut. I wanted the painting to go away, but there was no way that was going to happen. Instead I said, "I love it. Can we hang it right here, in your bedroom? I want it to be the first thing I see whenever I'm lying in bed here."

"The painting…is that what it's like, where you lived?"

I shook my head. "No. Not everyone in California lives on the beach and watches the sunset over the Pacific. I lived a half-hour from the ocean. And in Northern California, there are no palm trees on the beaches. It's too cold for palm trees along the ocean."

I walked the painting across the room, and propped it up on top of her dresser. My cell phone rang, and the caller I.D. said *Bobby Dylan*. "Excuse me for a second," I said. "It's Bobby."

Lena scoffed. "Tell the loser you're busy screwing his wife."

"I don't think I'll bring it up. I'm supposed to go fishing with him today."

"You're kidding. It's crazy that you and Bobby are buddies." Her voice trailed off, and I could understand why. She'd made herself vulnerable, had presented me with her homemade gift of affection, and I'd answered with plans to spend time with Bobby.

"It's just a fishing trip. Johnny's coming with us. Bobby's going to show Johnny how to fish." She looked unconvinced. I answered the call.

Dylan said, "Doctor, I have a question for you. Your boy Johnny is supposed to come fishing with us today. Is that right?"

"Yes. I asked you about it last week. You said it would be OK."

"Things have changed. I've got a problem with your kid."

"What's the problem?"

"I found some black short and curlies in Echo's bed this morning."

"You found what?"

"Black short and curlies. Italian pubic hair. They sure as hell aren't Echo's. Your son's getting naked with my daughter when I'm not here, and that's not OK."

My heart raced. "You don't know that," I said.

"I do know that. I asked my daughter to explain. She told me she had no idea where the hairs came from, but I can tell she's lying. Your son is having sex with my daughter. What does he think he's doing? Echo's 17 years old, for God's sakes."

I sat up in bed and bit down hard. Lena mouthed the words, "What's wrong?"

I shook my head at her and said to Dylan, "I have no idea if they're having sex. Let me talk to him about it."

"Tell your son to keep his pants on, and tell him to find a new girlfriend. If I see him around my house, I'll cut off his dick and stuff it down his throat."

The line went dead.

"Who's having sex?" Lena said.

"Bobby thinks Johnny and Echo are having sex in his house. He found black pubic hair in her bed." Lena's face soured. "Do you think they're having sex?" I squinted at her, looking for the truth in her eyes.

Lena looked ashen. "I asked Echo the sex question a couple of weeks ago, and she reassured me she was still a virgin. I believe her. She really likes Johnny, but she's a good girl. She'll keep her legs crossed."

"That was two weeks ago. Maybe she changed her mind. Bobby's proclaimed them guilty already. He said Johnny's not welcome at his house anymore. He said Johnny should find a new girlfriend."

"Echo and Johnny are inseparable. Bobby's such a freak, I'm telling you. He isn't an adult. He has the emotional reserves of a 15-year-old. He'll find out about us some day, and when he does, his silly friendship with you will be over, too." She climbed out of bed, reached for her robe, and said, "Your future lies with me, honey, not with Bobby Dylan."

"I know that."

"Do you?" She cocked her head to the side, a kindergarten teacher scolding a misguided child.

"I do."

"Echo and I are going shopping in Duluth today. Join us."

I shook my head. "I need to confront Johnny on this sex issue. It's best if I do it alone."

Another round of disappointment colored Lena's face. She left the bedroom and closed the bathroom door between us. The sound of the shower signaled that our conversation was over.

I leaned back on her pillows. Why couldn't she just be happy with what we had? I studied the colors and lines of her palm-trees-in-the-sunset painting. An oversimplified world of primary colors. Green fronds, red sky, blue water. Crisp borders without a shade of gray. Lena's dream, a two-dimensional fantasy in a three-dimensional world.

Johnny and I drove west on Minnesota Route 200, a two-lane highway that weaved in alternating left and right curves, forests guarding every bend. I chose a road trip for our confrontation about Echo and the pubic hair. Alone in the car, alone in the wilderness, there'd be no escape.

Outside the car windows, lakes outnumbered towns. Johnny had his earbuds jammed in his ears, and he pecked at his cell phone with both thumbs and ignored the passing scenery. We hadn't taken a trip together since we arrived in Minnesota, and the silence disconnected us.

"What are you doing?" I said.

"Texting Echo. She's trapped in a car with her mom on the way to Duluth, just like I'm trapped in the car with you on the way to wherever you're taking me. She's bored, and I'm bored. Watch out for deer, OK?"

I didn't appreciate the allusion to my past fuck-up. Since the minute Johnny buckled his seatbelt, he'd been distant, distracted, and non-verbal. The trip was no Norman Rockwell family outing. I'd kept our destination secret, and I slowed the car now as we approached it. I turned off the highway past a sign that read *Itasca State Park*, stopped the BMW at the far end of the parking lot, and killed the engine. Johnny looked up and said, "Now what, Dad? We drive a zillion miles past fifty thousand different lakes so we could wind up here, at some state park with another lake?"

"I want you to see this." I stepped out of the car and said, "Follow me." We hiked together until a well-worn path ended at a stream. A series of boulders poked up from the water and enabled us to ford across a tiny river that was about 20 yards wide. At the water's edge, a wooden sign read:

HERE 1475 FEET ABOVE THE OCEAN THE MIGHTY MISSISSIPPI BEGINS TO FLOW ON ITS WINDING WAY 2552 MILES TO THE GULF OF MEXICO

Johnny looked at the narrow stream, and reread the sign. At last, he said, "That's pretty cool." He stepped out onto the first boulder, spread his arms out wide, and hopped from stone to stone until he had crossed to the other side. He landed on the coarse gravel of the opposite shore, did a quick 360, and hopped back to my side.

"How many of your California friends have ever done that? Crossed America's greatest river in 25 steps or less?"

Johnny brushed it off. "None, but I suppose my Minnesota friends have. I'll ask Echo if she's been here." He frowned up at the sun. Perhaps satisfied he had time to linger, he plucked a long stem from a thicket of grass and fit it between his lips. He sat down on one of the boulders that poked out of the river.

I pulled a single sheet of paper from my pocket, and said, "I've got something I want to talk about with you. I think the setting is appropriate, because the grandest river in America starts here from this small stream. And the grand remainder of your life starts here, with the contents of this envelope."

"Are you kidding, Dad? You sound like a game show host. Just spit it out."

I unfolded the piece of paper and said, "This is your Hibbing High School transcript for the spring semester. Let me read you your grades:

Advanced Placement Calculus, A.
Advanced Placement English, A.
Advanced Placement Physics, A.
Advanced Placement U.S. History, A.
Advanced Placement Spanish III, A.

Health Sciences, A."

I looked up to witness Johnny's reaction. He raised one fist in triumph and said, "I knew my grades were looking good, I didn't know they would be that good."

"Couldn't be better," I said.

"Whew, that's a load off my mind. With college applications in the fall, that's the kind of transcript I needed." He stretched out both arms heavenward at the pristine North Country sky. "It was worth it, Dad. In every way, this move up here was prime. I might even have a chance at the Ivy League."

"With grades like these, you'll have a lot of options available to you."

"I'm so happy right now. I can't wait to tell Echo." He slapped at a mosquito on his left arm, and wiped a line of blood down the front of his gym shorts. "Thanks, Dad. This move to Hibbing was all your idea, and it was an awesome one."

"You're welcome." Now that the grade point news had cheered us up, it was time to confront the sex issue.

Before I could begin my interrogation, Johnny initiated his own. "Can I ask you a question, Dad?"

"Go ahead."

"That Angel chick. You know, Dom's daughter?"

"Yes?"

"The guy in picture with her. That was you, wasn't it?"

I picked up a twig and flipped it into the headwaters of the Mississippi. I didn't answer until the water carried it away out of sight. I wished Johnny's question would drift out of sight with it.

"Yes."

"It looked like a wedding picture."

"It was." I looked Johnny in the eye and said, "She was my wife. I married her when I was a kid."

"You said she died?"

"She did. When we were seniors in high school, I got Angel pregnant. She wouldn't have an abortion, and she decided to have the baby. The whole thing was such a botch-up. I wanted to go to college, get an education, have some good times. I had no business being a dad at that age."

"Where… where is the kid now?"

"There is no kid." I started talking faster, my speech pressured, the darkness of this buried story at last seeing the light of day. "Angel was a terrific girl, a dream girl. Smart, beautiful, kind. She was the number one student in my high school class."

"I thought you were number one."

"Nope. I was number two. Remember I told you there were two kids in my class who got accepted into Harvard?"

"Yes."

"Those two students were Angel and me. After she got pregnant, we told Harvard the truth—that we couldn't go, that we needed to stay closer to home and deal with it. We stayed in Hibbing to have the baby. When she was four months pregnant, Angel developed a rare bone cancer called osteosarcoma in her left femur—the thighbone. The doctors amputated the leg and hit her with maximum chemotherapy, but it didn't work. The malignancy spread to her liver, and was incurable. She died."

"How old was she?"

"Nineteen."

"Jeez. And the baby?"

"The baby didn't survive the cancer and the chemotherapy."

"Why didn't you tell me about this stuff before?"

I shrugged. "You didn't need to know."

"So you blew off Harvard to be a dad, and then it all fell apart."

"Yep. I enrolled at the University of Minnesota at Duluth the following year. The Harvard door closed."

"I'm sorry, Dad. That's a terrible story."

My eyes were dry. I'd cried my final tears over Angel years before.

"Next question," Johnny said. "What's going on with you and mom?"

"Your mother and I are heading toward a divorce."

Johnny chomped on the stem of grass, and looked north into the cumulus clouds that hovered over the Canadian border. "I figured as much. I shouldn't be surprised. I never saw you two hang out together for more than ten minutes at a time. Two separate bedrooms. And the fighting was ridiculous. You two argued like 5-year-olds. You two were a living advertisement for never getting married."

"We tried…."

"You tried to have the shittiest marriage in the world?"

"No, we tried. I tried."

"Spare me, Dad. And Echo's mom?"

"What do you mean?"

"I know you're doing Echo's mom."

"Doing?"

"Screwing her. Having sex. Whatever you old people want to call it."

Old people? I searched for the right words, somewhere up there in the treetops, among the sparrows and swallows. "Lena and I are friends," I said at last.

"Echo says her mom talks about you all the time. She says her mom is happier than she's ever been. Echo says her mom is in love with you."

"That's nice to hear. Time will tell what happens between Lena and me." I'd waited long enough. I blurted out, "Are you and Echo having sex?"

Johnny glared back. He threw another stick into the water and followed its progress downstream as if the future of the human race depended on it.

"Are you?" I repeated.

Still no answer. Johnny's tacit reply could only mean one thing. He and Echo were doing the deed. "Echo's dad called me this morning. He knows. He found your pubic hair in Echo's bed."

"So what?"

"He doesn't want you in his 17-year-old daughter's bed, that's what."

"That piece of shit. Why doesn't he just leave us alone? Everybody has sex in high school. It's no big deal."

"It is a big deal. I just told you what happened to Angel and me."

"Well, I'm not you. As much as you keep trying to make me into Nico Junior, I'm not you."

"Are you using protection?"

"Let it go, Dad. Leave me alone." Johnny sent a huge lugie on a river cruise to Memphis, and said, "This is so bogus. I'm trapped out here in the woods, facing the paternal inquisition. What are you going to do next, ram toothpicks under my fingernails until I talk? I want to go home."

"We're not done. I can't follow you around and make sure you're not having sex with Echo, but if you do have sex, you need to use birth control. Got it?"

"Yes, Herr General. I vill obey. Can we go now?"

"I want to talk about this summer. Your mother expects you to spend half your summer in California."

"No way, Dad. I'm staying here. I'm not leaving Echo."

"I repeat, your mother expects you to spend half your summer in California."

"And I repeat, no way."

"You're not going back to see your mother at all before school starts?"

"Nope. What kind of mother is she, anyway? Where is she in my life, day to day? If Minnesota has taught me one thing, Dad, it's that life is simpler without her around. Mom can come up north if she wants to see me so bad. I like it here. No one's calling me a lazy shit, and the 'Boy with the B's' is gone. I want to sleep in, hang out with my girl, and work at the hospital to make some money. I want to get my own car."

"Are you going to tell your mother that?"

"I told her on the phone last night. It's my life. I don't want to go back. If she wants to see me, Mom needs to come to Minnesota. I told her that. She just ranted about her job and how hard it is for her to get away."

Johnny hurled a handful of sand into the Baby Mississippi and said, "You and Mom need to clue in. I know more than you. I know who Johnny Antone is. You don't." He hopped across the remaining six rocks to my side of the river, and started alone down the path back to the car.

What could I say? Johnny paid off his parents in the currency we demanded: he turned himself into the straight-A student we'd dreamed of. Now he was determined to collect his just rewards, and follow his own dreams.

CHAPTER 14
BLOOD ON THE TRACKS

At dawn on a September morning I was scheduled to anesthetize a 28-year-old female for termination of her 8-week-old pregnancy. Termination of pregnancy is medical jargon for an abortion. I didn't love giving anesthesia for abortions, but I had no moral objection to assisting a woman's right to make that choice. The patient's name was Kendra White. When I met her in pre-op, Kendra was cheery and rosy-cheeked. If she felt any guilt over the abortion, she was hiding it well. Perhaps she was relieved to be dodging the responsibilities of motherhood. I didn't know, and it wasn't my job to ask.

I introduced myself, asked her the standard pre-anesthesia questions, and she signed her consent to proceed. I left the bedside to prepare my operating room for the anesthetic, and ran into Bobby Dylan. He had a dark expression, and pulled me aside into an empty conference room.

"Doin' some baby-killing today, Doctor?" he said.

"What?"

"It's bad business to get into around here. Doing abortions. Up here we've got a lot of good Christian people who believe that life begins in the womb."

I exhaled with bluster at this unexpected skirmish. I wasn't in the mood for a pro-life lecture from Dylan. "I'm not killing any babies here, Bobby. I'm just giving an anesthetic."

"You're aiding and abetting a murder."

"It's a first trimester pregnancy. There are thousands of these terminated in America every day. It's a legal procedure."

"But it's wrong,"

"You think it's wrong. I don't."

Dylan shook his head. "I thought you were a good guy, Doctor, but this is wrong. You know better. You're as bad as your kid, bringing your California amorality to town." His face twisted into a sneer. His upper lip was vibrating.

He was a rocket ready to blow. I'd seen enough. "I'm sorry you feel that way," I said. "I've got to get going." I shouldered my way past Dylan, and proceeded to my operating room.

Thirty minutes later the procedure was over. The gynecologist inserted a plastic hose through the cervix and suctioned the contents of Kendra White's uterus into a plastic bottle. There was no discernable baby in the bottle—no macroscopic sign of life—just a reddish collection of blood and tissue. I managed the woman's anesthetic drugs and her medical condition, and never looked at that plastic bottle for a second.

After Kendra White was awake and safe, tucked into her recovery room bed, I sidled up to Dr. James Saunders, the gynecologist who'd performed the procedure, and asked, "How much pushback do you get for doing abortions around here? Do you have a hard time finding nurses or anesthesia personnel to do the cases?"

"A few of the staff are opposed on a religious basis. I respect that. But there are enough staff who are OK with it, so I just work with those who are. Why?"

"Bobby Dylan gave me a hard time about killing babies."

"Oh, give me a break. He's a wackjob."

"He's been a decent friend to me."

Dr. Saunders rolled his eyes. "Take my word for it. He's a wacko. I never trusted the guy. I mean, Bobby Dylan? Maybe I'll change my name to Mick Jagger." He laughed at his own joke, and walked away.

The implosion of my relationship with Dylan concluded two days following Kendra White's abortion. There were no surgeries scheduled at the hospital, and he invited me to meet him for a hunting trip north of town. The sun was peeking inches above the pine forest east of Long Lake as I parked my car next to Bobby's truck. The leaves were on fire with autumn colors. We were 10 miles south of Bigfork, at the trailhead of an old logging road. I unzipped the long leather case that held Dom's 12-gauge shotgun, and unsheathed it. Like most Minnesota boys, I'd learned to shoot a firearm when I was in the 6th grade, and had shot my share of birds during my teens.

This morning the 12-gauge was loaded and ready. It was the first day of partridge hunting season, and I was looking forward to flushing a few fowl out of the brush. I buttoned the front of my jacket and stepped out into the freshness of the morning air. A blustery post-dawn breeze stung my fingers where they circled the metal of the trigger guard. It was 8 a.m., time for the ruffled grouse of Northern Minnesota to forage for breakfast. If my aim was true, a partridge or two would enjoy their last meal this very day.

Bobby Dylan jumped down from the cab of his pickup truck. He carried a beautiful firearm of polished walnut and glinting steel. He offered no words of greeting, and busied himself by loading shells into his double-barreled shotgun.

We still performed together at Heaven's Door twice a week, but our relationship had cooled since the pubic hair incident and Kendra White's abortion. We played our gigs, didn't talk much, and when we did, the conversation was strained.

It was my nature to try to make amends. When Dylan suggested the hunting trip, I saw it as an opportunity to mend our friendship. I wasn't mad at him. We worked together and we rocked together. I wanted us to get along. It was Bobby who had a bug up his ass about me. I was hopeful we could kill some partridge together, have a laugh or two, and forget about teenage sex and the morality of terminating a pregnancy.

Dylan shouldered his gun, and exhaled a thick cloud of Marlboro smoke. He took a second deep drag on the cancer stick and growled, "Let's go find us some birds."

No other words followed. No cordial "Good morning," or "How are you doing today?" He took off into the forest at flank speed, and I hustled to keep up with him. We marched single file up the trail under the orange and yellow canopy of the Chippewa National Forest. This old logging trail was two parallel troughs of dirt with a row of tall grass between them. A rugged automobile could forge up this trail, but the route was best suited for hikers.

"Beautiful morning, eh?" I offered.

Dylan still didn't answer, and I began to worry. Maybe he was tired, or maybe he needed caffeine. Or maybe Dylan was angry at me. Maybe he was as crazy as Lena described. I turned around and looked back down the trail, and began to devise exit plans.

Dylan never looked back at me. He tucked his shotgun under one arm while he lit another cigarette, quickened his stride, and offered no more words than an owl in a birch tree. The sky darkened, and rain began to fall. I turned up my collar, and struggled to keep pace with Dylan. He climbed farther up the hill until he finished the last puff of his second cigarette. We'd hiked half a mile from where we'd parked the cars. There was nothing around us except trees, an occasional chipmunk, and a canopy of gray sky. Dylan and I had never been more isolated from society, or from each other. This isolation was by design. He stopped with a huff, mashed the butt of his cigarette into the heel of his boot, and turned to face me. His face was wet with rain, and his eyes were wild. Dylan held his shotgun at his hip, and aimed it at the middle of my chest.

"I'm done with you, Doctor. I drove past Lena's house yesterday morning on the way in to work, and I saw a familiar automobile parked in the alley behind her place. Turns out that automobile was a certain black BMW that you don't see much up in this part of the country."

I held my breath and froze. I knew what was coming, and it wasn't going to be pretty.

"I was mighty curious and a bit agitated when I saw that there black car," Dylan said. "So I parked a block away and waited. Pretty soon, Lena's back door opens, and this dude pops out. A skinny guy, wavy hair, likes to wear sunglasses and pointy black shoes. Seems this dude looks a lot like one Nico Antone." He spat on the ground between us and said, "It seems to me a rebellious abuse of friendship, to be fucking your buddy's wife, does it not?"

He positioned himself between me and the path back to the car. I looked to the left and the right, and saw nothing but an infinite expanse of forest. I was alone in the woods with a jealous man holding a loaded shotgun.

"Did you think I was a dummy, that I'd never find out?" Dylan had a crazed look in his eye. His emphasis on the word *dummy* was loud and extreme. The word caromed off the tree trunks and resonated off the ceiling of leaves. I shook my head—not really a denial, but an action of disbelieving remorse. My heart thumped double-time while I searched my brain for a solution.

Bobby Dylan's black eyes burned into me with a glare I hadn't seen since our first meeting. "I wanted to corner you out here with no one around and no place for you to run to. You're a sorry-ass excuse for a friend, and you know it, you chickenshit sleaze ball. I'll never trust you again."

I chose my next words with great heed, walking on unseen eggshells. "I'm sorry you feel that way. I didn't tell you because I knew you wouldn't like it. But hey, man, you and Lena split up years ago. And you sleep with lots of other women."

"Don't give me any of your bullshit rationalization, Doctor Holier-Than-Thou. You're porking Lena behind my back. End of story. Hunting accidents, they occur. You know that, and I know that. Everyone knows that. Rainy morning. Man trips on a root. Gun goes off. Another man inherits a chest full of buckshot. No way to save you, so far from civil-eye-za-shun. No jury would convict me. You dig? I brought you out here to kill you. I killed men in Afghanistan, and I can do it again. I planned it this way, to fill your bony chest full of holes."

I was trapped. There was no way out of the woods except though the man. I curled my finger against the trigger of my shotgun, and wondered if I could shoot a man in cold blood.

Then it ended. Dylan fell back, withdrew his gun, and leaned it against his shoulder, the barrel pointed high into the darkening sky. He slumped down on a fallen trunk of a birch tree. His face lost its color, and his eyelids sagged. "Now I can't do it," he said. "I can't gun you down pointblank over this... this recreational fucking." He pointed down the trail, and said, "Just get out of here. Get out of my life, out of my hospital, and out of my town. Take your jailbait-loving son, get into that fucking German piece of shit car and ride off into the sunset. I don't ever want to see your repulsive mug again. The next time I might not feel so conflicted. The next time you might wind up with some buckshot up your asshole."

I wasn't going to argue. I backed down the path one step at a time, and kept the barrel of my shotgun aimed at the earth between Dylan and myself all the while. I rounded a curve in the trail. As soon as the stickman's outline disappeared behind the autumn foliage, I turned and ran full bore without looking back, a wiser man thankful for the breath in my lungs.

My census of friends had dropped by one.

CHAPTER 15
I'LL BE YOUR BABY

I drove back to town with one eye on the rear view mirror. With luck, Bobby Dylan, Afghanistan-War Posttraumatic Stress Syndrome veteran and Antone-hater extraordinaire, would not show up at my front door with second thoughts about revenge. The whole episode rattled me. What kind of psycho takes you hunting 30 miles from home, walks you into the wilderness where you have no car, no cell phone signal, and no defense, points a gun at you and says, "It seems to me a rebellious abuse of friendship, to be fucking your buddy's wife?"

A crazy psycho, that's who. The red flags had always been flapping around Bobby Dylan: the year in a psychiatric institution, the hijacking of Bob Dylan's name and life, the brash drug use, the searing "opt-out" confrontation in the operating room, and the intense friendship offered up in haste. Now, with equal intensity and speed, that friendship had turned into hatred.

I needed an ally. I drove straight to Lena's house. She needed to know what had just happened. She needed to know about this threat to our relationship. I ran up Lena's front steps and found her in the living room, face down on the marshmallow couch, crying into a towel.

What was going on? Did she know already? Lena looked up, her cheeks wet and her eyes wild, and said, "Echo is pregnant! She cannot have a baby now. She's still in high school, for God's sakes."

"What?"

"Johnny got her pregnant, what else? Echo is flipping out. I'm flipping out. She's locked in the bathroom upstairs." Lena grabbed a pack of Marlboros from the coffee table and lit a cigarette. I frowned. I'd never seen her smoke before.

I tried to sit next to her. Lena clamored to the opposite corner of the couch to maximize the space between us, and said, "Echo was nauseated. Her period was late. I asked her if she could be pregnant, and she wouldn't look me in the eye. I drove down to Walmart, bought a pregnancy test, and threw it in her lap. Echo took it into the bathroom. I heard the toilet flush, I heard the sobbing, and I heard her talking to Johnny on her cell phone. She locked the door and hasn't come out yet."

My thoughts spun like a roulette wheel, and the ball kept landing on OO. The tidy roadmap of Johnny's life was torn into shreds of parchment on a dirt floor, and no one knew that better than me. My teenage world imploded with Angel's pregnancy, and nothing good came of it.

Lena cowered on the couch, her hands shaking and the cigarette smoldering. What a mess. There was only one easy way out. I asked the obvious question. "Will Echo have an abortion?"

"Never. This family doesn't believe in abortions. Her dad will never agree to that."

"It's not his choice. It's Echo's decision."

She blasted thick blue smoke out through her nose, twin jets of rage. Where had she learned to do that, all of a sudden? "This family doesn't kill fetuses. No abortions. Echo will have this baby."

I was incredulous. "She's seventeen years old. Echo and Johnny are too young to raise a baby. She needs to get rid of the pregnancy."

"Get rid of it? Just like taking out the garbage? That's not going to happen. She'll have the baby. Bobby would kill her if she got an abortion."

"Bobby almost killed me today. He cornered me out in the woods, with his finger on the trigger of a 12-gauge shotgun. Bobby knows we've been sleeping together. He told me to get out of town."

"Oh, fuck that. Bobby would screw the crack of dawn if he could get up that early. He can go fuck himself. I don't care. He needs to crawl into a hole and stay there."

I had never heard her swear before, not even once. I was seeing an ugly Lena Johnson I'd never known. She stubbed out the cigarette in an empty wine glass, and repeated, "Fuck him."

I needed to get out of there. I had nothing to offer either of the Johnson females. I needed to go to Johnny. My kid needed his dad right now. "I have to leave," I said. "I have to go home and see my son."

"Go ahead," she said. "Get the hell out of here."

Her words were a splash of ice water across my face. There were no I love you's today. She didn't have to tell me twice. I left.

I raced home and found Johnny sitting at the kitchen table, his head in his hands. I could feel my heart breaking as I sat down across from him. Johnny's eyes were red-rimmed and wet. His jaw scraped the tabletop. "I'm so sorry, Dad," he said. "I messed up. I should have…"

I held back on the I-told-you-so lecture I had pre-loaded. Instead, I played the compassion card. "Don't beat yourself up, son. We'll get through this."

"No, we won't. What am I supposed to do now? Everything's screwed up. Echo won't see me. She won't answer my texts. She won't answer my calls. I love her, Dad. For the first time in my life, I love a girl. Then I screw it all up and get her pregnant. Now she's on another planet."

Johnny made no mention of the baby. All he could talk about was Echo. Losing Echo.

"It's too fresh," I said, searching for an angle to soften the pain. "Echo just found out about all this. Give her a few days to calm down."

"It's not that simple. Even when she does calm down, her old man won't calm down. He hates my guts already. What am I going to do?" Johnny reared back his head and howled at the ceiling.

I let him howl, and stared at the lines in the hardwood of the kitchen floor. What a terrible day. First I stared down a double-barreled shotgun, and now this.

Johnny stopped crying and wiped the tears away with the sleeve of his sweater. "Dad, I know what needs to happen now."

"What?"

"I need to marry Echo."

"That's ridiculous." The picture flashed across my mind: Johnny in a rented Hibbing tuxedo. Echo wearing white, her midriff bulging with child. My own lost youth reprised—the fireplace photo of Angel and me morphed into a photo of Johnny and pregnant Echo. I moved back to Minnesota to make Johnny's life better, and instead I'd turned him into Nicolai the Second. "No one's marrying anyone right now. You're too young. Give this some time, and we'll sort the whole thing all out."

Johnny picked up a plastic Minnesota Vikings cup from the table and hurled it against the kitchen wall with all the fury he could muster. The cup rattled to the floor. Vertical lines of Coca-Cola streaked the yellow paint and dripped into a brown puddle on the floor. He stomped off toward his bedroom.

"Stop behaving like a two-year-old," I said.

Johnny stopped halfway up the stairs and said, "I'm sorry, Dad. I'm just so sad right now. So sad." Then he marched back down the stairs and returned to the kitchen. He found a towel, dropped to his knees, and mopped the spilled soda off the floor. Johnny said nothing further and made no eye contact. When he was finished, he slinked back to the solitude of his room. I heard the bedsprings creak, and prayed the kid would fall asleep in minutes and find peace for the night.

Instead, Johnny called out from the second floor, "One more crappy thing, Dad. I called Mom, and she went ballistic. She told me it was all your fault for bringing me up here to live."

I wasn't surprised. When you threw gasoline onto a fire, the blaze worsened. "I'll talk to your mother about it. Get some sleep."

"Mom's arriving in Hibbing tomorrow. She said she's going to fix everything, because you're too lame to do it yourself."

The words hit me like an uppercut to the jaw. The situation went from awful to worse. Alexandra Antone would be venting her poison in the North Country.

CHAPTER 16
IDIOT WIND

I knocked back two bottles of Budweiser and three shots of vodka and fell asleep with the shot glass cradled in the fingers of my right hand. The sound of someone pounding hard on the front door woke me. I looked at the clock—it was 6:05 a.m. The banging on the door persisted. I walked to the window and pulled back the curtain. A lone figure stood on the stoop, a hood concealing the face.

It had to be Dylan in full vigilante mode. There was no way I was going to let him in. "Who is it?" I called out.

"It's Alexandra, you asshole. I'm freezing out here. Open up."

I turned the front lock, and Alexandra Antone blew into Dom's house like an unwelcome storm. Her boots tracked dirty snow over the carpet. She slammed the door behind her, peeled back her hood, and said, "Where's Johnny?"

"He's upstairs sleeping."

"I'm so wired and so annoyed right now. I flew into Minneapolis at midnight, rented a car and drove all night to this God-forsaken hellhole. I'm not going to let one more molecule of chaos infect our son's crumbling existence. I haven't slept in 24 hours, and I'm so angry at you I could scream. I can't believe how you've messed up this family."

"Wait a minute, I didn't..."

"Don't get defensive on me. You're the one who chose to move to Bumfuck, Minnesota. You're the one who let your son hang out with some loose trailer-trash Iron Range girl who wasn't smart enough to swallow a birth control pill once a day. And you're not capable of navigating our family out of this mess, either."

She threw her jacket on the couch and walked into the kitchen. "Do you have any wine? I need something to calm myself down before I engage these small-town cretins who want my 17-year-old to become the youngest father in America."

"There's no wine in this house. Besides, it's six in the morning. It's a little early for alcohol."

Alexandra extracted a Budweiser from the refrigerator, popped the top off, and chugged it down like it was the nectar of the gods. "This is all your fault, Nico," she said. "Couldn't you have looked out for him up here? I've never been as mad at you as I am right now."

"I'm mad at you, too. You were in bed with some stooge the last time I saw you."

She said, "I'm an adult. I can go to bed with whoever I want. I found someone who hit all the places you never were man enough to reach."

I felt like shoving the beer bottle up her ass sideways. "Don't talk to me like that," I said. "Get out of this house."

She tossed her hair back and laughed in my face. "I'm not going anywhere. I'm here to see Johnny. You're pathetic. You're the one who left me. You moved two thousand miles away and took our only child away from me. Johnny needs me right now. It's too late for your 'I'm the doctor and I know everything' bullshit. He needs me."

"I don't need you hollering at Dad," came a voice from the stairwell. Johnny stood there, looking down on us, his shirt rumpled, his eyes puffy, and his shoulders frozen in their slouch from last night. He glared at his mother, and she glared back. Nobody moved. This mother and child reunion invoked no hugs. This mother and child reunion was devoid of affection. I'd seen Alexandra suck the joy out of a room hundreds of times during my life, but this was even worse. There was no joy to suck out of Johnny.

"You look like hell, Johnny," she said.

"Thanks, Mom. Did you think that would make me feel better?"

"I'm not here to make you feel better. I'm here to stop this girl. She needs an abortion."

Johnny glowered. "She won't have an abortion. Her parents are both pro-lifers who'll never agree to an abortion."

"What is this? The fucking 1950's?" Alexandra ranted. "Teenagers who get pregnant can decide to have an abortion without their parents' consent. This isn't Kabul. What will it take? How much money will it take?"

"You're disgusting, Mom. You can't buy everyone. You can't control everything."

"Don't talk to me like that. I traveled all night to be here, and I demand you show me some respect."

"Whatever."

"Whatever doesn't sound like respect." She chugged the rest of the Bud, wiped her lips, and said, "Let's keep this simple, Johnny. Two things need to happen here: I want this girl to give up the baby, and I want you to move back to California."

Johnny mumbled an F-bomb under his breath. "The second one's easy, Mom. I'm not moving back. And the first one? Echo's not giving up this baby, and I love her. I'm going to be a teenage Hibbing groom like Dad was."

"Like your Dad? Your Dad sabotaged his youth by knocking up his high school girlfriend. He'd still be circling the drain if he hadn't met me."

"That's a lie, Alexandra," I said. "I'd already finished medical school when I met you. I had my life together just fine."

"You were a penniless research doc driving a ten-year-old car. I put you on the map."

"Right. I wouldn't know how to wipe my own ass if it wasn't for you."

"You're an asshole, so it wouldn't be that hard."

"Shut the fuck up, both of you!" Johnny screamed. "You two are just the same as you were in California. I can't stand it. Dad, I've been awake since 3 a.m. I've got to see Echo. I can't wait any longer."

"You're going to have to. It's way too early."

"Mom, you want to talk to Echo's mother, right?"

"I do."

"Then put down the alcohol, sober up, and let's go over to her house."

Alexandra smacked her empty beer bottle onto the coffee table. "You're a man of action, Johnny. You got that part of your personality from me. Let's go." She pulled on her jacket and flipped up the hood.

"It's six a.m., Alexandra," I said. "They won't even be awake yet."

"They'll be awake. Nobody sleeps when shit like this is going down. Let's go, Johnny."

"Dad, are you coming?"

"None of us should go over there now," I said. "Alexandra, you need to respect these people when you meet them."

"I will be the epitome of class and dignity. I'm a consummate deal-maker, and I win more friends with honey than with vinegar. Let's go, Johnny."

"Come with us, Dad," Johnny said. "You need to be there. Please?"

"I'll come," I said. For months I'd told Lena what a bitch Alexandra was. Lena was about to get a first-person demonstration. Alexandra was set to barge into Lena's house holding a bent coat hanger, intent on scraping out Echo's pregnancy with her own hands.

Our families would be at war, and the first shot was only minutes away.

All the lights were on when we arrived at the Johnson house. Lena answered the door, and Alexandra said, "Hello. I'm Johnny's mother. I just flew in from California. We need to talk."

Lena's hair looked like straw spewing from a scarecrow. Her face was a tortured mask. She shot me an inflamed look. Alexandra was the last person she wanted to see.

"I apologize for arriving unannounced, Lena," I said. "Echo wasn't returning Johnny's calls, and he really wants to see her."

Johnny cast a longing look up the staircase. "Is there any chance I can I talk to Echo? Alone?"

"It's not a good time," Lena said. "She's still in bed. She had a bad night."

"This is a difficult time for all of us," Alexandra said, peeling off her jacket and gloves. She was prepared to stay a while. She was on her best behavior so far, her voice lilting and syrupy. Alexandra was playing the scene like we were all allies. "I think it's important for us all to sit down and talk. I feel so bad that our two children have fallen into this pregnancy." She made it sound as if Echo and Johnny had tripped in the woods and plummeted into a booby trap.

"I'd offer you some coffee, but ...," Lena said.

"I'll pass," Alexandra said. "When do you think your daughter will wake up? I'd really like to meet her."

"This is not a good time. She needs to rest."

"I understand, but I did travel all the way from California to help Johnny. I can't very well understand the situation if I can't meet his girlfriend."

"Echo is pretty shook up right now." Lena said. "Having a conference with you at this time of the morning won't be high on her list."

The key to dealing with Alexandra was to avoid making her angry. Lena never read that owner's manual, and she was flunking Alexandra 101. Her refusal to let Alexandra control the situation was tantamount to a slap in the face.

Alexandra went from congenial to domineering in a heartbeat. She put her hands on her hips and said, "Listen, Lena Johnson. This is how it's going to be. It's no use stalling. My son is too young to be a father, and your daughter is too young to be a mother. I need your assurance that this baby is never going to be.'"

"Never going to be?" Lena said.

"It's time for an abortion. That's what families do when this sort of unfortunate thing happens."

"Abortion is not an option," Lena said.

Alexandra clucked her tongue and said, "How much is it going to take?"

"How much what?"

"Why money, of course. Will $10,000 make this pregnancy go away?"

"I can't believe you just said that."

"I'm prepared to pay $25,000. Now. Today. How can you refuse? That kind of money could change your life."

"No. That's not going to happen."

"$100,000 then. That's my final offer." Alexandra's tone was fierce, and the worst part of it was that she seemed to enjoy it.

"Stop it, Alexandra," I said. "This isn't going to work. You need to stop it."

"Leave me alone," Alexandra said. "Stay out of this negotiation."

"It's not a real estate deal, Mom," Johnny said. "Dad's right. Knock it off."

"I'm not leaving here without an agreement," Alexandra said.

Lena's mouth gaped. She was ready to erupt. She walked over to the front door, held it open, and said, "You need to leave. Take your money and stick it you know where."

Alexandra grew more enraged. "This is ridiculous. My son is not going to be a father at age 17. Your daughter needs to see a shrink if she thinks having a child at age 17 is the answer to this problem. I'll pay for it."

"Your money isn't going to make any of this go away," Lena said.

"Alexandra, you need to leave," I said.

"Stay out of this, Nico, you loser," Alexandra screeched.

"Stop screaming, all of you," came a voice from the second floor. There were footsteps on the staircase, and Echo appeared, dressed in a floor-length nightgown and pink slippers. Her arms were crossed over her chest, and her lips were pressed into thin pale lines. "I heard the whole conversation," she said. "Johnny, please get your mother out of our fucking house.'"

The quarantine on Johnson F-bombs had been lifted. Both Lena and Echo could swear like the crustiest of millwrights. The room was charged and ready to explode.

"Echo, can we talk?" Johnny said.

"Not until your mother leaves."

"Echo, let's start over," Alexandra said. "I've heard so much about you." It was a bogus flip-flop. Now that Echo was on scene, Alexandra was trying to turn it around—searching for warm and fuzzy instead of irascible.

"I heard everything you guys said," Echo repeated. "Get out of here. You and your money, get out."

"Can I say something?" Johnny said.

"No," Echo said. "Just leave. All of you."

Alexandra did not budge. The three women had reached an impasse. Alexandra's expression descended into a murderous glare. She wasn't in charge, and Alexandra hated not being in charge. "Echo, I thought you loved Johnny," she said. "Now you want to throw us out?"

"I will talk to you, Johnny," Echo said, compromising. "But your mother needs to leave first."

"Don't play it her way, Johnny," Alexandra said.

"No, Mom. I will play it her way. You need to go. Find a hotel and sober up. Leave us alone."

"How dare you say that to your mother?"

"Because I'm not your little boy anymore. I'm not afraid of you."

Alexandra frowned. The grim reality of this North Country morning was hitting her. Power had shifted. Her anger was not the foolproof weapon it was in California. "Ridiculous. I can't believe any of this." She stomped out, and the four of us stood alone in our predicament.

"I'm so sorry," I said to Lena. "That was awful."

"She's the nastiest woman I've ever met," Lena said.

"I can see why you guys left California," Echo said.

Johnny walked across the room and up the stairs toward Echo. She didn't retreat, and accepted his embrace. He whispered something into her ear. Echo nodded yes, and said, "Mom, can we be excused?"

"You may," Lena said. We watched Echo take Johnny's hand, and the two teenagers climbed the stairs out of sight. I was glad to see their bond unfractured. Lena lit up a cigarette. Her hands shook as she inhaled. "I've never seen a woman act like your wife," she said. "Who does the woman think she is?"

"I wish you wouldn't call her my wife."

"She is your wife. How in the world can I be involved with you, when you're married to a witch like that? She'll ruin my life, one way or another. I don't want that woman around my daughter ever again. Echo's a teenager, she's pregnant, and her life is a mess. She doesn't need to be harassed by your wife."

"Stop calling her my wife."

"Divorce the bitch then!"

I was blown away. Echo's pregnancy had turned Lena into a wreck. She blew a chain of smoke rings at me. "What's up with the bribes? Offering us huge sums of cash for an abortion? Sums of money like that are unheard of in our world. Bobby would kill her if he heard that. Last night he was screaming so loud I had to hold the phone a foot away from my ear. Bobby hates Johnny and he hates you. I'm so worn down by all this." She took another deep drag on her cigarette.

"Why are you smoking? Trashing your lungs isn't going to help anything."

"And you need to stop being my doctor. I need support right now, not criticism." She stubbed out the cigarette and said, "I can't believe any of this. Life was so good a couple of days ago, Nico. You and I were so good."

"It's all going to work out. Something positive will come of all this."

"I don't see how," she said. "I don't see how."

I returned to Dom's house, and Johnny followed me home later in the evening. He avoided me and retreated to the basement. I waited a few minutes before I went downstairs to talk to him. Johnny was sprawled on the couch, with a black knit cap pulled down over his hair. The unzipped bulk of a tan sleeping bag stretched up to his chin.

I sat next to his ankles and said, "You OK?"

"Oh, I'm just great. My girlfriend is pregnant and my psycho mother is orbiting. How do you think I am?"

I massaged the lumps of his feet. "I should have bought you a dozen condoms for your birthday instead of getting you a fishing rod."

"It's not your fault, Dad. I messed up. I didn't think it would happen to me." A Viagra commercial came on the television. Johnny said, "Viagra. Erections. Sex. Why is everything about sex? Sex screwed up everything for me." He changed channels from ESPN to ESPN2, where a Cialis commercial was airing at the same moment. "More sex commercials. The advertising media dangles fucking in front of every sports fan's face in America." He turned off the TV and said, "I talked to my buddy Andy back in Palo Alto. His brother Rudy got his girlfriend pregnant at college last year. The chick got an abortion. She never told her parents. She just got it taken care of. She and Rudy are still together. Rudy said it was simple, that it was like his girlfriend went to get a haircut or something. The abortion was that easy."

I'd seen dozens of abortions, and I knew they weren't as simple as a haircut. Some abortion patients went off to sleep in a flood of tears. I could make those tears disappear with a syringe of propofol, but with Echo's pregnancy that wasn't going to happen. "How's Echo doing?" I said.

"She's hanging in there. She went to her dad's tonight, but I'll see her in the morning. Echo's got a shift at the hospital. I was going to call in sick, but since she's working, I'll work too."

"Is that smart? Are you guys really up for orderly duty?"

"It was her call. Echo says helping other people will take her mind off her own problems."

"I expect she's right. Get some sleep, son."

Johnny went upstairs into his bedroom, and five minutes later I heard him snoring. I envied him. I wasn't so lucky. I was too wired by the events of the day—I couldn't calm myself. I couldn't sleep and I was lonely. I dialed Lena's number.

"How're you doing?" I said.

"Exhausted. Depressed."

"I miss you. Want some company?"

She sighed. "Sure. I'll leave the door open. I'm going to lie down. Let yourself in."

"I'll be right over."

I snuck into Lena's bed and stretched out alongside her. Her soft breathing soothed me, and I felt more at peace. I set my phone alarm for 6 a.m. so I could return home before Johnny woke up. I wrapped my arm around Lena, and cupped her breast in my palm. She cooed, "Thanks. I love you," and didn't wake up. I fell asleep without another word.

The bleating of my cell phone woke me from slumber. My first thought was that something was wrong with Johnny. I looked at my phone, and was surprised and dismayed by the caller ID. It was Alexandra. At 4:52 a.m. Alexandra was calling me?

I debated not answering. Nothing good could come from talking to Alexandra at this hour of the morning. Lena pulled a pillow over her head and grumbled her discontent. I picked up the call just to silence the ring tone.

"Nico?" Alexandra said, her voice edgy and pressured. "I'm sick. I thought it was some bad food I ate on the plane to Minnesota, or the crap beer I had at your house, but I have pain in my abdomen that won't go away. I'm sitting in the Emergency Room at the Hibbing hospital right now. I'm in the worst pain of my life."

She was hysterical, unable to finish a sentence between sobs. I sat upright in bed, my sleep invaded by her presence. Alexandra was the ultimate taker. I was the biggest piece of shit in the world until she needed medical attention, at which point I became exalted to the lofty role of Alexandra's Medical Helper. I was about to hang up, but her next sentence trapped me. "They say I need to have my appendix out. They're calling in some lumberjack doctor named Perpich to do the surgery."

"You're going to be OK. That lumberjack doctor is Michael Perpich, a colleague of mine who's very capable of taking out your appendix. I'd let him operate on me anytime."

"This can't be happening. With all the doctor friends we have in California, why do I have to get sick up here in the boonies where nobody knows who I am?"

I had no interest in listening to her complain. "Can you put the emergency room doctor on the phone for me? I'd like to talk to him."

"OK. Here he is."

After a short pause, a voice said, "This is Dr. Bellamy."

"Hi, my name is Nicolai Antone. I'm an anesthesiologist on staff."

"Sure, I know who you are."

"Thanks. I'm the husband of Alexandra Antone who you're attending to now. We're separated, and I have no interest in being at her bedside right now, but she called me. What's going on with her?"

"She had the onset of periumbilical pain and vomiting last night. She arrived at the E.R. at 1 a.m. Her fever was 102.1, and her abdominal exam was positive for peritoneal signs. The ultrasound shows an inflamed appendix."

"Does she need emergency surgery or can it wait?"

"She's stable. I have the surgeon coming in to see her. But knowing Perpich, he'll operate when the sun comes up."

"Who's on call for anesthesia?"

There was a pause on the line as Bellamy checked the schedule. He said, "Dylan. Bobby Dylan."

I scoffed to myself. They deserved each other, Alexandra and Bobby. They could argue about abortions at six in the morning.

"Thanks for taking such good care of her," I said. "Can you put her back on the phone?"

"Here she is."

I steeled myself, because one of my least favorite pastimes was telling Alexandra news she didn't want to hear. "It sounds like you will need to have your appendix out. You'll feel a whole lot better after the operation. They'll do it through a laparoscope. It won't be a big incision. You'll hurt less after the surgery than you do right now."

"Can you come in here and take care of me? I don't trust these people."

I looked at the clock. It was now 5:00 a.m. There were limits to my compassion. Alexandra had been kicking me for so long that I felt little obligation to service her. "No. I just talked to Dr. Bellamy, and they're doing all the right things. You'll be all right without me." I almost added, "You always have been."

"Please," she pleaded again.

"No."

"Fine," she said in an angry tone that made it clear that things were anything but fine. The line went dead. I curled myself around Lena, and tried to turn my mind off again. I had no such luck this time. My thoughts were rubber balls bouncing down an endless spiral staircase.

Lena stirred. "What was that all about?"

"It was my crazy wife. She's at the hospital. She needs to have her appendix out, and she's scared. Whenever Alexandra gets sick, she wants me to turn into her guardian angel, but I'm not taking care of her. Bobby's on call. It's his problem."

Lena rolled onto me and turned off her alarm clock. I liked the feel of her there, lying on top. "You sleep some more," she said. "I'm getting up. I have to be at work by six."

She kissed me then, and I drifted back into peaceful sleep.

My phone rang and woke me a second time. Lena was gone, and I was alone in her bed. The phone call was from Alexandra again. The clock read 5:58 a.m. What kind of drama was she spawning now? I answered the call and said, "What is it?"

Alexandra was hysterical, bawling into the phone. "Nico, I'm waiting outside the operating room at the hospital, and I have a problem."

"What's the problem?"

"The problem is this asshole named Bobby Dylan. He's not touching me in a million years."

"Why not?"

"You know why. He's the father of Johnny's girlfriend, and he's a dick. He's rude and stupid and he's not even a doctor. I can tell he's mad at me, and I don't trust him. I'm sure his wife and daughter told him all kinds of trash about me from yesterday. I refuse to let him take care of me. My surgeon tells me you're the only other option I have."

"That's not going to happen. There must be another anesthetist available. I'll call the charge nurse." I hung up and rang the operating room front desk. Roberta Selvo answered the phone. "What's the situation for anesthesia staffing this morning?" I said.

"Dylan's on call. He's here. He's going to do the add-on case, your wife's surgery."

"Is anyone else available?"

"No. It's a weekend. None of the other anesthetists are around. Sheldon, Avery, and Commons are all out of town. You're the only backup."

"Damn it. My wife is refusing to let Dylan take care of her."

"Are you available?"

"I can't be my wife's doctor."

"Of course you can. I've heard you two might be getting divorced, but she is the mother of your son. Can't you come in, just for this one case? Wait a minute. Dr. Perpich is right here. He wants to talk to you."

Dr. Michael Perpich's scratchy voice came over the phone. "Nico, we have a problem here, as you've heard. Do me a favor. Can you please give this one anesthetic? I reviewed the ultrasound, and she needs surgery. It's imperative there are minimal delays. I don't want this appendix to rupture, and I'm supposed to be in Duluth to watch my son's hockey game at one o'clock this afternoon. Your wife needs surgery, and before that can happen she needs an anesthetic."

Dr. Perpich was my friend. He was a gentleman and a humanitarian. It was hard to say no to Perp. I paced across Lena's kitchen and opened the refrigerator. My mouth was parched, and I plucked a bottle of orange juice from the top shelf. As I stood there, squinting in the bright light of the top shelf, I saw the day with clarity. This was an opportunity. "Very well," I said to Perpich. "I'll be there as soon as I can."

I returned to Dom's house before I went to the hospital. The water was running in the shower upstairs, a sign that Johnny was awake. He joined me in the kitchen a few minutes later. Even though Nordic winds were rattling the windows, Johnny wore his default uniform of Nike sweat pants and a T-shirt. His hair was wet and he hadn't shaved, but the bounce had returned to Johnny's step.

"Get any rest?" I said.

"Yep. I feel pretty good."

"I got a call from your mother in the middle of the night. She's in the hospital with appendicitis. She's going to have surgery this morning."

"You're kidding."

"Dr. Perpich is taking out her appendix."

"That's crazy. Are you going to take care of her?"

"I am."

Johnny shot me a doubtful look. "Will that be hard for you? To be her doctor?"

"I only have to spend ten minutes with her before she's asleep. I can handle anything for ten minutes."

"Can I see her before you start?"

"Of course. Are you ready to leave?"

Johnny checked his look in the living room mirror, ran his fingers through his hair, and said, "I am. I can't wait to see Echo again. Dad, can I ask you a question?"

"Sure."

"If Echo and I decide to keep the baby, can I count on you to help us out?"

"Help you out?"

"Yeah. We'd need money and a place to live for a while. Would you do that for us?"

I looked at my son's pleading expression. It was inconceivable that Johnny go unrescued, but it was just as inconceivable that he could be changing diapers nine months from now. "I love you, son, and I've always thought Echo was terrific. If you decide you want to go through with this, I'll stand by you. I think you're both way too young, but she's pregnant. If she keeps the baby, you're going to be a father. I'll help you out."

"Thanks. You're a great dad. Let's go."

I stood in front of the whiteboard and examined the surgical schedule. Alexandra's appendectomy was booked for Room #4. Michael Perpich was listed as the surgeon, and Bobby Dylan was still listed as the anesthetist. I found Roberta Selvo and told her, "I'm doing the anesthetic for my wife."

"Of course, Doctor." She erased Dylan's name and printed my name in its place. "The patient is in the operating room already. Dr. Perpich is in a bit of a hurry. He's been waiting almost an hour."

I remember every minute detail of that fateful day. I remember Bobby Dylan exiting the doorway of O.R. #4 as I approached the room. His head and face were covered with the surgical hat and mask. Dylan's eyes were hidden under the dark shadow of his brow. "Your old lady's ready to go," he said. "I put all the monitors on her because Perpich asked me to keep things moving. Her vital signs are normal. She didn't want me to take care of her, and I didn't want to take care of her. That's about the only thing the two of us agreed on."

It was our first meeting since Dylan had pointed the shotgun at me. There were no guns this morning, but the emotions were no less raw. He pulled off his mask to reveal a malevolent sneer. "Nothing's changed between you and me, Doctor. Lena's still my wife, Echo's still my daughter, and I still want you and your son to take your wandering pricks and go back to California." He brushed past me, headed for the locker room, and said, "By the way, your wife's a bitch. I see why you ran away. If you're lucky, she'll never wake up."

I frowned. It was an odd thing to say, but Bobby Dylan was an odd guy. I walked inside O.R. #4, and found Alexandra lying awake on the operating room table.

I took control of her anesthetic then, and my life was forever changed.

CHAPTER 17
TO SLEEP, PERCHANCE TO DIE

Alexandra reclined awake on the operating room table. Her eyes were closed, and she was unaware I'd entered the room. She was dressed in a faded paisley surgical gown, and she looked like a spook—her hair flying out from a bouffant cap, her eye makeup smeared from crying, and the creases on her forehead looking deeper than I'd ever seen them. I stood above her and felt distanced from the whole situation. I had little empathy for her sickness.

The circulating nurse that morning was Gina Littlefoot, a chatty Native American woman in her 60's. Gina busied herself trying to converse with Alexandra. Gina's verbal diarrhea sounded more like a monologue. "I think the air here in Northern Minnesota is so invigorating. You can smell the freshness. I've been to the West Coast and I remember the smog in L.A. was so opaque you couldn't see mountains that were two miles away. It's ironic that you could be in good health at home in California and then get sick when you visited us in God's Country. And our water Up North? I wish I could start a company to bottle our water and sell it all over the world. It's that wonderful."

Alexandra opened her eyes for the first time and moaned, "Oh, God. Can you people just get this over with? I feel like crap. When is Nico going to get here?"

"I'm three feet away from you," I said.

Alexandra's face lit up at the sound of my voice. She craned her neck to look at me and said, "You're here. For a change I'm glad to see you."

I ground my teeth. I turned away from her and said, "Give me a few minutes to review your medical records." She'd arrived at the Emergency Room with abdominal pain at 1 a.m., and an ultrasound had confirmed that her appendix was inflamed. Other than an elevated white blood cell count, all her laboratory results were normal. She already had an intravenous line in place, and she'd received 4 milligrams of morphine in the Emergency Room.

Dr. Perpich entered the room and offered me his usual professional handshake. "Thanks a lot for coming in, Nico. Are we almost ready to begin?"

"I still need to talk with Alexandra," I said.

"I'll be waiting in the lounge," he said. "Gina, call me when the patient is prepped and ready." He left, and I stood alone with my wife.

"Are you in pain?" I said.

Her eyes were dull, narcotized—pinpoint pupils under drooping lids. "I like the morphine," she said. "Please give me more."

I looked at the clock. It was 7:30 a.m. The door opened, and Johnny entered the operating room. He hadn't seen his mother since the night before, prior to her illness. It seemed wrong, this family reunion under the surgical lights, but I didn't have the heart to tell him to leave.

"Hi, Mom," he said, his face and his emotions hidden behind a scrub mask. Alexandra reached out her hand toward him. Johnny's fingers became tangled in the IV tubing that coursed from her left wrist. He pushed the tubing aside and massaged the skin of her arm.

"It's good to see you, John-John," she said with a giggle. "Mommy's a little sick. Daddy's giving me some real good drugs, and I'm floating high above the bed right now."

"You'll do fine, Mom. You have the best anesthesiologist in Minnesota."

She slurred her words. "He's the best anesthesiologist in the whole wide world."

I rolled my eyes. Alexandra had no aversion to mind-altering drugs. The door opened again, and Echo entered the room. She took a spot beside Johnny, and rubbed my son's back as he massaged his mother's arm. I was surprised to see

Echo in the operating room. She was the last person I'd expect to see at my wife's bedside.

Echo whispered something into Johnny's ear. He stepped aside and said, "Mom, Echo is here, and she has something to say to you."

Echo stepped up and covered Johnny's hands where he caressed his mother's wrist. "Mrs. Antone?" she said.

Alexandra blinked back at her. "Yes, dear?"

"I love your son."

"Good God, girl. Don't start talking to me about love. Not now. You and Johnny are babies yourselves."

"I love your son," Echo repeated.

"I can't listen to that right now. Please leave me alone."

I turned my back on all three of them. I was having a hard time enduring the mawkish drama of the Johnny/Echo/Alexandra sideshow. I stood at the anesthesia workstation and reviewed my checklist. The anesthesia machine, monitors, airway equipment, and necessary drugs were all set up and ready to go. I filled a 20 cc syringe with the sedative propofol and a second syringe with 40 mg of the paralyzing drug rocuronium. I turned back to the three of them and said, "Johnny, I need to start the anesthetic. You and Echo need to leave now."

I watched him stroke Alexandra's arm one more time. His girlfriend whispered something into Johnny's ear, and my son shook his head no. "Sleep well, Mom," he said. He leaned in and gave his mother a hug. He and Echo shuffled backwards, never turning their backs on Alexandra. Johnny clasped Echo's hand, and they exited together.

"I'm going to let you breathe some oxygen now," I said as I lowered the anesthesia mask over Alexandra's face.

She said, "Remember, no matter how much you might hate me, Nico, I'm still the mother of your child."

I took a deep breath, exhaled slowly, and injected the anesthetic into her intravenous line. The milky whiteness of the propofol disappeared into the vein of her arm, and Alexandra went to sleep. I opened her mouth, inserted a metal laryngoscope past her tongue, and slid an endotracheal tube into her windpipe. It seemed bizarre to connect the motionless body of my wife to an anesthesia machine. I listened to her lungs to confirm she was being ventilated. The metal disc of my stethoscope pressed against her left breast, a part of her anatomy I hadn't seen or touched for two years.

I felt dirty just being there. I couldn't wait to get this over with and move on with my life. I watched Gina prep the abdomen with antiseptic soap. Dr. Perpich reentered the room, his scrubbed hands held high in front of his face. The surgical tech was dressed in sterile gown and gloves, and she dressed Dr. Perpich in the gown and gloves he'd wear for the surgery. Together they draped the abdomen in sterile blue towels. Alexandra's midriff disappeared from view, reduced to a 15-inch by 15-inch square of exposed abdominal skin.

Michael Perpich operated with a calm precision and a lack of intensity, as if solving an easy crossword puzzle for the thousandth time. He inserted a hollow metal trocar through Alexandra's belly button, and insufflated carbon dioxide through it to convert her abdomen into a gas-filled balloon. Dr. Perpich inserted a camera lens through a second small incision, and a two-dimensional image of Alexandra's intestines appeared on the video screen. He inserted two additional long-handled surgical instruments through the abdominal wall, and spent the next twenty minutes dissecting the appendix from the surrounding tissue.

I managed the anesthetic as I always did, using standard combinations of narcotics, muscle relaxants, and anesthetic vapors. The surgery flashed by. Dr. Perpich closed the skin a mere 37 minutes after his initial incision. I turned off the anesthetics and ventilated 100% oxygen through the breathing tube. My patients usually opened their eyes within 5 to 10 minutes from the time the anesthetics were discontinued.

Five minutes passed, and Alexandra did not stir. Ten minutes passed, and she did not wake. I inserted a suction catheter into her mouth to stimulate her, but Alexandra slept on.

I double-checked my systems. No anesthetics were running, either through the IV or through the breathing system. I touched the twin leads of a nerve stimulator near the facial nerve lateral to her eyebrow. Her facial muscles contracted in a strong twitch, confirming her muscles were not paralyzed.

"Is everything all right?" Dr. Perpich said, as he watched and waited.

"She's waking up slowly, that's all," I said. "Let's be patient."

I opened an ampoule of Narcan, a narcotic antagonist that reverses the effects of morphine. I injected the Narcan into Alexandra's IV, and waited. Narcan was effective within two or three minutes. Two minutes passed, then three, then five. Nothing changed. Alexandra still didn't wake up.

Dr. Perpich asked again, "Is everything all right?"

I tried to act like I wasn't concerned. It was obvious to everyone that something was wrong. I said, "Let's go ahead and bring her to the recovery room. We'll let her wake up there."

Thirty minutes later in the recovery room, Alexandra lay motionless without spontaneous movement or eye opening. I stood as a vigilant soldier at her side, maintaining an outward calm as I pondered the grim reality in front of me. My wife was inert, senseless, and dependent on a breathing machine. I'd been the last person to speak to her before robbing her of consciousness. I could hear the nursing staff whispering in distant corners of the recovery room, no doubt discussing the damning happenstance of a man anesthetizing his estranged wife, and her not waking up afterwards.

Dr. Perpich stood watch with me, his arms crossed over his chest and a grim look across his face. "I'm concerned, Nico," he said. "I'm going to call our best neurologist to come in and take a look at her."

"I agree," I said. "It was a routine case in every way. I have no idea why she's still unconscious."

Perpich's face was blanched white, drained of all blood flow. He wasn't looking me in the eye, and his annoyance was apparent. Surgeons expect two things from their anesthesia providers: that the patients do not move during surgery, and that the patients wake up afterwards. I'd failed on the latter, and he wasn't happy about it.

The neurologist, Dr. Preston Mattson, was a three-hundred-pound giant with a ZZ Top beard and a shaved head. His attire of blue jeans, red plaid flannel shirt, and a white coat belied his "best neurologist" status. After Dr. Perpich and I recounted the clinical history, Dr. Mattson turned his back on us and began to assess Alexandra's condition. He manipulated her flaccid limbs and murmured, "No spontaneous movement." Mattson inflicted painful stimuli in the form of pinches and twists of the skin, and said, "No response to pain." He focused a flashlight into her eyes, and said, "Pupils unreactive to light."

His beard bobbed and his right cheek billowed as he chewed on something, either gum or a plug of tobacco. As the exam progressed, the bobbing and chewing accelerated. After fifteen minutes of deliberation, the neurologist turned to us and said, "I'm going to order a CT scan of her head to rule out brain injury. We should have the result within the hour. I'm also ordering a full panel of laboratory tests to rule out a metabolic cause for her coma."

Coma. It was the first time anyone had used the word. Instead of a delayed awakening from general anesthesia, my wife's diagnosis now turned on one horrific word.

Coma.

CHAPTER 18
INTO THE SUNSET

Alexandra was unresponsive after her surgery and no one knew why. The minutes following the horror of that discovery blended into my next problem. I had to tell our son what had happened to his mother.

Johnny was sitting in the staff lunchroom when I found him after Alexandra's surgery. "How's Mom doing?" he said without looking up from his phone.

"The surgery went well. She had acute appendicitis, just as diagnosed, and they took the appendix out."

"Can I see her yet, or is it too early?"

"It's a bit early. She's still pretty sleepy." Whatever was going on, Johnny didn't need to know about it yet.

Roberta Selvo walked up to our table and said, "Johnny, we need two orderlies to transport a patient down to the CT scanner."

The hair on the back of my neck bristled. This wasn't right. Johnny couldn't push his comatose mother down the hallway to a brain scan. "Can I talk to you?" I said to Roberta. I pulled her across the room. "This is a no go. The patient is Johnny's mother. He can't see her like this. He doesn't even know about her condition."

Roberta stared back. "Of course you're right. I'm so sorry. I'll have Echo take your wife down to the scanner."

"I'm going with Echo," I said. "Alexandra is still on the ventilator. I need to watch over her."

"Very well."

I returned to Johnny in the lunchroom. "When can I see Mom?" he said.

"Not yet. I'll let you know."

"Will she go home tonight?"

"No. She'll spend the night here." Beads of sweat coated my forehead and betrayed my fear. Johnny didn't bother to look up from his phone, so he didn't notice. I felt very protective of him. I needed to evade him for now. "I've got to go back to work."

"Let me know when I can see her, all right?"

"I will." I returned to the recovery room, where Echo Johnson waited at the foot of Alexandra's bed. She'd removed her mask. Her cheeks were blanched and her lips were pressed together in a thin line. Echo gripped the railings of the bed as if they were the top rungs of a ladder descending to hell. She knew the score. Echo was only a high school kid, but she'd worked at Hibbing General for two years. She'd transported patients to their hospital rooms after appendectomies. Transporting a comatose patient to the CT scanner after an appendectomy was an extraordinary event.

Echo kept her gaze focused on blankets that covered Alexandra's legs. I took the cue that conversation was off limits for now. I attached a ventilation bag to Alexandra's breathing tube, and squeezed the bag twice, pumping oxygen into and out of her lungs. "Let's go," I said. Echo's movements were robotic and zombie-like as we wheeled the bed toward the scanner.

We exited the recovery room and approached the elevators for our trip to the scanner one floor below. To my alarm, Johnny popped out of the locker room and stood wide-eyed and hopeful between us and the elevator. He flashed Echo his teenager-in-love smile.

Echo said, "Johnny, I'll meet you in the lounge when I get back from the scanner, OK?" Her eyes shifted from him toward the horizontal figure lying on the bed. Johnny followed her cue, and looked down at the patient. His eyes widened at the spectacle: his mother lay motionless and dormant before him, a plastic hose coursing between her perfect teeth.

"Mom?" he said, grabbing her by the shoulders. When she didn't respond, he turned to me. "What's wrong with Mom?"

"I was going to tell you."

"You told me she was still sleepy! What's going on?"

"We don't know. The neurologist ordered a brain scan. That's where we're headed now."

Johnny leaned over Alexandra's body and touched the blanched marshmallow of her cheek. "Mom!" he screamed into her ear. "Mom?" He steeled his jaw and turned to me again. "Can she hear me?"

"I don't know. We'll know more after the neurologist runs some tests."

"You did this to her. You screwed up the anesthesia in some way, to get rid of her."

"Johnny, don't say that to your father," Echo said. She held her palm out toward Johnny in a halting gesture. Her fingers shook like tree branches in a storm.

"You don't know them, Echo," Johnny said. "You don't know how they fight. You don't know much they hate each other. But what about me? Dad, how could you do this to me?"

"I didn't do anything to you. I promise we'll make every effort to help her get better. I'll come and talk to you as soon as we know more. I promise."

Echo and I resumed pushing the bed toward the brain scanner. As we rolled Alexandra's bed into the elevator, Johnny stared at us. The elevator door closed, and the three people Johnny cared most about disappeared behind panels of sliding steel.

One hour later I met with Dr. Mattson outside the Intensive Care Unit. Alexandra's clinical condition was unchanged. We stood over her body in a private ICU room, where her breathing was supported by the monotonous cadence of a mechanical ventilator. The neurologist crossed his arms and pushed his lips into a pout. His expression freaked me out. The news couldn't be good.

"What did the scan show?" I said.

Mattson raised one eyebrow. "The preliminary report on the scan is normal."

"That's good news."

"It is. The scan tells us there is no intracerebral bleed, no obvious stroke, and no discernable pathology. The scan gives us no explanation for her coma. I'm puzzled, as I'm sure you are, too."

Mattson's cell phone rang. He took the call, and his expression grew more and more serious as he listened. He hung up, bit against his lower lip, and squared himself to me. "That was the director of the clinical laboratory, telephoning me with Mrs. Antone's lab results. I have some very bad news for you, Dr. Antone."

"What kind of bad news?" I said, my voice reduced to a hoarse croak.

"Your wife's glucose concentration is the lowest the lab director's ever seen," Dr. Mattson said. "Her blood sugar is 2 mg/dL."

"Two? How could it be two?"

"I don't know. We'll need to draw a second sample and recheck it to confirm the hypoglycemia. The normal range for glucose is 60–100 mg/dL. If her blood level is truly 2, then I'm afraid that her low blood sugar explains her coma."

"We need to give her some intravenous dextrose. We need to draw another glucose level, stat, and then inject two amps of D 50. Get me a syringe." I wrapped a tourniquet around her left arm and located the cephalic vein at the crook of her elbow. The ICU nurse handed me an empty syringe, and I drew out a sample of Alexandra's blood to send to the lab. The nurse handed me two ampoules of 50% dextrose, and I injected the sugar into her IV as fast and as hard as a man could push.

We watched and waited.

The digital clock on the wall flipped to the next minute and then the next, as we stood vigil over Alexandra's motionless flesh. After five minutes, there was no change. I ground my knuckles into Alexandra's hard breastbone and said, "Alex, wake up! Can you hear me? For God's sakes, wake up!"

Nothing changed. The quiet in the room was haunting. Only the periodic purring of the ventilator broke the hush. "What do we do now?" I whispered to Dr. Mattson.

"She's been comatose since the surgery ended. That was three hours ago. If hypoglycemia was the cause of this coma, and it's almost certain that it was, then her brain has been deprived of sugar for a prolonged period of time. The damage is sure to be irreversible."

I leaned back on the wall and slid downward, a blob melting into the floor. I buried my face in my hands and screamed a loud "Nooooo" that bounced off the walls of the tiny ICU room and echoed into the ears of every human in that half of the hospital. Dr. Mattson laid his hand on my shoulder and tried to console me, but I was in a universe all to myself—a world of hurt, despair, and stigma. On my shift, on my watch, my wife had incurred the greatest loss a human could sustain. Brain cells died without glucose. Once they were dead, they never came back.

Mattson said, "I wish there was something I could do to make the situation better. I can't imagine how you must feel. The next step in my work-up is to order an EEG. Depending on the results of the electroencephalogram, we will decide what to do next."

I peeled my hands away from my face. Between hyperventilating gasps I asked the obvious question. "How did her blood sugar get so low?"

"I don't know. I'm going to contact my colleagues at the University of Minnesota and the Mayo Clinic for their opinions."

"I need to talk to my son before everybody in town finds out what just happened to his mom. He needs to hear this from me."

"Of course."

I stood, surprised that my wobbly legs supported me at all. I dreaded the confrontation with Johnny. I trudged back toward the O.R. with the sensation of a steel band encircling my chest. The effort required to inhale a single breath was overwhelming.

I found Johnny in the O.R. hallway. He was circling, a hamster bouncing off the bars of his cage. He planted his fists on his hips and said, "What's the deal? Is Mom going to be all right?"

The tone of his voice, his resentment and his scorn were too familiar—the reincarnation of Alexandra. My teenager son, who'd been in love with Minnesota, Echo, and life, had turned into a younger, male version of his mother.

I gave it to him straight. "Son, they did some tests, and they were all normal except for one: Your mother's blood sugar was very, very low."

"What does that mean?"

"That means her brain took a hit. She might not wake up."

"Not wake up? You said this was a really common surgery. You said it was going to be routine."

"It was."

"How could her blood sugar get so low?"

"I don't know. No one knows. The neurologist is calling the U of M and the Mayo Clinic for their expertise."

"You bumped her off. While she was under anesthesia, you bumped her off. What other explanation is there? Do you think people up here are so stupid they won't figure that out? I'm 17, and I figured it out." He laid his hands on my chest, and shoved me out of the way. "I'm going to the ICU. I need to see her."

"Johnny…"

"Leave me alone," He turned on me, and ran down the corridor toward the elevator.

Alexandra was dead, and Johnny was gone.

Every atom in my body was spinning out of control. I had no idea I could feel this awful. I staggered down the hallway until I found a vacant men's restroom. I locked myself inside, dropped to my knees on the cold tile floor, folded my hands, and prayed for the first time since grade school.

I didn't pray for Alexandra. Alexandra's ship had sailed into the sunset. I prayed for myself.

CHAPTER 19
TANGLED UP IN INSULIN

Dr. Roger Olson, the Chief Executive Officer of Hibbing General Hospital, sat at a small metal desk cluttered with papers. Snow blew in diagonal lines through barren branches outside the window behind him, a mobile collage framing the grim-faced Olson. Olson clamped his eyes shut in an involuntary spasm every twenty seconds or so. Between blinks, he focused his Norwegian eyes at me and said, "I have additional bad news regarding your wife's case, Dr. Antone."

"Hit me. It can't get any worse."

"Her EEG shows that she is indeed brain dead. But the most troubling findings are the results of insulin levels."

"Insulin levels?"

"Yes. Her blood insulin levels are extremely high—the highest our lab has ever seen."

"Why are the insulin levels so high?"

"I don't know, but the working diagnosis is exogenous insulin."

"Exogenous insulin?"

"Correct." Dr. Olson stared me down. His eyelids squeezed over and over, accelerating, pumping like window blinds closing and opening. Between blinks, his sapphire irises bore down on me with horrible accusing power. "It appears that Mrs. Antone received a massive overdose of insulin."

"That's not possible. There was no insulin in the operating room. I'm not stupid. I would never have done that."

"I'm not making any judgment calls, Dr. Antone, but I'd suggest you report this to your malpractice insurance company as soon as possible. And from my experience with the medical-legal system, I'd recommend that you don't discuss the sensitive medical details with anyone until you've met with a lawyer."

I slammed both palms down on Olson's desk and said, "I'm no fool. I did not inject insulin into my wife during anesthesia. I can't believe you just accused me of that."

"I didn't accuse you of anything. I just revealed the facts of the case to you, and I'm telling you: get a lawyer."

"I'm innocent."

"I hope there's an alternative explanation, Dr. Antone. I must tell you, though, that the word going around the hospital is that you and your wife were not on good terms. The word going around is that she cheated on you, and that you despised her. People are speculating that you had a motive to do this to Alexandra—to get rid of her."

"And lose my medical license and maybe even go to jail? Are you kidding me? I'll say it again: I'm not stupid. If I did this, I'd be certain to be caught. Where would that leave me? I'd never dare such folly. You've got to help me."

"We'll go over every nuance of Mrs. Antone's medical care with a microscopic eye to detail." The eyelids squeezed down hard, vise grips tightening. "The coroner will conduct an autopsy. Our peer review and quality assurance people will gather data. Be reassured, this is no witch-hunt. Our job is to discern the facts."

"The fact is I did nothing to harm Alexandra."

Olson raised one eyebrow. "I want to believe that, Dr. Antone. Really I do." He closed the folder that contained Alexandra's test results, folded his hands over it, and said, "Good day, Dr. Antone."

I made a return visit to my wife's bedside in the ICU, where I came face-to-face with the last person I ever expected to see in Hibbing. Beard Man, Alexandra's lover from California, sat perched on the edge of her bed. I watched as he stroked the skin of Alexandra's forearm and whispered into her ear. I was stunned. Our first meeting was one of the ugliest ordeals of my life. The circumstances of this second meeting were even worse. After all these years of marriage to Alexandra, why should I have to share the deathbed vigil with her hirsute lover?

I paused in the doorway and considered whether a quick one-eighty was the correct maneuver. Before I could exit, Beard Man looked up and saw me. "You," he said. He strode toward me with the predatory stride of a lion hunting food. Despite the modest fluorescent lighting of the intensive care room, the man wore sunglasses. A demonic beard tapered to a precise point under his chin. His hands drooped impossibly low, below his knees. He was a Neanderthal Satan in shades. Beard Man planted his right forefinger firmly against my chest and said, "You had to get even, didn't you? Did you think you wouldn't get caught?"

"I know it looks bad, but…"

"You're going down. I've already talked to the Medical Board of Minnesota and to the prosecuting district attorney for this county. They're coming after you. I'm coming after you. You're going to burn for this."

I peeled the accusing finger off my chest and pondered how to respond to the accusations. Before I could speak, there was a commotion behind me, and five young men dressed in white coats and blue surgical scrubs entered Alexandra's room. The lead man strode to the bedside, the clacking heels of his cowboy boots announcing that he was from out of town. A *University of Minnesota Hospitals and Clinics* nametag hung from his lapel. He extended his hand to me and said, "I'm Dr. Leroy McLean, cardiothoracic surgery, from the organ procurement team at the U. I need to speak to the Alexandra Antone's next of kin."

"I'm her husband," I said, a sick feeling mounting in my stomach.

"Your wife was signed up as a donor. We're here to harvest the organs, as soon as the coroner gives us clearance to proceed. This is the rest of my team: Dr. Harvey Olds and Dr. Samuel Ponds of surgery, Dr. Mike Giamotti of anesthesia, and Robert Gossamer, the lead transplant nurse."

The four men looked past me at the horizontal figure of Alexandra, a brain-dead fertile garden of useful tissues. They were sizing up their task, planning their next moves.

"Now? You guys are going to cut her up now?" Beard Man said.

"Who are you?" Dr. McLean said.

"I'm Frank Demitree, a close friend of Alexandra's."

"Mr. Demitree, our team is trained to extract the organs and tissues an individual has consented to donate. In Ms. Antone's case, her list included the heart, lungs, liver, kidneys, corneas, and Achilles tendons. The harvest procedure will be done in an operating room at this hospital. The vital organs will be transported back to Minneapolis via fixed wing transport as soon as we're finished."

"But after you do that, she'll be a carcass with an empty chest. She'll never come back."

"Mr. Demitree, I can assure you that Alexandra Antone has already been declared brain dead, and that she's never coming back. Removing a beating heart may seem like a fatal move, but in her case, it is a life-affirming move that will give years of survival to an individual with a failing heart. "

It was more than I could bear. I couldn't listen to the transplant team banter with my wife's lover for one more second. I needed to get away. I walked out of the room, only to have Beard Man follow me and grab me by the elbow.

"Murder, that's what this was," he said. "Mark my word, I will bring the fury of the legal system down on you. You killed her, and you're going down."

I batted his hand away and said, "Mr. Demitree, I'm very sad about what happened, but I did nothing wrong. Leave me alone." I turned to leave, but Beard Man had to have the last word.

"You're going to jail, Dr. Death. I won't rest until I've seen you in jail for Murder One."

My patience was exhausted. "To hell with you. You're nobody around here. Go back to California and climb under the same rock you were hiding behind when my wife found you."

"Alexandra loved me," Beard Man said. "You were a pathetic excuse for a husband and a miserable little cuckold. You deserve to be buggered by some convict in a prison shower."

This guy was asking to be punched in the nose. I could continue to trade verbal jousts, I could slug the man in the jaw, or I could leave now and try to put together the pieces of the rest of my life.

There was no way to win. I shut my mouth, slackened my fists, and walked away.

CHAPTER 20
NOBODY EXCEPT YOU

I sat on the edge of a wing-backed leather chair in the office of my newest ally, Edward Martinovich, Esquire, of Duluth, Minnesota. Mr. Martinovich stood behind a broad mahogany desk in his penthouse suite and stared through his floor-to-ceiling windows at the flat, snow-covered expanse of Wisconsin on the distant shore of Lake Superior. His college diploma from Carleton College, law school diploma from the University of Minnesota, and a dozen honorary degrees and professional society awards hung on the burgundy office walls. A plaque from the Croatian American Association honored him as their Man of the Year for 2012.

Martinovich was in constant motion. The shining toe of his black wingtip tapped against the carpet. The fingers of his right hand spun his platinum wedding band. His upper lip bounced as he sharpened his teeth on the corner of his moustache. Martinovich's attire belonged on Wall Street, not alongside the Great Lakes. The lawyer wore a slim-fitting ebony suit, a white shirt, and a powder blue necktie secured in a perfect symmetrical knot. His full head of jet-black hair was combed straight back. A pair of baby blue reading glasses perched on the end of a hawk-like nose.

I hired Martinovich when I learned of his reputation as a pugnacious courtroom brawler. He was the highest-priced litigator in the northern half of the state of Minnesota. I had money. Martinovich had moxie. I was a minnow swimming scared. Martinovich was a muskellunge poised to defend me. I was in deep trouble, and I needed the undisputed star of North Country courtrooms at my side.

I was disheveled and unshaven. I hadn't slept more than one hour any night since Alexandra's death. My attire was a wrinkled corduroy shirt and a pair of baggy blue jeans, and I looked like a ditch-digger in contrast to Martinovich's slickness. I didn't care about my appearance—I just wanted to stay out of jail. For the past hour I'd spewed out paragraphs of worry as I obsessed over every detail of Alexandra's demise.

Martinovich glanced at his Rolex and sighed. He'd listened to my version of the truth without speaking a word. He paced to the window again, knit his hands together behind his back, and watched the ore boats coursing in and out of the port of Duluth. Martinovich turned about to face me, and spoke in slow, assertive terms. "Yes, Doctor, I can help you. I love this case already. It's no doubt the highest profile medical malpractice case in the history of Minnesota, and as of yesterday it became more. As of yesterday, your case became the highest profile homicide case in the history of Minnesota. This is a great case. An important case. It's my kind of case. I reviewed the medical records and evidence last evening. Let me go over the pertinent legal issues with you, Doctor, and then let us outline a plan.

"You are charged with first-degree murder. These are the key facts surrounding your wife's death, as I see them: Fact #1: You and your wife were estranged. You were aware that she was sleeping with another man. It was well known that you were angry at her. This establishes motive.

"Fact #2: You administered general anesthesia to your wife for her appendectomy, and after the surgery she was brain dead due to hypoglycemia. The cause was an apparent administration of an insulin overdose. The prosecution will portray this as a premeditated insulin overdose.

"Fact #3: Her death could be construed as medical malpractice, because the standard of care would be for you, as her attending anesthesiologist, to protect your patient while she was asleep. If you inadvertently gave her the insulin by mistake when you believed you were administering a different medication, then you would be guilty of negligence. Negligence is not murder.

"Your plight worsened by a quantum leap yesterday after the discovery of Fact #4: Internet news services exploded with an additional tidy circumstance about your case. The value of Alexandra Antone's company and estate exceeds 90 million dollars, all of which now becomes the sole property of the surviving spouse, one Dr. Nicolai Antone."

"Everyone in the world who reads that crap gossip on the Internet will think I bumped her off for the money," I said.

"Yes. Money is a powerful motivator. All of a sudden what might have been a tragic, unintentional drug error becomes an arraignment for first-degree murder. The prosecution's case reads like this: You had the desire to kill your wife. You planned to kill Alexandra, you had the opportunity to kill her, and you carried out that plan in the operating room that day."

"But people have to realize it makes no sense. If I tried to kill her that way, I'd never get away with it. The blood on my hands would be apparent the minute I stepped out of the operating room. I'm too smart of a guy to kill my wife in this fashion."

"That may be true," Martinovich said with a smirk, "but unfortunately, 'I'm too smart to have done this' is not going to be a useful defense argument. Ninety million dollars buys a lot of lawyering. Perhaps you murdered her out of anger and greed, and gambled that an outstanding lawyer could convince the jury that you were innocent."

He sat on the edge of his desk, inches away from me, so close that I could smell the peppermint on his breath. "Have you ever heard of the Claus von Bülow case?"

"No."

"Claus von Bülow was a wealthy socialite who was tried in Rhode Island in 1982 for the attempted murder of his wife, Sunny. Sunny was found comatose, with a very low blood sugar and a high insulin level. Scenario sound familiar?"

"Yes."

"They found syringes and insulin in a locked closet in the von Bülow home. Claus von Bülow was found guilty of attempted murder, and sentenced to 30 years in prison. Alas, Mr. von Bülow hired the famed lawyer Alan Dershowitz to file an appeal. Dershowitz masterminded a successful defense, and Mr. von Bülow was found not guilty on all counts. Dershowitz described the case in his book *Reversal of Fortune*, which was also made into an Academy Award-winning movie. In that case, Mr. von Bülow paid for the best lawyering he could find, and walked away an innocent man."

Martinovich's chest swelled with pride. "The good news is that you too have chosen an outstanding lawyer."

"Do you think I killed my wife?"

Martinovich waved his hand. "I don't know if you killed her. I don't care if you killed her. My job is to convince a jury of Iron Rangers that you did not murder Alexandra Antone."

"You don't care if I killed her?"

"It's not my job to prosecute you. My job is to defend you. My mission is to assemble a sympathetic jury, devise a credible defense strategy, and present that strategy in a convincing, compelling manner so the jury will acquit you. It's not going to be easy, and it's not going to be cheap."

"I don't care how much it costs. I can't sleep. My son won't talk to me. Every news channel, newspaper, Internet news site, and Eskimo riding a dogsled is enamored with my guilt. I have no life. I'm dead."

"No, your wife is dead. You are quite alive. Play it my way, and there's a good chance you'll walk away from this a free man, with most of that $90 million dollars in your back pocket."

I wasn't sure if I liked Martinovich. The man was part shark, part huckster, and a good part blowhard. His persona reeked of self-absorption and egomania. I was trusting my life to this P.T. Barnum of the North Country. "Play it your way means what?"

"Play it my way means this: Fall on the grenade and avoid a murder trial altogether. We can establish which anesthetic drugs come in vials nearly identical to insulin. You testify that you gave the insulin by mistake when you meant to administer another, safer drug. Is that bad medicine? Yes. Is it malpractice? Without a doubt. Is it murder? No way. You will walk. So tell me, did you commit such a negligent act?"

"No, I did not."

"But it is possible, is it not? One can inject the wrong medicine by accident, can't they? A drug different than intended?"

"Yes, it's possible to inject the wrong drug by accident. I'm human. I've done 20,000 anesthetics, and every anesthetic involves multiple drug injections. I've injected the wrong drug 4 or 5 times."

"Excellent. Then we have a plausible means to keep you out of prison."

"I understand you'd like me to lie under oath to save my ass. The problem is that I won't do that. How can I claim that I injected insulin by mistake, when I didn't? I'm not going through life being blamed for Alexandra's death, with my son thinking his mother's death was my fault. I have to plead not guilty."

Martinovich nodded knowingly, a patient father listening to his son's description of how the muddy shoes had nothing to do with footprints on the rug. Then the attorney held up the thick packet of medical records from Hibbing General Hospital and said, "The evidence in here is damning. The warrant for your arrest is pending. You can expect to be in jail by the end of the week. Because of the gravity of the charges, the extent of your wealth, and the risk of flight, you can expect that no bail will be offered."

My gut sunk. "I can't go to jail. It can't be."

"It can be, Dr. Antone, and it will be." Then he said, in a slow, rhythmic cadence: "Because there is an enormous elephant in the courtroom—an elephant we will have to vaporize in order to win this case."

"And what elephant are you speaking of?"

"Mrs. Antone was awake when you started the anesthetic. She was brain dead afterward. During the time she was asleep, did anyone else inject anything into Alexandra Antone's bloodstream?"

"No."

"Then there is no one else. Nobody could have committed this crime except you. You are guilty because, to quote Sherlock Holmes, 'When you have excluded the impossible, whatever remains, however implausible, must be the truth.'

"Dr. Antone, there is no other explanation."

CHAPTER 21
HIGH WATER

I plummeted feet first into the ocean, the force of the fall submerging my face deep beneath the waves. I swam upward in desperate strokes until my nose and eyes broke the surface. I filled my lungs with precious air and flailed with all four limbs to stay afloat. The pull from below was powerful. A heavy weight clung to my ankles and tugged me downward.

"Help me!" I screamed to the empty sky. No reply came—there was no sign of another human. My boots filled with water, adding to the ballast dragging me toward the bottom. My arms ached with effort. My chest heaved. Salt water splashed across my gasping mouth. I tasted my inevitable fate.

A wave rushed toward me. Panic grew as the water crested and fell. I drew my last breath, closed my eyes, and felt the sea cover me once more. I yearned for oxygen as I held my breath. The seconds ticked on and tortured me until I could wait no longer. I had to empty my lungs and inhale in turn. I opened my mouth, and my airways choked and filled with salt water. My brain exploded, and I sank toward the ocean floor.

"No," I screamed, jerking my face away from the coarse cotton covering my stiff pillow. Bed sheets twisted around my sweat-drenched limbs. The jail cell was dark, the silhouettes of the vertical steel bars giving the room its only definition. I took in a deep breath, grateful to be alive. My heart thumped on, tormented by the nightmare. There would be no more sleep tonight. I sat up on one elbow, and took account of my circumstances.

The dream was gone and my lungs were dry. I was hundreds of miles from any ocean. The rough concrete walls that confined me were my prison and my shelter. Every night was a tedious ordeal. Rare bouts of sleep were interrupted by recurring dreams of suffocating, drowning, and death. Every night I fell to the bottom of the sea, over the edge of a waterfall, into molten lava, or into the depths of an iron mine. During waking hours, my room was a drab cocoon. I had no roommate, no alarm clock, and no one to fight with. My soul longed for only one thing.

Johnny.

I missed Johnny more than anything. I'd been in jail four months, and my son hadn't visited once. I had no access to email or a phone, so I relied on snail mail and prayers. I'd written Johnny thirty-one letters. He hadn't answered any of them. Each day I asked the prison guards about incoming mail, and each day there was no reply from my son. Johnny's anger was a wall between us, and I had no opportunity for an audience with him to explain away the facts.

In my months in jail, I'd had only two visitors: Edward Martinovich and Lena. Martinovich came every day, for logistical reasons. He needed my input to prepare my defense.

Lena was my beacon in the fog, the only person who cared about me. She visited once a week, and I craved her presence. In a world of pale green walls and iron bars, I lived to see Lena's face. With each sunrise, the prospect of Lena's next visit fueled my will to survive. She was my only portal to Johnny. Johnny was an orphan, and he chose to live with Lena. She became his chef, his chauffeur, his psychotherapist, and his surrogate mother. My knowledge of Johnny's life and times came solely through Lena.

The jail guard banged a metal cup on the bars of my cell and said, "The lady's here to see you, Doc. Freshen up. You've got twenty minutes." I combed ten fingers through my oily hair, and brushed unkempt waves off my forehead. I had no mirror and could only imagine how frightful I looked. I hadn't shaved in months, and shampooing was an every fifth day luxury.

Lena faced me from the opposite side of a Plexiglas barrier. She wore a white turtleneck and no eye makeup. Her face was a wan mask, a false copy of her former self. She wasn't enamored with the role of the prisoner's girlfriend. I hadn't seen a free world woman other than Lena in four months. Even a somber Lena was an angel to me.

"You look tired," she said. "Are you sleeping any better?"

"I'm hanging in there. How are the kids?"

"The pregnancy's perking along. Echo's still not showing much, so it's not too awkward for her at school. Her nausea is gone now that she's into her second trimester. We're meeting with an adoption agency out of Duluth this weekend. Echo goes to school, she comes home, and she studies. She's coping."

"And Johnny?"

"No change. He's a night owl, troubled and sad. He talks to me for an hour every night after Echo goes to sleep. He feels very alone."

"Does he talk about me?"

She looked uneasy. "Not often."

"What does he say?"

"He's mad at you."

"He thinks I'm guilty?"

"He does. Johnny's angry and he's embarrassed. One parent is dead and the other one is her presumed murderer. He believes the bloggers. Johnny believes you killed his mother."

"Is there anything I can do?"

She shrugged. "Get out of jail, for all of our sakes. Come home an innocent man. Be his dad again. As long as you're in here, Johnny will ignore you. He has to, just to survive."

"And you?"

"I'm tired, Nico. I'm tired of all this. Does your attorney have a plan? Are you ever going to be free?"

"Martinovich has a solid defense strategy. Yes, I believe I'll be free someday."

"I hope so. I want to move far, far away from here." She reached out her hand and splayed her fingers across the Plexiglas window between us. I extended my fingers against the glass on my side and matched them to Lena's across the barrier.

In my sensory-deprived world here in prison, she was my mooring. Before jail, I'd been stingy with my emotions for Lena. Behind bars, the wonder of her affection was clear. I emoted without reservation.

"I love you," I said. It was the first time she'd heard these words from me.

"Now you tell me you love me? Now that you can't have me?" Lena peeled her fingers from the window and folded them on the tabletop before her. She took in a long, slow breath, and said nothing. She stood and left without saying goodbye, and I felt more alone than ever.

I returned to my cell, stretched out on the cot, and closed my eyes. As I did every day, I replayed every detail of Alexandra's anesthetic in my mind. The gnawing in my gut grew. I was worn out and fatigued on the morning of Alexandra's appendectomy. I'd been overwhelmed and distracted by my disgust for her.

A solitary image from that morning haunted me. Inside Lena's refrigerator, next to the orange juice, next to the carton of milk, stood a full box of insulin vials. Echo's insulin vials. I'd seen those vials that morning before dawn. I could not remember what transpired after I held that refrigerator door. Had I closed the door and turned away? Or had I pocketed one insulin vial and taken it with me to the operating room? How badly had I wanted Alexandra vanquished? Could I have blocked all memory of the deed, the theft of the insulin, the injection of the insulin, and murdered my own wife in the operating room?

Perspiration soaked through my shirt. My body betrayed my guilt. I was Alexandra's killer. I was the assassin. Who else could have done it?

If I was ever to live as a free man again, my fervent hope was that Edward Martinovich was a magician.

CHAPTER 22
AT MY TIME OF TRIAL

The wind chill was minus thirty degrees Fahrenheit, and the sun had barely risen over the treetops. Dozens of Chevy, Ford, and Dodge SUVs with rusted-out fenders and billowing exhaust pipes carried denim-clad workers to their jobs in the mines of the Mesabi Iron Range. They drove past a circus array of media vans from CNN, ABC, FOX, NBC, and CBS, all parked on the streets surrounding the gray limestone walls of the St. Louis County District Courtroom.

I marched through this sub-zero morning air amidst the throngs of reporters and paparazzi, each pushing and shouting, jockeying for a better position to get the best photograph, or trying to provoke me to make some comment for the evening's sound bite. My face was close-shaven. My hair was cropped. I wore my best, and only, Giorgio Armani navy blue suit. My white shirt was starched, and the knot in my blue and red striped tie was tight. The heels of my dress shoes clacked on ice-coated pavement. The air smelled fresh and wonderful. Nothing inside the jail ever smelled fresh or wonderful. The breeze on my face was wicked and rare.

If I'd ever dreamed of fame, it had never looked like this—surrounded by a raucous crowd who thought of me as a notorious murder suspect. The juries of Twitter, Facebook, and TMZ had already convicted me. A loudspeaker across the street blared "No Sugar Tonight" by The Guess Who, a song that had become the signature soundtrack for the Alexandra Antone low-blood-glucose murder case. The rock song would air every time I entered and exited the courthouse. Like Ricky Vaughn walking from the bullpen to the pitcher's mound to the rocking of "Wild Thing" in the movie *Major League*, I left my incarceration van and entered the legal arena to the beat of my own anthem.

My armpits were drenched with sweat, my tongue was dry as a pinecone, and I felt like vomiting all over my Italian wool slacks. In the operating room I took pride in calm demeanor under pressure. When a patient tried to die on me, the correct synapses in my brain always seemed to fire to enable me to diagnose the problem and apply appropriate treatment. In the operating room, I was an expert.

In this courtroom, I was a melting candle.

The interior of the courtroom was jammed with non-Hibbingites—I surveyed a hundred faces and recognized no one. The individuals in the gallery buzzed like honeybees over a flower garden. Representatives of the state and national press populated the first four rows, the men conspicuous in their tailored suits and precision haircuts, the women cosmopolitan in their dress and make-up, more attuned to Vogue magazine than to the tundra of the Iron Range. The reporters scrutinized me and followed my every move. Pens scurried over sketchpads and fingers tapped on laptops and tablet computers.

Everyone I cared about was banned from the courtroom. Johnny, Lena, and Echo were all sequestered. As subpoenaed witnesses, they were not permitted to watch the trial until after they had testified.

Martinovich busied himself crossing out and underlining notes on a yellow legal pad. He wore a dark gray suit and a lavender necktie, and his hair was combed into a flamboyant pompadour. Martinovich paid no attention to me. I felt alone and exposed in the middle of the stark courtroom.

The bailiff strode to the front of the room and said, "All rise for the Honorable Judge Satrum." Judge Marcus Satrum entered from his chambers and seated himself atop the bench. He was a broad-shouldered hulk of a man with a thick head of white hair and a full beard to match. He eyed the crowded room with a proud countenance, as if presiding over a sensational murder trial was an every day occurrence. In truth, Satrum was accustomed to audiences far greater than this one. The judge was a former Iron Range hockey legend who'd played in the National Hockey League for the New York Rangers. Compared to Madison Square Garden, the St. Louis County Courtroom was a minor league venue.

Satrum wore the scowl of a man late for dinner. A deep diagonal scar sliced above his left eyebrow. A hockey stick to the forehead? A right cross from a barroom brawl? He looked like a grim executioner to me. I felt an immediate dislike toward the man.

According to Martinovich, Judge Satrum was going to be a tough cookie. During his NHL career Satrum had a reputation as a brawler, leading the league in penalty minutes five consecutive years. On the bench he was known to be an intelligent and fair judge who exalted brevity and pertinence in his courtroom. Satrum abhorred verbose and unprepared litigators. He'd never presided over a trial that had exceeded two weeks.

One way or another, I would know my fate within 14 days.

The prosecuting attorney was a local stiff named James Hamilton. He was a wide-body equipped with a pendulous gut that pushed his baggy white shirt out the front of his metallic blue suit. Hamilton carried his nose high and jutted his lower lip out in the fashion of Alfred Hitchcock. The man struck me as a confident prick, reveling in the media exposure and unprecedented attention from this sensational case. If I'd done nothing else in my life, I'd helped James Hamilton achieve his fifteen minutes of fame.

Hamilton stood at the podium and greeted the judge and jury. After a dramatic pause, he pointed a finger at me and said, "This man... Dr. Nico Antone... is a killer. Not only is this man a killer, he is a doctor who kills. Contrary to the Hippocratic Oath, which instructs doctors to do no harm to their patients, this man killed his patient. And not only did Dr. Antone kill his patient, this doctor killed a patient who was his wife. Contrary to the oath of holy matrimony, in which a man promises to love, honor, and cherish a woman until death do them part, Dr. Antone is a wife killer."

My heart rate climbed, and I knew the war had begun. This vile description was out there for the world to hear. Hamilton's declaration made me sound like the most evil creature imaginable. I wanted to wrap my fingers around his jowls and silence every whiny, accusing syllable.

Hamilton continued, "The evidence in this case will demonstrate, beyond reasonable doubt, that Nicolai Antone murdered his wife Alexandra Antone on the morning of September 9th. This murder was both deliberate and premeditated. You will hear testimony from medical experts who will pinpoint the cause of Alexandra Antone's death to an overdose of insulin. Dr. Antone alone attended to his wife on that morning. He alone had the opportunity to kill her. Dr. Antone willfully injected medications into his wife's veins that anesthetized her into a deep sleep, and then he willfully injected an overdose of insulin into Alexandra Antone's body that caused irreversible brain damage.

"The State will bring hard evidence on both the insulin level and the fatal low blood sugar level that killed Alexandra Antone. The State will provide witnesses to attest that no one other than Dr. Nicolai Antone had the opportunity to kill his wife. The State will provide witnesses that define the motives of jealousy, anger, and greed that drove Dr. Nicolai Antone to kill his wife."

Hamilton ceased his oration for a paroxysm of loud coughing. It lasted for twenty or thirty seconds, and served to dampen the force of his attack on me. "The man's a putz," Martinovich wrote on his yellow pad for me to read.

"A villain," I wrote back.

"I will bury him," Martinovich wrote.

"BURY HIM!" I wrote in capital letters. As I dotted the exclamation point, I pushed on the pencil so hard that the lead snapped off.

Hamilton recovered his voice and droned on. He concluded his opening statement with a rousing accusation. "Ladies and gentlemen of the jury, the question now before you is, 'did this man kill his wife?' It is no small thing to answer this question. It's a serious undertaking. You hold the fate of another human being in your hands, so I expect you to consider this question very seriously. But be assured that the State will show that one fact is not in question. A 41-year-old woman is dead and gone. And why is she dead? We will prove beyond a reasonable doubt that Dr. Nico Antone thought nothing of murdering his wife and depriving his only son of his mother." Hamilton pointed to me once again, and then he departed from the podium.

The Ghost of Nico's Future had spoken. I felt a hundred pair of eyes scrutinizing my every motion. I wanted to shrink into my oaken chair.

"Amateur hour is over," Martinovich wrote on his legal pad. Then he stood to address the jury. He looked calm, confident, and at ease. This was his stage, and Martinovich was as much an actor as he was a litigator. Game on.

"This is a simple case," Martinovich said in a soft voice. He made eye contact with each of the twelve members of the jury before he spoke again. "The evidence will show that insulin killed Alexandra Antone. The evidence will not show who gave her that insulin. The evidence will not show when she received that insulin.

"To convict Dr. Nicolai Antone of murder, the prosecution must show... must show... beyond reasonable doubt, that Dr. Nicolai Antone injected that insulin into Alexandra Antone. As you hear testimony in the ensuing days, you will not hear any testimony that establishes that fact. This is a simple case. A tragic insulin overdose killed Alexandra Antone. No one knows where the insulin overdose came from. No one... no one... will prove to you that Dr. Nicolai Antone gave Alexandra Antone that insulin."

I listened to Martinovich's powerful delivery, and marveled at his brevity. He'd framed the key issue in terms the blue-collar jury could well comprehend. No one was going to prove that I'd injected an insulin overdose into my wife. No one.

Would the jurors buy Martinovich's argument after they heard the witnesses testify? I squirmed in my chair. The waistband on my trousers was already drenched with sweat, twenty minutes into day one. As Martinovich sat down next to me, a wide bead of perspiration cascaded off my forehead onto the table in front of us. Martinovich pulled a pushed a box of tissues across the tabletop in my direction. He flipped his legal pad to a blank yellow page, and wrote, "Relax. You look like there's a torpedo up your ass."

"Nervous," I wrote, as I wiped the moisture off my face.

Martinovich patted my hand, and winked at me. "We will win," he wrote, and then he underlined the word win.

The first witness for the prosecution was Gina Littlefoot, the nurse who'd worked Alexandra's appendectomy case. I hadn't seen Gina since that day. She looked a decade older—grayer, more wizened, and very serious. She sat bolt upright in the witness chair. Gina wore a royal blue dress with a silver heart-shaped necklace across her slender neck—her look sleek and professional. Perhaps she'd made a special shopping trip to Minneapolis or Duluth to pick out her outfit. In Gina's world, this was her brush with celebrity.

James Hamilton said, "Ms. Littlefoot, you were the nurse in the operating room when Dr. Antone put his wife into her final coma, is that true?"

"Objection. Unfairly prejudicial," Ed Martinovich said.

"Let me rephrase," Hamilton said. "You were the nurse in the operating room when Dr. Antone anesthetized his wife, is that true?"

"Yes."

"How would you describe the interaction between them before she went to sleep?"

Gina didn't hesitate. "The interaction was cold and impersonal. I couldn't believe they were married to each other, from the way they acted. I tried to chat with Mrs. Antone, to help her relax. Dr. Antone did none of that. He ignored her at first. He looked through her medical chart, and spent time preparing his anesthesia equipment and his medications. After that, Dr. Antone talked to her for maybe two minutes about the risks of the anesthesia. Then he put her to sleep. You had no inkling that they were a couple. There… there was no affection between them."

I didn't look over at the jury, but I knew they must be studying me, curious about my reaction to these accusations. What kind of man could put his wife to sleep for surgery without any sign of affection? Was this the sort of man who could take marriage vows to a woman and later anesthetize her into eternal sleep? Was Dr. Nico Antone the sort of monster that could premeditate his wife's murder?

"Did you witness Dr. Antone injecting drugs into the patient's IV?" Hamilton said.

"I did," Gina said.

"Did you know what he was injecting?"

"No. No one ever does. Only the anesthetist knows what he's injecting. I mean, people can read the chart later to see what was injected, but in real time I had no idea what drugs he was using."

"Did you witness anyone else inject any drug into the patient?"

"Absolutely not. No way. No one else had an opportunity to do that."

"How many individuals were in the operating room during the surgery?"

"There was Dr. Perpich, Dr. Antone, myself, and Heidi the scrub nurse. Four. That's all."

"Did anyone else approach Alexandra Antone during the time she was asleep?"

"No. No one."

"Thank you. I have no further questions."

Hamilton sat down, and Edward Martinovich approached the podium for his cross-examination. "Ms. Littlefoot," he said. "How many times have you worked with Dr. Antone as the anesthesiologist?"

"I don't know. Maybe forty cases."

"Were there any complications during any of those cases?"

"Not that I recall. Not until this one."

"Very well. Is it your understanding that Alexandra Antone became brain dead due to an extreme low blood sugar concentration?"

"Yes."

"And is it your understanding that Alexandra Antone had an extreme low blood sugar concentration because she had an overdose of insulin in her system?"

"Yes, I heard that's what the lab tests showed."

"Did you witness Dr. Antone inject insulin into Alexandra Antone's IV that day?"

"Like I said, it's not standard for me to watch or monitor every drug the anesthesiologist injects. I wasn't watching everything he did. I mean, I was doing my job as a circulating nurse."

"Let me repeat the question. Did you see Dr. Antone make an insulin injection during the surgery?"

"I was busy charting and handing sterile supplies to the surgical team. That's what my job was."

"Let me repeat the question again. Did you see Dr. Antone make an insulin injection during the surgery? A yes or no answer, please."

"No."

"I have no further questions, Your Honor."

Gina Littlefoot returned to her seat in the gallery. As she walked past me, she looked straight down at the floor tiles in front of her. Gina had shown extraordinary composure on the witness stand, but now that she was done, she looked as if she was about to break into tears. I felt sorry for Gina. She hadn't done anything wrong. Gina Lightfoot had been dragged into the quagmire of this case by bad luck. She just happened to be in the wrong O.R. on the wrong morning.

Hamilton stood again and said, "The prosecution would like to call its first expert witness, Dr. Thomas Zender."

An ancient figure, a curled up Yoda of a man, hobbled toward the witness stand with the aid of a cane in each hand. Dr. Thomas Zender wore a coarse tan corduroy jacket over a wine-colored cardigan sweater. He took the oath with his head cocked, as if straining to hear the words.

Hamilton's first question was, "Dr. Zender, can you describe your training and expertise to us?"

"Certainly," the old man answered. He turned away from Hamilton, and faced the jury face on. His tone was grandfatherly and sage. "I'm the chairman of the Endocrinology Department at the University of Minnesota Medical School. I've been a practicing endocrinologist for 49 years. My research interests are in the field of diabetes medicine."

Zender continued for twenty minutes, revealing the details of his long and distinguished career—the hundreds of articles he'd written, the textbooks he'd authored, the medical journals he'd edited, and the boards he'd served on. Hamilton made sure the jury knew that Zender was one of the foremost experts in diabetes medicine.

After Dr. Zender stopped his well rehearsed, choreographed script, Hamilton said, "Based on your 49 years of practice and your experience teaching at the University of Minnesota, can you explain to the jury what happened to Mrs. Antone?"

Dr. Zender swiveled to face the jury box again. He licked his lips, and Grandpa Zender became a very hungry and very clever wolf about to feast. "Her lab tests were very specific. She had the lowest blood sugar level I can ever recall. She had a markedly high insulin level and a near-zero level of C-peptide. The triad of a low blood sugar, a high insulin level, and a low level of C-peptide is diagnostic of an injected insulin overdose."

"Slow down for us here, Doctor. Can you explain again how you know this was an injected insulin overdose?"

"Yes. Insulin causes blood sugar levels to go down. In this case, an extremely high insulin level caused the fatal low blood sugar." He paused there, to let this simple fact settle in to the jurors' minds.

"One questions whether the insulin overdose was from the patient's own body, that is, from her own pancreas, or whether the insulin came from outside her body." He paused again, until several of the jurors nodded their understanding. "The C-peptide level is how doctors determine where the insulin came from. C-peptide concentration rises with the body's own insulin production. A high C-peptide level with a high insulin level means the body is manufacturing excess insulin. A low C-peptide level like Mrs. Antone had, with a high insulin level, means the insulin came from outside the body."

"Tell us what 'from outside the body' means."

"It means that insulin was injected into the patient."

"Dr. Zender, can insulin be inhaled?"

"Yes. Recently the Food and Drug Administration approved an inhaled insulin, but only metered doses of 4 to 8 units of insulin can be delivered via the lungs. These small doses of inhaled insulin could never cause the extreme hypoglycemia found in Alexandra Antone's bloodstream."

"So it is your expert opinion that the insulin overdose was injected?"

"Yes."

Hamilton nodded in assent. He surveyed the jury. There were no looks of confusion. Dr. Zender had explained the topic in language anyone could understand. Now it was time to turn the discussion toward causation.

"How does low blood sugar produce brain death?" Hamilton said.

"Brain cells need oxygen to survive, and brain cells need glucose to survive. Deficient in oxygen, or deficient in glucose, brain cells will die."

"And after they die, can they be replaced?"

"No. When brain cells die, there is no back up. The brain dies."

"Were there any other abnormal laboratory values in Mrs. Antone's blood?"

"No."

"Any low oxygen levels?"

"No."

"Could anything else have caused her brain death?"

"No. There was no other explanation for her brain death."

I covered my eyes with my left hand as the ping-pong game of easy questions and damning answers continued between Hamilton and Zender. I wanted to shrink into a puddle of primordial slime on the floor under the table. The pen in my right hand had a mind of its own, as it doodled concentric swirls on the blank yellow legal pad in front of me. If only Dr. Zender would acquire a sudden case of Alzheimer's or perhaps die of natural causes before he nailed me any higher up the wall.

Hamilton concluded his dance with Zender, and turned the podium over to Martinovich for cross-examination. My attorney's first question, the key question in this trial, forced me to drop my pen and stop doodling. "Dr. Zender," he said, "In your expert opinion, when was the insulin administered to Alexandra Antone?"

"By all accounts, the patient's brain function was normal prior to her general anesthetic. Following the surgery she was hypoglycemic and brain dead. The insulin had to be administered after she went to sleep."

"Do you have a theory as to how it was administered?"

Zender pushed his lower lip skyward, almost touching the tip of his nose. "I can't be certain, but to push her blood glucose level as low as 2 mg/dL, it had to be a very large dose of insulin. In all probability it was injected intravenously."

Martinovich raised the amplitude of his voice into a shout, a resounding call that rivaled any Baptist preacher calling to the Good Lord on Sunday morning. "Is it possible, Dr. Zender, that the insulin could have already been present in the patient's IV prior to the time she was asleep?"

Zender blinked, unfazed by the question. "I'm doubtful of that."

Martinovich dropped the volume in his voice, and adopted the sternness of a high school principal interrogating a truant. "Let me rephrase my question. If someone injected a lethal dose of insulin into Alexandra Antone's IV bag before Dr. Antone arrived, is it possible that the patient could have been normal and awake prior to the anesthetic, but be brain-damaged once the insulin was infused during the anesthetic?"

"In my opinion, no," Zender said.

"I have no further questions at this time, Your Honor," Martinovich said. He sat down next to me and wrote, "The man is a bold-faced liar."

I was dismayed. The possibility that the insulin was present in Alexandra's IV before I arrived that morning was the central thesis in our defense strategy. Zender had pooh-poohed the notion as untenable, and Martinovich had let him get away with it.

Zender stepped down. Mr. Hamilton said, "For the next witness, the prosecution would like to call Dr. Jillian Ayers."

Dr. Ayers strode to the front of the courtroom. She was a thin woman dressed in a baggy cream-colored suit that hung on her bony frame like a slack sail from a yardarm. I knew her by her reputation as a professor of anesthesiology at the Mayo Clinic. I'd read dozens of papers she'd authored in the medical literature. Dr. Ayers was a well-trained academic and a formidable foe. Today she appeared cheery and self-assured. For her it was just another day answering questions in a courtroom—just another day collecting her expert witness fee of $700 per hour.

"Dr. Ayers, can you please tell the jury about your qualifications as an expert in anesthesia," Hamilton said.

"I attended college and medical school at Johns Hopkins in Baltimore. I did my anesthesia residency training and subspecialty training in neurosurgical anesthesia at the University of Chicago. I joined the staff at the Mayo Clinic 18 years ago, and I've been on the faculty there since that time."

Like Dr. Zender, Dr. Ayers spent twenty minutes recounting her considerable professional accolades for the jury, and droned on and on until it seemed as if she was God's advisor during the Creation.

At the conclusion of her speech, Hamilton said, "Very well. You've had time to review this case and form an expert opinion?"

"I have."

"Can you explain to the jury what happened to Alexandra Antone?"

"Before the surgery, the patient had a normal mental status and a normal blood sugar level of 88 mg/dL. Per the chart, the patient received 9 different injectable medications in the operating room before, during, and after the surgery. All the drugs were standard agents used during general anesthetics. All the drugs were given in standard concentrations."

"Could any of these drugs affect the blood sugar concentration?"

"No."

"Based on the anesthetic record of medications that were administered, when would you have expected the patient to awaken after the surgery?"

"There is variability among individual patients, but I would expected the patient to regain consciousness within 10 minutes."

"And based on your medical expertise and your review of the records on this case, why did the patient not regain consciousness?"

"Her blood glucose level was severely low. The lowest I've ever seen, in fact."

"We've already heard testimony from endocrinologist Dr. Zender that the low blood glucose level was the probable cause of her brain death. In your opinion, when did the patient receive this overdose of insulin?"

Dr. Ayers sniffed and nodded three quick times in succession, as if this was an elementary question that any first grader could answer. "It had to be sometime after the induction of general anesthesia and before the end of surgery."

"And how could the insulin have entered her body?"

"Insulin can be administered either subcutaneously or intravenously."

"Please explain to the jury what those terms mean."

"Subcutaneously means the injecting needle is inserted just under the surface of the skin. This is the way most diabetics introduce insulin into their own bodies. Intravenously means the injecting needle is inserted directly into a vein. Doctors in intensive care medicine sometimes use this method to treat diabetes."

"And what is a typical dose of insulin used to treat diabetes or hyperglycemia?"

"A typical dose would be from five to fifty units of insulin subcutaneously, or five to ten units intravenously."

"From your review of Mrs. Antone's chart, was there any mention of insulin being administered to her on that day?"

"No."

"Was there any medical reason to administer insulin in that operating room on that day?"

"No. Mrs. Antone was not diabetic, and she did not have an elevated blood sugar."

"Dr. Ayers, how is insulin packaged?"

"The most common package is a 10-milliliter vial."

"How many units of insulin are in such a vial?"

"The typical concentration of insulin is U-100, which means that there are 100 units of insulin per milliliter. A 10-milliliter vial would hold 1000 units of insulin."

"Dr. Ayers, you testified that a typical dose of insulin is five to fifty units, correct?"

"Yes."

"Have you ever administered 1000 units of insulin, an entire vial of insulin, as a single dose to one patient?"

"No. Never. No one would. One thousand units would be a massive overdose."

"And if 1000 units of insulin were injected into Mrs. Antone as a bolus, could that explain Mrs. Antone's low blood sugar of 2 mg/dL?"

"Yes."

"Would the patient show any signs of hypoglycemia if she was under general anesthesia?"

"No. The typical symptoms of hunger, shakiness, lightheadedness, sweating, confusion, or weakness would be masked by general anesthesia."

"You've read the coroner's report and the police report on Mrs. Antone's death?"

"I have."

"Then you're aware that no empty insulin vial was found anywhere in the operating room following the case."

"Correct."

"Do you have an opinion as to where the insulin came from?"

"Insulin is a standard medicine in every hospital. It's not a controlled substance like morphine or Valium that has to be locked up. Dozens of doctors and nurses have access to insulin."

"Do anesthesiologists have access to insulin?"

"Yes. Of course."

"Do you have an opinion as to where the empty vial of insulin went?"

"Objection," Martinovich said. "Speculation. Calls for conjecture."

"Overruled," the judge said. "You may answer the question."

"Anesthesiologists throw used vials into the pharmaceutical waste container in the operating room."

"But no insulin vial, empty or full, was discovered anywhere in the operating room after the case that day."

"Correct."

"Do you have an opinion as to why there was no empty insulin vial anywhere in Mrs. Antone's operating room?"

"I do have an opinion. Whoever gave the injection was trying to hide the evidence, hoping it would never be discovered."

"And where could you hide such an empty vial?"

"Anywhere. An insulin vial is small, no bigger than the cork from a wine bottle. The empty vial could have been hidden in the pocket of a scrub shirt and flushed down a toilet after the surgery. You'll never find that empty vial."

"We heard Dr. Zender describe how insulin overdose and hypoglycemia caused Alexandra Antone's brain death. From Nurse Littlefoot's testimony, we heard that no one other than Dr. Antone injected any drugs into Mrs. Antone in that operating room."

At this point Hamilton stopped and tapped his index finger to his temple, as if he had just put all this information together for the first time. "One man doing the injecting. A low blood sugar causing brain death. With a reasonable degree of medical certainty, can you conclude that the defendant injected the insulin?"

"Objection," Martinovich said. "Leading the witness."

"Overruled," the judge said. "You may answer the question."

Dr. Ayers looked over at me, and her face contorted into a smirk of superiority. She answered, "Yes."

"Is it probable, Dr. Ayers, that anyone other than Dr. Antone injected a large dose of insulin into Alexandra Antone's IV at any time?"

She rolled her eyes. "In a word, no. When you hear hoofbeats, you look for horses. You don't look for zebras. Mrs. Antone had a normal brain prior to her anesthetic, and she was comatose afterwards. I believe in Occam's razor, the scientific principle that the simplest of competing theories is preferred to the more complex. Occam's razor tells me that the man who injected multiple anesthetics into that woman also injected the insulin. Blaming the disastrous outcome on anyone else is absurd. There are no data indicating that anyone else can be blamed for the patient's death. None."

Hamilton nodded and raised one eyebrow, as if the whole case were being explained to him for the very first time. He seemed pleased. "Thank you, Dr. Ayers. I have no further questions."

Edward Martinovich stood, his hands splayed wide on the table before him. He boomed out, "Dr. Ayers, you have examined the medical records from Hibbing General Hospital. Correct?"

"Yes."

"Can you point out any specific evidence in the medical record that documents that Dr. Antone injected insulin into this patient?"

"As I just said, one can infer..."

"I'm not asking for inference here, Doctor. I asked you a specific question. Is there a page in the medical record that documents that Dr. Antone injected insulin?"

"No."

"Is it possible that someone other than Nico Antone injected insulin into Alexandra Antone's body?"

Dr. Ayers scowled in contempt. She furrowed her brow, and a frown blossomed across her angular face. "Anything is possible. In my expert opinion, to a reasonable degree of medical probability, the anesthesiologist is the only one who could do this."

"Dr. Ayers, were you there in the operating room in Hibbing, Minnesota the day of Mrs. Antone's final surgery?"

"No, I was not."

"Then you are cannot be certain who injected that insulin, can you?"

Even from across the room, I could see her pulse bounding in the temporal artery bordering her forehead. Her heart was rocketing at 160 beats-per-minute or more. Dr. Ayers looked like she was ready to explode like a Roman candle on the Fourth of July. Still she did not answer.

"You cannot be certain who injected that insulin, can you?" Martinovich boomed once more.

"With a reasonable degree of medical certainty, my opinion is that Dr. Antone injected the insulin."

Martinovich glared back at her. He'd asked the question twice. He chose not to ask it a third time.

"I have no further questions at this time, Your Honor," he said.

A wave of nausea overtook me. Martinovich had made both Dr. Zender and Dr. Ayers uncomfortable, but he'd failed to discredit the testimony of either expert. I checked the jury for their reaction at this point in the trial, and my heart sank. Of the twelve jurors, one was yawning, another was looking at his watch, a third had her eyes closed, and the rest of them were staring at the opposite wall in various states of boredom. These twelve men and women held my future in their hands, and they looked like they couldn't wait to leave the room for a cup of coffee and a smoke.

Hamilton took the stage again, to stack the next brick in the prosecution's wall. In a circus hawker's voice, he announced, "I call the prosecution's next witness, Mr. Frank Demitree."

The Neanderthal-like hulk that was Beard Man lurched across the courtroom toward the witness stand. He'd cleaned up his act. His beard was trimmed to a twelve o'clock shadow. His hair was cropped short, accentuating prominent elephant ears. He held up one substantial hand and took the oath. When he sat down he shot me a glower of disdain.

"In what capacity did you know Alexandra Antone?" Hamilton said.

"I'm the managing partner at Demitree, Greenberg, and Hawking, a law firm in Palo Alto, California. Alexandra Antone owned a major realty company in town, and I was her attorney in business matters." He sniffed and tipped his chin skyward. I could see the nose hairs inside his wide nostrils, and it made my stomach roil.

"What was your relationship with Alexandra Antone?"

"We were dating. After she and her husband separated, we began dating."

"Did Mrs. Antone ever mention her husband?"

"Not often. They were estranged, and they rarely talked. He lived here in Minnesota, and she lived in California. The only reason they were still married is that they had a child together."

"Was Dr. Antone aware that his wife was dating you?"

"He was."

"Describe how he knew that fact."

"One night last summer Dr. Antone made an unannounced and uninvited return to Mrs. Antone's California residence. He entered her home in the middle of the night and marched into her bedroom. Dr. Antone discovered Alexandra and me in bed together."

"How would you describe his reaction?"

"Insane rage. Jealousy. The man has a titanic temper. He held a fireplace poker over our heads and threatened to kill us."

"Dr. Antone threatened you?"

"He did. He said, 'For two cents I'd kill both of you right now, and no jury would convict me.' Then he smashed the bedside lamp with the poker, and stomped out the door."

I wrote on the legal pad, "That's a lie. She threw that lamp at me. I said nothing like that."

Martinovich scrolled back, "It's his word against yours. Impossible to refute what he claims. Damage is done. He's planted the idea in the minds of the jurors that you are a violent person."

Hamilton continued the questioning. "Why did Mrs. Antone come to Minnesota during the last days of her life?"

"Her son Johnny got his girlfriend pregnant. Alexandra loved her son very much. She wanted to be there for him. She was very scared and protective of her son's emotions about this pregnancy. Alexandra was worried that Johnny's dad was going to disown his son over it."

I'd heard enough. I blurted out, "You're a liar!"

Judge Satrum slammed down his gavel and said, "Dr. Antone, you will remain silent or I will remove you from the courtroom."

Martinovich put his lips against my ear and said, "Control yourself. You're hurting us big time. You need to be quiet as a totem pole."

I bit my lip and said, "I'm sorry, Your Honor."

The judge said, "Please continue, Mr. Hamilton."

"When was the last time you spoke to Alexandra Antone?" Hamilton asked Demitree.

"She called me just one hour before her appendectomy surgery. Alexandra was very upset. She was very scared."

"What did she say?"

"Alexandra was afraid to have the surgery in a small Minnesota town. She didn't trust the medical care. There was only one anesthesia doctor in the whole town that day, and that was Nico Antone. She was afraid he might still be carrying a grudge against her about the bedroom scene."

"How scared was she?"

"Alexandra said to me, 'I'm afraid Nico might try to harm me during the surgery and make it look like an accident.'"

"Objection. Hearsay," Martinovich said.

"Sustained," the judge said. "The jury will disregard the last statement."

Hamilton faced the jury, raised both eyebrows, and raised both hands palms up as if to say *I believe the man.* He turned to Judge Satrum and said, "I have no further questions, Your Honor."

I scribbled a note to Martinovich in hasty cursive, "The man is a lying bastard. You need to prove to them that he's lying."

Martinovich patted my hand, and strode toward the podium for cross-examination. "Mr. Demitree," Martinovich said. "Have you ever been married?"

"Yes. I've been divorced for three years."

"During the time you were married, did you ever catch your wife and another man naked in bed together in your own home?"

"No."

"If you did catch your wife in bed with a naked man in your own home, how would you feel?"

"This was different. The Antones weren't living as husband and wife. They were separated."

"They were still married, Mr. Demitree. And the house you were sleeping in was co-owned by Dr. Antone and Mrs. Antone. How would you feel if that happened to you?"

"Objection," Hamilton said. "Calls for speculation on the witness's part."

"Overruled," the judge said. "The witness will answer the question."

"I'd be angry," Demitree said.

"Do you think you might say some aggressive things? Things you may regret later?"

"I suppose, but…"

"Did you ever see Dr. Antone hurt his wife?"

"No."

"Have you ever seen Dr. Antone hurt anyone?"

"No. I haven't been around him enough to have had the opportunity to see him hurt someone."

"Then, given the fact that anger is a normal response to finding your wife in bed with a strange man, how can you say that Dr. Antone has a titanic temper?"

"I don't know. I just know he was rageful in Alexandra's bedroom that night."

"In point of fact, despite his anger, Dr. Antone left his house without hurting either you or his wife Alexandra, didn't he?"

"Yes."

"I have no further questions," Martinovich said, his voice dripping with disgust. He returned to his seat at my side.

"Very well," Judge Satrum said, glancing at the clock on the wall. "This court is adjourned for today. We will reconvene for tomorrow's session at 9 a.m." He tapped his gavel, and departed the bench.

I watched the jury file out of the room, and said, "Ed, what will the jurors think after hearing all that?"

"Who knows?" Martinovich said. "It's Hamilton's job to build a case for your guilt. There are holes in his argument. I can't wait to start punching back." The corners of his eyes crinkled. "Don't panic, Doctor. Remember, I don't have to prove that you didn't kill her. All I have to do is create uncertainty about what happened that day. All I have to do is create a gut impression that you might not have done it." He snapped his briefcase shut, and said, "Trust me, we're going to be OK."

"Are you sure?"

He winked at me and said, "I may not be right, but I'm never in doubt. See you tomorrow, Dr. Antone."

CHAPTER 23
OH SISTER

I returned to the courtroom the next morning and steeled myself for further onslaughts against my character and innocence. My throat was so parched I couldn't conjure enough spit to swallow. Four pitchers of water lined the table in front of me.

"The prosecution's first witness today is Rebecca Turman," Hamilton said.

Rebecca Turman was a Silicon Valley icon who handled the money matters of hundreds of Northern California's wealthiest entrepreneurs. She managed the assets of the Antone estate as a personal favor to Alexandra, who'd been her close personal friend. I hadn't talked to the woman since I moved to Minnesota.

Rebecca sat primly in the witness box, her spine erect, her makeup tasteful and minimal. She wore a masculine gray wool suit and a red necktie. Rebecca was money, and she knew it. She was accustomed to Silicon Valley boardrooms. A small town courtroom was no ordeal for her.

"Mrs. Turman, can you tell the jury how you knew Alexandra Antone?" Hamilton said.

"We were old friends. She was my realtor and I was her financial advisor. Alexandra helped me purchase my home in San Francisco and my seaside ranch near Pescadero. I helped her manage her money."

"When was the last time you saw her?"

"One week before she died."

"Describe the occasion, please."

"Alexandra consulted me regarding her financial future. She was planning to divorce her husband. There was a lot of money at stake. The Antone family net worth was in excess of $90 million dollars, almost all of which Alexandra earned in her capacity as a realtor and businesswoman. In a California divorce, half the community property money, or $45 million dollars in this case, would go to her ex-husband. She wanted to know how to best protect her assets."

"And what did you tell her?"

"I recommended a colleague who is an excellent divorce lawyer and litigator."

"Did Mrs. Antone consult with this lawyer?"

"No, unfortunately she died before that meeting took place. And now that Alexandra is dead, all $90 million of their community property estate is the sole property of her husband."

"Is it possible that Nico Antone had 45 million reasons to want his wife dead?" Hamilton said.

"Objection. Leading the witness," Martinovich said.

"Sustained," Judge Satrum ruled. "The jury will disregard the last remark. Continue, Mr. Hamilton."

"I have no further questions."

Hamilton yielded the floor to Martinovich, who marched to the podium in haste. "Ms. Turman, you were the Antone family accountant, correct?" he said.

"Yes."

"And you are uniquely qualified to comment on the family's financial affairs, correct?"

"Yes."

"Are you an expert on homicide?"

"No."

"Are you an expert on anesthesia?"

"No."

"When is the last time you spoke with Dr. Antone?"

"It's been over a year since I talked to Nico."

"Do you have any idea what Dr. Antone's emotional makeup was prior to his wife's death?"

"No."

"Do you have any idea if Dr. Antone was of the mind to kill his wife?"

For the first time, Ms. Prissy Silicon Valley bean-counter-to-the-billionaire-set looked rattled. "I don't know that, no …"

"No further questions," Martinovich snapped.

Rebecca Turman's face was candy-apple-red as she left the witness stand. I snickered. She was a rich bitch, in some ways a virtual clone of my wife. I had a hard time empathizing with the woman. It felt good to see her taken down a peg up here in the sticks of Northern Minnesota.

There was a din in the courtroom as the audience discussed the implications of this latest testimony, and the stupendous money at stake. The collective net worth of every citizen of Hibbing wouldn't total 90 million dollars. The Antone estate was an unthinkable sum. Every man and woman in the jury must be wondering the same thing: Would Nico Antone kill to acquire the sole possession of such wealth? What man or woman wouldn't be tempted by such an opportunity?

Hamilton summoned his next witness. "The prosecution calls Elizabeth Scipioni."

I ground my fist into my palm. Where had they found Elizabeth? She was Dom's daughter, and I dreaded facing her again. Elizabeth had nothing to do with Alexandra Antone's murder, and yet she had the power to turn the jury against me, big time.

Elizabeth Scipioni was a petite Italian woman, four foot ten inches tall at the most, with short white hair and olive skin that looked suntanned even in midwinter. She answered the oath with quick replies, scampered up the steps, and sank into the witness box. She was so tiny that only the top two-thirds of her face was above visible above the witness box railing.

"Mrs. Scipioni, can you describe for us how you know the defendant?" Hamilton said.

"I was his sister-in-law. He was married to my sister, Angel."

A hum of whispering erupted from the gallery. All testimony to date had centered on Alexandra and Nico

Antone. There had been no mention of a second marriage. Ed Martinovich wrote "????" on his legal pad.

"This was his first marriage, prior to his marriage to Alexandra Antone, correct?" Hamilton said.

"Yes."

"And where is your sister Angel now?"

"She's dead. Nico Antone killed her."

"That's bullshit," I shouted.

"Order," the judge said. "Dr. Antone, I warned you once before. You are not to speak. Mr. Martinovich, be advised that one more outburst, one more utterance, one more audible mumble from your client and I will have him removed from the courtroom proceedings. Do you understand?"

"I do, Your Honor. It will not happen again." Martinovich gripped my biceps with a firm hand and squeezed so hard I almost screamed.

The spectators were still rumbling about Elizabeth Scipioni's bold statement. Judge Satrum pounded his gavel in a run of staccato beats until the talking ceased. "Let me make this clear," the judge said. "This is not a marketplace. This is not the corner bar or the local coffee shop. This is a court of law. *My* court of law. There will be no disruption from the gallery or the offending individuals will be escorted out. If the noise persists, I am happy to try this case without an audience."

Silence returned at once. The judge said to Hamilton, "You may continue."

"Ms. Scipioni, please explain to the jury what you meant about Nico Antone killing your sister."

"Objection, Your Honor. Irrelevant."

"Overruled. I'll allow this line of questioning, but tread carefully, Mr. Hamilton."

Elizabeth's voice quaked as she answered. "Angel married Nico at the end of high school. Angel was a beautiful girl, the finest this town had to offer. Nico was handsome and cocky. He may not have been the best boy in town, but he always thought he was. Anyways, Nico got Angel pregnant, and they had to get married. It was a shotgun wedding.

"Two months after they were married, Angel got sick. She contracted a bad cancer, a bone cancer that started in her leg bone. My parents took her down to Mayo, and the doctors there had to amputate Angel's leg to cut the cancer away. It was awful what happened to her. She was such a beautiful young girl.

"Within another two months the cancer spread to her liver. It was so sad. The doctors tried chemotherapy, but the tumor didn't respond. Angel came home. She and Nico moved into my father's house. Angel was in constant pain as the cancer spread into other bones throughout her body, so her doctors prescribed a lot of pain pills, morphine they were. She had a hospital bed in the middle of my dad's house, for hospice care. Angel was doped up all the time. Keeping her comfortable was the merciful thing to do."

"How did she die?"

"I remember the details like it was yesterday. It was a Monday night. I sat with Angel all that afternoon. She was taking the morphine pills, but she was lucid, comfortable, and in good spirits. Angel had a wonderful attitude despite the rotten cards she was dealt. I had to leave at 6 p.m., and Nico took over for me at her bedside. At 10 p.m. that night, I got a call from Nico that Angel was dead."

"What happened?"

"There was a bottle of morphine pills on the fireplace mantle next to Angel's bed. I gave her two of the pills at noon because she said she was hurting. I didn't want her to be in pain. The morphine bottle was half full when I left her that day. Four hours later, my sister was dead, and that morphine bottle was empty."

"Did your sister take all those morphine pills?"

"I'm sure she did."

"Did you ask Nico Antone what had happened?"

"I asked him. He told me Angel said she didn't want to live anymore, that because she was in tremendous pain all day long, every day, and because there was no cure, Angel just wanted to fade away. I never forgot Nico's words. He goes, 'she just wanted to fade away.' Nico said he helped her take all forty morphine tablets. Then he held her while she fell asleep and stopped breathing. Angel died in his arms."

"What was your family's reaction?"

"My sisters and I were outraged. None of us had a chance to say goodbye. The decision was made without our knowledge, and Angel was gone. I don't even know if my sister made the decision or if Nico did. He told us it was her choice, but I've always had my doubts. I think he was tired of being married to an invalid. I think Nico was ready to go back to school and leave Hibbing." She pulled a handkerchief out of her purse, and blew her nose into it with a loud, honking sound.

The glint in Hamilton's eyes showed he was pleased with Elizabeth's testimony. Still he showed compassion, and seemed empathetic to how awful an ordeal it was for her to relive Angel's death. "Thank you, Ms. Scipioni. I'm sorry for the loss of your sister."

"I think about her every day. Still." Elizabeth Scipioni started to cry, and she dabbed the white linen hanky to her eyes to wipe away the tears.

I still thought about Angel every day myself. I'd relived that last evening with Angel countless times, through thousands of sleepless nights and thousands of lonely days. Angel was so weak, so frail, and so sad. She'd lost her will to go on. I would have felt the same way. Her arms had atrophied into fleshy matchsticks. Angel lacked the strength to reach for the pill bottle. Her fingers lacked the fine-motor skills to grasp a pill. I only did what she asked. I placed each pill against the leather of her tongue and held the glass of water to her parched lips. She swallowed, and I watched. Could Angel have done it without me? No. Did I kill her? I always believed Angel killed herself, but that was my fable. I had to live with the reality that my fingerprints were on that bottle of morphine.

After Angel swallowed that mouthful of pills, I climbed into bed next to her and told her I loved her. Her reply never came. She dropped off the edge into a soft snore. Within minutes, the snore went silent, and Angel breathed no more. I cried like I'd never cried before. I prayed for Angel's soul, and I mourned the blood on my rapier.

When it was Ed Martinovich's turn to cross-examine Elizabeth Scipioni, I sensed the circumstances were difficult. The witness was vulnerable and pitiful. Any effort by Martinovich to embarrass her would be unpopular. He needed to discredit Elizabeth in some fashion without being an ass himself.

He stood up from his chair, and did not leave the defense table. He spoke in a mezzo piano voice, a sharp contrast to his cup-rattling showmanship from the day before. "It seems that Nico Antone's role in your sister's last hours isn't very clear. Was anyone else present when she died?"

"No."

"With no one else there, isn't it possible his role could have been as passive as handing Angel a glass of water and a pill bottle?"

Elizabeth Scipioni pulled the handkerchief away from her face. Her mouth hung open in a perfect O.

"Objection," Hamilton said. "Calls for speculation."

"Sustained," the Judge answered.

"Ms. Scipioni," Martinovich said, "Let me rephrase my question. What evidence is there that my client killed Angel?"

"She was alive when I left. Four hours later Angel was dead. No one else was there but him."

"Isn't it possible that your sister took the morphine overdose on her own accord?"

"I don't believe that."

"I understand that you may choose not to believe that. But answer the question please. Is it possible that your sister took the overdose herself?"

Elizabeth shook her head back and forth, back and forth, and said, "Possible, yes. Likely, no."

Martinovich said, "I have no further questions, Your Honor," and he sat down.

Hamilton stood and said, "I have no further witnesses, Your Honor. The prosecution rests."

"This court will adjourn until 9 a.m. tomorrow morning, at which time the defense will initiate its case," Judge Satrum said. One firm tap of the gavel, and the day was finished. The judge left the room.

I tried to quiet the throbbing in my head. I'd started my day as a murder suspect, but now my predicament was worse. I was now a despicable man who'd killed not one, but two wives.

Martinovich growled into my ear, "Why didn't you tell me about your first wife?"

"I didn't think it was relevant."

"Are you kidding? That testimony destroyed you. It looks like you can kill a wife like most people swat a fly. It's a hell of a hole for me to dig you out of."

"Sorry."

"What else are you hiding?"

"Nothing."

"You worry me, Dr. Antone."

"I'm not hiding anything."

Martinovich placed one hand on each of my shoulders, locked eyes with me, and said, "Either way, I'll defend you to the end of the Earth, Doctor. Remember, I'm your biggest fan. Your biggest fan." He looked at his watch and said, "I've got to go. I've got a ninety-minute drive back to Duluth. It's important that your attorney sleep in his own bed once or twice a week, you know?"

Martinovich left the courtroom, bound for his Mercedes and a warm dinner with his family seventy-five miles away on the shores of Lake Superior. I was headed for my own depressing 6 X 8-foot jail cell. I remained alone there at the defense table, and my thoughts circled back to the image of Bobby Dylan, clad in faded green scrubs, walking out of Alexandra's operating room before the appendectomy.

Martinovich needed to prove that Dylan did it, not me. Dylan also had the opportunity, the motive, and the emotional makeup to murder Alexandra Antone in the operating room that day. My defense hinged on the jury believing he was guilty.

And Mr. Dylan would take the witness stand tomorrow.

CHAPTER 24
LONG BLACK COAT

I took my seat at the defense table the next day. Judge Satrum arrived at the bench, called the court to order, and said, "Today Mr. Martinovich will begin calling witnesses for the defense. Mr. Hamilton will have the opportunity to cross-examine. Looking at the list of planned testimonies, I've formulated a timeline for this trial. I expect the list of defense witnesses to require no more than three additional days of testimony. Closing arguments will require a fourth day, and we will send the case to the jury for a verdict following closing arguments. Let us begin. Mr. Martinovich?"

I sensed the impatience in Satrum's voice. The retired hockey star's trials were said to resemble athletic events, and I could see the parallels. There were two opponents and a time clock. When that clock ticked down to zero, the buzzer would ring. My fate would be in the jurors' hands within one week. These next days would be a competition to redeem my liberty or condemn me for life, and the specter of failure terrified me. All denial was stripped away. I was powerless. All I could do was watch and listen.

Ed Martinovich stepped to the podium. Today he wore a double-breasted brown suit with a white shirt and a maroon necktie. His level of poise was reassuring. He seemed cocky and confident, born for this moment. He said, "The defense calls Dr. William Sladen as our first witness."

Dr. William Sladen was the most renowned anesthesia expert witness in the United States. The week I was arraigned, my anesthesia chairman at Stanford advised me to hire William Sladen just to prevent the prosecution from claiming him. Sladen was renowned for his intellect and his domineering courtroom personality. His nickname was "Doc

Slayer," because he laid waste to every doctor he testified against. Lucky for me, Doc Slayer was on my team.

Dr. Sladen strode down the aisle like he owned the place. He wore a trim black suit and a navy blue necktie with red Boston Red Sox *B's* in a diagonal pattern. His hair was a wonder of white waves. After taking the oath, he broke into a big smile as he descended into the witness chair.

"Dr. Sladen," Martinovich said. "Can you inform us as to your medical training and qualifications as an expert witness?"

"Of course." He turned his toothy grin on for the jury, and said, "I graduated from Harvard College and Harvard Medical School. My residency and fellowship training in anesthesia were at Massachusetts General Hospital in Boston. I am a Professor of Anesthesia at Harvard Medical School." Martinovich led Dr. Slayer through a thirty minute description of the professor's list of outstanding medical accomplishments, the dialogue designed to convince the jury they were in the presence of a man with unequaled expertise in the world of anesthesiology.

"Excellent. And what materials have you reviewed in preparation for this testimony?"

"I've reviewed Alexandra Antone's medical records from Hibbing General Hospital, including the laboratory reports and brain scans."

"Very well. Have you formulated an opinion as to what caused Alexandra Antone's brain damage?" Martinovich crossed his arms and leaned back, delighted to hand the stage to Dr. Sladen.

"Her brain damage occurred during her general anesthetic. There is no doubt about that. The glucose and insulin levels are conclusive. She died from an overdose of injected insulin."

"Do you have an opinion as to when and where the insulin was injected?"

"I don't know when or where the insulin was injected. One possibility is that Dr. Antone injected the insulin into her intravenous line during the general anesthetic, as he has been accused. But there is another credible explanation."

"Enlighten us."

"Anyone who had access to Mrs. Antone's intravenous line that morning could have injected insulin into that line."

"We've heard testimonies that no one other than Dr. Antone injected any medication after Mrs. Antone went to sleep."

"I'm aware of that. It's my expert opinion that another individual who had access to the IV prior to the anesthetic could easily have deposited a large dose of insulin in Alexandra Antone's IV bag, before Dr. Antone arrived that morning."

"Really? How is that possible?"

"It's like this," Sladen said, addressing the jury eye to eye. "Mrs. Antone had a full liter bag of normal saline solution connected to her IV line at the beginning of the anesthetic. Normal saline is salt water, similar to a solution that one might use to store their contact lenses in. Normal saline contains no sugar. The entire bag of normal saline was infused during Alexandra Antone's hour-long anesthetic. The insulin could well of been injected into the IV bag before the anesthetic, and caused the coma that was evident when she did not awaken after the surgery."

"Do you have an opinion as to who could have done this?"

"The chart documents that the nurse anesthetist Bobby Dylan brought the patient into the operating room prior to Dr. Antone's arrival. Mr. Dylan had ample opportunity to inject insulin into her IV bag during that time frame. When Dr. Antone arrived, Dylan left the room. The insulin could well have been in the IV liter bag at the time he left the room."

I was flying high with the angels in heaven as I listened to Sladen testify. The most prominent anesthesia expert witness in the United States was here in Hibbing, telling everyone that Dylan gave the insulin. For the first time in the entire trial, someone was pointing a finger away from Nico Antone.

At cross-examination, Hamilton asked Dr. Sladen, "How much are you being paid to testify on Nico Antone's behalf?"

"I'm not being paid to testify on Dr. Antone's behalf. I'm being paid for my opinion."

"Yes, I see. And how much are you being paid?"

"I charge $10,000 a day plus travel expenses for a court appearance."

"Ten thousand dollars. That's a lot of money. How did you select that rate?"

"My rates are consistent with the hourly attorney fees in Boston, Massachusetts where I live and work. When I testify as a legal expert, I always charge the same rate as a first-rate attorney charges in my home town."

"And your expert opinion is that someone killed Alexandra Antone with an insulin injection, correct?"

"Correct."

"As an expert witness, is it your job to tell the jury who injected the insulin?"

"No. I wasn't there. I have no idea who injected the insulin."

"Correct. You were not there. Then how can you be sure that nurse anesthetist Bobby Dylan injected the insulin that day?"

"I am not certain that Bobby Dylan injected the insulin. It's only a theory."

"Only a theory. Dr. Nico Antone spent more than an hour in that operating room with Alexandra Antone during the anesthetic and surgery. Would you agree that Dr. Antone had the opportunity to inject insulin during that time?"

"Yes."

I frowned. Sladen's testimony was growing weaker by the second. He was looking more and more like some elite overpaid East Coast snob. *Come on, Harvard Doc. Stick your neck out a little, and stoke the fire of Dylan as the murderer.* I checked the expressions on the jurors' faces, and they weren't smiling. They didn't like Sladen. I could understand, because I didn't like the guy either. His big-city smugness was a major turnoff in this little mining town. Sladen laid the groundwork for our assault on Bobby Dylan, but he was smelling more and more like dirty underwear. I was ready for our highbrow East Coast expert to go away as soon as possible.

After Sladen stepped down, Martinovich shuffled through his list of witnesses and said, "The defense would like to call Johnny Antone."

I spun around toward the gallery seats behind me to marvel at the sight of Johnny walking down the center aisle. His eyes were fixed straight ahead at Judge Satrum. I hadn't seen my son for so long that I'd forgotten what a beautiful human he was. His hair was slicked back behind his ears in a style that made him look more like a GQ model than a high school kid. He wore a slim dark sport coat and a skinny black necktie. He was dressed to the nines for this nefarious occasion. It made my heart ache—it was as if Johnny was on trial as much as I was.

It was a controversial move, calling Johnny to the stand. He wore a lot of different hats in this trial: he was the son of the accused, the son of the deceased, and a Hibbing General Hospital operating room employee who was working on the day of his mother's surgery. All three of these roles made Johnny integral to the defense case.

As soon as Johnny was sworn in, he snapped his head erect and stuck out his jaw in defiance. He still hadn't ventured a look in my direction. Martinovich began with a series of questions that established Johnny's identity as the son of both the victim and the defendant. Then the footing grew stickier. "Can you describe your mother's mood when she arrived in Hibbing, one day before her surgery?"

"She was angry," Johnny said.

"Angry at whom?"

"Mom was angry at everybody. Angry at Echo because Echo wouldn't have an abortion. Angry at me because I got my girlfriend pregnant. Angry at Dad because he brought me to this town."

"Were you angry at her?"

"Not really. I mean, I didn't like the way she was screaming at everyone, but I'd heard her yelling a million times in my life. I'd gotten numb to it."

A million times indeed, I thought.

"Why did you move from California to Hibbing?"

"To switch high schools. Hibbing has an outstanding high school. My Dad graduated from Hibbing High."

"Don't they have outstanding high schools in California?"

"Yes, they do."

"Isn't it true that you and your father moved here so that your college application would come from Hibbing, Minnesota, instead of from Palo Alto, California?"

"Yes. We thought there would be less competition for me to get accepted into a top college if I graduated from a small town in Minnesota."

"Why didn't your mother move to California with you?"

"Mom couldn't move. Her job was selling real estate there."

"But your father relocated. And he had a job at Stanford Medical Center that he left behind, correct?"

"Correct."

"Can you describe your relationship with your father?"

Johnny looked over at me for the first time. I forged the smallest of smiles. *Come on, Johnny. Tell them how close we were.* "Dad and I were good before Mom's death," he said. "Dad would do anything for me."

"Have you ever seen your father act with violence toward your mother?"

"No way."

"Have you ever seen your father act with violence toward to anyone?"

"No."

"Have you ever seen your father threaten to harm your mother?"

"No."

Martinovich moved to a different topic. "Do you have any family or friends who are diabetic?"

"Yes. My girlfriend, Echo Johnson, is diabetic."

"Does Echo use insulin?"

"Yes. She wears an insulin pump every day."

"Who does Echo live with?"

"Echo's parents are separated, and she lives half of the time with her mom and half the time with her dad."

"Can you tell the court who Echo's dad is?"

"His name is Bobby Dylan."

"The same Bobby Dylan who was briefly your mother's nurse anesthetist?"

"Yes."

"Echo must have a supply of insulin somewhere. Did you ever see her vials of insulin at the home of either of her parents?"

"No."

"Did you ever look inside the refrigerator at either of Echo's houses?"

"Yes."

"Did you see vials of insulin there, inside the refrigerators?"

"I don't recall."

"OK, let's shift gears. Did you see your mother at the hospital on the morning of her surgery?"

"Yes. I went into the operating room to greet her, right before she went to sleep."

"She was awake?"

"Mom was sleepy, but awake. She knew who I was."

"Who else was in the room with you?"

"Dad, the operating room nurse, the surgical tech. And Echo."

"Why was Echo there?"

"She's an orderly at the hospital, just like me. I wanted to see Mom, and Echo joined me."

"Did you get close to your mother's body in the operating room that morning?"

"I gave her a hug."

"Did you inject any drug into your mother prior to her surgery?"

Johnny expanded his chest and snorted, "No. I did not."

"Did you see Echo inject anything into your mother prior to the surgery?"

"No way. That's ridiculous. She's an orderly. She never gets close enough to a patient's IV to do that. And besides, Echo would never do anything like that." Johnny's face turned crimson. He was flustered and there was nowhere to hide.

"Did you see Bobby Dylan at your mother's bedside at any time?"

"No. By the time I arrived in the operating room suite, my dad had taken Mr. Dylan's place at my mother's bedside."

"Can you describe your mother's emotional state in the minutes before she went to sleep?"

"She was doped up. High. She wasn't mad anymore."

"And your father's emotional state?"

"Dad was very professional. He gave me time to connect with my mom. He didn't rush me out of the room."

"Did he seem unusual in any way?"

"He was calm. Dad was all business, and he showed no emotion at all."

"Was he at all nervous?"

"No."

"Was he angry?"

"Not at all. He was as unflappable as ever. Cool, calm, and on task."

"Very well. Thank you, Johnny. I have no further questions, Your Honor."

It was Mr. Hamilton's turn at the podium. He focused his stare on a spot on the ceiling above Judge Satrum's bench while my son waited in silence on the witness stand.

Hamilton began the cross-examination by asking, "Johnny, did your father love your mother?"

Johnny said, "I don't know. Ask him. They were separated, so they didn't get along that great."

"Did your father's feelings toward your mother influence his decision to move to Hibbing?"

"I think so. They fought a lot. One night back in California he told her, 'I'm sick of you, and I'm sick of our bogus marriage.' The next day he and I agreed to move to Hibbing."

"Johnny, were you aware your father was having an affair with Lena Johnson?"

"Yes."

"Did your father ever talk about divorcing your mother?"

"Not to me."

"Did he talk about marrying Lena Johnson some day?"

"No."

"You said that when your mother arrived in Hibbing, she was angry at Echo, angry at you, and angry at your father. Was your father angry at your mother in return?"

"Dad wasn't very happy to see her show up in Hibbing. Mom was spitting venom when she arrived. She started drinking at 6 a.m., five minutes after she walked through our front door."

"Did they argue that morning?"

"They always argued. Mom blamed Dad for everything. She hollered so loud the walls shook. She said it was all his fault, my getting Echo pregnant and all. I was upstairs, and I heard Mom say something like, 'You're the one who let Johnny hang out with some trailer-trash Iron Range girl who isn't smart enough to swallow a birth control pill once a day.' Dad screamed back, 'You were in bed with some bearded stooge the last time I saw you.'"

"Let me ask you again," Hamilton said. "Was your father angry at your mother, the day before the surgery?"

Johnny looked over at me again. Had he betrayed me by sharing all this? I nodded to him. All he was doing was telling the truth under oath. Johnny sighed and said, "Yes, my dad was angry. He was pretty mad at Mom the day before her surgery."

"Very well," Hamilton said. "I have no further questions."

Johnny's eyes looked glazed and opaque as he left from the witness stand. There were no further looks in my direction. He wasn't seeking my approval or my validation. Johnny's journey through the gallery was a militaristic march that ended as he blew past the rear door and out of the courtroom.

I emptied my lungs. It had sucked, seeing my son on the stand, and he'd done nothing to establish my innocence. Johnny shared that I was a competent father. He described me as calm and professional prior to the anesthetic, but he'd also confirmed that I was an angry husband. Johnny had not seen Bobby Dylan at his mother's bedside. He had done nothing to establish Dylan's guilt.

Johnny's testimony hadn't helped me one bit. Johnny's testimony was a bust.

It was time for Bobby Dylan to answer some tough questions. I'd waited four months to watch Ed Martinovich joust with my enemy. At last we'd have Dylan where we needed him: under oath, exposed, and with nowhere to hide. Our defense strategy was built on Dylan's proximity to Alexandra's death. Our defense strategy was built on the possibility of Bobby Dylan's guilt. For me to look good, Dylan had to look bad, and he was going to look bad today.

Martinovich stood and said, "The defense calls Mr. Bobby Dylan."

Dylan appeared at the rear of the courtroom. He wore a blank sneer as he ambled past us. He was a caricature of superiority and self-righteousness. Dylan wore a pendulous knee-length black coat, an open-collared white shirt, and no tie. When he sat down in the witness box he erupted into a fountain of nervous mannerisms. Dylan ran his fingers through the orb of his fuzzy gray mane, rubbed his nose, and pulled on the wisps of his thin moustache. He closed his eyes and kept them shut, as if to dismiss himself from the reality of the courtroom in front of him.

"Mr. Dylan, you're a nurse anesthetist, correct?"

"Yes."

"And you were at work at Hibbing General Hospital the morning of Alexandra Antone's surgery, correct?"

"Yes."

"How much time did you spend attending to Mrs. Antone on the morning of her surgery?" Martinovich said.

"I never attended to Mrs. Antone," Dylan said. His eyes remained closed. I could see his eyeballs circling behind the lids; the thin layer of skin cells a flimsy barrier protecting him from Martinovich.

"We've heard testimony that you were alone with her in the operating room."

Dylan's eyes sprang open, black beads floating in bloodshot whiteness. He said, "I told you, I never took care of her. I was scheduled to be Mrs. Antone's anesthetist, but when I met her in the preoperative room, she refused to consent to me as her anesthetist."

"What did you do at that point?"

"Nothing much. I brought her to the operating room as a favor to Dr. Perpich. Dr. Perpich had a bug up his ass to keep things moving along so he could get to his son's hockey game in Duluth that afternoon. I didn't do a damn thing to Alexandra Antone. I left her there in the operating room when her husband arrived. The woman was awake and neurologically intact when I left her."

"Did you start her intravenous line?"

"I did not. She already had an IV in place when I met her. It was started in the Emergency Room before she arrived at the O.R."

"Did you inject anything into Alexandra Antone's IV?"

"No. I injected nothing into Mrs. Antone."

Martinovich was calm, his icy stoicism a marked contrast to Dylan's twitchy behavior. Martinovich had anticipated this denial. His work today was to entice Bobby Dylan into a blunder, a gaffe, or a misstep that would expose his guilt. "Were you upset at Alexandra Antone before you met her?" he said.

"Hell, no. I'd never seen the woman before the day of her surgery. Her husband Nico used to tell me that she was a pain in the ass. My daughter Echo told me Mrs. Antone was nasty and threatening the night before her surgery. Both Nico and Echo were right. Mrs. Antone was bitchy and condescending when I met her. I can't say that I liked her much, but I didn't care enough about her to be angry."

"Were you angry at Nico Antone on the day of his wife's surgery?"

Dylan shrugged, and didn't answer right away. "No," he said. His countenance suggested the truth was less monosyllabic.

"Mr. Dylan, how would you characterize your relationship with Dr. Antone?"

"We used to be friends."

"You used to be friends?"

"That's right."

"What ended your friendship?"

"He was boffing my wife. I didn't like it and I told him so. It wasn't cool, what he did to me."

"Were you jealous about that fact?"

"I didn't like it. This here's a small town. Lena and I are separated but not divorced. Nico knew I still cared about my wife. Did it bother me that my so-called-friend was sleeping with my wife, and that he concealed that fact from me? Yes, it did."

"Dr. Antone's son impregnated your 17-year-old daughter. Were you angry about that fact?"

"Yes, I was upset about the pregnancy."

"When Dr. Antone's wife Alexandra showed up in Hibbing, she requested that your daughter get an abortion. Is that true?"

"Yes."

"How did you feel about that?"

Dylan cocked his head to the left, and donned a look of deep introspection. "I didn't like the abortion talk. I'm morally opposed to killing babies. But I see where you're going with this. Even if I didn't like Alexandra Antone or her views on abortion, I'd never try to kill her."

"You and Dr. Antone had similar jobs at the hospital, correct?"

Dylan scowled. "No, that's incorrect. We had the same job."

"But he's a physician and you're a nurse anesthetist."

"So what? I could do everything he could."

"People call him 'Doctor.' Does anyone call you 'Doctor?'"

"No."

"Were you jealous about Dr. Antone's job superiority over you?"

"No. Like I said, I could do anything he could."

"Dr. Antone gets paid a lot more than you do to do the same work. Is that true?"

"That's true. It makes no sense to me, but it's true."

I listened, spellbound. Dylan was confirming a broad spectrum of negative emotions toward Alexandra and me—each emotion a potential motive for killing Alexandra and framing me. I looked at the jury, and they were more engaged than they'd been at any point in the trial. Two white-haired ladies in the front row were wide-eyed. A freckle-faced ginger in row two was stroking his chin. Their civic duty had turned into a legal thriller.

"The evidence and testimony to date indicates that someone injected insulin into Mrs. Antone," Martinovich said. "Do you have insulin in your house, Mr. Dylan?"

"I do. My daughter takes insulin every day. She keeps it in the refrigerator."

"Do you have access to that insulin?"

"Access?"

"It's not locked up, is it?"

"No."

"You could remove it from the refrigerator at any time, if you chose to. Correct?"

"Yes."

Martinovich stepped over to our defense table, where he'd earlier hung an IV bag and intravenous tubing from a metal pole. "Your Honor, I'd like to ask permission to wheel this IV pole across the floor to where Mr. Dylan and the jury can inspect it at close range."

"Proceed," Satrum said.

Martinovich pushed the IV line on its pole toward the witness stand. "Mr. Dylan, is this IV setup similar to the what you use in the operating rooms at Hibbing General?"

Dylan leaned forward and inspected the equipment. He rolled the intravenous line in his fingers, and said, "Yes. It looks like our equipment."

"What about this rubber nipple at the bottom of the IV bag? What is this nipple used for?"

"We can use that nipple as an entry port to inject medications into the IV bag."

"You just poke the needle through the nipple and inject the medication into the bag. Correct?"

"Yes."

"Did you inject any medication into Mrs. Antone's IV bag?"

"I already told you. No."

"Did you inject anything into her IV line?"

"I already told you. No." Dylan looked like he wanted to drive his fist through Martinovich's eye socket.

"Could you have injected insulin into the liter bag when no one was paying attention?"

"I did not inject anything into her or into her IV."

Martinovich chewed on the inside of his cheek, and squinted at the witness. Then he went for the jugular. "Is it true that you spent one year in a South Carolina VA hospital inpatient psychiatric ward?"

"Yes."

"Why?"

"I had some issues after my tour of duty in Afghanistan. They called it Posttraumatic Stress Disorder. I just had a hard time coping with life stateside. I got treatment. I'm OK now."

"You're OK now. Mr. Dylan, what is your real name?"

As if a switch had flipped, Dylan turned from a determined adversary into a vibrating mass of tics once again. His eyebrows bounced. His tongue lashed across his upper lip. The fingers of his left hand fidgeted with his ear. At last he answered, "My name is Bobby Dylan." His reply was bold and confident. There was no shortage of bravado.

"Were you born with that name?"

"No. I changed my name."

"Why did you change your name?"

He picked at his nose. "Because I wanted to. People change their names every day."

"Are you are the same Bob Dylan who recorded hundreds of songs and sold millions of albums?"

Dylan's eyes narrowed. It was such a simple question— an obvious trap. There was no way this nurse anesthetist in a Northern Minnesota mining town was the world famous rock and roll legend. Every soul in the courtroom, every soul on Earth knew that. Yet Mr. Dylan sat silent, as if solving a mystery.

"I didn't hear your answer, sir," Martinovich said, looking toward the jury box, and seeking a bond with the jurors at this critical moment. He asked again, "Are you the Bob Dylan who recorded hundreds of songs and sold millions of albums?"

I watched with anxious anticipation. This was it. Mr. Dylan would hang himself here and now. Dylan would repeat what he'd claimed to me months earlier at the Zimmerman residence, when he'd asserted that he was indeed the famous Bob Dylan who'd toured the world. Declaring his fantasy under oath, the man would be exposed as a psychotic dreamer and a blatant perjurer. Dylan was crazy, a man capable of snuffing out Alexandra with an insulin overdose.

Everyone would realize this as soon as Mr. Dylan answered
the question.

Mr. Dylan opened his mouth and said, "No. I'm not the
same Bob Dylan who recorded and sold millions of albums."

The words fell as a roundhouse hook to my jaw. Mr.
Dylan did not establish himself as insane. He'd somehow
separated himself from his delusional world. His claim that he
was the famous rock star was supposed to be the tipping
point in this trial.

But Dylan had not acted psychotic.

"I have no further questions," Martinovich mumbled,
looking sallow and confused. He sat down next to me and
wrote on the yellow pad, "That went well."

"Went well?" I wrote. "He was supposed to come across
as psychotic. That didn't happen."

Martinovich wrote, "Let's talk after."

Hamilton began his cross-examination. "Mr. Dylan, did
we hear you testify that you never injected any medication
into Alexandra Antone's IV at any time?"

"Correct. I injected nothing."

"Did you inject any insulin?"

"No. I did not."

James Hamilton said, "Thank you, Mr. Dylan. I have no
further questions."

The brevity of the cross-examination shocked me, but it
made sense. Hamilton didn't want Bobby Dylan to appear
guilty. Hamilton needed to make the jury forget Bobby Dylan,
and the best way to do that was to get rid of him. Bobby
Dylan shuffled his way from the witness box toward the
gallery. He shook his head and grimaced as he walked past
Martinovich and me.

Martinovich leaned into me and whispered, "We're in
good shape, Doctor. Dylan stunk up the courtroom. He
reeked of guilt, and made the neon "Reasonable Doubt" sign
flash on and off at a thousand candle watts. He owns a
refrigerator full of insulin, and he's a jealous cuckold who was
alone with the deceased minutes before the surgery. Dylan's

our case. The jury can sense it. Now it's your turn. I want the jury to see you as a loving husband and healing physician who wouldn't step on an ant—a refreshing contrast to Mr. Dylan the mental patient."

"But Dylan didn't come across as a delusional mental patient."

"Are you kidding? The man was a mess on the stand. Trust me, we're in good shape. Now it's your turn. Our fine jurors can't wait to hear the sound of your voice." Martinovich stood and said, "The defense calls Dr. Nico Antone to the stand."

My fingers were icicles as I laid my hand on the Bible. I took a discerning look at the witness chair as I walked toward it. The seat was a collection of wooden slats assembled at 90-degree angles. The rose-colored seat cushion was faded and worn, polished by hundreds of men and women who'd sweated their way through their ordeal under oath. I'd waited months to tell my story. It was time to paint my version of the facts into a pastel landscape twelve jurors would find comfort in.

I folded my hands and awaited the first question. Martinovich promised he'd pitch nothing but lob balls across the middle of the plate so I could hit home run after home run. Our job was to convince the jury I was a model citizen and an intelligent, honest, and trustworthy physician.

Mr. Dylan sat in the last row of the gallery. Now that he'd finished testifying, he was no longer banned from the endgame of the trial. Dylan's scowl was gone, and he had a bemused look on his face.

Martinovich commenced the interrogation. "Dr. Antone, can you tell the jury about your education and medical training?"

I faced the jury and made eye contact, as Martinovich had instructed me. He advised me to converse with them as if we were all sitting around the fire at a ski lodge—to imagine I was telling them an interesting story. I tried to follow his advice, but my body was rejecting the notion of the ski lodge.

My body knew it was on the hot seat in a courtroom. With my hands folded in front of me, I could feel the pulsations of my radial artery at the wrist. My heart rate was nearing 180 beats per minute. My hands were tremulous, but I controlled my vocal cords and made a cogent reply. "I'm a local boy. I was born here in Hibbing. I graduated from Hibbing High School."

"You were an excellent student. Is it true that you were accepted to Harvard for college?"

"That's true."

"But you didn't enroll at Harvard, correct?"

"Correct. I got married to my first wife, Angel. As was described earlier in this courtroom, Angel became pregnant, and we decided to stay closer to home and get married."

"Can you tell the jury about your education after you left Hibbing High?"

"Yes. I completed four years of college at the University of Minnesota at Duluth, four years of medical school, also at the University of Minnesota at Duluth, then a one year internship and four years of anesthesiology training at the University of Minnesota in Minneapolis."

"That's a great deal of education. Where did you work after you left the University of Minnesota?"

"I moved to California where I did subspecialty training in cardiovascular anesthesia at Stanford. I was on the Stanford anesthesia faculty for ten years before I moved back to Hibbing."

Ed Martinovich beamed, proud to be talking to Hibbing High School's most over-educated graduate. "I think the jury would agree with me that you are a highly trained, intelligent man, Dr. Antone. If you planned to overdose your patient Alexandra Antone with insulin, if you were to drive her blood sugar to near zero and thrust her into a fatal coma, would you expect such a misdeed to be discovered?"

"Of course. There would be no way to conceal that sort of crime. If I did this crime, if any anesthesiologist did this crime, he or she would be caught as soon as the blood test results were revealed. Only the stupidest doctor in the world would believe this was an effective way to murder someone."

"Thank you, Doctor. I agree with you. Can you describe to us what happened prior to Alexandra's surgery that day at Hibbing General Hospital?"

"Sure. It was a Saturday, and I was off duty. I was asleep when my wife called me on my cell phone and asked me to come to the hospital to give her anesthesia for her appendectomy."

"Was it your plan to be her anesthesiologist that day?"

"No. It was her idea. Alexandra demanded that I take care of her. I was not on call, and I had no intention of giving anesthetics that day."

"So you were not scheduled to attend to her?"

"I was not."

"The day before, you had no knowledge that Alexandra was to have emergency surgery the following morning. Is that true?"

"Yes."

"Is it even remotely possible that, prior to her phone call, you could have been planning to murder her that day?" Martinovich teased out the syllables to the word "remotely" over several seconds, emphasizing the absurdity of the notion of premeditated murder.

"No, it's not possible I could have planned to murder her."

"When the surgery was scheduled, the scheduled anesthetist was Bobby Dylan. Correct?"

"Yes."

"And your wife told you on the phone that she wanted you to take care of her, instead of Mr. Dylan?"

"Correct."

"Why did she want you to take care of her?"

"She had two reasons. Number one was because Dylan was not a doctor. He's a nurse anesthetist. Alexandra did not trust him or his skills. The second issue was that our two families were in the midst of a major conflict. Our son

Johnny had gotten Mr. Dylan's daughter Echo pregnant. Alexandra was adamant about Echo getting an abortion, and Mr. Dylan was strongly anti-abortion."

"Did you agree to do the anesthetic at that point?"

"No. I refused. I tried to arrange for another anesthetist, but there were no others in town. Then the surgeon, Dr. Perpich, talked to me on the phone and pleaded with me to do the case so he could take out the appendix before it ruptured."

"And so you came in to the hospital for this unplanned, emergency anesthetic. When you arrived at the operating room, what did you find?"

"I found Mr. Dylan in the operating room, attending to Alexandra, awaiting my arrival."

"Did he have an opportunity to inject insulin into Alexandra Antone's IV bag before you arrived?"

"Yes. I've thought about that question a thousand times, because Alexandra received an insulin injection from someone, and I wasn't the one who gave it to her. Mr. Dylan had the opportunity to inject a very large dose of insulin into Alexandra's one-liter IV bag of fluid before I got there. She was awake with a normal blood sugar before I anesthetized her. During the hour she was asleep, I infused the entire liter of IV fluid, which is standard anesthetic care to keep the patient hydrated. This liter of fluid must have contained the lethal dose of insulin. Mr. Dylan knew I was coming in. He knew how easy it was to set me up, to frame me."

"Why? What would be his motivation to frame you?"

"He hated me. He was angry because I sleeping with his wife, even though they were separated and their marriage was over. He was angry because my son impregnated his 17-year-old daughter, and had in Dylan's words 'ruined her life.' He was angry because we had similar jobs at the hospital, but because I'm a physician and he's a nurse anesthetist, I got paid a lot more to do the same work. And Mr. Dylan was angry at my wife, who showed up in Hibbing hurling insults at his entire family and demanding that his daughter get an abortion, which Dylan was morally opposed to."

"Did he ever display violent behavior toward you?"

"Yes. On a partridge hunting trip two days before Alexandra's surgery, Mr. Dylan confronted me about my affair with his wife. He pointed a loaded shotgun at me, and said he'd taken me on the hunting trip out into the woods with the intention of shooting me. Dylan said, 'hunting accidents happen all the time. It would be that easy.'"

"And what did happen on that hunting trip?"

I looked over at Mr. Dylan in the gallery. He was still sporting that faraway smile, as if my entire testimony was a bizarre hoax dreamed up by a desperate defendant. His flippant body language made me more determined to pin the murder on him.

"Nothing happened. Dylan changed his mind, and he let me go. I got out of there as fast as I could, and I never saw him again until the day of Alexandra's surgery."

"Dr. Antone, did you kill your wife?"

I took a deep breath. "No. I did not."

"Dr. Antone, did you inject a bolus of insulin into your wife while she was anesthetized?"

"No. I did not."

Martinovich broke into a warm, fatherly smile, and said, "Thank you, Dr. Antone. I have no further questions." He left the podium and took a full twenty seconds to walk back to his seat. I knew Martinovich wanted my last sentences to hang in the air like the final chords of a symphony. We needed the jury to believe those final sentences, and it was crucial those words had ample time to sink in.

I was feeling more relaxed now, as blissful as I'd felt in any minute since the legal proceedings began. It was therapeutic to tell my story to the jury. My guilt was drifting away like smoke from a bonfire. Every single juror must know that Mr. Dylan was the true suspect.

Compared to Martinovich's languid exit, Mr. Hamilton's jaunt to the podium was swift and agile. He began the cross-examination by asking, "Dr. Antone, were you planning on divorcing your wife?"

"I hadn't made a decision. We were living apart, but no one had filed for divorce."

"Did you have hopes to reconcile your marriage? To get back together?"

"No."

"In fact, you had a serious girlfriend, correct?"

"I was dating someone. Yes."

"And that someone was Lena Johnson, correct?"

"Yes."

"And you were sleeping with Lena Johnson, correct?"

"Yes."

"In fact, you were in bed with Lena Johnson just hours before you anesthetized your wife for her emergency surgery. Is that true?"

"Yes." I wriggled in my seat, my bliss pulverized and my palms drenched with sweat.

"Did you and Lena Johnson ever talk about a future together?"

"Not much. We enjoyed each other's company. We tried to stay in the present. To enjoy the friendship we had."

"Dr. Antone, how much was your salary as an anesthesiologist in Hibbing?"

I sucked in a quick breath. I didn't welcome this line of questioning. "My income varied," I said. "It varied with how many cases I did each day, and on how many days I worked."

"Can you give me an estimate, Doctor? An approximation of the income from your Hibbing job?"

"It would be in six figures. I might make $250,000 a year."

"We've heard testimony that your wife's business interests were very valuable. In fact, that her net worth was in excess of $90 million dollars. Do you recall that testimony?"

"Yes."

"Did your wife start her company after she was married to you?"

"She did."

"Were you aware that her company was community property, that is, that the company belonged to both of you?"

"Yes."

"Were you aware that you would be sole owner of your wife's property if your wife were to die?"

"I… I wasn't sure about that. I'd have to ask a lawyer."

"Ninety million dollars is a lot of money, isn't it, Doctor?"

"Yes, it is."

"It's a lot more money than $250,000, your yearly salary, isn't it?"

"Yes," I hissed. I hated Hamilton right now. I wanted to reach out and squeeze his doughboy neck until his bloodshot eyes bugged out of his head.

"We heard testimony that you are highly educated, Doctor. If I do the math correctly, I figure 13 years through high school, 4 years of college, 4 years of medical school, and 6 more years of internships, residencies, and fellowships after med school. I've got you down for 27 years of education. Does that sound right, Doctor?"

"That's about right, yes." At least he'd stopped grilling me with incriminating questions. He was acknowledging my intellect, and I warmed to it. Perhaps the worst was over.

"Would you say all that training made you a smart man? A highly educated doctor?"

"It did."

"You learned a great deal about many diseases, didn't you?"

"I did."

"You learned a great deal about diabetes, didn't you?"

"I did." My fists tightened. He was about to twist everything, and I had no alternative but to spar with him.

"You learned expertise about many drugs in your training, didn't you?"

"I did."

"That would include an expertise in the drug insulin, correct?"

"Yes."

"Anesthesiologists sometimes need to use insulin on their patients, correct?"

"Yes."

"Why do anesthesiologists give insulin to patients?"

"When diabetic patients have elevated glucose levels, we give insulin to decrease the blood sugar."

"When do you give this insulin?"

"It depends. Sometimes it's before surgery, sometimes it's after surgery, and sometimes it's in the operating room during surgery." I was trying my best not to let him trap me into damning admissions, but the questions were so simple that no anesthesiologist could lie in answering them.

"In your career, how many times have you administered insulin to a patient?"

"I don't know. Too numerous to count."

"So on any given day, if you were to inject insulin into a patient, it could be part of an anesthesiologist's routine day."

I leaned forward and barked at him, "I would never inject insulin unless the patient was diabetic. I would never inject insulin unless the blood sugar was significantly elevated. There's no way I'd inject insulin into any other patient." A bead of sweat rolled across the bridge of my nose. I wiped my sleeve across my face, and tried to steady myself.

A bemused smile crossed Hamilton's face. He knew he was getting to me, and he was enjoying my ordeal.

"Where would you find vials of insulin at Hibbing General Hospital?" he said.

"They would be in the refrigerator at the nursing station. They always keep insulin refrigerated."

"And do you have free access to that refrigerator?"

I sighed. "I do. But so do a lot of people. Every nurse and physician in the operating suite can go in and out of that room."

"We've heard testimony that Lena Johnson's daughter Echo is an insulin-dependent diabetic. We've heard testimony that there are vials of insulin in the refrigerator in the

Johnson's kitchen. Have you ever looked inside the refrigerator in the Johnson's home?"

"Yes."

Have you seen the insulin in their refrigerator?"

"I don't recall." My heart rate jumped. I'd just lied under oath. I slowed my breathing, and prayed I could hide my guilt.

"You never saw insulin vials at the Johnson house?"

"Correct."

"Dr. Antone, when did you discover you were going to have the opportunity to give your wife anesthesia for her appendectomy?"

"When Alexandra called me from the hospital in the middle of the night and asked me to take care of her. And as I already testified, I refused to do the anesthetic. I didn't want to take care of her."

"But Alexandra called you back, right? She didn't take no for an answer, right?"

"That's right. She refused to let Bobby Dylan give her the anesthesia. Alexandra put Dr. Perpich, the surgeon, on the phone, and he pleaded with me to come in. So I did. It wasn't my idea."

"Where were you when you received that phone call?"

"I was at Lena's house."

"Did you sleep with Lena that night?"

"I did."

"Could you have removed insulin from the Johnson refrigerator that morning?"

"I told you I never saw any insulin there."

"But you were in the same house as Echo Johnson's insulin supply? That morning?"

"I didn't touch their insulin." I was breathing fast and shallow. My heart was thumping. The faces in the courtroom behind Hamilton blurred into a blur of brown and gray. I couldn't look at the jury at all.

Hamilton everted his lower lip in a doubtful pout. "Doctor Antone, how much time elapsed between that phone call, the phone call that established that you would have the opportunity to anesthetize your wife, and the actual beginning of the anesthetic?"

I bristled. "I wish you'd stop calling it an 'opportunity.' It wasn't an opportunity, it was just an anesthetic. Only an anesthetic."

"Very well. How much time elapsed between when Dr. Perpich convinced you to do the anesthetic, and the actual beginning of the anesthetic?"

"I talked to Perpich about 6 a.m. The anesthetic started at about 7:30, so it was about an hour and a half."

"So you had ninety minutes. An hour and a half. What did you do with that time?"

"I got out of bed, got dressed, and went back to my house. I had breakfast with my son, then he and I drove to the hospital together." I cringed. It all sounded so awful. What kind of father sleeps at his girlfriend's house, and then goes home and has breakfast with his teenage kid, who had been at home alone?

"Was ninety minutes enough time to plan the anesthetic?"

"I guess so."

"Was it enough time to plan an intentional insulin overdose?"

"Objection," Martinovich bellowed. "Argumentative and badgering the witness."

"Sustained," said Judge Satrum.

Hamilton seemed unfazed. He let a full minute tick by before he offered up his next question. "Did you give your first wife an overdose of pills, Dr. Antone?"

"No. I did not."

"We've heard testimony that the pill bottle was empty at the hour when she stopped breathing. Did you watch her take an overdose of pills?"

I ground my teeth together. Couldn't they just let Angel sleep in her grave? "Yes. I was with her at the end."

"So you were there with your wife as she took in the excesses of medication that ended her life?"

"I was there with her. Yes."

Hamilton's eyes narrowed. "So we agree that you were there with your wife as an excess of medication ended her life. Now which wife are we talking about, Dr. Antone? Angel, or Alexandra, or both of them?"

"I'm talking about Angel," I said, leaning toward Hamilton. "Only Angel!"

"I have no further questions, Your Honor," Hamilton said, and he retired to the prosecution table.

I stood from the chair and made my way across the courtroom. I tried to keep my head high, my shoulders back, and my countenance indifferent, but inside I felt like an abject failure. How could all my years of education culminate in this wretched mess?

Martinovich asked permission to approach the bench, and he and Hamilton conversed with Judge Satrum. After the attorneys stepped down, the judge said, "The defense has requested a recess and a break in the trial until Monday morning. I deplore delays, but I've heard their request and have acquiesced. This court will reconvene at 9 a.m. on Monday. I remind the jurors that they are not to discuss this case with anyone, or read anything about it." He tapped his gavel once, and left the room.

Martinovich approached me, and exhaled a mighty breath. "I asked for a recess because we need to regroup, Doc. That was ugly. I never second-guess myself, but it would have been better if we'd never put you on the stand. Hamilton made you look guilty. We need a weekend off to help the jury forget those last answers. I need to rethink my strategy."

"I didn't mean to get rattled up there. I couldn't help it."

"Forget it, Doctor. It's over. Next week we'll make it all better. We have to."

CHAPTER 25
MY BLUE-EYED SON

That weekend the worlds of the Antone and Johnson families scraped bottom once more, while I sat rotting in jail oblivious to the events outside. At dawn I was scratching the stubble on my chin and replaying every sentence of the prosecution's case against me. After another sleepless night, I understood why people got hooked on downer drugs. I could not relax. I heard an iron gate creak outside, and my guard announced, "You have a visitor."

"This early? Who is it?"

"He says he's your son."

A visit from Johnny? I sat bolt upright.

"The young man is waiting in the visitation room."

What had changed? Johnny had spurned me for months, and now he showed up uninvited? Whatever the reason, this was the best news to come my way since I'd been locked up.

Johnny's hair was tousled in wild disarray and his lips were cemented into a troubled frown. He denied me a smile or any sense of fond reunion. It had been four months since our last conversation, and everything was different. How could he be comfortable, divided from his father by bulletproof glass?

"Thanks for coming, son. It's good to see you."

The dam broke, and Johnny burst into tears. "It's not good, Dad. It's so terrible. Echo's in the hospital. They won't let me in to see her. I've got no one now."

My mouth hung open. "What happened, son? What happened to Echo?"

"She crashed in her dad's fucking snowmobile. She's all messed up, maybe dying. The doctors said she bled into her abdomen. I don't know any more than that. The surgeon— your buddy Perpich—took Echo into the operating room. I had to wait outside in that same stupid waiting room where I waited during Mom's surgery. They won't let me see her. I'm so scared. Mom is dead. You're in here, and I'm all alone in the world. Lena can't help me. She said I should come and see you."

Johnny wiped his wet cheeks with his shirtsleeve. He raked his fingers through his hair as the words poured out. My heart was breaking. At a time when my son needed me more than ever, the Great Wall of Glass divided us. There could be no hugs, no touch, and no shoulder to cry on. All I could do is listen, and his news sucked the breath out of me.

"I'm sorry, son," was all I could say.

"Oh, Dad, what if I lose her forever?" He dropped his face onto the tabletop and covered his head with his arms. "My life is shit. Just shit."

I closed my eyes. After all the horrors I'd lived through in the past few months, I never dreamed it could get worse. Watching my son melt in front of me was unbearable. "Johnny, I love you."

"I don't care, Dad. That doesn't help right now." He buried his face in his hands and rolled his head back and forth. "What am I going to do?" He sneered at me. "I want to be with Echo. Only Echo. Don't you get it?"

"I do, but…"

"It's not fair. I'm only 17 years old. I have no mother. I have no father. All I have is Echo and Lena."

"You still have a father."

"What, like this?" He waved his hand at the barren visitation room. "For a twenty minute visit in a jail room? You're no good to me in here."

"I will get out of jail."

"When? In fifty years?"

"No. Soon. After the trial."

"Don't think so, Dad. I've been following the newsfeeds on the Internet. You're cooked. You were in the operating room alone with Mom. You hated her. You wanted Mom's money. You killed your first wife. It's all there. You're cooked."

"Son, I need you to know two things about me and forget all the other static. One, I love you. And two, I did not kill your mother."

Johnny rubbed his shirtsleeve across his face, and dried his eyes. "I believe number one. I wish I could believe number two."

"You need to believe me, and you need to hang in there. I'm sure Lena will continue to take care of you. She needs to be there for Echo right now. Can you go back to Lena's house? That's still the best place for you. She'll look out for you until I get out of here."

"You're never getting out of here, Dad."

"Have a little faith, Johnny."

"Whatever faith I had is gone. I don't know what I'm doing here. You can't help me. I've gotta get out of here." Johnny spun around and stomped out of the room. I watched the door slam behind him, and I felt more empty than ever. Johnny had returned, tantalized me with his presence, and left me without a promise.

I returned to my windowless room, and feared that nothing would ever be the same. I couldn't shake the sorrow in Johnny's voice. My son was an eighty-year-old in a teenager's body. He'd dealt with a lifetime of loss in one lousy winter.

Poor Echo. The prospect of motherhood at age 17 was a stark predicament, but motherhood was a trifling inconvenience compared to a critical snowmobile crash. What if she died?

What about Lena? She'd kept both Johnny and Echo above water since Alexandra's death. She'd taken in Johnny as if he was her own son, and attended to his every need. What if Echo died? Would Lena still accept Johnny as a surrogate son?

Lena visited that afternoon, and my concerns were validated. She looked sallow and moribund. She wore a white sweatshirt with the hood pulled up. Furrows I'd never seen creased her forehead and circled her mouth. She leaned back in the chair and distanced herself from me. Her gaze flickered about the room and her eyes refused to focus on me.

"Johnny was here this morning," I said. "He told me about Echo. How is she?"

Lena shook her head and said, "She's in the ICU. She's alive, but it was awful."

"What happened?"

"It was Bobby, that shithead. He and Echo had a blowout argument about Johnny, and she ran out of his house. Echo didn't have the car keys, so she jumped on his snowmobile and headed west out of town. She lost control on a trail east of Hibbing and rammed into a tree. The paramedics brought her to the hospital, and Dr. Perpich operated on her. Her asshole father gave her the anesthetic. Can you believe that?"

"Jesus. Couldn't somebody else take care of her?"

"Bobby was on call, and no one else was available. It was lunacy. Echo runs away from him, and yet Bobby winds up sticking a tube down her throat at one o'clock in the morning."

"What were her injuries?"

"A ruptured spleen and a torn uterine artery. Dr. Perpich said if he hadn't clamped off the blood supply to the uterus, she would have bled to death. She needed a ton of transfusions, but she'll survive."

"What about the pregnancy?"

"Gone. All gone. And all future pregnancies are gone. They had to take her uterus out. She was bleeding that much."

"What? They did a hysterectomy?"

"Yep. Can you believe that?"

I was blown away. Beautiful young Echo, sterile at age 17? Unthinkable. Anything I said would only trivialize the damage. I stayed silent and waited for Lena's next move. The seconds passed, and I grew more worried. Lena would take this loss hard.

"It's like God is punishing us," she said at last. "For everything."

"I'm so sorry."

Lena Johnson said nothing more. She wiped her eyes with a handkerchief, turned her back on me and left me there alone.

CHAPTER 26
ASK NICO …

A third unexpected visitor arrived the following morning. On the freedom side of the Plexiglas barrier sat none other than Mr. Bobby Dylan. On this Sunday morning he wore a black bolero, a long black suit coat, a white shirt and a razor-thin scarlet necktie. His eyes were swollen and red.

There was no one I was less interested in seeing. "Why are you here?" I said.

"I won't take up much of your time," he said.

His words were absurd to me. Who had more time than a man in prison? I had nothing but time. "Why are you here?" I repeated.

"To set things straight. My daughter almost died yesterday. Because of you, she's still alive."

I frowned. The man was as bizarre as ever. "What are you talking about?"

"Echo was in an accident. She blew out her spleen and her uterus."

"I know."

"She lost the pregnancy."

"I heard."

"She lost 80% of her blood volume before she got to the operating room. Her blood pressure was unobtainable on arrival. My own child was my surgical patient, and she was dying. I had to keep her alive, and I couldn't think straight. In my mind's eye I saw the newspaper headline: 'Anesthetist loses his daughter in operating room disaster.' It was gonna be like what you went through, giving your family member an anesthetic and watching them die in front of you."

"It sucks."

"I ordered up that Massive Transfusion Pack you developed for the Blood Bank. I gave her the MTP, and it worked. I pumped in the 6 units of blood, the fresh frozen plasma, and the platelets as fast as I could, and we saved her. Echo lost the pregnancy, she lost her womb, but she didn't lose her life. I didn't lose my daughter. And I'm here to thank you."

"I did nothing."

"My daughter is alive. She's alive because of what you taught me. From this point forward, everything has changed for me. I feel different about you. I cannot hate you. I'm sorry I said all those things about you in the courtroom. It says in the Bible, 'Do not judge, and you will not be judged. Do not condemn, and you will not be condemned. Forgive, and you will be forgiven.' Luke 6:37."

I didn't buy any of it. I didn't trust the guy. "What you're saying doesn't change anything. I still think you killed Alexandra. I still think you hate my guts because I slept with your wife." It felt good to say it to Dylan's face.

"I couldn't care less about you and Lena at this point. Me and Lena were done. I was doing ladies all over this town. I was a hound, and you moved in on my ex. So what, man? So what?"

"So you trashed our friendship, scared the hell out of me in the woods, killed my wife and framed me. Then you had a fight with your daughter, and she ran off and crashed your damn snowmobile into a tree. You feel guilty as hell about everything, and I don't care. Will you get out of here? I can't stand looking at you. Your apology can't bust me out of jail. You're the one who should be inside here, not me. I should be out there in the real world, lying in bed with your wife."

Dylan's face darkened. "That's mean, Nico."

"I don't care. Fuck you, Bobby." I spat at the Plexiglas, and the gob hung there between us. He shook his head at me and said no more. He pushed back his chair and left the room. I pulled my shirtfront out of my pants and wiped the spit off the window. I felt stupid. I'd acted the part of a low-life prisoner to the max, but I was pissed off, and I deserved to be.

One hour later, Johnny surprised me by visiting a second time. He looked calmer and steadier. This time he wore a button-down blue Oxford shirt and khaki pants—full prep school regalia—an abrupt change from his customary tee-shirt and gym clothes. I liked the wardrobe upgrade. I didn't even know he owned clothes like that.

"How's Echo doing?" I said.

"She survived, but she can't stop crying. No one wanted to have a baby right now, but now that Echo can't ever have one, she's devastated. It's awful."

"There's nothing you can do but be kind and supportive. She's going to have to grieve."

"It's all my fault," Johnny said.

"No, it's not. You didn't wear a condom, and Echo got pregnant. That's the extent of your involvement. You didn't make her argue with her dad, and you didn't make her jump on that snowmobile."

Johnny pulled a piece of paper out of his pocket, and said, "I came here today to show you something. It came in the mail last month, but I wasn't talking to you then. Take a look. It's what you wanted." He unfolded the paper and pressed it up against the Plexiglas between us.

I squinted to read it in the dim light. It was a letter addressed to John Antone, dated December 10th. The first sentence of the letter read,

The Admissions Committee of Harvard College is pleased to inform you that you have been accepted in the Early Action Program for admission next fall.

I read no further. "Wow, Johnny, this is incredible. I didn't even know you'd applied to Harvard."

"How could you know? You're stuck in here. I just took care of business myself. My counselor convinced me to apply to Harvard. My grades were at the top in my Hibbing class, and my SAT scores were great. The curling helped. How many top applicants are curling champions from Minnesota? But none of that was enough. Remember you told me once, that it takes a gimmick to get into a top college?"

"Right."

"I had a gimmick no one else could match."

"What was that?"

"You. Mom. September 9th. Our family is famous, or infamous. My essay was about what happened that day, the worst day of my life, and how it changed me. I wrote about the intense feelings I had, how I got through it, and how I'm a better man for it."

My joy vanished. His Harvard acceptance letter was written in blood.

The corners of Johnny's mouth turned up. "See? I'm just like you, Dad. First, the teenage pregnancy, and then the admission letter to Harvard."

"Look at me. You don't want to be me. Are you going to Harvard?"

"Hell, yes. I'm not you."

"I'm proud of you."

"Do you think Mom would finally be satisfied?"

"I'm sure she's smiling up in heaven."

Johnny closed his eyes for a long moment, and blinked back tears. When he opened them and said, "There's one more thing, Dad. Something kind of weird. I got this bogus text message today, but it's really for you."

"Who's it from?"

"I don't know. It's from some local number I've never heard of."

"What does it say?"

"Let me read the thing, so I get it right." He took out his phone and pulled up the text. "The message says, 'Ask Nico where the cefazolin went.'"

"It says what?"

"'Ask Nico where the cefazolin went.' What's cefazolin?"

"It's a drug."

"Does the message make any sense to you?"

"Not really. I'll have to think about it."

Johnny glanced at the clock on the wall, and he sighed. "I gotta run now, Dad. I'm glad I saw you, I guess."

"I'm always glad to see you. Come visit as often as you can. Congratulations on Harvard. You've got what it takes, son." I flattened both of my hands against the glass. Johnny matched them, his fingers mirror images of mine. He couldn't conjure a smile. He folded the letter into his pocket.

Back in my cell, I flopped onto my cot and stared at the stained acoustic tiles of the ceiling. Echo crying in an ICU bed, the Harvard letter, Johnny's fingers against the glass—each of these pictures spun through the Instagram of my mind. A year ago, I'd have given anything to see my son marching toward success beneath a Harvard Crimson banner. It'd been the Antone family quest, to move to Hibbing and beat out tens of thousands of faceless high school kids from around the U.S.

I tried to make sense of the mysterious text message. *Ask Nico where the cefazolin went.* I obsessed over every syllable of the curious sentence. In my mind I saw a small window off in the distance—a weathered pane of stained glass, cracked open no more than a millimeter. That crack... that seam... admitted a sliver of light into my darkness. What if there was a clue, buried somewhere in the hundreds of pages of Alexandra's medical records? It was a long shot, but I had to pursue it. There was so little time.

I banged on the bars of my cell, and cried out, "Guard! Guard! I need to speak to my attorney."

CHAPTER 27
IT WAS NEVER SUPPOSED TO BE LIKE THIS

I found my seat at the defense table on Monday morning. I'd envisioned the conclusion of this trial for months, and now that it was here, I was as panicky as a man blindfolded before a firing squad. I'd watched Ed Martinovich preen and pontificate without success in this courtroom for days. It seemed he was driving me headlong into the brick wall of a guilty verdict and life imprisonment. I'd go to jail, and Ed Martinovich would take a long vacation to Florida.

After Johnny's visit I asked Martinovich to deliver the volumes of Alexandra's medical records to me, and I stayed up all night rereading every page with new eyes. My salvation had to be somewhere in those pages. I met with Martinovich this morning, and together we scripted our agenda for the courtroom day.

Behind me, Bobby Dylan sat in the same seat he'd chosen for the last session. He appeared unruffled after his bitter meeting with me the day before. The skinny man was in rare couture this morning, decked out in a red flannel shirt and bib overalls. He wore a yellow farmer's cap with the words *Mesabi Mining and Trucking Company* stenciled across the front in black script letters. As I watched, the bailiff approached Dylan and peeled the hat off the curly bush of his hair.

Johnny sat two rows behind me. He looked tense and pale. The sad saga of this awful North Country winter had ended his adolescence. Johnny made eye contact, and I was pleased to see him acknowledge me with a nod of his head.

Judge Satrum settled into his chair and the trial resumed. Martinovich stood and announced, "The defense calls Lena Johnson to the stand." Lena worked her way down the aisle, her back erect and her posture perfect. She'd undergone a striking metamorphosis. Lena wore thick mascara, blue eye shadow, and ruby lipstick. An ellipse of cherry rouge freshened each cheekbone, and her swirling silver blond mane completed a garish visual that recalled Marilyn Monroe in her prime. She wore a form-fitting black dress, adorned with the golden scarf I brought her from California.

She seated herself, and stroked her temples with the forefinger of each hand. I watched her for a sign of affection, but Lena had no interest in me this morning.

"Mrs. Johnson," Martinovich said. "We've already heard testimony that you and the defendant Dr. Antone were close friends. Can you tell us about your relationship with him?"

"We were dating," she murmured in a hushed tone.

"Mrs. Johnson," Judge Satrum said. "You will need to speak up so the jury and the court reporter can hear you. Do you understand?"

"I do, Your Honor."

"You and the defendant Dr. Antone were lovers. Correct?" Martinovich said.

"Yes."

"Did you know the deceased? Mrs. Alexandra Antone?"

"I met her once."

"Can you tell us the details of that one meeting?"

"She came to my house the day before she died. My daughter was pregnant with her son's child. Mrs. Antone wanted to talk about the pregnancy."

"Was she excited about the pregnancy?"

"No. She tried to talk us into an abortion."

"How did you feel about the abortion proposal?"

"I rejected it. She wasn't happy, and she left."

"Can you tell us where you were when you heard that Alexandra Antone was to have surgery?"

"I was at home. There was a call in the middle of the night."

"A call?"

"She, Mrs. Antone that is, called Nico on his cell phone."

"And where was Dr. Antone?"

"He was with me. Dr. Antone was at my house."

"What time did she call?"

"It must have been 5 a.m."

Martinovich paused for a long, long while, giving the jury ample time to ponder what the witness and defendant were doing together at her house at five in the morning. "And what happened at 5 a.m.?"

"Nico told her he wasn't going to do the anesthesia for her. He told her that Bobby Dylan was on call. Then he hung up."

"So Dr. Antone refused to anesthetize his wife. Is that what you heard?"

"Yes."

"If you were planning to kill someone during their anesthetic, don't you think you'd agree to do that anesthetic?"

"Objection," Hamilton said. "Speculation."

"Sustained," the judge said. "The jury will disregard counsel's last question."

Martinovich continued. "What happened next?" he said.

"I got up for work," Lena said. "I'm a nurse. My shift at Hibbing General started at 6 a.m."

"And what did Dr. Antone do?"

"I don't know. I think he went back to sleep."

"So you went to work. Did you work in Alexandra Antone's operating room that day?"

"No. I was assigned to be the float nurse that day."

"And what does a float nurse do?"

"The float nurse helps out in all the operating rooms. We give breaks and assist other operating room nurses as needed. I worked most of the morning helping out in operating room #5, where Dr. Davidson was doing colonoscopies."

"Your husband, Bobby Dylan, was the anesthetist scheduled to attend to Alexandra Antone. Did you witness him at Mrs. Antone's bedside?"

"I did."

"What time did you see him with Mrs. Antone?"

"Right after my shift began, at about 6:30."

"Did you witness Bobby Dylan and Mrs. Antone talking to one another?"

"Yes."

"What did you hear?"

"The conversation wasn't friendly. Bobby woke her up to tell her about the anesthesia, and she got pretty agitated."

"What was she agitated about?"

"I heard her say, 'You're not taking care of me in a million fucking years.'"

"She used those words?"

"She did."

"Did you witness Bobby Dylan injecting anything into her IV?"

"No. I did not."

"Can you describe the relationship between your husband, Bobby Dylan, and your boyfriend, Nico Antone?"

"Bobby hated Nico. From the moment he found out Nico and I were lovers, he was furious at Nico."

"Was Bobby furious enough to inject insulin into Alexandra Antone's IV bag? Furious enough to frame Nico Antone for murder?"

"Objection," Hamilton said. "Calls for speculation."

"Sustained," Judge Satrum said. "Do not answer that question, Mrs. Johnson."

"Was Bobby Dylan jealous of Dr. Antone?"

"Oh, yes. He was jealous because Nico was sleeping with me. He was also jealous because Nico was an anesthesia doctor, and Bobby was only a nurse anesthetist."

"Was your husband... mentally unstable?"

"He was. He spent a year in a mental hospital after his tour of duty in Afghanistan. He tells people the diagnosis was Posttraumatic Stress Syndrome, but the truth is he had a nervous breakdown."

"A nervous breakdown?"

"Yes. He was in a straitjacket for days at a time. He was belligerent and violent. The doctors wouldn't let me visit him for the first month after he was hospitalized. Bobby improved after a lot of medication and five rounds of electroshock therapy, but he's been damaged goods ever since. He always had an edge to him. He's always been a bit crazy."

"Were you afraid of your husband?"

"Yes. I couldn't live with him anymore. He scared me."

"Mrs. Johnson, let me change topics." Martinovich peered over the top of his reading glasses, and looked straight at the witness. "Mrs. Johnson, please direct your attention to the video screen, where I'm projecting a page from Alexandra Antone's medical record." The screen lit up with a black-and-white magnified copy of a document from Alexandra's chart. Martinovich said, "We're looking at a page of the Physician's Orders. Please direct your attention to order #14 in this list of orders written by the surgeon. Can you read Line #14 for us?"

"It says, 'Administer Kefzol 1 gram IV.'"

"What is Kefzol?"

"An antibiotic."

"And what does IV mean?"

"Intravenously."

"Who signed that order?"

"Dr. Perpich."

"And can you read to us the time he signed that order?"

"It says, '0610'."

"And whose initials are written adjacent to order #14?"

"The initials are L.J."

"Are those your initials?"

"Yes."

"And what is the time stamp written after your initials?"

"It says, '0620'."

"Does that mean that you administered Kefzol to Alexandra Antone at 6:20 a.m. on the morning of her surgery?"

"Yes."

"What does it say below your initials?"

"It says, 'Done.'"

"Done. What does that mean?"

"It's an indication that I gave the Kefzol, at 6:20 a.m."

"Where was the patient, Alexandra Antone, at that time?"

"She was in the preoperative area. She hadn't gone into the operating room yet."

"So even though you did not work the appendectomy surgery in Operating Room #4, you did care for Alexandra Antone on the morning of her surgery?"

"Not really. I just administered the antibiotic."

"And this was part of your assignment as the float nurse?"

"Yes."

"But you were Alexandra Antone's nurse, for this one medication. Is that true?"

"Yes."

"How did you give the Kefzol?"

"I injected the dose into her IV slowly over 5 minutes, as ordered."

"Did you talk to Mrs. Antone at that time?"

"No. She was very sleepy. She'd received morphine in the Emergency Room."

"Did you inject insulin into her intravenous bag instead of Kefzol?"

Lena jerked her head back and said, "No. I did not." She looked over at me, and said, "This is ridiculous. What are you trying to do to me now, Nico?"

I shook my head, and met her gaze. All I wanted was the truth. Lena frowned back at me, and shook her head in return.

Martinovich watched her with solemn attention for several seconds, and then said, "I thank you, Mrs. Johnson. I have no further questions at this time." Lena looked ready to explode. Her face clouded further, and I could see her chest rise and fall faster and faster as her indignation grew.

It was Hamilton's turn. The pudgy prosecutor rolled out of his chair and made a hasty approach to the podium. "Mrs. Johnson," he said. "Can you describe your relationship with Dr. Antone?"

She clenched her teeth and said, "I loved him," with loud emphasis on the word loved.

"And was it your impression that Dr. Antone loved you in return?"

"I thought he did, yes."

"Did Nico Antone ever talk about his relationship with his wife?"

"Sometimes."

"What did he say about her?"

She stared down the jury and said, "Nico told me they fought all the time. He told me that Alexandra was a bitch, and he moved to Minnesota to get away from her."

The hair stood up on my neck. *Why would she tell the jury that?*

"Did Dr. Antone love his wife?"

"Nico didn't ever say anything like that." She stopped and chose her words with care. "He didn't like her very much. He told me many times he wished she would disappear from his life."

My jaw dropped. *What was she saying? What the hell was she doing?*

"Is it possible that Dr. Antone envisioned a life with you, and wanted to rid himself of his wife?"

She cast me an evil look, and said, "It's possible, yes."

My heart was a jackhammer in my chest. My lover was dropping a noose over my neck.

"Did Dr. Antone have access to the insulin vials your daughter stored in your home refrigerator?"

"He was in my kitchen many times."

"He was in your house on the morning of Mrs. Antone's surgery. Was the refrigerator locked?"

"Of course not."

"Is it possible that he opened the door of the refrigerator and removed a vial of insulin the morning of his wife's surgery?"

Lena muttered an inaudible syllable. She closed her eyes and her head quivered in a tight vibrato.

"I didn't hear you," Hamilton said. "Is it possible that Dr. Antone opened the door of your refrigerator and removed a vial of insulin that morning? Is it possible that after he got the phone call about anesthetizing his wife, Dr. Antone removed a vial of insulin from your refrigerator and took it with him to the hospital?"

She opened her eyes wide, and blurted out, "Oh, Jesus, this is so awful I can hardly say it. The day after Alexandra's surgery, when I looked into my refrigerator, there had been a full box containing ten vials of insulin, but now the box was opened and there were only nine vials left."

Hamilton's eyes widened at his good fortune. "Nine vials? And one vial was missing?"

Lena clawed at her cheeks with her fingertips. "Yes. One vial was missing. I kept this a secret for so long, but I just can't... I can't lie, Nico. I can't." She covered her face with both hands and cried real tears.

Hamilton inhaled through a gaping mouth, raised his eyebrows in triumph, shot a lethal glance at me, and said, "I have no further questions at this time, Your Honor."

Lena stepped down and walked across the floor like a tightrope walker, her footsteps balancing on a narrow line. She looked beaten and drawn.

Lena had fried me. Any reasonable doubt had floated out the window. She'd professed love for me, and then in the same breath she'd told everyone that I wanted my wife dead and that I took the insulin from her house.

I was dead meat. Dead.

I turned to watch Lena exit through the rear door of the courtroom. Bobby Dylan turned his back on her as she passed him. Johnny watched her with a look of abject horror. After Lena walked out the door, Johnny looked over at me and shook his head in disgust.

I leaned into Martinovich, and scribbled on his legal pad, "Fuck her. Stick to the script." He nodded in assent, and I saw a gladiator's ire in his eyes. He turned around to confirm that a certain diminutive, balding, white-haired physician had returned to the courtroom. Dr. Thomas Zender was sitting one row behind us. It was a risky move, but I'd convinced

Martinovich we needed to bring back the prosecution's expert witness for further questioning. Zender had incriminated me at his initial testimony. He'd insisted the insulin could only have been injected during my anesthetic. Giving Zender a second opportunity to repeat the accusation seemed unwise, but I believed this geriatric fossil was the vital cog in my hope for acquittal.

"The defense would like to recall Dr. Thomas Zender," Martinovich said.

The courtroom was quiet as the old man took the stand. He looked so frail that I prayed the man had enough stamina to hang in there through another round of questioning. Dr. Zender leaned his two canes across the railing next to the witness chair. His eyes were distorted, warped crescents behind the Coke-bottle-thick lenses of his eyeglasses. He had a new nervous tic this morning, his neck jerking leftward every second or two, his ear approaching his shoulder in an irregular rhythm.

I leaned forward, my sweaty palms folded as in prayer. "Help me, Dr. Zender," I murmured to myself. "Be my savior this very day."

Martinovich addressed the witness with respect. "Dr. Zender, you testified earlier in this case, in this courtroom. As you recall, your testimony asserted that Alexandra Antone's brain death was attributable to an intravenous injection of insulin during her general anesthetic."

"That is correct," Zender said, his voice a coarse rasp. He reached up and adjusted his red bowtie with both hands. The tie moved from a 30-degree tilt to the right into a 30-degree tilt to the left.

Martinovich touched a button on the podium, and projected an image onto the video screen hanging on the courtroom wall. A magnified copy of Alexandra's anesthetic record appeared for all to see. Martinovich said, "Dr. Zender, this is a copy of the anesthetic record from Mrs. Antone's surgery on September 9th. In the lower right-hand corner of this form, I call your attention to the line that reads "Surgery End Time." Do you see that line?"

Zender screwed his face up, studied the video screen, and said, "Yes, I do. The surgery end time was 8:30 a.m."

Martinovich said, "Agreed. Now I'm going to show you another page from the medical record. The page on the screen is the summary document from Mrs. Antone's laboratory report from Hibbing General Hospital. Have you seen this document before?

"I have. I reviewed these lab tests in detail."

"I call your attention to the time stamp at the top left hand corner of this page, which documents the time and date when these blood tests were drawn. Can you read the date and time of these blood tests to us?"

Zender said, "The blood was drawn at 11:05 a.m. on September 9th."

"So if the surgery ended at 8:30 a.m., and these blood tests were drawn at 11:05 a.m., then two hours and thirty-five minutes passed between the conclusion of surgery and these tests. Correct?"

"Yes. The blood tests were drawn in the Intensive Care Unit, when the doctors were trying to determine why Mrs. Antone was not waking up."

"You testified in this court that these toxicology blood tests were diagnostic for an overdose of injected insulin. Do you still agree with that assessment?"

"I do."

Martinovich paused for theatric effect, and scratched his head as if mining deep thoughts. I was on the edge of my seat, waiting for the fateful confrontation. Martinovich was shuffling the deck and toying with dealing out the cards, but at the moment no one in the room was anteing up. No one had a clue where Martinovich was going. I watched the lead juror stifle a yawn.

"Let's take a closer look at the toxicology blood tests, Dr. Zender. These tests revealed a multitude of other drugs that were present in Mrs. Antone's blood, in addition to the insulin. Correct?"

"Yes."

"The patient had just finished anesthesia and surgery, and there were multiple drugs administered in the operating room. Correct?"

"Yes."

"Could you please read to us from the toxicology report, and tell us the names of all the drugs found in Alexandra Antone's bloodstream?" Martinovich said. He puffed out his chest now. He'd dealt out the cards, and he knew where the ace lay.

"You want me to read the whole list?" Zender said, with incredulous wonder.

"The whole list. Yes."

Zender adjusted his glasses, and started reading off the video screen. "The tox report shows the following drugs were present in Alexandra Antone's blood: propofol, midazolam, fentanyl, lidocaine, morphine, promethazine, succinylcholine, rocuronium, glycopyrrolate, ondanstetron, neostigmine, atropine, naloxone, meperidine and insulin. There were also trace amounts of cocaine, cannabis, and alprazolam."

Martinovich nodded in assent, and turned to face the jury. "Thank you, Dr. Zender. Let me ask you a question: do you see the drug cefazolin on that list?"

Zender scrutinized the video screen for thirty seconds, and then he said, "No. There is no cefazolin."

"Can you tell us what cefazolin is, Doctor?"

"Yes. It's a common antibiotic."

"Do you know any other names for cefazolin? Brand names?"

"Yes. Cefazolin is also known as Ancef or Kefzol."

A ripple of mumbling began in the gallery behind me. It began as a buzzing din of illicit whispers, punctuated by a low-pitched curse or two. I wanted to turn around to view the audience's reaction, but the wordplay on the courtroom floor at that moment was too riveting to ignore.

Martinovich said in a bold, theatrical voice, "Dr. Zender, if Kefzol is cefazolin, is it true there was no Kefzol in Mrs. Antone's bloodstream?"

Zender took off his thick spectacles and chewed on the earpiece as he pondered. He blinked twice, and said, "No. There was no Kefzol in Alexandra Antone."

"In your expert opinion as a pathologist and the interpreter of Alexandra Antone's toxicology report, if the blood tests show no Kefzol in her bloodstream at 11:05 a.m., could the patient have received one gram of Kefzol at any time in the preceding five hours?"

Zender furrowed his brow, and pursed his lips until the color left them. He cocked his head back and uttered the single, damning syllable, "No."

"If someone documented on the medical record that they injected one gram of Kefzol, what would be your expert opinion about that fact?"

Zender blinked hard and said, "I would say the medical record was false. No Kefzol was ever injected."

"Is it possible that insulin was injected in place of the Kefzol?"

"It is possible, yes."

I closed my eyes and bit down hard. Martinovich sat down next to me and squeezed my hand. It was Mr. Hamilton's turn to cross-examine Dr. Zender. At the prosecution table, Hamilton looked perplexed. He rose to his feet and said, "I have no questions for the witness, Your Honor."

Judge Satrum said, "Dr. Zender, you may step down."

Dr. Zender wobbled off the witness stand, and had no sooner escaped the well when Ed Martinovich said, "The defense would like to recall Lena Johnson to the stand."

Lena was ushered back into the courtroom. She floated down the aisle, her face a porcelain mask. She fingered the golden scarf as she sat down on the wooden chair. Her gaze was directed downward. The anger Lena had unleashed on me minutes before was gone. She was subdued, tranquilized, stuporous. She bit her fingernails. Lena Johnson, my lover, the changeling, would not look me in the eye.

"Mrs. Johnson," Martinovich said, "we've already heard sworn testimony from you this morning. Once again, I'm projecting a page from Alexandra Antone's medical record onto the video screen." The screen lit up with a black-and-white magnified copy of a page from Alexandra's chart. "We are looking at a page of the Physician's Orders. Order #14 in this list of orders from the surgeon, Dr. Perpich, reads, 'Administer Kefzol 1 gram IV.' Do you see that?"

"I do," Lena said in a faint whisper.

"Let me read to you from the transcript of your testimony from earlier this morning:

Mr. Martinovich: "Does that mean that you administered Kefzol to Alexandra Antone at 6:20 a.m. on the morning of her surgery?"

Mrs. Johnson: "Yes."

Mr. Martinovich: "What does it say below your initials?"

Mrs. Johnson: "It says, 'Done.'"

Mr. Martinovich: "Done. What does that mean?"

Mrs. Johnson: "It's an indication that I gave the Kefzol at 6:20 a.m."

Martinovich stopped reading. "Mrs. Johnson," he said. He glared at her. He was circling for the kill. Lena, precious Lena, was backed into a corner.

"Mrs. Johnson," he repeated. "We have a problem here. Dr. Zender just presented laboratory evidence that there was no cefazolin, no Kefzol, in Mrs. Antone's body. Where was the Kefzol?"

"I don't know."

"You don't know? According to your signature in the medical record, on which you wrote 'Done,' you injected the Kefzol into her IV at 6:20. The laboratory tests reveal insulin in her blood, not Kefzol. Mrs. Johnson, did you inject insulin into Mrs. Antone's IV bag instead of the antibiotic Kefzol?" He boomed out the question at a frightening amplitude.

"I... I think I need a lawyer," she said. "I don't want to answer any more questions."

Martinovich ignored her stammering non-answer, and went for broke. "You thought Bobby Dylan, your estranged husband, was going to do the anesthetic on Mrs. Antone. You knew that if you injected your daughter's insulin into Alexandra Antone's intravenous liter bag, the insulin would be infused during Mr. Dylan's anesthetic and you'd kill two birds with one stone. Mrs. Antone would be brain dead from the insulin and your estranged husband would be blamed because he was the one who put her to sleep. Isn't that correct, Mrs. Johnson?"

Lena's lips trembled. Her eyes were wide and wild. She pawed like a savage at the golden scarf around her neck. Judge Satrum looked down on her, his brow creased in dismay.

Satrum's got to stop this, I thought. He can't let this skewering go on. But the judge let the scene conclude, perhaps because he was as dumbfounded by the play as everyone else in attendance.

"But Dr. Antone screwed up your plan by doing the anesthetic instead," Martinovich said. "Your dream of having Alexandra Antone and Bobby Dylan out of the picture was gone. Your dream of sipping Mai Tai's on a tropical island with Nico Antone at sunset was gone. Instead, Nico Antone sits in this courtroom accused of murder, a crime that you committed. Am I right, Mrs. Johnson?"

Lena looked at me for the first time. Tears poured down her cheeks and she said, "I'm so sorry, Nico. It was never, never supposed to be like this."

She was right. It was never supposed to be like this.

CHAPTER 28
THE ROAD NOT TAKEN

Seven months later

I spent so much time locked behind the steel bars of the St. Louis County Jail that I'd memorized the smell of captive men. I memorized the cracks and texture of every wall that denied freedom. I recalled every flake of dandruff on every guard's lapel and the steady cadence of their polished boots on the cement floor. As many hours as I spent inside, I never gave a cursory inspection to the exterior of the place. On this fateful day, I ambled down the cracked concrete sidewalk, past the dandelion-invested lawn, to the gray limestone entryway to my old prison.

I signed in with the guards, accepted an insincere greeting from a familiar face or two, and followed the guard who directed me to the visitation room. As many times as I'd faced Ed Martinovich through this same bulletproof glass, and as many times as I'd endured depressing dialogue through the telephone that hung on the prisoner's side, I'd never spent one second in the visitor's chair.

"Twenty minutes," the guard said, and he stepped back into the corner of the room behind me. A door opened on the far wall, the door that separated the jail cells from the visitation room, and Lena Johnson stepped out.

She wore an ill-fitting orange jump suit that enveloped and disguised every wonderful curve of the body I still dreamed of every night. Her hair was chopped into an unkempt boyish cut. She wore pink-framed plastic eyeglasses, a dubious adornment I'd never seen before. Her mouth was creased into a tight-lipped, grim line. Lena made no attempt to smile. She didn't look sad. Hers was the face of a sphinx.

She looked into my eyes and didn't blink. I hadn't seen Lena in months, and she'd never looked worse.

"Hello," I said.

"Hello yourself," she answered. "I didn't think you'd ever visit."

"I think about you a lot," I said.

"I think about you a lot, too. They're moving me to Mankato tomorrow. They say I can't have a fair trial here."

"I heard. That's why I'm here."

We stared at each other for a long time. Her irises were tiny green dots at the end of a warped tunnel, behind the refraction of these new lenses. Her jaw hung slack. It seemed Lena had grown a second chin since I'd seen her last. She wasn't beautiful any more. She was damned hard to look at, a puppet propped up in a chair.

"Will you come to the trial?" Lena said.

I shook my head in denial. "I already sat through this trial once. I'm not up for reliving any of it. I'm here to say goodbye."

"I never loved anyone like I loved you, Nico," Lena said, with the flattest affect imaginable. Then she started to cry. I wished she would stop, but the tears kept coming, and the words poured out with them.

"It could have been so great, Nico. You and me, sitting under a palm tree in California, just like in my painting."

"How could you do it, Lena?"

"You were never going to divorce her. I was doing you a favor. The woman was standing in your way. She was standing in our way."

"You didn't have to kill Alexandra. I was yours already."

She shuddered. "It wasn't just about you. Why do you think everything is about you? I wanted what she had. Money, cars, status, California. I wanted out. All my life I wanted out, and I never had a chance until you showed up. We could have had it all, Nico. I could have been so good for you, so much better than Alexandra ever was."

Lena dissolved into her chair. She buried her face between her elbows and lowered her face against the tabletop. The graying roots of her once-bleached hair shook as she wailed into the table's polished metal surface.

I was dumbfounded as I watched her performance. I knew then that I'd made a mistake visiting there. I should've left town without seeing her, without risking a confrontation. I was feeling worse by the second, and needed to escape. Lena looked up at me, her eyes bloodshot and crazed, and said, "You know I will always love you." She kissed the fingers of her hand, and blew the kiss across the glass toward me.

I exhaled through clenched teeth. I couldn't stand one more second of this. "Goodbye," I said, and set the phone back in its cradle.

I settled into the cockpit of my BMW and drove away from the village center. The water towers and mining company signposts of Hibbing filled my rear view mirror. The elms, maples and birch were beginning their transition to autumn red and gold. Five minutes outside of town along Highway 37, a road sign read, "Duluth 75 miles." Beyond Duluth lay Minneapolis. Beyond Minneapolis the road stretched west to California. A stack of my clothes and a computer bag filled the back seat. I had little else to show from my Minnesota misadventure.

A turboprop commercial airliner flew overhead and circled low over the treetops. The asphalt ribbon of the airport runway stretched along the right side of the highway, and the plane raced against my car in a parallel path toward the terminal. I slowed and turned into the airport driveway as the plane's wheels touched down. The incoming flight was right on time.

I parked at the curb next to the terminal and walked through the sliding glass door into the lobby. There was no doubt I was still in the North Country. The entryway was guarded by a stuffed black bear standing on two legs, its jaw fixed in the act of a fearsome and perpetual roar. The antlered head of a once-mighty moose cast a shadow from its mount above the water cooler on my right.

Johnny and Echo stood side-by-side near the observation window at the far side of the lobby. Beyond the glass, the plane taxied to a position fifty feet away from them. The propellers slowed their spin. Johnny saw me approach, held out his right hand toward me and said, "Hey Dad."

I pulled the handshake into a hug. "This is it, Harvard guy. Are you ready?"

"I'm pretty excited. I'm glad I'm not going out there alone."

Echo remained behind him, her body eclipsed by his. She'd been cool to me from the moment I'd walked out of jail and her mother had taken my place. In some absurd construct, I was to blame for everything. If I hadn't fallen in love with Lena, Lena would never have killed Alexandra, and Echo would have a mother here at the airport today. Both Johnny and Echo were motherless children now, a tragic coincidence that strengthened their bond. That bond would continue in college. Echo was bound for Boston University, a mere three miles from Johnny at Harvard.

"Are you excited for Boston?" I said to Echo.

"I'm ready for a fresh start," she said. "In this town I'm as guilty as my mother." She clutched at Johnny's hand, and looked out the window at the waiting airplane. Echo Johnson was a macabre celebrity, the daughter of the suspected murderer in a small-town scandal that caught the attention of the entire nation.

"I'm proud of you both," I said.

Echo's face lit up for the first time, not at my comment but at something behind me. I turned around to see the stickman form of Bobby Dylan approaching. Echo threw her arms around his neck. Dylan picked her up off the floor and spun her, her white sneakers tracing a circle against the dark décor of the lobby. Still carrying her, Dylan extended his hand to Johnny, and said, "Keep those East Coast prep school pricks away from my daughter, OK?"

"I won't let her out of my sight," Johnny said. He shook Dylan's hand for a prolonged time, neither man in a hurry to let go. I mistrusted the peace between them. I'd heard Dylan had dropped his vendetta against Johnny after the trial, and that Johnny had made a good faith effort to get along with Echo's sole caregiver.

I wasn't going there. To me, Dylan was a cancer. I was more than capable of carrying a grudge. There was no love between me and Bobby Dylan.

"Lord knows you two are the smartest couple ever to graduate from Hibbing High School," Dylan said. He turned to me and said, "If these two stay together, I'd better get used to lookin' at your face again, Doctor. How have you been?"

"I'm fine, thanks." I couldn't conjure a fake smile, and this wasn't the time or the place for an honest answer. This moment belonged to Echo and Johnny. It wasn't the time for me to make a scene. I'd avoided all contact with Dylan since the trial. I hadn't returned to Hibbing General and hadn't gone near an operating room.

I'd lived as the recluse father of a high school senior. I'd shunned interaction with the populace of Hibbing except for cursory chats with the clerks at the Super One Foods grocery store or Walmart. My sole objectives were to reclaim my relationship with my son and to protect my sanity. The horror of the murder trial was behind me, but I trusted no one.

I'd lived the past seven months walled up inside Dom's house. I spent my time reading, watching television, gardening, and writing the words on this page. I cooked meals for Johnny and sometimes for both Johnny and Echo. I knew my son spent time with Echo at Dylan's house. I knew the two men had reconciled, and I couldn't change that. Johnny's relationship with Echo was vital. If Bobby Dylan filled a niche in Johnny's life for that reason, so be it.

I was no dope. I had an unfailing memory, and my recollections of the man always flashed back to two searing images: Dylan leveling a shotgun at me out in the woods, and Dylan smirking at me from the back row of the courtroom gallery when I was a roast pig turning on a spit. Encountering Bobby Dylan dredged up pains I'd already buried. I wanted no part of Bobby Dylan.

The boarding announcement sounded over the public address system. Echo said goodbye to her dad and joined the line at the gate. Johnny and I stood alone, toe-to-toe, in the center of the lobby. Chills ran up my arms. My son was a man—a man turned loose on the world.

"I'm proud of you," I said. "You've got what it takes, Johnny."

"Can I make one request before I get on that plane?"

"Sure. Go ahead."

"I'm not 'Johnny' any more. From now on I'm 'John.' Got it?"

"No problem. Got it."

"I love you, Dad." He hugged me and squeezed hard.

"I love you, too, John."

We clung together until a voice over the loudspeaker said, "Last call for Delta Flight 4590 to Minneapolis-St. Paul." My son pulled away from me and joined Echo in line. I watched them move through the security checkpoint and walk out onto the tarmac hand in hand. They climbed the stairs onto the tiny plane and disappeared inside the door. The flight attendant pulled up the stairs and sealed the plane shut.

I was happy for Johnny. We'd gambled for his success, and his success seemed secure.

The plane taxied out to the runway. The propellers gunned in acceleration. Flight 4590 sped down the runway and lifted off, its tail wings disappearing into the powder puff cumulus clouds above God's Country. I felt the tingling emptiness in my fingers where I'd touched my son's hand minutes before. I dreamed of this moment ever since we arrived here from California. I dreamed of this moment ever since Johnny first rolled over in the crib. The moment had come and gone, and now I stood there in a Northern Minnesota airport lobby alone. I had nobody, and the next phase of my life was as opaque as the cloud that had just swallowed my son.

I needed to disappear, too—the sooner the better. I heard Bobby Dylan's nasal breathing from ten feet behind me. He was still watching the sky where the airplane had flown off. I took a step toward the exit, and he moved sidelong to block my path. His facial expression had changed from celebratory joy to soulful remorse. "I'm sorry about everything, Doctor," he said. "Can we start over? Can I buy you a burger or something?"

I recoiled. The man was clueless. The blur of our previous friendship was a bad dream, erased by the worst year in my life. Apologetic words weren't going to heal the rift. Blocking my path out of the terminal was the coda to all the craziness. I tried to stride past him again.

Dylan scurried in front of me and said, "Hey, Doctor, give me a chance. Can I show you something?" He pulled a cell phone out of his pocket, and held it toward me at eye level.

"What's this?" I said.

"Read it." He pushed the screen into my face.

The phone displayed a text message. The message was addressed to Johnny Antone. The words read, "*Ask Nico where the cefazolin went.*" The date of the text was January 19th.

"It was you?"

"It was me."

"Ed Martinovich tried to trace that phone number. It was unlisted."

"It's a throwaway phone I bought at Walmart. I didn't think it would be smart to have my name mixed up in the evidence."

"That text was the breakthrough that pointed us to Lena. That one sentence turned my life around. Because of that text, I'm free."

Dylan turned his palms up, as if to catch the compliment. "You knew she did it?"

Dylan shook his head. "No, I did not know."

"You didn't know?"

"I did not know. All I knew was that I didn't kill your wife. In the beginning I was sure you did it, and I thought they caught you fair and square. But after Echo survived that snowmobile crash, it was like a curtain lifted. I stopped hating you. I laid awake that night wishing you were innocent, and the Kefzol question popped into my mind. I knew Dr. Perpich always ordered prophylactic Kefzol before every case. Who gave the Kefzol? What if whoever gave the Kefzol never really gave it? What if that person gave insulin instead? I didn't have access to the medical records, but you did. I wanted to look for the cefazolin in the blood tests. If the cefazolin was in your wife's blood, then my theory was wrong and you were the murderer. If there was no cefazolin, then ... Poof." Dylan bit off the invisible shackles between his wrists. "You'd go free."

I shook my head in amazement. "I can't thank you enough. You sent your wife to jail. You sprang me out."

"You weren't guilty. She was. It's that simple. Say no more." Dylan slapped me on the back. "How about that burger?"

"I can't."

"I'm sorry to hear that. We miss you at Hibbing General. You were a damn smart doc. All the best." He extended his hand, and I shook it this time. I welcomed the warm roughness of his grip.

"Thanks. For everything."

"No prob, Doctor."

Dylan turned to walk away. I called out after him, "Bobby, can I ask you one last question? Something that always gnawed at me?"

"Sure. Shoot."

"Why Bobby Dylan? Why try to be someone that you're not?"

He shrugged and blossomed a wry smile. "I didn't want to be the millionth Robert Johnson in this world, Doctor. Would you?"

"Good point. I'll have to think about that one."

Dylan crossed the parking lot and climbed into his Chevy pickup. He started the engine, rolled down the window, and said, "Tell you what, Doctor. Me and the boys are playing Heaven's Door tonight. We could use a bass player. Why don't you join us, one last time?"

"Thanks, Bobby, but I've got a 2,000 mile drive ahead of me, and I need to get as far as Minneapolis by tonight."

"OK, I had to ask. You're always welcome, if you're ever back in town."

"I appreciate that." I fit myself into the driver's seat for the long journey. I looked over at the passenger seat, where a much-younger Johnny Antone sat when we arrived in Hibbing a lifetime ago. I could still picture him sitting there with the breeze from Highway 61 fluttering through his hair.

I fired up the engine and tried to ignore the ache in my stomach. As awful as jail had been, the prison of this one-man road trip toward the checkered flag of loneliness in California was almost unthinkable.

I put the car in gear and eased it toward the airport exit. I leaned on the brakes at the stop sign when I reached Highway 37. The highway was flat and empty to the left, and flat and empty to the right. Both roads traced a narrow stripe of pavement through a corridor of trees. The sun was setting low behind the woods in the west. The clouds to the east were painted in shades of orange and yellow. A flock of Canada geese flew overhead in a V-formation, their leader guiding them south with a distant honking. I'd soon follow them.

There was a rumble as the red Chevrolet truck pulled up alongside me at the stop sign. Dylan flashed me one of his crooked grins. He brought his hands up into view and twiddled his fingers in the ecstatic movements of an air guitar solo. Then Dylan's left hand abandoned the imaginary fret board and morphed into a thumbs-up motion. He flashed me one more zany smile, and he made the left turn down Highway 37 back into town.

I sat there and watched Bobby's taillights grow smaller along the narrowing road toward Hibbing. Another loss on this rollercoaster day.

I idled the engine there at the airport exit. Two road signs faced me from the opposite side of the highway. The first sign had an arrow pointing to the right, and read: *Duluth 70 Miles, Minneapolis 203 Miles.*

The second sign had an arrow pointing to the left and read: *Hibbing 6 Miles.*

I stared at the words on the two signs until my eyes blurred, then I dropped my forehead against the steering wheel with a resounding thump. The jumbled emotions dancing through my head disappeared in a single instant of certainty. I looked up to see the tiny image of the red truck, now just a fleck in the distance. I looked in the opposite direction and saw the ribbon of highway that led back to California.

Life is a series of choices. I stuck my forefinger into the crook of the steering wheel, spun it hard to the left, and turned down the road toward Heaven's Door.